A Kept Woman

Frankie McGowan

ISBN: 978-1-911445-04-3

First published in Great Britain 1998 by Victor Gollancz.

This edition published in 2013 by Endeavour Press Ltd.

Printed and bound in Great Britain by Clays Ltd, St Ives plc.

Endeavour Press is the UK's leading independent publisher.

We publish a wide range of genres including history, crime, romance, historical fiction and thrillers.

Every week, we give away free e-books.

For more information about our titles, go to our website:
www.endeavourpress.com/our-books/

Or sign up for our newsletter at:
www.endeavourpress.com

Also by Frankie McGowan availably from Endeavour Press:

My Mother's Wedding

Chasing Shadows

Another Way

Unfinished Business

A Family Affair

A Better Life

The Italian Lesson

Table of Contents

Chapter One

The faint sounds of the shower behind the closed door on the other side of her bedroom roused Serena from sleep. Stretching out a hand she fumbled for the lamp-switch, forcing one eye open to examine the bedside clock. The slim black hands swam into focus as she pulled it nearer. A groan escaped her as she registered the unearthly hour. She clutched the clock to her chest, snapped the light off and let her head fall heavily back on to the pillow.

Six o'clock. Even without knowing it was not yet dawn or the activity in the bathroom, she knew before she opened her eyes that there would be an empty place beside her. A familiar tug of disappointment flickered but it was over in moments. It had been a long time since she had allowed herself to hope things might change, that her day might start in a more leisurely, more intimate way.

She pushed the clock away and rolled over to enjoy at least the warmth of the crumpled sheet where Stephen had been lying, her tousled blond hair trailing across a foaming pile of white lace pillows. A rush of blue silk framed the bed, falling from an antique corona high above and held in place by gold ombras on either side.

The pleasure of waking to see Stephen's dark head still next to her, curling herself contentedly into the curve of his back before the day began, had never seemed a certainty. These days she thought of it as a rare bonus. She gave the covers a tug, pulling them up under her chin.

Outside it was still dark and rain was beating in a steady downpour competing with the wind for attention. The swathes of heavy silk that looped in graceful arcs across the sash windows were not enough to muffle neither the sound nor that of the bare branches of the trees in the square outside bossily dipping and plunging against a blustering wind. It was, she thought, a delicious feeling lying in bed protected from it all, even if she was alone.

Across the darkened room Serena could see a thin yellow line under the door of the bathroom. A subdued rose glow from Stephen's dressing room cast just enough light by which he could dress without disturbing her. At least that's what they both agreed it was doing, but she knew with a resigned sigh that it was nothing of the sort; he simply hated talking first thing. Today he would have to not mind. His hours were becoming ridiculous.

Serena sat up on one elbow, pushing her hair out of her eyes as the bathroom door opened and Stephen's dark shape filled the doorway.

"Hi," she called drowsily. He paused and came over to her, one towel wrapped around his waist, rubbing his hair dry with another.

"Sounds ferocious," he indicated the storm rising to a howling pitch outside.

"I missed you," she yawned, reaching for his hand. It was cool, still damp from the shower. "We couldn't sell your ticket at such short notice. Melanie says I should divorce you."

"Mercifully, what Melanie says doesn't interest me," he returned, giving his hair one last vigorous rub with his free hand.

"Oh, give her a break," Serena replied. "She's been a very good and loyal friend to me. And you know you like her. You just don't like the way she argues with you."

"If she argued, I wouldn't mind," he protested. "She isn't logical. Serena, you haven't woken up just to nag me about bloody Melanie?"

She ignored him. "Would I? What happened last night?"

"Usual stuff." He pressed the ball of his hand into his eye. "Malcolm let the meeting drag on fretting about losing Bretil's interest — he's just not getting back to us. 'Fraid it's going to be like this for a while," he warned her.

Serena closed her eyes. "So what's new?" she grumbled. "Nothing for it. I'll have to take a lover."

"Then you'll have to get him past me," he said, sinking down on the edge of the bed.

She opened one eye and squinted up at him. "Not if you continue to live at the office, I won't."

He smiled, slipping his hand under the sheet and between her thighs. She gave a sleepy growl. "Forget it, Buster," she said, removing his hand. "I can't be bought that easily."

"No?" He sounded amused. For a second she held his gaze, torn between wanting to pursue what he'd started and knowing only too well that he would resist if she pushed it. From the moment he had opened his eyes, she knew his mind had been focused on the day ahead.

She let him stand up, trailing her fingers away from him. "Believe me, my precious," he said, "everyone's got their price." He leaned over and dropped a kiss on her mouth. "Even Melanie. Tell her I'll write an obscenely large cheque and a grovelling apology."

Serena gave him a lazy smile. "Excellent. I love it when you talk dirty. Actually it was a bloody awful concert. I rather envied you having an excuse not to turn up."

He walked towards his dressing room. "Not if you'd been where I was, you wouldn't." He massaged the back of his neck with the towel. "Even a god-awful concert has to be more interesting than waiting for Malcolm to make a decision, unless it's saying yes to a weekend with any of Rupert's relatives."

"So how is the beautiful Rupert?" she asked, seizing the moment to air what was really on her mind. She lifted her head to pummel the pillows into a more comfortable shape.

"Still beautiful, still useless." He stopped, his hand on the doorframe, briefly resting his forehead against it. He sounded detached from it all. She wondered how it was possible for him to stay so calm. Rupert Chawton Browne had been personally hired by Malcolm Brisley Jones, the chairman of Draycott Mendes Merchant Bank where Stephen was head of Corporate Development, for no better reason than Rupert's family name stretching back to the Normans, and his future held an earldom. Not to mention, Malcolm's weekends assured in stately homes around the country. This blatant social mountaineering had resulted in ludicrously long hours for Stephen, unravelling the problems created by the harmless but inept Rupert.

"Honestly, darling, you should put a stop to it. First bloody Malcolm foists that idiot on to you. Then you have to find him something to do which he screws up the minute he opens his mouth and then you have to spend time you could be spending with me — oh all right, I agree last night it was with Melanie, but at least she works for a good cause — bailing him out. And what's happened to that poor girl hired to be his secretary? Exactly. Four weeks she lasted and she was so bored she resigned."

"Hey, hey," he interrupted, "calm down. If Malcolm gets off on greasing up to Rupert's family, at least he's not interfering anywhere else in my life. There are enormous compensations."

Serena slumped back on the pillows. It was hopeless. Perhaps it was why he was so successful. Nothing distracted him from the main event in his life — his job. No use pretending otherwise. It wasn't that Serena and the children came lower down the list. They were just on a different one.

"Well, you're going to kill yourself at this rate," she finished morosely. "The children won't have a father and I hope Malcolm will be satisfied when I'm a widow."

He laughed. "But such a wealthy one!" he insisted.

"What good will that do me?" she retorted as he dropped the towels to the floor. "There's only a limited number of clothes you can buy in black."

"Nonsense. Turn yourself over to Paula — she'd regard it as a challenge. Or that idiot Miranda. That's all they think about."

Serena wrinkled her nose. "Not Miranda. Poor girl's in a bad way — that bloody husband of hers."

She stopped. Partly because Stephen was even less interested in the woolly Miranda Hooper than he was in Paula, but mostly because after the concert the night before, Miranda had clutched her arm and begged her to take her home. She was feeling too distressed to face the dinner that Melanie had spent weeks arranging and had made Serena promise to stay silent about the cause.

It was an interlude Serena could have done without, but Miranda's stricken eyes and white face made it impossible for Serena not to help. As they sat in the back of Miranda's chauffeur-driven car, she told Serena that she had just discovered her husband's affair.

Stephen paused in the doorway. "Oh? What's he done now? Screwed the nanny?"

"Stephen," she remonstrated. "No. Forget it. It's just that I had to miss Melanie's dinner, so you'd better add another nought to that cheque. She's furious with me, but what could I do? Miranda needed me and made me promise not to tell anyone."

He gave a grunt. "Know your problem? You're too soft. Every time he plays away from home, Miranda comes sobbing to you. And every time you drop what you're doing and listen to her. And what difference does it make? You know perfectly well that Miranda is an airhead and if she had a brain cell that functioned beyond Bond Street, she might pay more attention to her marriage."

He closed the door. He was right, she thought glumly. How on earth had she found herself in the role of counsellor to someone who basically didn't want to be counselled? Serena knew Miranda was silly, but she could be amusing, and her anguish each time she discovered another act of infidelity appeared so genuine that, while Serena knew she should harden her heart to Miranda's gulping description of the Hoopers' complex relationship, each time she saw Miranda's tear-stained face, the frantic gulping of whiskey, she could not bring herself to turn away. Last night, not turning away had cost her both Melanie's fury at the missed dinner and not getting to bed until nearly one o'clock in the morning.

However, there was no point in hoping that someone as disciplined and level-headed as Stephen would understand that. He believed in tackling problems head on. She could not imagine him bothering to repeat advice to someone who had turned it down the first time. And he was right. Of course he was. Lucky Stephen, so single-minded as he was. And they still hadn't resolved the mistreatment of his time by Malcolm.

Five minutes later, dressed in a pinstripe suit, pale blue shirt and navy silk tie, Stephen emerged from his dressing room to pause only long enough to pick up a black leather wallet lying on the bedside table.

Serena, now wide awake, watched him as he briefly checked its contents. It was a pity, she thought, that Mrs Owen couldn't see him. Stephen's immaculate appearance was her handiwork. Olwen Owen had presided over Serena's household for the last seven years. Such was her regard for the proper order of things that she had never invited Serena to call her anything other than Mrs Owen and frowned disapprovingly when Chrissie, the nanny who had joined them two years before, had fallen easily into the habit of addressing their employer by her Christian name, apparently encouraged to do so.

But it was Stephen whom Mrs Owen really claimed as her employer. Within weeks of her becoming housekeeper to the Carmichaels, Serena guessed that the attraction was not working for a good wage and reasonable hours, it was Stephen. Stephen, who featured frequently on the financial pages of the papers, who dined regularly with the Chancellor and members of the cabinet. Even more satisfying to Mrs Owen's notions of grandeur was the Chancellor's visit to Belvoir Square where she, Mrs Owen, was charged with overseeing the caterers.

If that hadn't been obvious evidence enough, it was visible in her devotion to his wishes. The care of his Savile Row suits and the laundering of his handmade silk shirts had become a cause in her life, fussed over with the same degree of ferocity with which she tyrannized the handful of people regularly employed by Serena in the running of their London house, but who were left to Mrs Owen to supervise.

These days the sight of Mrs Owen carefully arranging Stephen's clothes in colour-graded lines raised nothing more than a resigned sigh from Serena, who thought her devotion to his needs excessive. The military precision with which she hung his suits in the closets, the ones Mrs Owen liked to tell Mr Owen may well have been designed to Mr Carmichael's own specifications, was equally ignored. Particularly since Serena had discovered that Stephen rather approved of such meticulous attention to detail.

She did however draw the line at having Mrs Owen take control of her own wardrobe. Beyond the practicalities of organising laundry and dry cleaning, Serena firmly excluded her from her dressing room and was amused, if a little surprised, when Mrs Owen made no objection.

"Gives her more time to devote to you," Serena teased Stephen, who simply grunted and told her that he was sure she had everything under control. Very occasionally Serena would gently remonstrate with Mrs Owen when her zeal for her job threatened to mobilize a mass walk-out of the rest of the staff. When the last cleaner the agency had sent to assist Mrs Owen on her daily trawl through the house, ferreting out every rogue speck that might lurk in an unsuspecting corner, had stalked out midway through hoovering the stairs, Serena assured her housekeeper that as long as the house was clean and tidy she didn't mind the odd mite of dust.

"Mrs Carmichael," had been the indignant response. "You don't understand these people — and indeed why should you? You have no training. Demand more than you need and you'll get the standard you expect. Accept less and they will take advantage."

Serena hesitated, on the point of reminding Mrs Owen that she had managed quite well for seven years without the luxury of such extensive staff, but she stopped. Serena knew that Mrs Owen's son-in-law had just been made redundant and was, according to Mrs Owen, eating her out of house and home, and decided this wasn't the moment to add to her stress. Cranky and snobbish she might be, but Serena knew she was excellent at her job and that was, in the end, all that mattered. Especially to Stephen.

So she agreed: they'd be lost without her and the cleaners came and went. The florists who supplied fresh flowers to the Carmichael household twice a week continued to silently fume while Mrs Owen inspected every bloom. The caterers who were brought in at least once a week when the Carmichaels entertained continued to grit their teeth as Mrs Owen examined the ingredients they used and found an outlet for their fury by inviting her to sample any of the hors d'oeuvres which had been accidentally dropped in the sink.

Only the gardener, responsible for the profusion of roses, lavender, geraniums and peonies that clustered around the small lawn that stretched along the terrace at the rear of the house, ignored her. In Mrs Owen he recognized a woman wielding power disguised as devotion to her employers. And in the end, because they liked Serena, who paid well and was sympathetic when they privately grumbled to her about the housekeeper, most of them continued to work for her.

It was her dedication to Stephen's welfare that had prompted Mrs Owen the day before to sever all links with the current shirt service they were using, when they did not, in her view, achieve the perfection Mr Carmichael's shirts deserved.

Serena sat up in bed with a guilty start, remembering she had promised to relay this change in domestic affairs to Stephen, who she knew would have no interest in it and nor could she blame him.

"Oh God," she muttered. "Stephen?" she called, halting him as he began to close the door. "Totally forgot. Mrs Owen's in a pelter about your shirts. She fired Personal Valet yesterday."

He paused in the doorway, gazing blankly back at her. "Who?"

"Her latest find. Don't look like that. They've lasted six weeks. The last lot were slung out in one. This, let me tell you, is progress. Leave her a note will you? Say 'quite right' or something."

Stephen leaned his head against the doorframe and sighed. "Can't you just tell her for me?"

"It isn't the same. Oh go on," she cajoled him. "One line, that's all. I know she can be a pain, but she does get things done." He grunted his assent. "Love you too, Grumpy," she teased. "Hey, come back, I haven't finished."

But he hadn't heard her. She scrambled out of bed on to the polished landing, calling down to him in a whisper so that Harry and Louise, still asleep on the next floor, would not be disturbed. "I bet you've forgotten. Chrissie's weekend off. I'm leaving early so I'll be at the cottage by six."

He nodded and went on down the stairs.

"And lunch at my mother's on Sunday," she added, "try for a twenty-three-hour day instead of twenty-four." She blew him a kiss and returned to bed. After that she followed his movements in her head because two flights of stairs blotted out further sound filtering between Serena's bedroom and the breakfast room.

She knew Stephen would drink one cup of black coffee which he would take with him into his study, gulping it down while he ran his eye over the endless reports he would be dealing with that day, and then he would let himself quietly out of the house having stuffed into his briefcase those reports that projected how the Nikkei, Dow and FTSE might have overnight altered the worth of banks across the world.

It was six-thirty. Stephen's driver would be waiting outside to open the door of the car and hand Stephen the *FT* as he eased his tall, lean frame into the back seat, before walking briskly round to take his seat behind the wheel. A quick flash of black and chrome — unlikely to be seen by anyone else in the square since most of its residents would not yet have left their beds — and the black Jaguar would head north along still dark and mostly deserted streets towards the City.

Less than twenty minutes later, Stephen would climb out of the car at the main entrance to Draycott Mendes. The day ahead would see him making financial decisions that ensured that his employer was infinitely richer at dusk than he had been at dawn.

*

Stephen's impatience was not easily aroused, largely because he surrounded himself with people who made sure it wasn't, but it could be instantly mobilized by a job inexpertly or carelessly completed. Serena regarded this as a virtue. But not everyone agreed.

"The trouble with Stephen," Serena's mother had once told her in a rush of honesty, "is that he's a man in a hurry and expects everyone to keep up with him."

"Well if that means he hates accepting less than the best when the best is achievable for want of a little extra effort, then yes, I suppose he is," Serena had replied. "He hates time-wasting. It's why he's so successful. You can't help wanting the best when he's around. Look at you," she teased, "don't think I haven't noticed that you pat your hair when you hear him come in."

Margot Armitage, Serena's widowed mother, said nothing. It was true her son-in-law had an unsettling effect on her but it was not his approval she was seeking; patting her hair was to disguise the fact she was taking a deep

9

breath to help her stay silent. She just wished he wouldn't — sometimes — be so punctilious in his dealings with her. His courtesy to her was faultless, but in all the years she had known him, she had never felt she knew him. Not properly.

Not having any other children and only her sole living relative, her widowed cousin Isabel, by which to judge these things, Margot was never quite sure if she was expecting too much from her daughter's husband. Isabel disliked both her daughters-in-law intensely, so had found no trouble at all removing herself from Gloucester and moving back to her home in Scotland when her husband had died. In the circumstances, she regarded Margot's situation as fortunate.

Margot's visits to her daughter's home amounted to two or three a year, including Christmas, although she saw more of Serena and the children when they came to visit her, so perhaps, she thought, Stephen was more approachable than she had come to believe. Clearly he loved his children even if he expected more from them than perhaps they, or at least Harry, could deliver.

At nine, three years younger than Louise, Harry, with his pale blond hair and quiet and gentle nature, was slower than his sister who had inherited Stephen's dark good looks, lean body and quick mind. Stephen, Margot could see, found it hard at times to disguise his impatience when Harry failed to understand his maths homework.

"Harry," Stephen would order him, "concentrate. You can do it. Don't confuse boredom with not being able to do it. Of course you can. Now try again and stop thinking about the — whatever it is on that computer. Serena? I thought he was only going to be allowed that stuff at the weekends?"

On Harry's part, the minute his father walked in the room, he went from frowning concentration on one of his computer games to a touching eagerness to show him what he had been doing, to boast a little of what he had achieved, suffused with pleasure when Stephen smiled and nodded his approval.

Louise was a different matter. She adored Stephen and took her father's approval as a matter of course but their strikingly similar temperaments led to loud clashes, which, of course, Serena did her best to diffuse without alienating either of them. At the moment, rock concerts were Louise's passion and Stephen's blunt refusal to allow her to go to them alone, her fury.

"Take no notice," Serena wearily told her mother, who had witnessed one of these loud and noisy exchanges. "Stephen won't budge and she knows it. Just listen ..."

Margot obediently craned her head towards Stephen's study where she could hear her granddaughter yelling: "Everyone's going. *Everyone*. Even Sophie Belton and she's really sad. I'll be utterly humiliated. *Utterly*. I hate you."

"I hope you won't be saying that when you get a new saddle for your pony," came Stephen's untroubled voice.

Serena sighed as a split second of silence was followed by squeals of delight.

"There you are. I do everything I can to stop her wearing him down when he comes in — honestly, Ma, he's working the most killing hours. I try and stop Lou from nagging him, but she doesn't listen. What can I do? And then of course he undoes all my good work by spoiling her."

To Serena, Stephen had always been the most extraordinary man. Supporting him, protecting him, was as much a part of that as loving him for himself.

When Melanie Westfield had said she spoilt Stephen, she looked surprised.

"Why shouldn't I?" she asked. "Anyway, it's not spoiling, it's supporting ... If I didn't completely organise this side of his life, how could he find the time to be so successful? And if he wasn't so successful," she patted Melanie's cheek, "how could I nip off to New York with you next month to shop?"

Melanie sniffed. "You might joke, but I honestly don't know how you stay so calm when he expects you to drop everything at a moment's notice."

But Serena did. Stephen's success was their success and she found it incredible that anyone would think she found it arduous to be there for him. She knew he could be — and usually was — hard on his staff who

11

had been known to arrive late at night in Belvoir Square straight from their desks bearing papers and reports that Stephen had asked for. Their day, which had started for most of them at seven o'clock that morning, would be about to come to an exhausting end. But he was harder still on himself.

Only Serena noticed the tired lines around Stephen's eyes when the drinks he offered them looked like going on for a bit. Somehow she would manage to see his staff to the door without them realising they were being eased out and the next day talked of Mrs. Carmichael's warmth and charm. Stephen, however, saw nothing unusual in the hours his staff worked. If you made an effort, he reminded her, you got noticed and got on. Making an extra effort had got him a first at Cambridge. Pushing that extra inch secured him a place on the corporate ladder the week after he graduated.

It was what Serena had noticed about him when, aged nineteen, she had first seen him making an effort. The only one exerting himself to talk to the very dull wife of a tedious but titled landowner at the equally tiresome drinks party to which Serena had been invited. Escorted by the besotted Hon Johnny Bishop, who couldn't understand why, instead of marrying him, she wanted to start a degree course at university after a year doing very little but attend such parties.

Well, perhaps it wasn't the first thing she noticed about Stephen. The first was purely physical. It was like being slung from her pony when she was ten; a severe jolt followed by disorientation, the inability to grasp what had happened.

She had never experienced such a feeling before. Certainly the devoted Johnny had not aroused the force in her that led to sleepless nights and loss of appetite. Curiously she never wanted to feel it again. A *coup de foudre* was all very well in books but in reality she recalled it as just being bloody painful, especially when she surveyed the competition for Stephen Carmichael's attention.

Later, when the Hon Johnny had been consoled by someone more appreciative of the stately pile waiting for him in the Midlands and Serena had moved in with Stephen to his minuscule flat, the panicky feeling of having a permanent temperature left her, and was replaced by an obsessive need to make Stephen see it had not been a mistake.

For days on end her enthusiasm for hoovering, dusting, shopping, making love and plans for their future blotted out the fact that it had been Stephen's urging that had brought her to this mews just off Sloane Square, to the united disbelief of her parents, university lecturers and friends.

Being in love with Stephen was a full-time job and looking after him made finding time to discover paid employment utterly hopeless. Each morning for the first week she scrambled out of bed to cook him breakfast and kiss him goodbye.

"It's just me being a boring bugger," he told her apologetically, as she stood in the tiny kitchen cleaved out of a space no bigger than a broom cupboard, the hem of one of his old rugger shirts just covering her bottom. She was clutching a frying pan and an egg.

"I just don't eat breakfast," he told her ruefully. She looked aghast. "And the space between getting up and leaving is when I do all my thinking for the day. It's me, I know it's me," he groaned, "I'm just uncivilized first thing."

Serena flung herself, still clutching the frying pan, at his middle, burying her head in his chest, and asked him to be honest. Had it been a mistake?

"God no. Don't be such a goose. You? A mistake? Never. But," he untangled himself from her clasp, "the eggs just could be."

So she trained herself to stay where she was until he had left the house and learned to immerse herself in his life in other ways, which was a daunting task since they had little money.

"That's all right," she reassured him when he pointed this economic fact out to her. "I'm brilliant at being poor. Honestly, if we hadn't inherited all that stuff down in Wiltshire, my mother used to say we would have had to sling ourselves on the parish."

Far from being reassured, he had seemed shocked. "How does your mother pay the housekeeper ... and what about the cook?"

It was Serena's moment. She might, she told him, be the gently nurtured and only child of a minor baronet but she was adept at stretching meagre resources to great effect. The staff, she explained, stayed out of habit rather than any desire to make money. When they retired, a small trust fund would pay them a pension. They would not be asked to go, just not replaced when they left. It was the way things were done in old families such as hers.

"I'll cook when you have people to dinner," she told him. "It'll be brilliant."

"Can you cook?" he asked, having only the eggs and the odd salad to go on so far. "I mean properly?"

She wrinkled her nose thoughtfully. "Yes," she said confidently. "I mean," she went on, beset by honesty, "probably. Heavens, there can't be that much to know, can there?"

Pregnant with her first child, and not being of a domestic disposition, they were both astonished to see how good she became at being Stephen's wife. She learned to cook, and listened when his colleagues came for drinks or dinner and worked out the right questions to ask, making them feel smart and powerful and eventually more than happy to include the young Carmichaels into their social lives and Stephen on to their list of those to consider when the right moment came along.

Serena did it for Stephen. It gave him such pleasure, he seemed more relaxed than when she had first known him and she wanted him to be happy. It was his future they were investing in. And of course, she agreed with him, hers too.

Eventually her parents came to support her decision and even developed a cautious regard for Stephen on the grounds that he appeared to love their daughter and that his determination to succeed was confounding all the critics. However, they thought it unnecessary to let anyone know the deep inroads they had made into the whiskey decanter when they first realized Serena had thrown away her chance of getting a degree and marrying a title.

Her mother had seen her daughter somehow carrying on the family tradition, producing fine books on works of art that would be in keeping with the chatelaine of a stately home. Instead Sir Stafford and Lady Margot Armitage maintained a brave and united front when Serena and Stephen had married hastily but beautifully in the parish church near their home in Wiltshire.

The bride wore a dress of moiré silk and was attended by four tiny bridesmaids wearing white dresses trimmed in blue, garlands of flowers in their hair. The groom looked impossibly handsome and *Tatler*, who covered the fairytale occasion for their diary pages, tactfully refrained from mentioning that the bride was also four months pregnant.

Their lives moved rapidly on, which in later years Serena would say was the reason she managed to hang on to her sanity after her first child died a day and one night after she was born. They named her Anna. Serena had held her just once, staring brokenly into the tiny still face that was her daughter, not knowing how such terrible grief could be endured.

Less than a year later they brought Louise home to their new house in Holland Park where two years on Harry was conceived. Then, without telling her, a surprise he said, when the children were five and two, Stephen had driven her to this house in Belvoir Square, all five floors of it, with a pretty garden square opposite and just around the corner from Kensington High Street.

Chapter Two

"Melanie?" Serena tucked the phone under her chin, pulling her robe on with her free hand. "I know, I know. I'm truly sorry. It was a kind of crisis that I wasn't expecting."

"Huh," Melanie muttered. "Miranda's a walking crisis. Who is it this time? Oh don't bother — I know you won't tell me."

"Not won't," Serena said, "just can't. I want you to say the evening was a huge success and that you're not going to be vile to me."

"You don't deserve it," Melanie told her severely. "Anyway, ready for the meeting?"

"Absolutely," Serena replied promptly, relieved that Melanie was, as ever, not going to sulk about the previous evening. But then Melanie never did. "Minutes at the ready. Can't wait to see Paula swanning around in her committee outfit. What? Paula might not have something made for the occasion? Her only problem is that she won't know who to have dialled first, the Red Cross or Armani."

Melanie gave a shriek of laughter and then checked herself. "Hey, while I'm on, what excuse did Mr Carmichael give? We could have got another fifty grand if he'd been around to sweet talk that German banker."

As usual Serena felt defensive at the lack of understanding about Stephen's punishing hours. "Locked in meetings and I won't hear a word against him. Anyway he's left you a cheque."

A sound like a *hrumph* came down the phone. "You're far too forgiving. If it had been the first time … oh all right. I love him to bits. Better?"

"Not much. But as I do, it hardly matters. Hey, must dash. Sounds like a minor earthquake going on upstairs."

An hour after Stephen had left the house, Serena's day began. She could hear Chrissie, Louise and Harry's nanny, making the first of the usual several attempts to rouse Louise, followed by a sharp thump as Harry dived from whatever piece of furniture was doubling as a launch pad on to the centre of his bed.

She pushed back the covers, took a quick shower and dressed in record time. Before she reached the floor above she was already calling out to Louise to get a move on. Chrissie called good morning and went back to her own room to dress as soon as she heard Serena round the bend in the stairs.

It was a practised and familiar routine. When Chrissie, a good-natured, easy-going young girl from Yorkshire, arrived two years before, Serena had explained that in spite of what her agency might have said about being given sole charge, that was not her intention. It had worked out well. After some initial reservations that the glamorous banker's wife with her charming smile and warm manner might turn out to be just another rich bitch, Chrissie had accepted that Serena Carmichael had no intention of relinquishing her children to anyone else unless her husband, or her commitments to the charity *Babyways*, of which she was a founding member, demanded her time.

The best of it for Chrissie was that she got chunks of spare time that others in her nanny circle did not. Most of this time was spent with her new boyfriend, which was fascinating for Louise, who Serena knew spent hours fantasising about such a trophy for herself. She was now asking Chrissie endless questions about a lad who appeared to Serena to be perfectly nice but of so few words, and it was hard to understand why Louise found him so riveting. Serena could hear her as she reached the next floor.

"Where did you go? You were awfully late. Are you engaged?"

"Buck up, LouLou," Serena called to her daughter who was standing on one foot, her pyjamas crumpled, leaning against Chrissie's open door. "Chrissie doesn't need an inquisition into her private life at this time of the morning, do you, Chrissie?"

"I'm not," Louise retorted as Chrissie, grinning, fled to the bathroom. "It's … it's just girl's talk," she finished airily, trailing back into her own room.

Serena waited to make sure that Louise had at least made an attempt to start the day before opening Harry's door. She ducked as he sprayed his space gun in her direction, firing at imaginary aliens.

"Where are you going?" demanded Harry, lowering the lethal-looking weapon, eyeing her black skirt and the blue tailored jacket she was holding over her arm. "Why are you dressed like that? Why have you got make-up on?"

"Committee meeting," Serena explained, swooping him into a hug, letting him go as he wriggled from her grasp. "*Babyways* at St Biddulph's." She dropped her jacket on to a chair while she opened drawers, pulling out clean socks and pants, throwing them on to the bed behind her.

Harry lost interest in his mother's charity work and returned to dealing with the alien forces from another planet while Serena moved around the room assembling his uniform. With a final plea to get a move on — repeated to Louise who was still sitting on the edge of her bed gazing in disgust at her school skirt — she picked up her jacket and disappeared downstairs to start their day.

Stephen's note to Mrs Owen was lying on the table. Serena grinned as she took in the two scrawled lines. She moved it to where it would be seen as soon as Mrs Owen came in and then began the familiar routine of putting on coffee, dropping sliced bread into the toaster, placing eggs into a saucepan and pouring juice.

"Oh LouLou, just *try* and eat something," she pleaded fifteen minutes later, depositing boxes of cereal on the table for Harry to choose from. Louise yawned, rubbed her eyes and surfed idly through breakfast television, ignoring everything her mother put before her. "You'll be keeling over by ten if you don't. You haven't touched your egg."

"Daddy doesn't have breakfast," Louise argued, tossing her dark bob out of her eyes as she turned the volume up to listen to some disembodied voice interviewing *One Direction* at an awards ceremony the night before, "so why should I?"

"Because Daddy has breakfast meetings," Serena replied calmly, determined not to be drawn into an exasperated exchange by Louise's current

passion for thinness. It was absurd. She was, at twelve, as lean as her father
— tall too — a softer version of his dark good looks. Harry was as blond
as Serena was, but showing no sign of taking after either of his parents in
height. At nine he was small for his age, almost fragile, and with a gentle nature, unlike Louise's more fiery one. Louise, just like Stephen, was impatient
to get on with life. Harry, like Serena, was more content to observe.

Louise was arguing that she could eat when she got to school.

"Your school does not provide breakfast, and if it did," Serena persisted,
raising her voice a fraction, cutting off Louise's next protest, "you would
have to be there by eight and you wouldn't like that."

She piled yoghurt and chicken salad into Louise's lunchbox telling Chrissie, who was stifling a yawn as she dragged a bomber jacket over her jeans,
to make sure LouLou at least ate the orange she had peeled en route to
school.

"I am gross already," Louise wailed to an unimpressed audience. "No
one seems to care that I am obese — or," she added catching sight of the
chicken, "vegetarian."

Serena ignored her, telling Harry, who had sat through this familiar family
scene every morning since the beginning of term, to eat in a civilized
manner and stop spilling cereal everywhere. Harry carefully retrieved the
spaceship figure promised on the side of the box from the depths of the
slivers of corn, scattering brown dust everywhere.

He licked his spoon before letting it clatter back into the bowl and
scrambled away from the table. The usual last-minute frenzy of finding lost
scarves and donning coats was more frantic than usual since Serena was
casting around for the minutes of the last *Babyways* committee meeting —
the ones, she had assured Melanie less than half an hour earlier, that she
had to hand. She checked her diary was in her bag and swooped the entire
family before her across the kitchen, through the hall and out of the house.

As they piled out they passed Mrs Owen hauling her thin frame up the
stone steps in the manner of one who was overweight and not at all well.
Serena guessed she lied about her age, but even so she couldn't be more
than sixty and, if her robust dealings with everyone who came under her

scrutiny were anything to go by, her claim that she was not an entirely well person could not be taken very seriously.

All the way up to the door she grumbled about the traffic and Mr Owen's refusal to get a car with an odds-on chance of starting first time in the morning. Serena took a deep breath, accustomed to Mrs Owen's belief that all forms of transport conspired to make her life a misery.

"Oh poor you," Serena sympathized, trying not to sound rushed. "Why don't you have a cup of tea, relax. I'll be back later — I want to leave by four if I can, oh, and there's a note from Stephen. Says you should work for him at the bank," she grinned, hoping to distract Mrs Owen from her favourite theme, but failing.

"Oh, I agree," she gave in, as Mrs Owen reached the door. "Dreadful. I know, the tube's no better. Poor you."

At the bottom of the steps Chrissie was arguing with Harry about leaving his computer game at home. Louise was looking on with a saintlike expression on her face. Serena turned to kiss Louise goodbye and with a sigh put her bag on the pavement. "OK, Lou, what is that?" she demanded, eyeing a strange lump around Louise's waist which would have gone undetected if Louise had not been so obviously clutching it. Serena held on to her arm as she tried to sidle past Chrissie and into the car away from her mother's curiosity.

"Nothing. Stop fussing. I'll straighten it in the car."

Serena regarded her steadily. "Open your coat, Lou," she commanded.

A short eye-to-eye tussle ensued before Louise, who her grandmother once said could sulk for England, complied and revealed a skirt rolled thickly over at the waist to bring the hem a more fashionable four inches above her knees.

"If you just listened and sent me to a decent school, I wouldn't have to look so *sad*," Louise retorted bitterly as she unfurled the skirt to its regulation length. "It's gross."

"Oh c'mon sweetheart," Serena smiled, sympathetically wrapping her arms around Louise, "it isn't anywhere near as bad as some and it isn't for ever."

"Feels like centuries," grumbled Louise, allowing her mother to give her a hug. "Just remember, it won't be my fault if I grow up to be dys … dysfunctional."

"No danger of that, dear, unless you get chucked out of school for wearing the wrong uniform," Serena assured her, and waved her off as Chrissie manoeuvred the car around the square.

Serena, now running late, hurtled across London to Hampstead to decant Harry into his prep school, knowing that her chance of reaching George's consulting rooms by nine-thirty was fading unless every light between here and Cromwell Road was in her favour. She called Paula Van Stuckley from the car to warn her that she might be late. Then, as she slowed for the lights at the Marylebone flyover, she stabbed out her hairdresser's number and had her highlights put back half an hour in case the meeting ran over.

After that she called Christie's and told them she would stop by just after lunch instead of before to pick up the package containing a first edition of Yeats, which she planned to give Stephen for an anniversary present the following day.

Her day re-organised, Serena felt better. The drive back across town at the tail end of the rush hour was serenity itself compared with the beginning. Serena chose to go through Hyde Park as far as Kensington Gate, relieved to have time to think.

In her head, she checked off a list of what needed to be done before she drove the children down to the cottage later that day. Chrissie had asked to leave straight after dropping Harry, so that she could get to Yorkshire just after lunch, where her parents were preparing for her sister's wedding the next day at which she was to be a bridesmaid. Serena suggested she take Monday as well. Chrissie's family were close-knit and she suspected that her mother would be glad of Chrissie's company for an extra day after the emotional upheaval of parting with one daughter and the other living in London.

Mrs Owen, of course, would not leave before she had piled Serena's car with enough food to feed the entire Cotswold village for a fortnight, ignoring as she always did the fact that Mary Walton, who looked after the

Carmichaels' country home, would be blithely stocking up both fridges in the cottage.

Every Friday Serena would discuss with Mrs Owen what she needed for the weekend and each time Mrs Owen would say, "Perhaps you should let me decide what you need. You're so busy." Serena would agree, knowing that at the cottage the devoted Mary would gaze in silent disapproval at what she saw as a criticism of her housekeeping skills, but knowing much of Mrs Owen's Friday raid on Harrods Food Hall would most welcomely wind up in Mary's own fridge on Sunday night.

Domestic life was Serena's concern but it had been years since the minutiae of it had troubled her. If Mrs Owen wanted the pleasure of telling everyone that the Carmichaels could not survive without her, she saw no reason to deprive her of it. She was far more preoccupied with persuading Stephen to take it easy. Even the promise that he would get to the cottage after dinner was not one she had much faith in, although curiously she had total faith that Stephen meant what he said when he said it.

Thirteen years of marriage — exactly thirteen the next day — had left Serena more calmly in love with Stephen than gripped in the grand passion that had engulfed her when she married him. The passion that had made her abandon university and a career rather than risk losing him to other distractions had been softened by familiarity and two children. He had not lost his physical attraction for her, or his ability to interest her. That, lately, was the problem.

It was just tiredness, she consoled herself, and the bloody Chancellor sending mixed signals about the Budget, that had limited more passionate moments. Stephen so badly needed a holiday. She had organized a whole month in Cap Ferrat earlier in the summer, but after four days installed in their villa, and endless phone calls going to and from London, she knew it wasn't going to work.

"Never mind, darling," she soothed, as he flopped down on to a lounger on the villa terrace. "They'll get used to making a few decisions without you." She saw immediately she had said the wrong thing and groaned. "I mean until you get back," she amended. Harry was splashing wildly in the pool with Chrissie, while LouLou, one eye on her mother, ogled the deeply tanned fourteen-year-old son of their neighbour. The noise repeatedly drove Stephen into the house to escape so that he could hear what various people in London, New York and Tokyo were saying to him on the phone.

"We'll go away, just the two of us, when the children are back at school. Bloody bank," she finished, moving around to massage his back when he rejoined her for the fourth time in an hour. "They don't deserve you. Why can't stupid Rupert take some of the load?"

"Why indeed?" Stephen muttered, reaching out for his mobile. "Try asking Malcolm that." He punched out the number of the bank and waited. "Harry," he called to his son who was shouting triumphantly as he raced Chrissie across the pool, "keep it down. I'm working."

Serena caught Chrissie exchanging a guilty grin with Harry as he pushed his drenched hair out of his eyes and swam silently to the edge of the pool. His father had now noticed Louise attempting to squash in beside her new swain in a swing seat meant for one on the shady terrace of the house. "Serena?" Stephen muttered under his breath, "can't you stop Louise from behaving like such a trollop … Barbara?" He turned away to talk to his office.

He left the same night. Serena and the children came home three weeks later as planned, having spent the rest of the holiday without him.

*

Serena turned the car into the side road alongside the hospital and began searching for a meter. The suggested break without the children had not of course taken place. Her hopes were now resting on a New Year holiday with Stephen once Christmas was over and the children were back at school, but she would not, she told herself, slotting money into the machine, hold her breath.

She gave a sigh, inched her way between parked cars and ran across the road to the entrance of St Biddulph's. Once inside the swing doors of the glass and chrome building, she walked across the marble floor to the lift. The fourth floor — the Wendover Wing — was where the monthly committee meeting of *Babyways* was to be held for the first time, in George

Kincaid's office. She would think about Stephen later.

It had been Serena's idea to switch committee meetings to the eminent consultant's rooms at the hospital. Of late, while the committee had met just as often with just as effective results in raising money for neonatal equipment, Serena had felt it was sliding more into an excuse for lunch at each other's house or a fashionable restaurant where they gossiped about their own and each other's lives. They were, she knew, losing sight of why they were meeting in the first place.

"Awareness," she told George Kincaid when they had all met up at a fund raising dinner about a month before, at the home of Paula Van Stuckley, "isn't just about raising money, is it? It's about making sure that every new mother knows what can be done to help premature babies. When I suggested we formed this charity I was thinking only about Anna and how she might have been saved. But I wanted to raise awareness as well of how many babies could be saved for want of the right equipment. And we don't do that. And you know why? Because we're not organized properly. We should have meetings that are conducted on a professional basis, and that could be done if we met in a businesslike way, no fancy lunches, just coffee at most, at the Wendover."

She refused to acknowledge the pained expression on the eminent consultant's face. George Kincaid was gynaecologist to a clientele drawn from *Debrett's*, including two members of the Royal Family. He was adored by all the mothers who came under his private care at the Wendover Wing, all of whom he pronounced, had produced, without doubt, the most beautiful babies he had ever had the privilege of bringing into their well-shod world.

George, who looked rather good for his fifty-four years, wore designer suits and had his hair cut every six weeks by a hairdresser so fashionable he featured more on morning television than in his own salon. George loved fund raising evenings when his Angels, as he smilingly referred to them, brought their rich husbands and sometimes, as in Serena Carmichael's case, their rich husbands' even richer bosses from which he would be the sole beneficiary, his reputation as the leader in his field enhanced. His knighthood, in his view, became even closer, not to mention the forthcoming interview in *Vogue*.

There was only one blot on George's perfect horizon. His kingdom, where he bowed and scraped to no one, where the mere mention of his presence in the building sent nurses scurrying to their stations and new mothers for their mirrors, was his exclusively. If he was obliged to allow the *Babyways* committee to invade it, he would be forced to do a little bowing and scraping himself and that would not help his standing at all. Gracing their fund raising efforts was one thing, but all these women traipsing across his empire, poking their noses into what he was doing with the money they had raised, was just bloody outrageous.

He began to arrange his features into an expression of pained regret, and might have succeeded in deflecting Serena, had it not been for Malcolm Brisley Jones, who was attending the party in the hope that his pretty but bored second wife might be invited on to the committee. Unfortunately for George, Malcolm, who privately had earmarked Serena to help him in his cause, had taken the opportunity to slide his arm round her waist while he listened to her proposal and broke in: "Splendid idea. Business-like. That's what I like. The direct approach. Oh c'mon, George, what's the problem with that?"

George swallowed hard and accepted defeat gracefully. Having only recently passed under mental review those colleagues who could not boast a group of fundraisers with such influential address books to advance their work or personal glory, he summoned an astonished laugh at Malcolm's question.

"Problem? Why, no problem at all. I was just surprised because I've been thinking much the same thing myself. Splendid. Good. I'll just have a word with Paula to see if we can start next month."

Serena waited until George had found his hostess before turning to Malcolm and giving his arm a squeeze. "You're a wonder," she grinned conspiratorially. "He would never have agreed if you hadn't said something."

"Oh stuff," Malcolm disclaimed, but she could see he was pleased. She just hoped he wouldn't now suggest the dreadful Mrs Brisley Jones should be foisted onto her in exchange. But Malcolm was too busy feeling warmly charmed by Serena to recall the point of his presence at this party, or to notice if her manner towards him was a little cooler than he was used to. He liked her. She wasn't one of those women who tried to make him feel he should be inviting her on to the board. You could talk to her; she made him feel comfortable and clever. The way she always remembered small details about him made him feel that if it hadn't been for Stephen — not to mention his own new wife — well, who knows what might have happened?

Nor did she exploit private moments to berate him about how hard he was making her husband work, or why he was being lumbered with carrying the burden of the tiresome Rupert Chawton Browne, which was a relief. Wives could sometimes be such a nuisance — but not Serena.

Few understood, as she obviously did, the reassurance value Rupert's name gave to the investors who trusted Draycott Mendes with their assets. But then she must know that her own family name had never harmed Stephen's progress. Without it, all the brilliance with money, the clear hunger for success, would have made it a much harder journey for Stephen. He looked good at parties, but few mothers would have been thrilled to have their daughters married to a struggling young banker still trying to recover from the fall-out from a spend-thrift father, and with no connections worth mentioning.

No doubt about it, Serena understood these things. So what if Rupert couldn't tell the yen from the dollar? Malcolm dismissed the faint guilt he had been feeling about Stephen with relief. If there was an asset around here it was Serena.

Meanwhile George Kincaid, ostensibly listening intently to Paula congratulating him on his brilliant idea of moving *Babyways* into the Wendover, watched the mildly flirtatious exchange between Serena and her husband's boss. He was angry that he felt a pang of frustration at the ease with which she got things done, and always had, as far as he could see. Paula might have grabbed the chair when Serena had gracefully declined but it was Serena who quietly kept the charity buoyant. She made him wary.

As he watched her across the room, he saw her turn from Malcolm and slip an arm through Stephen's as he joined them, but she was still smiling at something Malcolm was saying. There was a depth to her that wasn't always obvious in the light easy manner she adopted on such occasions. It was easy, when you first met her, to fall into the trap of thinking that she was like the others. Like Paula here, with her eye constantly raking the room for someone grander to talk to, or that absurd woman Miranda Hooper who had spent the entire evening not letting her husband out of her sight, who would do better to curtail the time she spent in Harvey Nichols spending his money and pay more attention to what he was doing with any number of women while she was shopping. It was easy to flatter them into acceptance of anything he suggested. Not Serena.

She would gently arch an eyebrow with a look that was amused at his obvious manoeuvres when they gathered for their monthly meetings. Or she would frown and ask inconvenient questions, like why were they buying such expensive equipment which would be overtaken by even newer technology in a year or two, when it might be cheaper to lease it, or why couldn't St Biddulph's use their mailing system to send out flyers for *Babyways* and save the charity a fortune in postage?

It just showed, he thought, what time and money could do. She was now, by any standards, a beautiful woman. He'd known her for years; since Anna, in fact. Not that Anna was one of his babies. Too late for that. He'd just picked up as best he could the consequences of a negligent and elderly country GP who had failed to spot the danger signs. No one in their right mind would have allowed Serena to travel up to London in that condition had they known. They met because he was on duty that night and afterwards, through gratitude — although God knows he'd done nothing — or the shared distress of a lost child, she had stayed with him. He had said to "go home, grieve and learn to want another child." Within three months she was back, pregnant with Louise.

Sometimes, even now, he could see a flash of pain in her eyes. She had all the weaknesses and strengths that came with being a rich man's wife. A warm charming woman, unaware that getting her own way was the result of being able to afford having her needs met — the first to deprecate her own efforts and the last to claim credit. Down to earth and amusing, she looked better now than she did when he first knew her. And she got her way where the charity was concerned. While he might envy the ease with which she did it, and find the fact that he had to switch off the practised charm when he dealt with her, the outcome of her activities was always to his advantage. He just wished she liked him more.

In this he wasn't entirely correct. Serena knew that George was vain. It amused her. It was however his skill that kept her loyal. And she could tolerate most things if someone was the best at their job.

"After all," she explained to Stephen, "I don't have to live with him. I'm not overkeen on Mrs Owen either, but I don't have to live with her. If they can do the job they're meant to do, you shouldn't hold a personal view against them. And he is good."

And he was. You couldn't miss George's success. The lift doors opened on to a carpeted corridor, on either side of which were the private rooms where new mothers and their babies were nursed in careful comfort until they were ready to go home.

Serena passed the nursing station and nodded a pleasant good morning. Further along she slowed her step to glance into the room where Louise and Harry had been born. Not the same room, where George Kincaid had broken the news to her that her first daughter had not survived. That was on another floor, one she could not bear to see ever again.

It was because of Anna, now buried next to Serena's father in the peaceful graveyard next to the church in Wiltshire where she had married, that Serena had become a prime mover raising money for a premature baby unit, relieved it was now a reality, just wishing — oh God, how she wished — that it had been there for Anna.

At the end of the corridor she pushed open the light oak door and joined the meeting that was just being called to order by Paula. Serena took in the white double-breasted coat dress and the security tag Paula was wearing on a slender gold chain around her neck and did not dare look at Melanie who, in any event, had bent her copper-coloured curls over her notes, apparently afflicted by a troublesome cough.

An hour later, as the meeting broke up, Serena had to agree to chair a meeting on Monday morning at her house to discuss the cabaret for the Easter Ball at Hurlingham.

*

As she let herself into the house Stephen's secretary phoned to tell her that Stephen would be taking her to dinner. She would need her passport and would not be home until Monday morning. He would collect her at five. Could she pack a weekend case for him?

Serena let out a shriek. "*Five?* Impossible. I mean, oh heavens, what do I mean? How can I be ready by five? What about the children? I've got a meeting on Monday. I'll have to call Melanie. Oh drat the man. Why didn't he *tell* me?"

"Because it wouldn't have been a surprise, would it?" Barbara replied woodenly. Serena ignored the obvious sarcasm. It was a nuisance that Barbara was so potty about Stephen, but Serena had grown used to that. And of course Stephen's habit of turning her plans on their head.

"Isn't he amazing?" she demanded of Melanie twenty minutes later, having despatched Mrs Owen to pack Stephen's case. Melanie's silence told her that amazing was not the word she would have used. Melanie much preferred her own husband's predictable way of doing things and his reassuring habit of consulting her before he made plans that might affect hers.

"Didn't you tell him it was Chrissie's weekend off?" Melanie demanded, torn between irritation that Stephen had not turned up for the charity first night she had so carefully planned and the pleasure of seeing the size of the cheque Serena had delivered from him to compensate. "How can you go just like that? You *are*? God, it's you who's amazing. Yes, yes, OK. I'll chair the meeting if you're not back. What about LouLou and Harry — want me to have them? Oh right, fine, fine. Go on, shoot. You've only got an hour as it is. Serena ...?"

"Yes?"

There was a pause. "Oh, nothing. Have fun."

Chapter Three

Lucky, is how most people described Serena Carmichael, and she would agree. Cushioned from having to make decisions no more taxing than whom to invite for the weekend or whom to get to speak at a charity fund raising lunch, most people assumed her view of life was one seen from the comfortable confines of two well ordered homes and marriage to a man who provided so much it was unthinkable that independent gestures, such as a job of her own, should be considered.

A mellow Georgian town house rising to five floors in Belvoir Square in Kensington provided their home during the week. Glebe cottage, a charming house in the Cotswolds took over at weekends and Christmas and the long summer weeks when they weren't abroad, which, Serena's mother argued, was a misleading term for something approaching a small manor house.

Not a whiff of scandal touched their name and no one had ever heard the smallest whisper that Stephen was anything but utterly faithful to his wife. It was what made Serena both an object of envy and a name to be courted. She was an honourable, if penniless, name to the union, which few had expected to survive given the groom's reputation of being as fond of women as they were of him. There was much speculation about how the squeaky clean twenty-year-old with, in those days, more wit than beauty would cope with such a man.

Thirteen years later they had confounded the critics. Serena had never regretted her decision to marry Stephen, and if she ever gave it a thought, she would have wondered only why anyone would think she might. Stephen brought energy to her life that had delighted her and which, to the dazed young girl she had been, was all that she needed as proof that life with Stephen could only get better. And it had.

At five, Chrissie had long departed for York. Serena had despatched Louise and Harry to friends rapidly organised without her children's consent, but knowing that, unless Louise had switched allegiance and now had a new best friend, they were with their favourite people until she got back.

Her cases were waiting in the hall. Mrs Owen had hastily transferred as much as possible of the mountain of food she had assembled into the deep freeze, and her dismay at such a wasted effort was mollified by seeing Mr Owen's car parked outside waiting to collect her and a considerable portion of the fruits of her afternoon's labour.

Serena was on the phone when she heard Stephen come in and quickly brought her conversation with her mother to a close. She could hear him greeting Mrs Owen. The word "shirts" floated through, and Stephen's voice saying, "Absolutely right. Couldn't agree more."

She stifled a laugh. "Ma? Sorry. Stephen's here ... must dash. I'm really sorry about lunch on Sunday. No, no. It's my fault, I should have reminded him," she lied. It was easier. "He's so busy," she rushed on. "It's our anniversary tomorrow, he's actually being very thoughtful."

Her mother's polite "of course" came just as Stephen strode into the kitchen. He couldn't have heard but Serena instinctively turned her shoulder towards the window to shield them from each other. Thirteen years had not softened Lady Armitage's view of her son-in-law who had, as she saw it, robbed Serena of many choices in her life.

It was a subject no one in the triumvirate touched on. Stephen did not because it no longer seemed relevant. Serena, from not wanting to revive old reproaches and unable to explain to her mother that she had never regretted the lack of a degree. Her mother, because she was afraid she might lose Serena and the children if she expressed her opinion that Serena should make her voice felt more often in the marriage.

"I do have a voice," Serena protested. "How could I not? I want what Stephen wants. I love making him happy."

There remained an unspoken collusion between the two women — that Stephen should not be troubled by the fact that his mother-in-law found him charming but the restless energy that appeared to still earn her daughter's admiration continued to leave her unsettled.

"Darling," Serena exclaimed as she rang off and turned to hug him. "You're a perfect angel. Where is it? Rome? No it can't be. Too far. Please tell me, it's Paris?"

He laughed at her eagerness and kissed her before looking at his watch. "Buck up, car's waiting, plane's waiting and most of all I'm waiting."

It was of course Paris. Lights from cars and street lamps were reflected in the wet pavements as their driver navigated the stream of cars on the Périphérique, competing aggressively for space with the usual Parisian indifference to traffic conditions as they circled the Arc de Triomphe and hurtled along the Champs Elysées towards their destination.

A thin mist had followed them from the airport, clinging to buildings, hovering in trees, presenting a mournful view of Serena's favourite city.

"Shame we didn't get married in April," she commented, turning back into their bedroom at the Ritz from where she had been peering down at the Place Vendome. "I mean instead of November."

"Grateful little soul, aren't you?" Stephen called from the sitting room where he was using the phone. "I seem to remember you were not keen to wait at the time. Barbara? What news? See if he's there. I'll wait."

Serena broke off the affectionate retort she was about to make. She stared down into the street. Her one consolation was that, while Stephen's umbilical cord to the office remained intact, even he couldn't get back there tonight. Unless he hired a plane that is, as there were no more flights to London.

She strolled through to join him, slipping her arms around his waist, rubbing her chin on his back, releasing him only when he gently pushed her away as the person he was waiting for came on the line.

"Tell them the airport's closed down," she mouthed as she left him to run a bath, pinning her hair up as she walked between bathroom and bedroom, preparing for the evening ahead. She had plenty of time. Stephen never made just one call and always received several back.

Through the closed door she could hear the phone ringing incessantly as she soaked in the bath. His mobile seemed to be active as well. Later, while

Stephen had gone down to the lobby to collect a package that had just arrived for him, she called each of her children to make sure they were OK.

Louise immediately demanded to know why she was ringing. She was thrilled at any opportunity to be away from her mother's watchful eye and cheered up enormously when she realized she was not being summoned home. Harry, on the other hand, had been expecting her call, his usual need for reassurance only too obvious. He liked to know exactly what was happening and when it was going to happen.

She was ready, except for her dress, and was wrapped in a silk dressing gown when Stephen finally appeared, loosening his tie, slipping off his jacket. He yawned. It was faked. Serena knew the body language. She waited.

"Everything all right?" she asked lightly, looking at him in the mirror. She adjusted her hair, already perfectly in place. "Uh-huh. Small hiccough with something just before I left. Barbara's sorting it out. Mmm, you smell good," he said, kissing the nape of her neck and dropping his cufflinks on to the dressing table.

"And has she?" Serena asked as he moved away. She sat very still and pretended she had no suspicion. Maybe she could cheat fate that way.

"Sort of," he said, disappearing into the bathroom, emerging seconds later, pulling his shirt over his head and dropping it to the floor. "Small change of plan. Nothing spectacular."

"So," she said, engrossed in examining her face in the mirror. "Am I going to be told or do I have to guess?"

He was rummaging in his jacket pocket before he flung it on top of the rest of his discarded clothes.

"Honestly, Serena, it's nothing. It just happens that they've managed to set up a meeting with Jacques Bretil. You know, the guy from Banque Commerciale? The old man told him I was in town and he's delaying leaving for the country just to have lunch with me tomorrow. It's an amazing stroke of luck."

"*Stephen*," she wailed, turning to face him. "How can you say that? It's our weekend. Can't someone else go? It's not fair. Why you?"

He crouched down beside her and took her hand, gazing intently at her. Serena glared at him. "I love it when you sulk," he teased. "Hey," he coaxed, stroking her wrist. "It's not so bad. Just one lunch on your own and a browse around the shops without me dragging behind you getting bored and bad tempered. C'mon, we've got two whole nights here and we don't have to get the plane back until Sunday evening …"

"*Sunday*? You said Monday. And when have I ever dragged you round the shops? Just that one time in New York, and never again. *And* I've got Melanie to cover for me *and*," she emphasized the word each time, "the children could have come back on Sunday *night* which is much better for them *and*—"

She stopped as Stephen produced a small white box from behind his back and held it out to her. It was tied with thin gold ribbon. "What's that?" she asked, staring at it, knowing perfectly well all the possibilities that it contained, hanging on to her position for just a little longer.

"Present. Well, go on, open it."

Inside a pair of pearl and gold drop earrings glinted back at her from a box marked Van Cleef & Arpels. Serena's shoulders sagged in defeat as she lifted the earrings from their velvet pillow. He worked so hard. She would not be here unless he did. He was waiting for her to understand. She repeated it in her head like a mantra.

"You idiot," she said crossly, throwing the box at him. "They're beautiful and you're infuriating and … oh damn you. Go to your silly lunch. Just leave your Amex behind."

He kissed her on the mouth. "I'll make it up to you," he promised.

Serena gazed steadily back at him, fixing her new earrings in place. "You'd better," she murmured, getting up and pushing him gently backwards towards the bed, sliding her robe off as she went, "and it had better be good."

It was a familiar but practised intimacy that satisfied her on a number of levels. Not least was that Stephen was back to his normal self. It had been almost two weeks. Her beautiful earrings got tangled up in her hair and they were of course a little late arriving at the restaurant. They agreed with the maître d' that traffic in Paris was becoming impossible.

Over dinner she gave him the Yeats, which he adored, reaching for her hand to kiss it. Later they took a cab to the Eiffel Tower because over dinner they had argued as to whether you could see right through to the top if you stood square underneath, and neither triumphed because it was too dark to tell.

After that they strolled back in contented silence, their fingers entwined, not bothering to check the time, threading their way through brightly lit but nearly deserted streets. After all, it was November and they could see their breath on the cold night air.

At the Pont de la Concorde they crossed the river, pausing slightly because it was Paris and they were lovers, but the river was swollen and dark. Stephen pulled the fur collar of Serena's coat up around her ears and wrapped his scarf around her. They gazed down into the murky depths of the Seine, swirling angrily away below them.

"Scary," shivered Serena. "Not romantic at all. We need warm sunshine, *bateaux mouches*, accordions, artists and poets ..."

Stephen began to laugh. "Accordions I can't do, but I might be able to help you with poetry." He delved into his coat pocket, retrieving the slim volume of Yeats. "Now where is it ... ah, here," he said, finding the page he wanted. "*I heard the old, old men say, all that's beautiful drifts away, like the waters.*"

"That's romantic?" she protested. "What a let down you are. Anyway I got that book to make you happy, not depress me," she scolded, taking the leather volume from him and trying to slide it back into his coat. The wind whipping across the bridge was not conducive to standing around quoting Irish poets in the middle of Paris.

"Of course it is," he objected, taking the leather-bound volume from her hands. "Honestly," he said severely. "This is the last time I take a married woman to Paris for the weekend. Romance is all you think about. Where's your soul? Now listen to this." He held the book above his head, walking backwards, while she made ineffectual grabs at it, laughing and ordering him to stop. He began quoting from memory, "*When you are old and grey and full of sleep and nodding by the fire, take down this book ...*"

"All right, all right," she begged, breathlessly sagging against the parapet, "I give in. Anything but your idea of romance. Name your price."

"A kiss," he said, and pulled her to him.

She shrieked but complied as two passers-by, heads down against the biting wind, glanced curiously at them and hurried on.

"You drive a hard bargain," she announced as they moved on.

He gave her an odd look. "There you are," he said, "I've proved another point."

"And that is?" she asked, taking his arm, burying her face for warmth against the sleeve of his coat, turning so that they could continue their progress across the bridge. Stephen carefully stored the book in his coat pocket and then reached down, lightly tugging one of the earrings he had just given her. She looked up as he chuckled.

"As I said, my precious, everyone's got a price."

She gave him a push. "Bastard," she said, companionably.

*

She skipped shopping and lunch and went instead for a stroll along the Boulevard St Michel, stopping at a small café overlooking the Seine and settling herself outside. She chose a table in the corner, shielded on one side by a glass partition. The damp mist from the day before had given way to a bright but still sharply cold day.

Serena felt peaceful. For a long time now she had felt Stephen slipping away, caught up in his work, sliding further into his own world. Even if it was just for a day, Paris had been enough to restore something of the old Stephen to her. Serena decided that she adored Paris. She paused. It was true but not quite as true as it sounded. She adored being away from London, with just Stephen, everything out of reach. It was so surprising how, in a matter of hours, you could create a world of your own that no one knew about, just the two of you.

By the time she ordered her second coffee, Serena was not only able to forgive Malcolm, and even Stephen's mild duplicity in getting her there, but she was now a fair way to being grateful to the unknown Monsieur Bretil for making it necessary. The waiter placed the coffee and a glass of mineral water in front of her. She smiled at him and then slipped a pair of sun-glasses on. After that she wound her wide cashmere shawl close up to her ears because she felt suspended there and didn't want to go inside. There she waited until she guessed Stephen would have finished lunch and her weekend could resume. She avoided the word she knew was more accurate. Her life could resume.

Ever since she had met him, Serena had waited for Stephen to breathe life into her world. She glanced at her reflection in the glass. She saw a very different woman to the one who had met Stephen all those years ago. Then she was generally regarded as striking rather than beautiful with her wide mouth and not quite straight nose. She had a warm, humorous charm inherited from her father, and a bone structure from her mother that would last longer than more youthful good looks.

All of which, during that long painful summer when she had first seen him, she would willingly have traded in for a dash of the glamour her rivals exuded. She was tall with wide-set grey eyes and a sweep of blond hair which, in those days, fell in a tangle of curls around her shoulders. Her hair was her one small rebellious part she protected against the rigid social code enforced by the hostesses to whose parties she dutifully came. Refusing to have the waves tamed by a good hairdresser, as her mother kept urging, allowed her to keep a mind of her own.

Her name, however, was of far greater importance to such hostesses than her hair, or the fact that her fortune was clearly much less impressive than the family into which she had been born.

None of this, she decided, was any use while trying to keep Stephen Car-michael focused on her. What she needed was glamour, and in the privacy of her bedroom she made several attempts to achieve it. After one misera-ble evening watching him charm someone else, she barricaded herself into her bedroom and got to work with the spoils of her trawl through Harvey Nichols' beauty department. After ten minutes she anxiously eyed the star-tling effect the deep lines of blusher and the kohl-ringed eyes had created and pouted into the mirror.

Somehow glamour was not the word it inspired. "Harlot," she told the mirror frankly. She began to scrub it all off, giggling helplessly at her reflection. Then she binned most of her unsatisfactory choices and went back to the store to buy two very tight, very short black dresses instead. Since her legs were long, even she could see these were her most helpful asset. All the way to the drinks party that evening she begged God to let Stephen be a legs man.

She was swept along by her own feverish attempts to reinvent herself, purely to compete with the line of women who routinely seemed to cling to Stephen. She didn't notice for quite a while that his interest in her was already stirred. At the time she knew only that he was causing a commotion by being seen regularly in the company of the youngest daughter of a cabinet minister. The girl's mother, however, had other plans for her daughter than to be hitched to the uncertain star of a man with charm, but no money.

Serena, who heard all this on the grapevine, could have kissed the girl's mother for despatching her daughter to New York for a year. She was, however, scornful of someone unable to see what an amazing man Stephen Carmichael was, but even she could see that Stephen's late father hadn't helped his younger son's chances of impressing an ambitious mother.

Trying to conceal such a background would have been impossible. Everyone said it was to Stephen's credit that he made no attempt to do so, even if he did not go out of his way to promote it. No one, of course, said it to his face.

Wilfred Carmichael, Stephen's father, came from a family where the money that had set him up for a life of travelling, gambling and womanizing, came from a win on the football pools by his grandfather. It was he who had raised Wilfred and his brother when their mother and father abandoned them. When he died, he left his money divided equally between his grandsons.

Wilfred's brother died driving the extremely racy sports car he had bought with some of his inheritance, leaving Wilfred, at not quite nineteen, his brother's sole heir. It enabled him to enter the social circle of gamblers and drinkers who helped to ruin him.

Stephen's mother, Jasmine, had married Wilfred, fifteen years her senior, in the teeth of her family's opposition. She had been dazzled by his charm and disregard for convention. Stephen was still in his first year at Cambridge when Wilfred dropped dead in a night-club in Nice. The debts he left were considerable. But these were nothing compared with the legacy of his reputation.

This only served to intrigue Serena all the more. She saw what others failed to see beyond the obvious ambition and social charm and unfortunate parentage. Stephen was clever. Stephen listened. He attended carefully to what was being said. His dark head bent slightly to one side, absorbed, interested, confidently challenging any economic or business strategy he found flawed, and upholding his own theories.

She thought he was amazingly brave. His quiet air of confidence seemed light years away from the gauche and noisy boys who were her friends.

His critics — and there were some, even at that stage of his life — regarded the way he went about business as quite often too reckless, but as he mostly emerged unscathed, a grudging respect, if not an acceptance of him, was obvious. Serena watched all this, knowing those who were dismissive of him had their dislike also rooted in the ease with which Stephen attracted women.

Serena disliked it too, but for different reasons. The question of his professional future did not, however, concern her. All she saw was a man with a plan where she had none, other than the one laid down for her. He made her question the careful structure of her life thus far and the possibility — hitherto unexplored or even thought of — that she was following a design not of her making.

Finally Stephen took her to dinner and encouraged her to discover if all that was laid out ahead of her was indeed her wish, or whether she was just being obedient and loyal to those who had conceived these plans.

"You're awfully like me," he told her, when they eventually went to bed together about a month after Serena had taken up her place at Bristol, and three months after she had first met him. "Only you don't allow yourself to do what you really want to do. You just want everyone to be happy."

"I don't," she cried, horrified in case she had been a disappointment to him but thrilled that he should regard her as daring as himself when she knew she was no such thing. "I mean I do. Want everyone to be happy, I mean. What's wrong with that? It's just that you know what you want and … and go and get it."

"Well, maybe you just don't know what you want yet?" he said, rolling over to glance at the bedside clock.

But she did know. She simply lacked the courage to tell him. She feared he might take fright if she confessed, not sure that she wanted to say something so important so soon.

Lying awake long into the night in her narrow bed in the cubicle of a university dorm room, she would try to unravel why her future no longer seemed as clear to her as it once had. She watched the daily unfolding of student life, feeling remote from it all. Wrapped in a duvet she thought of him incessantly. His lean face, the shock of dark hair falling into his eyes, the way he continually tossed it back.

She wrote his name in the margins of her essays. She found the street where he lived in the A-Z and traced the route from the nearest tube. She memorized the times of trains from Bristol Parkway to Paddington.

Other girls on her corridor crowded into each other's rooms, sharing confidences which she did not feel at ease with, bored, not only by students who tried to attract her attention, but by university life itself.

When she phoned him and oh — the joy when he phoned her — he would tease her when she hesitantly started to tell him of her uncertainty. Then he would say he had to rush, tell her she was the magic in his life and hang up, leaving her more uncertain about his feelings for her than ever.

She took to walking for miles through the town, schooling herself not to think of Stephen, trying to determine what would be best for her, what her parents would say — and that did matter, because Serena truly loved them. But until Stephen came along — with his sharp intellect, the way he seized life and made her feel she had been only half alive until she was with him again — she had never really known what she wanted.

For months, she remained on the edge of other students' concerns, distanced from their world, waiting only for the moments when she could escape to London to be with Stephen.

She smiled inwardly and signalled to the waiter for the bill. Here she was, more than a dozen years later, sitting in a café by the Seine, still waiting.

*

Stephen was already at the hotel when she got back, which surprised her. It was not quite three-thirty but Jacques Bretil, with a wife and two children waiting for him at his country home in St Emilion de Croix, a two-hour drive from Paris, had kept the lunch brief.

Stephen looked exhausted but his eyes were bright, triumphant. He was holding a glass of brandy. His tie was loosened, his shirt sleeves pushed back.

"How did it go?" she asked, pulling her scarf off and shrugging out of her coat.

"Ace," he crowed, putting the brandy glass down and swinging her around. She could smell the wine and garlic on his breath. "In the bag. Aren't you proud of me?"

"Of course," she laughed, as he nuzzled her neck. "Tell me all. Stephen? Stephen, stop it, what are you doing?"

"Celebrating," he muttered, as he pushed her on to the sofa from where they both slid in a frantic heap on to the carpet. Serena's protests were silenced in the shock of being so ruthlessly taken.

The practised skill of the previous evening was absent. An explosion of raw lust, shameless in its ferocity and over in minutes, left Serena feeling bruised, somewhat bewildered and Stephen sound asleep on the floor, as she eventually eased herself away to gather her scattered wits and clothes.

Chapter Four

Serena readily acknowledged that she was in the fortunate position of being a wealthy woman because of Stephen.

"Left to me," she would cheerfully insist to anyone who suggested her own contribution to such a successful life was not exactly insignificant, "we'd be surrounded by books, living in a freezing house somewhere in the depths of Wiltshire, chopping up furniture for firewood."

It was an exaggeration that nearly always drew a disbelieving laugh from her audience, but she was right about Stephen. Stephen, who was passionate about life, filled theirs with indisputable evidence that he was clever as well as successful. A discerning eye and a talent for investing in new young artists brought him to the attention of serious dealers. A wine cellar was stocked with vintage champagnes and clarets bought at auction. His children were sent to expensive schools and his library was that of a man who was well read with perhaps a weakness for the Irish. MacNeice, Yeats, Joyce and Synge crammed the shelves.

He was fond of saying he loved Paris because it was where Synge met Yeats for the first time. His Irish roots were another enthusiasm, although he knew it had been at least four generations since a pure Irish strain had been evident in his family. He said it was because they were mavericks, or rebels, that they appealed to him but Serena decided after much teasing on her part that he was just saying it. Stephen's own need for order and his respect for the established manner of doing things contradicted this.

He had brought them from a cramped little mews house to their present splendour through his genius for getting what he wanted, a regard for the discipline of hard work as the route to success, driven most of all by a contempt for his father's dissolute lifestyle.

When Serena met Stephen, it was long after his father's death. The Stephen she met had lived on his own for five years, ever since his second year at Cambridge when his mother had departed to set up home in Tuscany with only a vague suggestion that, if he was at a loose end, he would be welcome to join her in her mountain home.

True, Stephen was not destitute. In a rare show of strength against her husband when she saw what was happening, his mother had insisted that Wilfred set up a small trust for each of her sons which was enough to support them in reasonable comfort until they found jobs. That, plus the division of the sale of the rambling Victorian house in Norfolk, where Stephen and his brother had been brought up, had cushioned the risk of both her sons having no chance of success at all in life, but it was only a small fraction of the money Wilfred had squandered.

Serena had expected Stephen to feel grateful that his mother had stepped between him and hardship. Indeed, his anger was directed almost solely at his father.

"Didn't he leave you anything?" she asked, feeling uneasy at such a blaze of bitterness.

"Oh, certainly," he said. "A huge struggle to survive."

Serena looked bewildered. "But you had some money and a flat ..."

"But not the future I was entitled to," he interrupted angrily. "The one he could have provided if he hadn't put himself first. My mother was hopeless with him."

"But, Stephen, he drank, what could she —"

"Do?" He finished her sentence. "If she'd divorced him years before, she would have got far more, rather than hanging on to a man who cared nothing for her. You have no idea what it was like trying to shake off his reputation. The only decent thing he did was die abroad so that for the last few years no one knew just how bad he'd become."

Serena said nothing. In the end she decided that if this clever and wonderful man had been left with only memories of a miserable childhood, contempt for his father and indifference to his mother, then they'd both done him a favour by getting out of his life, allowing him to make a success of it. She wondered how he could feel anything towards his surviving parent. But they remained in touch and continued to antagonize one another whenever they met. She admired Stephen for such loyalty.

Jasmine Carmichael, known to everyone as Minnie, was something of an artist in her own right. A tall lean woman with strong hands, her loosely assembled hair streaked with grey, she was indifferent to fashion and never wore make-up. Those who knew her could never understand what she had in common with Wilfred. Now established in a small villa in Lucca, she was happier than she had been in years. She had been able to live economically enough to return to her first love of painting, making enough from modest sales to make abrupt and infrequent trips to London to see the younger of her two sons.

Stephen's older brother, Toby, figured in their life even less. Serena had met him only twice in her life. He lived in Cape Town and had not attended their wedding. On both occasions the brothers clashed over their view of Wilfred. Toby was more inclined to favour his mother's indifference, believing that Wilfred had not been deliberately irresponsible, for it was just the way he was. During one heated exchange — when Stephen and Serena were living in Notting Hill — Toby had arrived with their mother to inspect Harry, then just a few weeks old.

He argued from the depths of one of Stephen's burgundy striped *fauteuil* chairs, deplored the values of the moneyed classes who were, he asserted whilst savouring the bouquet of particularly mellow claret from his brother's cellar, blinkered to the real world. His sister-in-law glanced uneasily between the brothers. He would, he continued, have preferred to have been given the money spent on his education, and, rather than getting a useless degree, have used it doing something more in keeping with what he did best.

"And that," Stephen furiously relayed later to Serena, after a tense family evening, "is trailing around the world, living off other people and then criticizing how they live. God, I wish he'd go."

It was plain to her even without that impassioned outburst that none of the Carmichaels cared overmuch for each other's company. His mother had attended their wedding, giving them one of her paintings and told Serena

— watching Stephen as he moved among the guests — that Stephen was his father's double.

"His father's?" Serena repeated, swinging round to look at Stephen as he stood, looking impossibly handsome in his morning suit and dove grey necktie, lightly clasping a glass of champagne. He was talking to his boss and his boss's wife.

"Mmm," Jasmine nodded. "A fondness for the good life."

"Heavens," Serena's eyes widened. How little she knows her own sons, she thought, amazed at such a judgement. Where Wilfred was indifferent to amassing money, simply unloading it at the nearest casino, or more often a bookmaker when enough certainties had failed to romp home at Goodwood, Longchamps or Kentucky, Stephen worked long hours and devoted himself to structuring a career that would shield them both and their unborn child from an uncertain future. She wondered if Stephen even knew how to place a bet he was so opposed to it.

Serena felt a surge of pride for Stephen, so responsible, so anxious to make something of his life, a pride she knew was not shared by his mother. Why couldn't she see, wondered Serena — too polite to say so and indeed not knowing her mother-in-law nearly well enough to point it out — that it was Toby, with his footloose wanderings, and at that time disentangling himself from the second of what would eventually be four marriages, who clearly evoked the spirit of their dead and — shocking to Serena — unlamented father?

In an attempt to get to know her mother-in-law, Serena had politely enquired after her own family. But Minnie did not seem inclined to reveal much. The only child of rather bohemian parents, she'd married, not anticipating that the wild young man who had captured her imagination in her youth would become a tiresome, drunken liability in middle age.

Apart from lamenting the lack of relatives on both sides of the family, Minnie was obviously bored by Serena's interest in her history and wandered off to find someone to refill her glass and provide more stimulating conversation. If she was interested in getting to know this thin, blonde, already pregnant wife of her son she showed no sign of it, and as Serena was fighting down waves of nausea, longing only to escape to find somewhere to lie down, they parted, each feeling the other could have tried harder.

Still, long hours at the office, and longer evenings throwing dinner parties they could ill afford for those who would be likely to remember Stephen as the man they most wanted in their company or on their side when the right openings showed themselves, had reaped a rich harvest. At not quite forty, Stephen was a significant player in the financial markets across the world and invitations for the Carmichaels to dine with the Chancellor and to spend a weekend at Dorney Wood demonstrated that his star in the City was well in the ascendant.

Slowly Serena had come to realize that Stephen's hunger for success was his driving force. Not for a moment did she doubt that she and the children were loved, but it was many years now since she had acknowledged that her marriage would survive only if she gave Stephen the room he needed to power his way to the top.

She also understood his relentless need to fill their homes and their lives with tangible proof that he was going somewhere. It would be untrue to say Serena would have been as happy if she had to hesitate about writing a cheque or charging shopping to Stephen's account; it simply never occurred to her that life with Stephen would have resulted in anything less.

*

After their weekend in Paris, Serena's hope that Stephen would cut back on his hours was short-lived. Christmas was spent in the country, but the holiday they had planned in the New Year to Antigua once the children were back at school was cancelled at the last minute.

"Antigua?" Stephen looked blank. "Oh God, sorry, Serena, I forgot. Hopeless. Look, why don't you go with … I don't know … Melanie. Well, OK, not Melanie. For Christ's sake, Serena, I can't. It's just not on at the moment."

Serena fell silent. It was after midnight and they were in the drawing room. For the past week, Stephen had been locked in his own study on the floor below until the small hours. Last night he hadn't come home at all, spending what little was left of it in the hotel where he had been in negoti-

46

ation with business associates sorting out the havoc caused, once again, by the hapless Rupert Chawton Browne.

"Rupert's OK." Stephen sounded impatient. "Just a twit."

"Then if he's so hopeless why's he in banking?"

"Not hopeless, just not very committed. Told me he would prefer to have been a farmer."

"Not much call for tilling the soil in the square mile," she snapped, and instantly regretted it. "But he's making a good job of spoiling the tills," she added drily, in an effort to stop the exchange plunging, as it did so often these days, into acrimony.

Her weak joke fell into silence. He just gave her a distracted grunt, directing the remote control towards the television, snapping it between channels looking for a City update.

"Sorry." He turned to her as the screen dissolved into blackness and he tossed the controller to one side. "What did you say?"

"Nothing important," she said, handing him a drink. This had to stop. Rupert's move to head up a specially created department dealing in offshore developments removed him from Stephen's immediate sphere, but the chaos he'd left in his wake remained undetected because of Stephen. Serena knew from the odd remark he let fall that once again he had moved quietly and efficiently to repair the damage. It was Serena who was exasperated, at his indifference towards a man being rewarded for incompetence.

"Of course he's rewarded," she cried. "Anyone else would have been turfed out. I would have thought hanging on to his job was ample reward."

"Just a toy to keep him amused," he said. Serena looked down at him sprawled beside her on the sofa. "And out of the way."

She was struggling to keep her temper. "The trouble with you," he said, his eyes closed, "is that you spend too much time wondering what everyone else is doing, while some of us keep our eye on what matters. What does it matter about Rupert? He's simply cosmetic. A joke."

Serena started to protest that he wasn't a joke to the outside world. Because of Stephen's discretion or indifference, Rupert was publicly regarded as an asset, because Malcolm treated him as such, and it was all so unfair.

But Stephen just yawned.

"God, don't let Malcolm hear you say that. He's had a hell of a day. Feeling rather foolish having fielded Rupert in the first place."

No wonder Stephen was so successful. Unwavering in what he wanted, untouched by other people's trajectories.

Part of her was pleased that Stephen had taken to seeing Malcolm in a less heroic light than in former days, but she worried in case his new habit of mocking the chairman's reverence for titles and his pleasure in spending weekends in stately homes no matter how cold, great or small, might slip out in an unguarded moment.

"Look, Stephen," she said, trying not to sound like a whinge, knowing instantly she had failed. She saw the lines around his mouth beginning to clench. She persisted: "I was only thinking of you. Ever since Paris you've been working your socks off and that bloody lot are not even remotely grateful ..."

Stephen gave a tired shake of his head. "And all the work you bring home is ludicrous. I worry, that's all. I'm entitled to worry, aren't I? Stephen, are you listening to me?"

"Yes, yes, yes." He struggled to his feet, putting his glass down with a snap. "I'm listening. It's just a particularly tricky time. You wouldn't understand." He cut across as she opened her mouth to question why it was tricky.

"Can't talk about it, you know the rules. Look," he said, rubbing his eyes and letting his fingers drag down his face. "Why don't you buzz over to Rome, do some shopping, eh?"

She glared at him. "Is that all you think I do? For God's sake, Stephen, give me some credit. How could I leave? You're under pressure. It's no fun for me either at the moment. You snap my head off all the time. Yes you do. Next time I see Malcolm, I shall bloody well tell him."

She stopped as he rolled his eyes to the ceiling. "Look," she said, dropping into her role of appeaser. "Ignore me. As if I would say anything. It's just tough on me as well. I hardly see you ..."

"All right, all right." He picked up his drink and tossed it back. "I understand, only ..." his voice dropped to a more gentle tone, "not now, eh?"

She knew that voice. She couldn't win. She forced a smile.

"No, of course not. Not now. Bed?" she invited, holding out her hand for him to pull her to her feet.

"In a minute," he said, as she stood up. "You go on. I'll be up later."

*

She had hoped to celebrate Stephen's fortieth birthday at the end of January on a sun-drenched beach, but, deprived of this, Serena planned a party instead. She phoned Barbara, his secretary, and asked if she would just remind Stephen that he was due home by seven on that day, in case he threw in any more meetings, and if possible to make sure that Stephen left the office on time.

Barbara's voice was chilly. "I'll do my best of course, Serena. But Stephen doesn't always tell me about the meetings he arranges. I can only vouch for those I organize."

Serena stopped. "Of course," she agreed, "I only meant you could remind him." She replaced the phone.

She toyed with the idea of ringing Malcolm's secretary but she could be worse than Barbara where boss' wives were concerned. Then she remembered that Malcolm's second, much younger wife was far worse than her. And they were coming to this party, younger wife undoubtedly bringing with her all her pretensions of style and precedence that she had acquired on her second marriage. Last time they had all dined together at Malcolm's house, in order to further Mrs Brisley Jones's quite naked ambition to inveigle herself into the world of fundraising and to remove Paula from the chair of *Babyways*, Serena had decided that such an ill-matched couple couldn't last.

The young wife clearly fancied Stephen. You could see it, and Malcolm was miserable. Good, she thought, with unaccustomed but long-overdue venom. If he went home to the silly woman earlier than was his custom, she might not have to keep turning up at his office and dropping in on poor Stephen.

"And Stephen," Malcolm's wife cooed, indicating his place next to her, "you here." Her breasts straining against a too-tight dress, she clutched a piece of paper from which she was instructing them where to sit. Serena darted a look at Malcolm.

Poor old Malcolm, thought Serena, taking her place much further down the table. "Serena, next to Rupert, and Malcolm," his wife wagged her finger at him, "you're not to flirt with Paula."

The discovery that his personality and fine mind were not, after all, enough to maintain his new wife's interest once they were married, came as a bit of a surprise once the honeymoon period had worn off. Serena was annoyed with herself for feeling the first pang of sympathy for him since he had left his first wife — a nice, quiet woman who, Stephen had said, fulfilled that old maxim: I owe my success to my first wife and my second wife to my success.

"Don't waste your sympathy," Stephen said later, as they drove home. "His own fault. How can you get to know anyone if you only see them in expensive hotel suites and discreet apartments? They never went out publicly until he'd truly unloaded Maria and the tabloids couldn't push him into resigning, even when he's been screwing her on the office floor. Still," he said, loosening his tie as he drove, "her uncle's related to a duke somewhere along the line — he can console himself with that."

Weeks later, planning Stephen's party, Serena frowned at the list in front of her. If there had been any way of not inviting the Brisley Joneses she would have willingly used it. This should be a party for their own friends, but Stephen had said he wanted them included. At first Serena had been surprised but now she was worried. These days Stephen made very little attempt to be diplomatic about his boss.

Being tactful about Malcolm had been a tedious enough business while Stephen had admired and, she assumed, respected him. But the arrival of Rupert Chawton Browne, the endless deference to his silly wife and the task of bringing Jacques Bretil to heel while Malcolm sweated in London seemed to change all that. It had also stretched Serena's mild temper to unreasonable lengths. Even so, Stephen insisted that Malcolm, with the bird-witted wife and the dozy but rather sweet Rupert in tow, should be at his party. Serena had argued in vain against it.

What worried her more were the increasing arguments they were having over things that would once have been resolved without rancour. Indeed, now she thought about it, at one time they wouldn't have argued at all. Certainly not about Stephen's job.

About a week before the party, Melanie asked them out to dinner. "Just us, you know. Charles was saying he hadn't seen Stephen for such a long time."

"Snap," Serena replied. "Tell Charles I've put in a request for a recent photograph."

"That bad, eh?" Melanie asked, sympathetically.

"No, not that bad. Just … oh, I don't know, Mel, just different. I'll be glad when this contract is over. God knows what it all means, but Stephen's really taking the strain."

Stephen had asked Melanie to start without him if he was delayed, and by the time he arrived the three old friends were well into discussions about the forthcoming birthday party.

"Richard Van Stuckley wants to say a few words," Serena told them, forking up lasagne, "but that will be about work and how many times he beats him at squash …"

"And that would be?" grinned Charles.

"Ball park figure?" she asked with a straight face. "About twice. I'll say one thing for Richard, he's an old schmoozer, but he does speak well."

"Let's just hope the party boy doesn't jet off somewhere," Melanie put in. "With his present record I hope you've got Barbara on full alert."

Serena laughed. "God, she's a pain. But she'll make sure. Anyway, Stephen's looking forward to it. He won't forget."

Stephen chose that moment to arrive. "Sorry, sorry, sorry," he said, kissing Melanie and shaking Charles' hand. He bent and kissed Serena and all the exasperation she had felt at his late arrival melted. He looked shattered.

"So what's the gossip?" he asked, as Charles poured him a drink.

"Nothing strenuous." Melanie sat down again and picked up her fork. "Just wondering if we might all get in some skiing before Easter. Serena says you need a break."

"Does she?" Stephen glanced at Serena. "She worries too much. I'll get away just as soon as the Budget's over, but this," he waved the hand holding his glass to embrace the company, "is about as much free time as I'm going to get until then."

Melanie glanced at Serena, who was absently pushing food around her plate, and then back to Stephen. "You mean except for your party?" Melanie said.

Stephen looked blankly at her. "Party? I'm sorry, remind me."

Serena let her fork clatter to the plate. "Really, darling, you must be tired. Your birthday party, of course. It's not every day you're forty, is it?"

Briefly he closed his eyes. "Oh, that party. Sorry, darling. Of course. Wednesday, isn't it?"

"Thursday," Serena contradicted him.

"I meant, Thursday," he said.

Melanie glanced at Charles. "Now," her voice sounded overbright, "who's for coffee?"

*

The following Thursday, the day of Stephen's party, Malcolm Brisley Jones' secretary phoned to apologize and to say Malcolm couldn't make it after all. She didn't give a reason and Serena didn't ask for one. This did not cheer her as she thought it would. She knew Stephen would be irritated, especially as the secretary had phoned her first and not him.

She phoned Stephen's office to let him know but he wasn't there. Barbara was expecting him at around midday. She didn't tell Barbara about the chairman, she guessed she would know anyway — there was little you could keep quiet in a bank like Draycott Mendes.

Meanwhile, the florist and her team were already working downstairs. Caterers would be installed at midday. Chrissie was going to make sure the children disappeared after Stephen had opened their presents. Dress from Bruce. Hair. She ticked off the list in her hand. Charles Westfield was going to propose the toast after Richard Van Stuckley had made his speech. Paula phoned Serena just after breakfast to say that Richard was only too pleased to have been asked. As he had offered himself, ruling out more appropriate candidates like Charles, Serena assured Paula that Richard was the perfect choice.

She wondered if Paula knew about Richard's infidelities. Certainly she could not have known that the last one had been the subject of one of her rare rows with Stephen. Rare for those days, at least.

Serena had not known that Richard Van Stuckley, senior member of the cabinet, charming and urbane, upholder of family values, had taken his mistress to Glebe Cottage, Serena and Stephen's country home. Serena's fury when she discovered this had alarmed Stephen. Knowing she was right, clearly furious with himself for having been so stupid, he simply stared back at her.

"Paula can be an absolute pain at times, but she is loyal to him and considers herself a friend of mine," Serena stormed. "And it won't do you any good if that bloody girl dumps to the *Sun* and our cottage is plastered across the tabloids as a 'Minister's love nest', will it?"

Denied the use of the cottage, Richard Van Stuckley had blamed its loss on Serena. He never said this, but she knew. He was, however, nervous that she might tell Paula, so he remained outwardly as pleasant and attentive as only an adulterous husband can be.

At eleven, she was dismayed when another guest dropped out. A close colleague of Stephen's at the bank was needed urgently at the same meeting as the chairman which meant that the chairman's deputy would undoubtedly be ringing any minute to cancel as well.

Serena started to feel nervous. At this rate it was likely that Stephen would also be summoned and not show for his own party. She called Barbara again, but this time she got the junior secretary who said Barbara had gone to lunch and Mr Carmichael was expected any minute.

She left a message for Stephen to call her at the hairdresser's. She might still be able to get him to wriggle out of the meeting if she got to him before Malcolm did.

George Kincaid rang as she was leaving the house to tell her he'd just had a bright idea and wouldn't it be marvellous if the Prime Minister's wife would open the new baby unit? Disappointed it was not Stephen, knowing George was trying to get past Paula who wanted the newest royal bride to do the honours, she felt cross at being delayed and used like this.

She promised to talk to Stephen. She could have called the PM's wife's office herself; but she knew Stephen preferred to do this. Sometimes, he said, you need an excuse just to gauge the mood of the moment. A social reason was always useful.

There was a pleasant buzz of activity as she finally left the house, hurrying because she was now running behind schedule. The caterers were well underway, Mrs Owen scrutinizing their every move.

Simon, her hairdresser, whizzed her through in record time, keeping two clients waiting at the backwash so that he could ease Serena's schedule a little. She left a handsome tip discreetly tucked into the pocket of his skintight trousers. She picked up her dress from Beauchamp Place and headed home. It was almost five.

The drawing room was already piled high with Stephen's presents. Chrissie would have organized the children's tea. Mrs Owen, who was staying overnight to help with the party, would be lording it over the caterers. Soon the house would be awash with plump winter roses, the scent of lilies and a string quartet playing Vivaldi.

All Serena had to do was check everything was in place, and then be ready by seven-forty-five before the first guests arrived. Still no word from Stephen, and the junior secretary had said Barbara had been asked to help out in the chairman's office. And no, Mr Carmichael wasn't at the meeting. She was quite, quite sure.

Serena breathed a sigh of relief and switched off the car phone. She manoeuvred her way through Knightsbridge into Kensington, and swung the car into Belvoir Square. The chance of Stephen doing a no show at his own birthday now safely deflected, Serena was mulling over the merits of the PM's wife as opposed to a royal bride for the grand opening of the prem baby unit. Neither seemed to her to be suitable. A more glamorous person would pull the press. Maybe that American actor she had met at the Duke's dinner party last week? He would certainly be a draw. She reached into the back of the car to collect her parcels, slammed the door and then set the alarm. Maybe, she mused, a few famous mothers with their offspring would make a much better picture. She'd deal with it after the weekend when the party was out of the way.

It occurred to her, as she approached the shallow steps leading up to her front door, that there were an unusual number of cars in the square. Dark saloons. Two of them had drivers. Both were staring straight ahead. The caterer's van stood silently by the kerb. The florist's jaunty rose-pink van was parked further away. As she put the key in the lock the door was pulled open from the inside. She knew that something was wrong. Serena stared at the woman in front of her.

"Natalie," she exclaimed, leaning forward to embrace the dark-suited woman who was standing there, "what brings you here so early? Goodness me, you gave me a fr —"

Her voice tailed off. Natalie Silverman, senior partner in the law firm, Beresford Wright, Stephen's lawyers, took her arm and pulled her gently into the house. A series of images flashed before Serena. Frozen moments that she would remember for the rest of her days.

Mrs Owen's pale, stern face by the door that led to the kitchen, clutching a cloth in her hands. Harry's school blazer hastily thrown on top of his school bag. Silence when the sound of her children's voices should have been filling the house. Stephen's study door open, papers everywhere.

She could see the backs of two men dismantling the computer, wires trailing everywhere and snaking across the floor. Two more stood in the doorway of the drawing room. The clock was pointing at five to five. Serena wheeled around dropping her parcels.

"Natalie, what is it? Don't frighten me. Is it Stephen? Oh my God, he's had an accident? But why are you ...?"

"Serena, you must be calm." Natalie was still clutching her arm. Confused, jumbling thoughts crowded in on her, as she allowed herself to be ushered into the drawing room. One of the men came forward.

"Mrs Carmichael?"

"Yes?" Her voice was cracking. It came from a great distance. She knew she was holding on to Natalie. She didn't know why.

"Have you any idea where we might find your husband?"

Serena looked at Natalie and back at the man. She remembered later that Natalie's eyes were filled with fear. "Stephen?" she repeated. She felt stupid. She couldn't think. "His office. Here — I mean later he'll be here. It's his birthday. Why? Please, for God's sake *tell* me."

The second man came forward and motioned Natalie to make Serena sit down. "Mrs Carmichael," he addressed her, "I'm sorry to have to tell you, we have a warrant for your husband's arrest."

Serena gazed at him. Slowly she shook off Natalie's supportive arm. She wanted to stand up straight. For some reason she couldn't. She tried to speak, but the words were caught in her chest. Her eyes flashed around the group. She thought her handbag had fallen to the floor.

"Don't be so absurd. Arrest my husband? Is this some kind of bad joke?" But even as she said the words, she knew it wasn't, and as the man slowly shook his head, Natalie's hand closed over hers and a noise like a gun being fired echoed in her head.

Chapter Five

Serena was sitting on a rock. In the distance she could see Stephen standing on another, much taller one, staring out to sea. She was puzzled because he was holding a candle in the way he had once held a tiny white coffin. As she watched, the flame kept going out. Of course it did, because he wasn't shielding it from the wind whipping off the waves that were lashing angrily upwards, dragging at his feet, before their long fistfuls of foam fell back into the darkness.

She wanted to stand up to tell him, warn him that the flame would only keep going if he protected it with his hand, but she couldn't move. And then, without warning, he threw the candle into the blackness ahead of him. There was a roaring noise as it plunged down into the waves, a sound that made no sense because the candle was so small for such a thunderous sound.

She tried to scream to make Stephen look at her, but her voice was strangled in the back of her mouth. The weight of the candle separated the waves into a rolling valley, towering over and engulfing her. She couldn't run and she couldn't see Stephen any more. She began to scream.

Her eyes flew open. It was still dark. She groped for the light beside her bed, her hair damp with sweat, straining to hear if Harry or Louise had woken. Her hand found the small gold alarm clock. It was four in the morning. The house was silent.

No one stirred. She slumped back on the pillows. She didn't know which of them she had been dreaming about. Anna or Stephen. She often dreamed about Anna. Her lost child was sometimes smiling at her. Sometimes she was not Anna, but Louise, but she was always being held by Stephen, just as he had held the small white coffin — carrying it into the church where no one had been allowed to touch it except for him.

57

She hadn't meant to go to sleep but neither did she felt guilty that she had given in to exhaustion. She had stopped thinking of anything other than the paralysis that had gripped her. Her day had started at seven with a comfortable familiarity. It had slid almost seamlessly into night, and this brief moment of oblivion had marked the start of the day. The next day. The day after the terrible shock. She could hardly bear to think of it. A whole day not knowing where he was, terrified that he might be dead. And the silence. The dreadful silence that roared in her ears. She had not left the house since she had been driven to and from City police station in the early hours of the morning after Stephen disappeared. She began to shake; huge gulping sobs racked her body. Sheer fear. She wanted Stephen. She wanted him now, now, now. She stifled a scream and swung her legs to the floor. Holding herself steady, she stood up and moved stiffly towards the window.

Below her was a scene that was bizarre and frightening. They were still there, still waiting. All waiting for Stephen. All night the press corps were encamped outside the door and the police inside it. By that time the bank had admitted something was wrong, that an unspecified amount, but of seismic proportions, had gone missing from several accounts along with Stephen Carmichael, the head of corporate development, and the Fraud Office had put out an alert for him.

Before this revelation, the fact that the Fraud Squad had raided the home of a prominent merchant banker and that he was not available for comment was, however, sufficient to fill a five-minute slot on most channels with library pictures and a live on-camera report from outside the bank.

Sky News was well into it by midnight, with live coverage from outside Serena's house. Their lights eerily illuminating the deeply respectable square, the inhabitants of which were already locking themselves away from such a scandal behind tightly drawn blinds and closed front doors.

Shortly after one o'clock in the morning, the TV crews were rewarded when a weary, but stony-faced Detective Inspector Donald Trewless emerged from the house. He refused to comment, beyond that he hoped to be able to interview Mr Carmichael shortly, but admitted he was waiting for Mr Carmichael to contact him before his wish could be fulfilled.

Malcolm was filmed arriving home, rushing to his front door through the throng of waiting reporters. The door was swiftly opened and shut behind him, his housekeeper clearly having been instructed by phone as he approached.

The front steps of Draycott Mendes became the backdrop against which all stories on the Stephen Carmichael case were introduced. The aggressively entwined D and M hammered out in brass script on the wall of the bank became, by early morning, synonymous with seedy goings-on, sleaze and a list of household names reputed to be clients of the bank. It was later established that company accounts, rather than individual clients, would bear the loss of this multi-million-pound discrepancy in the books. Privately, speculation had begun that they would never know for sure how much was missing.

The most prized shots were of Serena arriving home in the small hours accompanied by an exhausted Andrew Beresford. He helped her push her way through the clamouring throng pressing her to answer questions, look in their direction. Wooden-faced, perfectly groomed, emotions intact, she ignored them and the door closed firmly behind her.

At three, Serena was persuaded by Chrissie to go and lie down, where a mixture of shock and exhaustion overcame her. She dozed for a few minutes, preferring the nightmare she had emerged from to the one she was facing.

Mechanically she went into the shower and turned the taps full on. Immediately a gentle knock came on her bedroom door. Oh God, she'd forgotten. The policewoman protecting her from the press outside the door, but much more likely monitoring her in case she tried to phone Stephen, or slip away or do herself in.

She crossed to the door and opened it a few inches.

"I'm sorry, Mrs Carmichael, I just wanted to check you were OK. Can't you sleep?"

Serena stared curiously at her. "Sleep?" she repeated. "No. Dozed. That's all."

"Tea?" the young woman asked anxiously. "Would you like a cup of tea?"

If it meant she would go away and leave her to her shower and to think, then she could make all the tea in China. Serena gave a weak smile. "Yes. Thank you. That would be welcome."

By morning every paper splashed the story that a well-known merchant banker was missing. Headlines on breakfast television were dominated by it. ITN's lunchtime bulletin irritated its rivals by finding brief footage of Stephen at a society wedding six months before, Serena smiling beside him as they walked towards the side entrance of St Margaret's in Westminster. The marriage had been honoured by the presence of members of the royal family.

By six, the BBC weighed in with several interviews — bank staff who claimed to be variously "shocked" or suffering from "disbelief". One said "Stephen was a workaholic, a bit of a loner in many ways." By nine, all interviews had been vetoed on the orders of the bank, who, in their panic, had not had time to brief their employees. Andrew Beresford had also threatened to slam injunctions on the entire staff for prejudicing his client's right to a fair hearing when he came forward, as he confidently predicted he would.

Deprived of this, the media turned to film of Glebe Cottage, shots of Cambridge where Stephen had performed so brilliantly and the house where he grew up. Nothing was left unearthed. Wilfred, Jasmine and Serena's parents were hauled in.

By the following evening, Serena had stopped watching the news, and shortly after she followed suit with the papers. Melanie was let in early next morning, after the police had established that she was likely to be more of a help to them than a hindrance, to be with Serena until her mother arrived from the country.

Harry and Louise were kept upstairs by Chrissie, with orders not to let them see any news bulletins, answer the phone or catch sight of any newspaper. Serena had taken them both into her room and explained that Daddy had been delayed somewhere but hadn't been able to tell anyone yet where he was. As soon as he phoned, she would tell them. Louise gave her a level stare. Serena lowered her gaze and turned to Harry, but still holding

Louise's hand.

"OK, darling?" Harry just nodded and slid his thumb into his mouth.

Mrs Owen was told not to speak to reporters and to cancel any staff due at the house for the time being. Mr Owen arrived to sit it out with his wife in the kitchen.

"There's been a mistake, a dreadful mistake," Serena told the silent Owens and Chrissie. It was the first of many weeks when she would repeat this explanation. She knew, even the first time, no one believed her. But they would, she vowed, they would.

*

Three o'clock. The house was silent. Serena pushed herself, still fully clothed, to a sitting position. Not as good as last night when, closed up with Seconal, she had slept for six hours. But better than the five days after she had been told, when she couldn't sleep at all. Hadn't wanted to. Wouldn't have known how to.

Across the room the door to Stephen's dressing room was slightly ajar. Through the gloom Serena fixed her gaze on it, seeing him in the doorway, dressed immaculately, Mrs Owen's best efforts showing in the crispness of the shirt collar, the impeccable shine on the handmade Lobb shoes. The perfectly groomed merchant banker ready to take his place on the corporate ladder, driven there by the man the bank employed to chauffeur him day or night.

If it hadn't been so tragic, she reflected, she might have laughed at Mrs Owen's face when fraud squad had trawled through his wardrobe, searching for disks which Draycott Mendes claimed were crucial to their pursuit of a successful prosecution.

"Who knows?" one of them told Serena when she asked what they were looking for. "People store information in the oddest places. Won't be long now, Mrs Carmichael."

Serena had stood, rigid with rage, as they went through her husband's most personal possessions with an indifference to their worth that made her want to lunge at them and snatch them back, smooth their surfaces, and remove all traces of such a violation.

"If you have a complaint, Mrs Carmichael," one said stiffly, polite but devoid of any measure of regret when she raged at him for scattering cufflinks from the drawer of the miniature *armoire* sitting on Stephen's dressing table, "you only have to speak to my superior officer."

She slammed the door in his face and locked herself in the bathroom. There was nowhere else. Each day the house was crowded with detectives mobilized by the Serious Fraud Office. She never saw the financial investigators brought in when Draycott Mendes had first suspected Stephen might be doing the unthinkable, or the case controller, a lawyer who cared only for documents, paperwork, computer disks and who never saw the frightened, white faces of a family like the Carmichaels.

Those same people who had been secretly brought in by Malcolm, unwittingly alerted by the hapless Rupert, who as usual stumbled into a file that made no sense to him, and for once took his clumsiness to Malcolm's deputy to unravel rather than Stephen. All of them closing in on Stephen, silently waiting to trap him.

Malcolm. Malcolm with whom they had dined only a few weeks before knew, absolutely knew that the man he was entertaining so lavishly in his own home was under investigation on his instructions. Serena pushed her hands into her chest. The tight compression was preventing her from breathing. The man Malcolm had praised so publicly ... she stopped. Had he? Her mind raced over that evening. Of course he hadn't. His manner had suggested it, implied it, the mere fact they were in his house being entertained by him fuelled it, but no — her mind went in slow motion over the evening — no, he had never actually said a word in Stephen's praise.

How could he have been so devious? How could they have believed Stephen would not know? Stephen, so sharp, so clever, would have sensed danger, seen the trap waiting for him and the odds they were stacking against him. Of course he fled. If Malcolm could be so treacherous, not ask him, after all those years of loyal and selfless devotion, to explain the discrepancies, Stephen would have seen he had little chance of his innocence being recognized. She repeated this not only to herself but to anyone who questioned her. It had to make sense, she urged herself. It had to.

It seemed to Serena that every room in which she sought sanctuary was filled with strangers searching, unearthing, storing documents or papers that might hide clues to Stephen's whereabouts, his extravagant living and, impossible though they all knew it to be, the money.

Serena leaned her head against the cool white tiles of the bathroom and took several deep breaths. Even then, the ever present policewoman tapped and asked if she was all right.

"Go away," Serena shouted through the door. "Do you think I would damage myself and leave my children to your mercy?"

"We know you wouldn't do that, Mrs Carmichael," the woman said, patiently ignoring the implied claim that her children would be ill-treated by them, "but you must know that until your husband comes forward, we have to know if he tries to contact you."

Serena opened the door and stood back so that the woman standing outside had a clear view into the white and blue tiled room. She gestured with her hand, inviting her to step in. "Of course," she said stonily, "my husband always phones me while I'm in the bathroom. As you can see it is completely wired for such occasions. Now, you have searched me for phones, and clearly the bathroom does not have one. You would have found it, would you not, in your endless search if there was one installed in here. Please," she asked wearily, "just leave me alone, will you?"

But they didn't. A saner, more rational voice that hovered just below the surface of her anger knew they couldn't. They couldn't because the lawyers who were running the show had squeezed every possible hiding place on to the search warrant. She doubted there was a cupboard or drawer they would be denied access to because it was written down on the piece of paper they kept showing her when she asked if they were allowed to be this intrusive. Thank God at night they left only a presence outside her door. For that she was torn between gratitude that they kept the press at bay, and sickening fury at the invasion of her life. But she was not ready for the saner voice. Not when her bank accounts were frozen, when Stephen's picture flashed on every news bulletin. Surely to God, it would end soon?

*

"She doesn't say anything, sir," fretted the policewoman. "She doesn't acknowledge me at all. Couldn't Bob sit with her? She might talk to a bloke. Looks the type, if you ask me."

"Meaning?"

The policewoman defended her impression of a woman she had only just met. "You know, blonde, elegant, used to being a rich man's plaything."

But Serena wasn't the type, and the young policewoman, trained in trauma therapy, was ordered back to her post to sit silently with this composed woman and while away the hours as best she could.

Serena wasn't being deliberately unhelpful. She wasn't used to being forced to stay at home, not doing her usual errands, her pristine house treated like a drug greenhouse rather than a doll's house.

It was routine to the police, who now invaded her house, but a shock to Serena, to witness the measures she had to live with in the quest to get her husband to call them. To find him. Anything.

Her phone calls were monitored and a system to track any call, should it come from Stephen, was hooked up to landlines and mobiles and the fax line. Phone records were checked for calls overseas — to Europe, the States, Russia.

Until all of this had been put in place, Serena was asked not to leave the room unless accompanied by the policewoman. A fierce argument followed because Serena refused to see her children in the presence of the police, and a compromise was reached.

All phones upstairs were disabled on, they assured her, a temporary basis. Just a few hours. Serena's mobile phone was commandeered and she was asked if she would bring the children downstairs while their rooms were searched. "Is that necessary?" she asked stiffly. The young detective nodded.

"You won't need the children," she added. "You won't question them, will you?"

He shook his head vehemently. "No. Absolutely not."

At first Serena had allowed Natalie to monitor TV coverage, but the words "missing banker" threatened to break her resolve to appear as dignified and as calm as Andrew had instructed her to be in front of all these people. "Once more," she told Natalie wearily, "and I'll throw up in front of everyone."

CNN had a full report on the missing merchant banker and the man on CBS looked suitably grave when he reported the theft of millions of dollars from the London bankers Draycott Mendes. This had had a sharp effect on the Dow and later in the programme the "60 minutes" correspondent in Wall Street reported excitedly on the loss.

The German news channels concentrated on the effect of the theft on Draycott's European banking partners, for once relegating their views on the uncertain health of British livestock to a less noteworthy slot. The French exploited the fact that Banque Commerciale supremo Jacques Bretil, who had so recently been only too happy to delay leaving for the country in order to lunch with Stephen Serena though bitterly, had been a business associate.

Monsieur Bretil, she observed, the man so impressed with the negotiating skills of Monsieur Carmichael. He had hesitated only long enough to un-screw his pen before signing over to Draycott Mendes a lucrative contract on behalf of his bank, and now protested he had met the man only once. Malcolm Brisley Jones, he said, had been responsible for fielding Stephen on behalf of the bank.

No one mentioned, Serena noted, that Stephen had been feted by Malcolm for rescuing one of Rupert's botched jobs. A huge bonus had come his way. She stopped. Ashamed of herself, but she couldn't resist the question. Had it? Had it really been a bonus?

The Italians, far too busy in the midst of their monthly task of selecting a new prime minister, said Serena often wore Armani and Valentino and found footage of her carrying a Prada handbag.

"Try and think, Mrs Carmichael." Serena gazed stonily back at the man, who wearily repeated for the sixth time that he was just doing his job. "At no time did your husband discuss his concern about money going missing from accounts … I know, I appreciate that, you would have mentioned it, but it's surprising how people suddenly remember …"

"I won't suddenly remember it," she said, equally wearily, "because he never, ever mentioned such a thing to me."

The same voice asking the same questions. She had been giving the same answers now for days. How many days? Five, six, ten? She had to ask Chrissie just to be sure. She wouldn't look at the paper. Every day, even now, so many days later, something was still on the front page and Stephen was still in hiding.

*

"Let them stay with Melanie," begged her mother. "They can't stay here like this. Let them go to school."

"I can't," Serena said. "How do I stop those vultures taking pictures? What will it look like? Just think. Two privileged children being dropped off at their expensive schools, while their father is wanted for lifting millions from his company?"

"That police officer, you know — oh, whatever his name is — he said the press aren't allowed to take pictures of children no matter what their father has done."

Serena leapt to her feet and gripped the fireplace. "I don't care. I don't trust anyone. They stay here until … the fuss dies down, or," — she took a deep defiant breath — "until I hear from Stephen."

She turned and looked beseechingly at her mother. "Sorry. Sorry, sorry." She sank down beside her.

Margot reached out and tried to grip her daughter's hand. It was cold, unresponsive. Margot tried again, leaning forward, speaking quietly, but with urgency.

"Serena? Listen to me. The children need to get out of here. There must be some way. Watching you suffer is purgatory for them. Of course, they know you're suffering. You're in such pain, you can't see it but they can. Believe me …"

"No, no, no. The children stay with me. They need me."

Margot slumped into silence. The children could, *should* leave the house. Margot had been in Belvoir Square now for over a week and was desperate for the children to experience normality. Even the doctor had said so. There was nothing to stop them going back to school, seeing their friends. That detective had said the police would make sure they reached school safely.

Not quite agreeing that a police escort for two ordinary children was her idea of normality, Margot had thanked him as politely as she could. But they weren't normal any more. Nor would they ever be. Not now. They would always be the children of "disgraced banker, Stephen Carmichael", just as Serena was now routinely described as "wife of", when once her name was prefaced by "society beauty".

So many footnotes to history were being created as each day passed. Margot longed for her husband to be there, tell her what to do. Stafford would have known. Known how to deal with their beloved daughter, to reassure her that her daughter's mind was not hovering on collapse. She gave herself a shake.

Only a fool would believe in Stephen's innocence. An innocent man would not allow his wife to suffer in this way. Watching Serena waiting for anything, clinging so stubbornly to the belief that Stephen would phone any minute or walk through the door, Margot longed, more than anything she had ever longed for in her life, that he would, to ease her daughter's pain.

Margot wanted to say more than ever "he was never right for you, I never understood him". But such an admission, not such a great surprise, was unnecessary. What was it Detective Inspector Trewless had said? "Bottom of the sea or South America." She had chosen to ignore him, repeating her daughter's phrase. "I'm sure my son-in-law will make contact. He is not a criminal. Now if you'll excuse me, my daughter needs me."

And her daughter did. Maybe she didn't want her mother, but she needed someone to lean on. She hadn't mentioned it, and Margot had refrained from drawing her attention to it, but the phone, which rang incessantly, was rarely for Serena. And was anyone surprised? Their friends had been questioned by the Police, reputations were on the line, professions to be considered. In a world bound so tightly with finance and the ease with which suspicious fingers could be pointed, who could blame a little reserve until the dust had settled?

It was an excuse. Margot wondered just how many real friends Serena could rely on. Apart from Melanie, who would have moved in if Serena had not prevented it, not many were braving the press corps to see her. Two or three had called, had hugged her, agreed there must be a rational explanation and tried not to exchange uneasy glances while Serena was in the room. Nice women, bewildered at what had happened, but hopelessly incapable of offering comfort.

The door of the drawing room, where she was sitting with her daughter, was pushed cautiously open. Margot looked round to see the solemn face of Harry framed in the doorway.

"My precious," she greeted him with a smile. "I was just coming to find you."

Serena turned at the sound of Harry's entrance. His small anxious face mobilized her into action in a way that her mother's entreaties failed to do. She held out her arms and Harry ran to her. Margot rose quietly from her seat and went in search of Louise.

For days now, Louise had been ushered back upstairs to amuse herself as best she could in her own room. It was Louise's unquestioning acceptance of her lot that concerned Margot. Louise was a rebel, but at twelve she had to have something to rebel against. In her world it was her mother, the restrictions on her life, the imagined restraints, that she kicked against. Without her mother's attention, she did not know how to rebel.

Harry had taken to watching television with a concentration that was as fierce as it was unconvincing. It unnerved Chrissie. He'd also taken to asking for a night light and more than once Serena had dozed off on her bed only to be woken by Harry curling up beside her.

"It's not his father that's troubling him," Chrissie finally told Serena, with a bluntness that astonished Margot but won her silent admiration, "It's you. He doesn't know how to react any more. I doubt he's heard two words of what's being said on the box, and that's a fact. He's in denial ... I know, cranky shrink stuff. But it's true. I know Harry ... no, not like you know him. Course not. But he needs you to notice him."

Serena looked shocked. Chrissie was red in the face. "Sorry, Serena, it had to be said. Don't think I don't understand."

"Do they know?" Margot asked Chrissie, as Serena went in search of her son.

"Louise does," she answered, thoughtfully. "She knows what's being said but she doesn't believe it. Harry can't quite grasp it, that's why he's so withdrawn."

Margot now found Louise, staring silently down into the garden four floors below her bedroom window. She looked around as her grandmother came in and then went on silently contemplating the empty space. Margot slipped an arm around her shoulders and gave her a squeeze. "I'm all right." Louise responded to the gesture with a gruffness that did not fool her grandmother.

"I know you are," Margot replied, mustering a cheerfulness that exhausted her, "It was just me that needed a cuddle. I do wish all these people would go away, don't you?"

Louise continued her examination of the view from her window. "They won't until Daddy gets back." She paused and then said in a strangled voice, "I've missed Alice's party as well."

"Darling," Margot cried. "When was it? Oh, why didn't you say?"

Louise shrugged. "Saturday. Last Saturday, I mean, two days ago. It doesn't matter," she struggled on fiercely. "Can't stand her anyway. She's such a cow."

"LouLou!" Margot checked back a rebuke. No one had called to ask if Louise was OK. Certainly no one called Alice. Louise was right, Margot sighed to herself. Indeed. What a cow.

*

Melanie picked Louise and Harry up just after seven that night.

They were smuggled out of the house with the help of the police and their neighbours, a quiet, retired Colonel and his wife, who agreed instantly to allow them to lift the children over the garden wall that divided the two houses, and from there into the cobbled street that ran alongside it leading to the mews behind Belvoir Square. Undetected by the press waiting at the front, Melanie and Charles Westfield were waiting in their car to speed Louise and Harry to the safety of their own house in St John's Wood.

Serena watched her children's progress, hugging them both and promising to see them the very next day. Her mother was right, she was thinking only of herself. The children would be better off if they could go to school. But not from this house.

"Mum?" whispered Louise, as she was about to be lifted across the wall separating the two houses. "Come with us, don't stay here."

Serena kissed her and gave her a fierce hug. "Don't worry about me, darling," she whispered back. "I have to stay here, just in case ... in case Daddy calls, needs me."

Louise hesitated. "He will, won't he, Mum? Then it will be all right again, won't it?"

"Absolutely," Serena whispered back. "Take care. Yes, yes, she's coming." She stepped back as the pleasant-faced young officer, perching on the dividing wall trying not to wreck the roses due to reach their prime in a few months' time, reached down to lift Louise off the ladder to join Harry already being whisked across the next wall and out to Melanie's car.

Dear God, Serena covered her face with her hands as her children disappeared into the night. What is happening to us? Stephen. *Stephen.* Where are you? Why are you doing this?

Chapter Six

Serena mouthed a silent thank you at the picture emblazoned across the newspapers of the cabinet minister who had been discovered in a discreet hotel with an indiscreet young model who, it appeared, felt compelled to reveal over three pages of a tabloid newspaper how treacherously he had behaved towards his wife.

Overnight, the chaos enveloping the house in Belvoir Square was up-staged by a major government scandal. News teams were rapidly rede-ployed to push the doorbell of the arrogant MP trying to bluster his way out of a mess of his own making. The phone in Serena's house no longer rang incessantly. The doorbell fell largely silent. With no progress in locat-ing the missing banker, and Serena's continued refusal to grant interviews, the cold and bored press corps vanished.

The few visitors who called to offer comfort dwindled. It was beyond her to even discuss it, but Serena knew there was widespread anxiety among those who had been called on by the police to discover if anyone had had a clue as to Stephen Carmichael's activities.

It was the very good-natured but talkative Emily Painswick-Smith who let it slip.

"God, to think Paula could imagine for one second that anyone would think she was one of Stephen's confidantes," Emily marvelled. "I mean re-ally. She practically had to go to a health farm for an entire week to recover from the suggestion."

Her hand flew to her mouth. "Oh Christ, sorry, Serena — Melanie, don't look like that, you know exactly what I mean — I don't mean for one second Stephen is guilty. I just mean that Paula and Miranda and a few others ... well, we're all bound to be caught up in it. After all we all see each other, lots of our husbands work in some way with him ... not that I would

71

ever not stand up for you." She looked around frantically, knowing she was digging herself in even deeper, and proceeded to make it worse. "No one believed for a moment — at least not until the police started asking all of us if we thought you knew where he was ..."

Melanie stared at her lap. Serena stared out of the window. She didn't have to be told. Poor, blundering Emily. She turned and smiled.

"Forget it, Emily. I know what the police are asking. And I know you'd never desert me."

After Emily had gone, Melanie walked silently over to Serena and wrapped her arms around her. For a moment they stood hugging each other and then Melanie gave a sniff and pushed her away.

"C'mon," she ordered. "Where's the Scotch? We'll drink to Paula's downfall and Miranda's face-lift sagging."

In spite of herself, Serena smiled.

*

The daily calls from the police and Melanie continued. Eventually the children came home, and without a press corps to note their every move their lives resumed a kind of routine that, curiously, helped.

Andrew Beresford's role was restricted to the battle with the banks to keep Serena afloat once it had been established that she was not implicated in Stephen's fraud. Mrs Owen continued to arrive each morning at eight, alighting from her husband's car with a haughtiness that she could not shake off, having dealt with the press corps for so long, and her "I have no comment to make" no longer necessary.

"Thank God for that," Margot said, as Serena came back into the room from her routine meeting with Donald Trewless.

"For what?" Serena asked, lowering herself into a chair.

"All those dreadful people," said Margot, peering out into the strangely deserted square as the detective's car drove away. "All rushed off to plague the life out of someone else. Still, maybe now we can get back to normal."

"And what would that be, exactly?" Serena asked, drily.

Margot looked flustered. "Darling, I didn't mean ... I meant being left alone ... Oh, you know what I mean," she ended, crossly.

"I know. Don't get your hopes up just yet. Inspector Trewless says not to be fooled. They'll be back."

"Back? But why? Surely they've got enough pictures of the house? You're not going to be interviewed, are you? What for?"

"Well, after a bit, what they do is come back when the fuss has died down and think that you'll be ready to talk to them — yes, I know, complete waste of time in my case, but there's still the big picture to take."

Margot looked blank. "Big picture?"

Serena made a fuss of pouring herself more coffee. "Of course," she said lightly. "When Stephen comes home."

Her mother's mouth opened and then closed. Whatever she was going to say was left unsaid. Instead she nodded vigorously. "Absolutely," she said stoutly. "Of course."

Serena wasn't fooled. Her mother had never felt easy with Stephen. She wondered how long it would be before she blurted out what she really wanted to say. Serena was afraid of that moment. Once said, she would be moved to defend Stephen to the one person she needed most. There was no one else.

She folded her arms on the table and gave Margot a small smile. She knew she should tell her mother she looked tired, that the exhaustion etched on her face was dreadfully unfair, but she had nothing left for anyone.

During the day she longed for night so that she could stop making an effort. She walked from room to room, drinking endless cups of coffee until the children were finally persuaded to go to bed. Then she could escape to her own room to be alone without someone following her, her mother anxiously trying to make her eat, the children watching her face waiting for a smile.

Haunted by images of Stephen lying dead somewhere, or with amnesia wandering in some strange city, it was as well none of her family could see her hands shaking as she opened his closet to stroke his jackets, wrapped herself in his dressing gown, buried her face in the soft towelling robe with its faint smell of his aftershave. Certainly, no one was to witness the moments when she crouched on the smooth grey velvet carpet, the blue silk curtains locking out the darkened square, rocking herself, moaning like a wounded animal.

*

"Well, missing or not, I can't live on thin air."

Chrissie sighed deeply and went on reading the morning paper. She had hoped to be clear of the kitchen before Mrs Owen grabbed her.

"I said to Jim, 'We're the ones suffering.'" Mrs Owen leaned forward, lowering her voice. "She doesn't live in the real world, that one. Never had to wonder where the next penny's coming from. And it's not as though I was being paid a fortune either. I could have gone long ago, but I could see she was hopeless and I'll say this for him, he always said thank you, left me notes, stuff like that. Not that I ever thought you could trust him. Wouldn't be surprised if there was another woman involved, would you?"

Chrissie ignored her but Mrs Owen, in the absence of anyone else on whom to unload her complaints and resentments, was not easily rebuffed. "I said to Jim, I said, 'I am a loyal person, everyone knows that. Her ladyship,'" she nodded her head in the direction of the drawing room where Serena was closeted with Andrew Beresford, "'knows it, but I've got to live and where's my salary going to come from, that's what I want to know?'"

She paused, looking with annoyance at the back of the paper held up to Chrissie's face. She tried another tack. "It's all right for you, you live in. No bills to pay …"

Chrissie abruptly lowered the paper. She missed her sleep. She was acting as counsellor, nanny and comforter to them all. She'd been up since six that morning dealing with a tantrum from Louise, rescuing Margot trying to get breakfast underway and vainly attempting to get Serena to at least eat some toast.

"If," she said, making no effort to erase the irritation from her voice, "you're asking me where the money's coming from to pay me, then I haven't a clue and if you must know, living in doesn't help. It's all right for you, you go at the end of each day, I'm here. Asking for money at this moment is stupid. Anyway, it's only a day or two over for God's sake. Besides, who's to say he won't turn up any minute and straighten things out?"

"Turn up? *Turn up?*" Mrs Owen looked scornfully at her. "Oh my dear, that's the last we've seen of him. Mark my words. South America's my bet — he's left all his winter clothes, that's how I know."

"Then maybe you should tell the police your theory," suggested Chrissie, returning to her paper. "Or Serena." She deliberately turned the page with a huge rustle. She had always found Mrs Owen irritating, with her grand ways and petty power-games. Now she had a growing suspicion that the housekeeper's daily encounter with the group of journalists she pushed past with such hauteur was just more fuel for her self-importance. Tension, and dealing with two scared children, had dealt a severe blow to Chrissie's sense of humour.

"Look, Mrs O, Serena's driving herself nuts not knowing where the stupid sod is, and I'm exhausted from checking to make sure Harry's in his bed each night. He's taken to creeping in with her when he hears her crying. Poor little mite. Frankly I'd give a month's salary for a good night's sleep, let alone ask where it is."

Mrs Owen scraped her chair back and gave an irritating little smirk. "Oh, I'll tell you where it is, my dear. Vanished. Along with him. Get paid? You're wasting your breath, you'll see."

"You're the one who's concerned about money." Chrissie retorted. "I haven't said a word. Look, I know you're worried, but stop asking me questions to which you've obviously got all the answers."

Whatever Mrs Owen was going to say was silenced when the kitchen door opened. Harry walked around the scrubbed pine table, his elbow sliding along the edge until he reached Chrissie. He was sucking his thumb — a baby habit which Serena had told Chrissie he'd grown out of.

"Hi, you," Chrissie said, ruffling his hair as he reached her. Gently she removed his thumb from his mouth. "What's up?"

Harry said in a flat voice: "Mummy's crying."

*

Miranda Hooper's drinks party to welcome Ryland Holt, newly appointed chief executive of the Wall Street financiers, Bagelhoff Sherman, to his new posting in London was surprisingly short of people who were prepared to admit they knew the Carmichaels well.

"She's a sweetheart," said Ryland's wife, Meryl, in her flat East Coast drawl. "I met them when they stayed with the Barkers out at East Hampton. How's she taking it?"

"Quite badly, I'm told," said Miranda, who had tied Serena's phone up for days and nights when her husband, with whom she was once again reconciled, had admitted to an affair. "But I was never a particularly close friend. Now, have you met Paula and Richard Van Stuckley? The sweetest couple."

"Played squash with him a few times," Richard Van Stuckley was heard telling Ryland. "Never really knew him well on a social level. She was the ambitious one. Quite a toughie, I'm told."

"One sits with her on the odd committee," Paula Van Stuckley told Meryl. "I only know her through George Kincaid. Have you met George? Oh, you must."

Whilst being chauffeured home, Meryl asked her husband if he had noticed the noise at Miranda's every time Serena and Stephen were mentioned.

"Noise? What noise?"

"The noise of rats disappearing into the woodwork. Frankly I liked her and I might just call her up."

Ryland leaned forward and pressed the button that activated the glass screen between them and the driver.

"Honey, I'm here to sort out Bagelhoff's cock-ups, not to fuck things up. I need those guys. OK?"

Meryl pulled a face at him. "OK, but it stinks."

"Money always does, sweetheart. So what's new? By the way, get the Van Stuckleys over to dinner. He may be going to the Treasury."

*

The sight of the betrayed wife of an MP might well distract the public gaze from the shifty behaviour of a missing banker and the misery of the banker's wife, but it didn't, Serena told herself, stop the litany of horrors waiting for her each morning.

All Stephen's assets were frozen. Even if Stephen had stayed to protest his innocence, the bank, with enough documentary proof that irregularities on a vast scale had emanated from accounts controlled by Stephen, had found no difficulty in having an injunction granted in their favour since he had fled the country.

Everything was under threat. The house, the cottage, the ponies, the cars. All bought, claimed Draycott Mendes, with defrauded funds. The bank's revenge had been swift and savage. Pressure on the police to find Stephen had become their mission. Serena suspected it was because they felt such fools it was the only way to assuage their anger.

"Nothing of the kind," said Andrew Beresford. "They simply want to pile the pressure on you to flush Stephen out once he knows — if he knows — what his actions have done to you and the children."

She couldn't bring herself to believe Stephen would ignore their plight. But apparently he could. She returned to her fear that he might have killed himself but, as Donald Trewless pointed out, kindly but firmly, someone planning to end their life does not take their passport, empty their bank account and buy the new wardrobe of clothes which Amex receipts showed that he had in the two days leading up to his disappearance.

"What do you mean?" Serena whispered, when Andrew Beresford took her through the debts. "They can't take the house away ... Can they?"

"You have no assets of your own — yes, I know, but a few pictures and some family silver and furniture is not going to pay off the amount missing. It's still being counted. Between us, my dear, I doubt they'll ever know the final figure. Whatever Stephen did — OK, or didn't do — had a knock-on effect right across the board. It will be months before they unravel the mess. It runs into millions."

Serena gasped. "Millions? Impossible. Andrew — there's been a terrible mistake. Show me? Where are the millions?"

"Probably in a Swiss bank account," he told her bluntly. "He's been planning this for some time."

"You don't know that," she said stubbornly. "He's had a breakdown. This isn't like Stephen. We lived well, but they were bonuses."

Andrew just gazed at her. Her hair was pulled back from her face, she wore no make-up. He noticed that her hands shook and that the skin around her eyes looked like parchment paper.

"I don't believe it. If that were the case Stephen would have made sure he protected me and the children — he would have made some provision. The house. That's it. If he were planning all this, he would have put the house in my name."

Andrew shook his head. "I'm afraid it wouldn't have made any difference. It would have had to have been done at least five years ago and with no evidence that any fraud was going to be committed. The evidence for the funds going walkabout starts a good seven years ago. It would have been seen by the courts as intent."

"Surely to God, the court can't blame me and the children?"

"The courts are not interested in you and the children — not yet. They're on the side of the victim."

"But I'm the victim," cried Serena.

"No you're not. The bank is."

*

Serena's cash flow dried up at an alarmingly quick rate. The daze she had been wandering around in had diminished, to be replaced by blind panic that rose up to the roof of her mouth and left her breathless.

Bills that would normally have been paid by banker's order from Stephen's account were starting to be returned to her for payment. Mrs Owen had finally broached the delicate subject of her salary which had not turned up in her account. Nor had Chrissie's, who had said nothing.

Serena was mortified. She found Chrissie upstairs, folding Louise's scattered clothes.

"You should have said something," she scolded her, "I'll pay it from my own account immediately."

"Serena, honestly, I'm fine," Chrissie protested. "I'll end Mrs Owen, see if I don't. Surely to God, she can manage for a week or two?"

Serena gave her a quick hug. "Nonsense, she's entitled to be paid and so are you ... Chrissie?"

"No," Chrissie stopped her. "Don't say it. I know. But as long as you can feed me I can hang on for a bit."

Serena walked slowly downstairs. Absently she picked up Harry's computer game and his discarded trainers. Hang on for a bit? She didn't have the heart to tell Chrissie just how bad things were. Later, sitting huddled in an armchair in her room, it occurred to her that Mrs Owen had been patronizing. She had called her "dear".

Charles Westfield came over that night. He wrote out enough cheques on her behalf to ward off tradesmen who on another occasion would have been happy to wait for payment. Chrissie and Mrs Owen were paid up to date.

"I hate this," Serena mumbled, shuffling a sheaf of letters, all polite but all unmoving in their demands. "I know I should be grateful and I am, but it's not what I want. I wouldn't have asked, only Melanie insisted."

"Quite right, too," Charles replied, not looking up from the kitchen table where he was busy writing. "Just a little temporary help from a friend until you're back on your feet. No big deal, is it?"

Serena watched him silently as his pen scrawled across a sheaf of bills. "And ... of course Stephen will put it all right when, well, when things settle down."

Charles glanced up at her. "Of course," he said heartily. "And a very large dinner will be extracted as well."

She looked bleakly at him. This was difficult for both of them. She, because she was humiliated and he, because the furious exchange he'd had with Melanie earlier hung over him. Charles had to fight back a strong impulse to tell Serena to stop it, stop believing in Stephen. But Melanie was appalled at the idea.

"Do that and what have we got on our hands?" Melanie stormed. "Serena a basket case — God help us, Charles, she's practically that now — and those children upstairs in trauma? That's what we've got. They're OK, because she's OK. I mean it, Charles, don't say a word. Just make her take some money — oh for God's sake, just pay whatever will keep her afloat. Anything. Charles, she'd do it for me."

"But I wouldn't do what he's done," Charles protested. "He's a ghastly prat. God knows how she never suspected. She's not stupid."

"No, not stupid. Just loyal. I mean, look at the way she gave up all those evenings to sit with Miranda Hooper when Simon left her. You remember when she rang at the last minute and said she couldn't come to the Mozart — and I know for a fact she was really looking forward to it — because Miranda phoned her at six screaming and crying down the phone that she couldn't cope? And where is Miranda now? Telling anyone who cares to listen that she wasn't a particularly close friend of Serena's. And look how she stuck by Paula when Richard was holed up at the cottage with that ludicrous secretary or whatever she called herself. And Paula never misses a trick to bad-mouth Serena. Serena wouldn't ever be so disloyal."

"That's not loyalty," he said, "that's breeding."

"Well, breeding or no breeding, at the moment we're all she's got."

Charles paused in the act of pouring himself another drink.

"Us? What about all her other friends?"

Melanie grimaced. "Exactly. Tell me about it."

Faced with the burden of being Serena's only friend struck Charles more forcefully than he cared for. He was by nature an indolent man, leaving the cherishing and nurturing of their joint friends to his wife. But now that Melanie had pointed it out to him, it struck him that she was right. His innate sense of decency that she had been so easily abandoned roused such sympathetic anger in him, but it wasn't enough to chide his friends.

Serena knew that too. For a brief moment their eyes locked. Charles felt ill at ease. He could have murdered Stephen.

"Of course," she said valiantly, as Charles repeated that Stephen was bound to surface soon. "As a matter of fact Andrew has fixed for me to see Stephen's bank manager. I'll pay back everything. No, I will. Bless you, Charles."

*

Ireland. That's where he is. Serena stopped pacing up and down as the thought struck her. Why hadn't she thought of it before? Not South America as the police suspected. But Ireland. He loved his Irish roots.

She began to feel excited. She chided herself for being stupid. She of all people, not to have worked it out. She was in her bedroom, once again trawling through Stephen's belongings, looking for clues. Not in the way the police had, but something more intimate, something that would guide her to where he was.

Only that morning she had told Melanie that she knew he was alive.

"I would feel it, here," she said, pressing her chest, "Or here," she continued, placing her hands against the side of her head. "I was so close to him, I would know. If it were Charles, wouldn't you feel it too?"

Melanie shook her head. "Serena, don't raise your hopes. That's all I'm asking."

"Hopes? God, Melanie. What else have I got? Every time I turn round something else rotten has happened. Look at this." She reached over and pulled a file towards her. "Here, read these. I keep them for the police."

Melanie read the first one. "Are they all the same?" she asked, aghast at the violence of the language, the unfounded accusations against Serena written down as evidence on the letters before her. She handed them back, brushing her hands on her skirt.

Serena put them back in the file. "More or less. You can't believe complete strangers would write such filth. Trewless says anyone in the news attracts cranks. And I'm certainly in the news."

Now she sat down on the side of the bed and tried to school her mind to think straight. The copy of Yeats that she had given Stephen had gone. To anyone else it would have been meaningless. But to Serena it was her clue. All that admiration for rebels and dissidents must have been true. She had scoffed at the idea and laughed when he said he thought the missing peer Lucan was holed up in the Wicklow Hills.

"You could hide there for years, grow a beard, say you're a writer and who would disbelieve you?" She could hear Stephen saying it, remember where he was sitting, what he was wearing.

Somehow she would go there. When the dust had settled. She was afraid for Stephen now. Supposing he decided to just come back? He wouldn't stand a chance. So much evidence logged against him. Now she wanted to be the one to take the risk, go to him.

She was prepared to wait. Irrationally she felt more buoyed than she had for weeks. The children began to relax, and Margot felt Serena's less bleak demeanour was sufficient to make a hasty trip back to her own home.

Serena could no longer avoid telling Mrs Owen and Chrissie that she would have to let them go. The scene with Mrs Owen was less painful, even after ten years, than it was with the dear, loyal Chrissie.

"No more than I expected, of course," Mrs Owen said tightly. "I can't work for nothing. I'll be off then. No point in hanging around."

"No, of course not," Serena agreed, hurt by the older woman's eagerness to go, and not a little puzzled by it too. "I mean if you want a reference ..."

"No ... no, that won't be necessary," Mrs Owen interrupted, "I may be doing something quite different, so it wouldn't be relevant, if you see what I mean."

"I wish I could give you a bonus or something," Serena continued awkwardly, "But as things stand at present, it's not possible. But I do have a little gift for you to remember us by."

She reached out and picked up two parcels lying just behind her on a small console table. Both were gift-wrapped, the first with a label written in Louise's familiar rounded hand: "To Mrs Owen, we'll miss you, lots of love LouLou and Harry." Inside, as Serena knew, was a red wool scarf patiently knitted by Louise and a clay dish made in Harry's crafts class which he had brought carefully home and insisted on wrapping himself.

"Oh very kind, I'm sure," Mrs Owen said, stuffing the present into her bag.

"And this is from us ... I mean, me." Serena held out the second gift. "No, open it when you get home. I think you'll like it."

It went the way of the first one, rammed down the side of Mrs Owen's capacious bag. Serena wondered if the delicate porcelain figures, always admired by Mrs Owen in the past, would survive the journey to their new home.

"Come and see us, stay in touch, won't you? You've always been so dependable." Serena rushed on, not quite knowing how to end the interview, so anxious was Mrs Owen to be gone.

"Well, goodbye." Mrs Owen stuck out her hand and grasped Serena's for a brief second and then walked rapidly out of the room.

"I think she's got a heart after all," Serena remarked to her mother by telephone, describing the scene. "She really was very overcome. God knows how Chrissie will take it."

Chrissie offered to stay on without pay for the near future for Serena looked a little more certain, but Serena refused to hear of it. "You are the most special person to us," Serena told her gently and gratefully, "but you have a life to lead, and I have no idea any more when mine will return to normal. I can care for the children myself and my mother is more than willing to help out if I get stuck."

They looked at each other and began to laugh.

"Give me a break," Serena begged, "I'm not that hopeless." She put her arms around Chrissie and hugged her. "Come and see us, stay as our friend whenever you want and write to the children. That, I really would appreciate."

"As if I wouldn't," sniffed Chrissie, wiping her eyes with the ball of her hand.

*

While Serena had become accustomed to knowing that Interpol were searching for her husband, she saw no reason to let anyone know that she was searching for a copy of the *Irish Times*. Whenever she could slip away, usually after dropping the children at school, she would park the car, pray she wasn't being watched and slip into a newsagent in Kensington High Street that usually held copies.

She knew it was madness that was gripping her when she pored through it, not at all certain what she was looking for, but she felt somehow there would be a clue, a sign, something small that only she would recognize.

It became her obsession, trawling through the lines of personal ads, news items that might tell her something, speak to her. And then she saw it.

A small box on the personal column. It started with a line from *Down by the Salley Garden* followed by: "When you are old and grey, take down this book." After that it said: "Interested? If you want to contact me, write to me," followed by a box number.

She thought she would never breathe again. It was Yeats. The line Stephen had quoted in Paris on the bridge that she had protested about.

It was Stephen.

Chapter Seven

Jasmine Carmichael had never enjoyed an easy relationship with her daughter-in-law. She did not despise Serena or even dislike her. She simply felt puzzled by her. Once, on a rare visit to stay with her family in Belvoir Square, she watched while Serena, who was not in her view daft or submissive, shushed the children and coaxed her husband into a good mood, when she would have told him to stop sulking. There was also a suggestion that Serena deferred to him a little too easily. Her admiration for him was readily detectable.

Jasmine observed it all while appearing absorbed in what her grandchildren were telling her, or studying a new addition to Stephen's art collection. Privately, she thought her son would benefit far more from less enthusiasm from his wife and a measure of humour in its place, but honesty compelled her to acknowledge that her own relationship with him had hardly improved when she had given way to frankness. Maybe Serena had tried that. But she doubted it.

So Jasmine had kept her own counsel. Once she had been tempted to advise Serena to love him less, help him more to laugh at himself — but it was easier to remain silent. She assuaged her conscience now with telling herself it would have been pointless. After all, a mother's view is rarely that of a lover's.

Neither of her sons pleased her much, but at least Toby, racing through marriage after marriage ... Jasmine had to stop and think of his present wife's name. Martha? Marty? What was it? Something like that. Oh no, Marlee, that's it. Stupid name, stupid woman. Where was she? Oh yes — Stephen. At least Toby had not inherited Wilfred's weakness for wanting what he couldn't have. She winced. Stephen had simply taken it a stage further. She would not have admitted it to anyone but Jasmine knew, as Serena refused to believe, that her son was guilty. She felt a most terrible sense of failure.

Stephen, so clever but so furious with the world. For days after his arrest Jasmine had switched from terror not knowing where he was to fury that he could have been so incredibly stupid. Such a hard son to live with and even harder to live up to, especially once he was married. So who would have listened to an old woman who knew her sons so much better than their wives? Her husband never had. But what was the point in torturing herself now? There was work to be done.

As Jasmine hauled herself from the bench, the late afternoon sun exploded and fell from sight behind the valley that ran between the hills surrounding her retreat. It was April and the evenings were still cool. She stretched her back, pressing her fingers into her aching hips to ease the stiffness that sitting so long in one position had produced, and pondered what to do next.

She was a woman of stern principles. Even while grappling with the knowledge that her missing son was now regarded as a criminal, Jasmine knew she must support Serena. How, was more difficult. In the last few weeks, she had discovered that Serena, the one person she wanted to support, was not easy to help.

Jasmine's grandchildren were, of course, another matter, and there she took her duties seriously, interested in their progress but lacking the kind of warm affection showered on them by Margot. But then, unlike their maternal grandmother, she hardly knew them.

Occasionally the children paid a brief visit to their grandmother whilst en route with their parents to somewhere more exotic. Stephen called her Tuscan farmhouse isolated; Jasmine argued that it was simply peaceful. She lived contentedly, enjoying a freedom and peace her turbulent years of marriage to the profligate Wilfred had denied her. She surrounded herself with a pleasant clutter of canvas, paints and comfy sofas, spread over with brightly coloured woven blankets. For company she had two large dogs of indeterminate breed, dominated by a very thin cat who forced them to patrol the house looking for a place to snooze that did not disturb her.

Every birthday and Christmas Jasmine's grandchildren dutifully wrote to thank her for her rather odd gifts. A roll of canvas for Harry because she had noticed he was rather good with colour. An embossed antique leather box — quite empty as Louise pointed out in disgust — bought at a Sunday morning market in the old town square.

To her surprise Serena had rather warmed to the charm behind these gifts, but in the face of Louise and Harry's lukewarm reaction and Stephen's irritation at his mother's eccentricity, she placated them all by pointing out that Jasmine lived off the proceeds of her paintings and was not rolling in money.

"And whose fault is that?" Stephen demanded. His mother, having rejected all offers of financial help, had left him constantly exasperated every time they spoke. Finally he had slammed the phone down in disgust. "Fine, if she wants to live a peasant's life, let her. She's utterly selfish."

"Why do you get so upset about it?" Serena soothed. "You can't possibly feel conscience-stricken over someone who refuses help. It's not as though you've ignored her, is it? And besides, I think she prefers living like she does — you know, simply. No fuss."

"That's all very well you knowing, but the world doesn't, does it? Honestly, what does it look like? Thank God she's doing it where no one can see her."

Jasmine had wasted no time in phoning Serena, once the police had satisfied themselves her fugitive son was not barricaded in her loft or the small barn where she kept her car. Unlike Toby, who had fired off a furious letter to his sister-in-law pointing out the many ways in which his life had been disrupted and reputation stained, Jasmine had immediately offered to come to London.

At the time Serena was too bewildered to register the novelty of Jasmine seeking her out, and assured her she was surrounded by a lot of people. It was perfectly true. The police and the press had made sure she wasn't left alone for a minute. As for friends, who of them had really believed her when she protested that it was amnesia, maybe a breakdown, that was at the bottom of all this? At least Minnie had never made any pretence about their relationship, she thought, as she suppressed her disappointment when the post bringing Minnie's letter registered Lucca and not Dublin.

Jasmine's latest letter to Serena was, as ever, mercifully lacking in sympathy, restricting her observations to what she could do of a practical nature. It did not escape Serena that Jasmine was not protesting Stephen's innocence.

"At this distance it is difficult to offer a lot," she wrote briskly. *"I do of course feel for you and cannot imagine what Stephen must be thinking of, letting you go through all of this. I really had hoped by now some news would have emerged. If I thought I would be of use I would come to London, but I doubt it. Besides you have so many friends who must be driving you mad with their constant presence, but even so, are obviously more helpful, knowing your life on a day to day basis as they do, which of course I don't."*

Serena lifted her eyes from the page and gazed out on to the garden. It looked a little neglected. So was she. *So many friends.* She gave a mirthless laugh. She had taken to living in the kitchen now that Chrissie and Mrs Owen had gone. It was warmer and cheaper. The children were at school. Andrew Beresford was due to call her later, and Melanie had been deflected from making a daily visit by Serena telling her she would be locked up with him for most of the day.

It had taken an effort. Melanie's staunch support was not a surprise to Serena, but if Melanie was shielding her, then Serena knew that the time had come to usher Melanie back to her own life. Letting Charles Westfield pay some bills had been agreed in the days when she was expecting to hear Stephen's voice at the end of a phone. Gently deflecting her friend from the front line of her life became a necessity, and Serena knew that, unless she convinced Melanie that she was coping, she might lose her altogether.

Melanie's own life was bound up with all the people who were now shunning Serena. Business, friends, children and weekends were all woven seamlessly into each other's lives. The strain on the Westfields of supporting Serena was one she wasn't prepared to risk. She liked the Westfields too much and valued their friendship too deeply to watch them make such a sacrifice and inevitably come to resent her.

Nor did she want Melanie to know about the sale of her own paintings and some jewellery left to her by her grandmother which had taken place the previous week, discreetly through Andrew Beresford, to pay for the children's school fees.

Schools. Serena sighed. Louise was suffering. Little girls, she thought savagely, can be such bitches. Old enough to know what had happened, they knew why their parents were discouraging them from including Louise. And could you blame them? Serena pondered. With the press snapping at the heels of many of their friends, they were protecting their own children and families from scandal.

Louise had already asked to be taken away. Louise was bright. She was like Stephen — quick, sharp and proud. She didn't want her classmates' sympathy any more than she wanted their derision. The headmistress was used to the effect divorce had on her girls and adept at recognizing when money was a problem. Stoic in the face of grimly ambitious parents of unambitious daughters, and caught between her duty to protect the interests of all her pupils, she was holding rigidly to her line that normality in Louise's life was paramount. But it wasn't easy when she could see the child was being excluded, and the defiant way she dealt with the rejection.

Each afternoon, she watched as Serena ran lightly up the stone steps into the square wood-panelled hall where girls were instructed to wait until they were collected, and each afternoon she heaved a sigh seeing both mother and daughter greet each other and move away quickly. They exchanged a brief smile with those who tried awkwardly to pretend all was well, and when the Carmichaels were out of sight they turned to each other to speak in hushed whispers about the ghastliness of it all.

Having collected Harry from his school, Serena's heart was torn apart by the sight of Louise standing alone by the doorway, pretending to be absorbed in a book. She was learning, in such an agonising way, just how cruel the world can be.

She's not even prepared for it, Serena thought, bleakly waving at Louise who scooped her school bag up from between her feet and pushed her way towards her mother. I have failed her, Serena told herself, as Louise approached her. I shielded her and spoilt her. She doesn't know where to start. It isn't her fault, it's mine.

"Hi, my baby." She hugged her as Louise slid into the front seat, throwing her bag in the back on to an indignant Harry who set up a howl. "Want to stop off at the book shop and choose something?"

"No thanks," said Louise politely. "I've got rather a lot of homework."

Meaning, I want to stay in my room again. Serena wasn't fooled. The school wanted to talk about an assisted place, maybe enter her for a scholarship place when she was thirteen. Serena resisted taking it further. To do so would be to acknowledge Stephen's guilt. And to admit he might not be back. Besides, Louise didn't want to stay.

Harry was faring slightly better. His friends were too young to understand the full scale of how his little life had been disrupted and were not interested. But Harry was slow. As Minnie had spotted and Serena had tried to convince Stephen, Harry was never going to be the academic Stephen dreamed he would be. Scholarships and assisted places were not in order.

Unable to bring any new solutions to her children's immediate future, Serena resumed Minnie's letter.

"I hope you will not be silly about this and refuse all offers of help. You have the children to think of. It isn't a great deal but I do have a small reputation as an artist and the tourists are good about the rubbish I pass off as art. The money would go to the children in the end anyway, so they may as well have it now.

"Perhaps instead of birthday presents, they would like me to send tickets for them to stay here during the summer — you too of course — but I was rather thinking about the small respite you might get if they were safe with me. I leave it to you to let me know."

She folded Minnie's letter and began to stack the breakfast dishes into the machine. Later she would call her mother but for the moment she would try and deal with the disappointment of not having a reply to her letter to Ireland. Serena had been having huge misgivings about her hasty action, terrified she might have unwittingly led the police to Stephen by her coded letter to him in Ireland. The waiting was unbearable, but wait she did, because she had no other choices open to her.

The day ahead stretched before her with unanswered questions, self-doubt and recriminations to keep her company. Why couldn't he confide in her? Had she been so wrapped up in her own world of children, fund raising and entertaining that she hadn't noticed her own husband tottering on the brink of a breakdown? Believing for all those weeks that it was simply Malcolm putting a terrible strain on him, the burden of the incompetent Rupert Chawton Browne being laid at his door. All of that must surely have been the cause of all those rows towards the end. And in a way it was. But not in the way she had thought. Why did it not occur to her he was in trouble?

Round and round, her thoughts swirling into a jumble that left her head pounding, her eyes red with weeping. Her mother, Melanie, Andrew, Natalie Silverman — all had tried to tell her she was not to blame. But she shook her head impatiently. Clearly she hadn't been the loyal, supportive and loving wife that evidence suggested she had been.

The questions stopped her in her tracks, dominated her days, prevented her sleeping. They hadn't needed such a lifestyle, she knew that now. Her own childhood, growing up in Wiltshire, had been simple and driven by harsh economic facts. They might have had a title to their name, but the family publishing business that had been so prosperous at the turn of the century had not survived in the progressive, aggressive conditions that prevailed in the years that followed and the changing tastes of a fickle public. But she had been happy. She had been happy, too, with Stephen, when they had nothing. She could have been happy with less than they acquired.

Now that she had time to think about it, why he did it was not a mystery to her. Serena had simply misread the signs, of that she was sure. The arrival of Rupert less than a year ago was when Stephen had begun to be more critical of Malcolm, shrugging off any suggestion that he cared about the astonishing rise of Rupert's star. It was she who had been indignant, but seeing Stephen take it in his stride she had simply replaced indignation with admiration that he was so single-minded about his career, and took her cue from him.

Checking the dates given to her by the fraud squad she was not surprised that while the start of his fraudulent activities was tracked back as far as the year they visited, it was the arrival of Rupert that had generated the cracks, and carelessness had set in.

But she knew she had an ace waiting to be served. It was contained in a letter winging its way to Dublin, signed using her middle and maiden name, Mary Armitage, so that Stephen would know it was her.

As the days passed and the cryptic letter she had sent to the box number in Ireland went unacknowledged, she fluctuated between hope and despair. Sometimes she stared at herself in the mirror and looked for signs of derangement. God knows, she told herself, it would be no surprise.

But she knew Stephen. Oh, perhaps not this Stephen who had become a stranger. Sometimes she plunged into total panic when images of their life together began to blur. Like a faded photograph. She struggled to get a clear picture of Stephen, but he remained out of focus, out of reach.

*

The children had gone to bed. The kitchen was silent except for the sound of the dishwasher humming gently. On the table in front of her a mug of coffee had grown cold. The flowers from the garden sitting in the centre of the scrubbed pine table were beginning to wilt. Absently, Serena rose and carried them into the laundry room where she threw the withered blooms into the waste bin and emptied the yellow dank-smelling water down the drain. She rinsed the glass vase and left it on the draining board to dry.

Ten o'clock. Too early for bed and too late to call Melanie or her mother. In the last few weeks her concentration had deserted her. It was no longer unusual for her to read whole paragraphs in the paper without absorbing even a general meaning of what she had read. She picked up the remote control for the television. A raucous gale of laughter from a late night chat show filled the room and a chanting football crowd competed with an overexcited commentator on another channel. She switched it off.

Perhaps she should reply to Minnie's letter or fix the hem on Louise's school skirt. The doorbell ended her need for a decision. Surprised, she pressed the intercom.

"Serena? It's me. Richard. Am I disturbing you?"

Richard Van Stuckley at this time of night? Richard Van Stuckley at all was a shock. Paula had made no attempt to get in touch with her and she herself was not his favourite person. Not after her ban on him using their cottage. Hurriedly she pulled her hair from its combs and glanced in the mirror as she ran up the stairs from the basement, pausing only to throw open the door of the drawing room and turn on the lamps.

No one would be able to report back that she was reduced to living in her kitchen and that she looked a wreck.

"Just an impulse." Richard smiled as she led him into the now more welcoming room that had been closed up for weeks. There was a faint musty smell that comes from a room that has not been used, the curtains were undrawn and an old copy of a morning paper was still lying on one of the tables. Smoothly, Serena picked it up and binned it.

"How nice to see you," she lied. "Let me get you a drink."

As she handed him a tumbler of whiskey she could smell brandy on his breath and saw that his eyes were just a little bloodshot. Dutch courage to come here, she thought contemptuously. She moved towards the windows and pulled the cord to draw the curtains, shutting out the night and prying eyes.

"How's Paula?" she enquired, returning to join him but not remotely interested.

He waved his hand indifferently. "Fine, I expect. Don't see a great deal of each other."

She resisted an impulse to point out that if he spent less time with his secretary he would have more to devote to his extremely silly wife. Instead she smiled and said:

"I expect you've been busy."

He nodded and took a gulp from his drink. Serena moved to a sofa opposite the one on which Richard was sitting and hoped this visit would not last long. If he had been sent to spy he was wasting his time. If he had come to offer help she would have been astonished. For a while Richard described his busy life, the several mentions in the paper that his career had excited, and Serena deftly dealt with any enquiries about Stephen.

"If I had any news, I would be delighted to tell you," she said quietly. "But there isn't. I'm sorry to be so boring."

She wanted him to go and hoped he hadn't noticed the quick glance she threw at the clock. He looked at her and tossed the rest of the whiskey down his throat. She moved to refill his glass but he was there before her.

"No, no," he waved her back to her seat. "If you don't mind, of course?"

She shook her head and he lifted the decanter to replenish his glass. It was then she began to feel wary rather than bored. Instead of returning to his own seat, he sat down beside her, too close. She moved back, which didn't escape his notice.

"Look, Serena," he massaged the heavy tumbler between his short fingers and turned to face her. "I know we haven't always got on. But it's rotten what's happened. To be frank," he went on earnestly, "I've only just discovered that the girls have not been seeing much of you."

She opened her mouth to speak, but he interrupted.

"Oh don't pretend with me, Serena, we've known each other for too long. Don't defend them." Richard sailed on, ignoring her bewildered look. "You're worried that I've come to pry into your life, I can see that. Well, I haven't. And I was livid with those papers who misquoted me. Dreadful scum. They'll invent anything. Anyway, I thought I'd drop round myself, to see if maybe I could help in some way. I know we haven't always seen eye to eye but you're so alone now, I thought you might need someone to talk to, depend on."

Serena was surprised but quite touched. Of all the people she had once known she would not have thought Richard would have had any time for her. Clearly she was wrong. "It's kind of you, Richard," she smiled more warmly at him. "But Andrew Beresford is handling everything for me. But thank you anyway."

He stretched round to put his glass on the table behind him and took her hand. She was too astonished to pull it away.

"Serena." He moved even closer. "I know what you're going through. I'm sure Andrew handles everything beautifully, but he can't be here for you, can he? Not for all your needs. It would be so easy for me to help you, and no hardship either. You know I've always thought you were a very beautiful woman."

He was obviously drunk and harbouring several hideously erroneous illusions about her. She was acutely aware of being alone in the house except for the children. It was imperative that he went. She attempted to stand up to signal that the visit was now over, but he wouldn't let go of her hand.

"Richard," she tried to sound firm. "I appreciate your coming here, but believe me I am not in need of the kind of — comfort you're suggesting. Now you must go, Paula …"

She suppressed a scream as he pulled her down beside him, pinning her against the sofa. "Bugger Paula," he muttered, trying to pin his mouth to hers.

"Richard," she pleaded, twisting her face away from him. "Get off me. This is ridiculous. Please. Richard —" Her voice rose to a scream as she felt his hands grip and grind into her breasts.

"That's right," he panted, trying to control her pounding fists. "That's it. Fight me for it. I've always wanted you … My God," he screamed, suddenly releasing her. "You *bitch!*" His weight was too much but with a last furious lunge she had grabbed the decanter of whiskey and hit him with it on the only bit of his body she could reach. The centre of his back. The contents spilled down the expensive cashmere jacket and dribbled on to the white silk sofa.

It was the respite she needed. With a twist that wrenched the breath out of her body, she wriggled off the sofa and raced into the hallway and made for the front door. Her hands shook as she released the catch and then, trying to steady her nerves, she walked back to where Richard was shaking his jacket, squirming around to feel his back. From the doorway she said breathlessly:

"Get out. Directly opposite you will see a dark saloon. The driver and his passenger are detectives. They watch me the whole time. If you don't go quietly, one word from me will have you arrested."

"You stuck-up fucking bitch," he spat at her. "No man will ever touch you. You'll be sorry. Fancy you? I was doing you a favour. Anyone can see you're desperate for it. Your loss. And any ideas you might have of telling what's left of your friends that I came on to you will be laughed at. Who's going to believe you," he jeered venomously. "A fucking crook's wife?"

"Out." She could hardly breathe and she was shaking uncontrollably. As he pushed past her out of the house, she shrank back against the wall. His shirt, suffering as much as his jacket from her desperate action, left a trailing aroma of alcohol in his wake. As he reached the bottom of the steps, she knew he had seen the car parked opposite, and also knew the effort it must have taken him to walk at a normal pace and not to race for the safety of his car.

Swiftly she closed the door and slid slowly to the floor, her eyes tightly closed, fighting to control the frightened and angry gasps that were exploding in her chest. She was desperate for what he had to offer, but not from him. Only ever from Stephen.

Her only consolation as, minutes later, steaming hot water poured through her hair and down her body, was that Richard had believed the dark saloon, owned by her neighbour, was that of a fraud squad detective. And later, as she swabbed the silk sofa and the carpet, trying to eliminate the smell and the damage, that the moonless night had made it impossible for Richard to know if it was empty — which it was — or not.

She was not surprised to read some days later a reference to Richard's friendship with Stephen being dismissed as mere acquaintance.

"A few games of squash," he was reported as saying. "Didn't really know him on a social level. I gather it was Mrs Carmichael who pushed him. Very ambitious for her husband. Quite a toughie, I'm told."

*

It was because she felt humiliated by the scene that she had at first tried to deal with it herself. What, she argued, could be gained by distressing her mother? What good would telling Don Trewless do? After all, Richard would deny it. But most of all, in her weakened emotional state, her judgement had been scrambled and she felt she was somehow to blame.

In the end distress, mingled with rage at such an assault, proved too much, and Melanie was given a stammering and largely incoherent account of what had taken place. Even as she poured the details out she could feel the weight in her chest beginning to dissolve.

She had expected Melanie to be deeply shocked. But she wasn't.

"Not surprised," Melanie snorted. "He'd screw a Belisha beacon if it stopped flashing long enough. Why didn't you just tell him to get lost?" she asked. "Laugh at him. The prat."

"Laugh at him?" Serena exclaimed. "Let me tell you, it was no laughing matter."

Melanie was instantly contrite. "Sorry, Serena. I'm just so angry that he started on you. He did it to Jane Marshall when she and Paul split up for a bit."

"No?" Serena exclaimed. "What happened?"

"Much the same. The old 'you must be lonely' routine. She told me she started sobbing and screaming and then the au pair came downstairs and Richard pretended to be trying to console her and it would have worked except the au pair didn't know who he was and thought he was attacking Jane. So she started hurling books at him, until Jane had to beg her to stop."

Serena looked awed. "Good God, he must be so fed up with solitary women all over London beating him up."

She and Melanie began to giggle. When the unusual sound of their mother convulsed with laughter drifted to the children's ears, they both turned up to investigate.

"It's just the idea that someone who is the pits thought I would give in to him. Christ, Mel," she groaned later on. "What do I look like? Easy meat?"

"Rubbish," Melanie retorted angrily. "You know you don't. You're not to blame in any way and you weren't sending out the wrong signals letting him in. What were you expected to do? Scream like Snow White and lock the door against someone you've known for years? He's so up his own backside he probably thinks we've all got the hots for him. Any one of us on our own would be a target. Frankly I think you're wrong, we should take a stand over this."

But Serena was adamant. "No, listen to me," she pleaded. "If you blank him you'll have to cut Paula out as well and it isn't her fault — oh, I know she's a prat, but the point is that if you blank her it means Miranda will then be put on the spot and Charles will be dragged into it because he works with Bill Hooper. See?"

The mention of Charles's business life being affected worked on Melanie. Serena was relieved when she saw the uncertainty on her friend's face. "Honestly, Mel," she said. "It was just the need to tell someone and I feel so much better already. I just felt so grubby. Truly, much better now. Promise."

*

"Left to me I would like to see Malcolm's nails pulled out without anaesthetic."

Andrew Beresford glanced up surprised. Serena glared back. "It's true. I do. Stop looking at me like that. It isn't fair, it shouldn't just be me. He should be suffering the worst possible agony, because if he hadn't been so foul and unfair to Stephen, this would never have happened. Would it?"

Andrew stayed silent. He knew this would pass. Serena's passionate outbursts against the world were preferable, he had decided, to her silent misery, the dead look in her eyes. She was thin now. Too thin.

"Believe me," he said, as she resumed her jerky pacing across his office. "He's going through his own personal hell. If you saw him, you'd know he's suffering."

"How can he be suffering?" she cried bitterly. Andrew winced as she replaced the small Chinese vase she had absently picked up.

"He's got so much to answer for and he's still sitting in his bloody office with his ghastly wife telling everyone how he feels so betrayed. *Betrayed?* How has he been affected? Tell me, will you? No, I'll tell you. No way."

"Well, he might still have to resign."

Serena laughed out loud. She placed the palms of her hands on the highly polished oval table and leaned across to him. "Resign? *Puh-leese.* Not till he's got several directorships lined up and a handshake to melt Midas in his pocket."

She sat down abruptly, coiled her legs around each other and wrapped her arms tightly around herself. She hunched forward, choosing her words carefully.

"I'm sorry," she sighed. "Ignore me. Look, Andrew," she looked up and gazed directly at him. "It's really good of you to continue acting for me. I won't pretend I have the faintest idea how I'm going to pay you, but believe me I will."

He shook his head impatiently. "Nothing to pay. No, seriously. God, you're an argumentative woman all of a sudden. All right, all right, sometime when you're back on your feet. But not now. Besides, I'm not sure there's much more I can do after the hearing."

Serena tried to keep her voice steady. "When's that likely to be?"

Andrew shrugged. "I'm going as fast as I can. Mid-July is looking likely. I want to get it in before the summer recess."

Serena just nodded.

Later that day Andrew Beresford arrived home to find a parcel had just been delivered. Inside he gazed at an original L. S. Lowry that had once hung in Serena's hallway, an inheritance from her father.

"On account," said the note, signed with a flourishing S.

"Shit," he groaned. "Bloody women."

*

Serena reached home from Andrew's office just after midday. She had left before the post that morning and now she scooped the handful of letters from the mat.

Her bag dropped to the floor along with a sheaf of bills, as she held the one with an Irish postmark. She couldn't read what it said, she didn't care. It had come. Clutching the slim white envelope, she hastily crossed to the window. The square was deserted. She whirled round looking for somewhere to be safe. If she drew the curtains she might be suspected.

The house was silent. She was expecting no callers. She stared wildly round and then raced upstairs to her bedroom. She picked up the phone and heard the familiar click as the intercepting device activated. She crossed the room and closed the door of the bathroom behind her.

She read the single sheet of paper with its cheaply printed logo and short message. There must be a mistake, she thought frantically.

Thank you for your interest in joining our little group. Sadly as you are in London and we meet in Rafferty's just off O'Connell Street, it is unlikely you would be able to attend our meetings. However, do drop in should you ever be in Dublin.

It was signed Anona Fitzgerald who had thoughtfully enclosed some literature on where the devotees of the respected and distinguished poet could share their thoughts on the great man, while taking advantage of the proximity of a snug little bar to help lubricate their musings.

The letter slipped out of her fingers. She leaned her head against the cold marble tiles and slid to the floor.

Not Stephen. Not Stephen at all.

*

"I've tried." Andrew's voice was quietly furious. "Look, Serena, she hasn't said anything that is untrue. She's entitled to her opinion."

"Opinion? God help me, Andrew. What did I ever do to her? Why? Oh my God, the children. Can't we sue her?"

"For what? Telling a filthy tabloid what it was like working for the man the world's police are looking for? Did you have any idea she'd go to the papers?"

"Idea? Are you serious? None. She was housekeeper here for seven years and she was paid on the dot, holidays honoured, we gave her decent presents at Christmas and on her birthday. Why? I mean what on earth can she say that would interest anyone?"

Serena was shouting, pacing up and down with the phone in one hand, dragging the other down over her eyes. No wonder the knocker remained silent, the press interest diluted. They didn't need her any more. Not with such treachery on her doorstep. Louise stood in the doorway of the kitchen listening, her face pale and solemn. Serena could do nothing to protect her. Harry began to cry.

"What does it say?" Serena whispered, turning her back on her children.

Andrew wasn't sure. All he knew was that *The Daily Messenger* had paid Mrs Owen a fair sum of money to describe life with Serena Carmichael, whom they referred to in the next days' centre spread as *A Kept Woman*.

The feature, ghosted by a staff writer, was a concoction of fantasy and cringing cliché.

She wanted only the best from those who worked for her… I had to change dry cleaners practically every week because she never thought any of them were good enough. Same with other staff, she would check everything after they'd gone and woe betide me if it wasn't up to her standards. She was a stickler for things like that. Money was no object … Children were indulged … Friends were glamorous from showbiz to politicians … Holidays … cars … Paris for clothes, never worked a day in her life, glorified hostess, that's all.

Words to justify the headline poured across the page in a giddy list of adjectives — spawned to hide just how little Mrs Owen really could reveal about life in the Carmichael household.

No word about the money she had paid to send the Owens on holiday when Mr Owen had been ill, Serena noted. Or the cheque for three months' mortgage that had been slipped quietly into her treacherous housekeeper's account when Mr Owen lost his job and they fell behind with payments. A memory lapse about the time the cottage had been turned over to Mrs Owen's son and his wife when they couldn't afford to go away and their marriage was cracking under the strain — as was the cottage after the damage inflicted on it by the little Owens who had accompanied their parents. All of which Serena had repaired without mentioning the cost to the unruly family, and certainly not to Stephen, who had been against the offer in the first place.

Serena chose not to retaliate. It was what the paper wanted and what Serena knew would simply prolong the agony for them all if she did. Chrissie had fired off a letter to refute everything Mrs Owen had claimed, but it was put on the letters page and did not provide the burst of glamour that the housekeeper's tales had, and went unremarked.

Her only solace was Mrs Owen's quite untruthful claim that the Carmichaels' disagreements were often over friends.

"Mr Carmichael," it read. *"Came to me one day to tell me that his best friend, the MP Richard Van Stuckley, wanted somewhere to work with his secretary on a top secret government paper and asked me to make sure the cottage would be well stocked with food and wine. He told me not to trouble Serena with his private arrangement with Mr Van*

Stuckley because even Mrs Van Stuckley — for security reasons — shouldn't know. But Mrs Carmichael flew into a rage when she found out and he wasn't allowed to stay there again."

What goes around comes around, sighed Serena. She winced when she thought of the scene in the Van Stuckley house when that was revealed. Richard, who had claimed in several interviews that he was barely acquainted with Stephen, would be mortified. And Paula? Poor, deluded Paula.

Melanie just sniffed. "Paula had it coming," she snarled. "God, Serena, you should have seen her the other day at the committee meeting —" Melanie stopped.

Serena had quietly resigned from the committee, knowing it was expected of her, and only Melanie and the newly arrived Meryl Holt, invited by Paula and Miranda to join the *Babyways* committee, had voted against accepting it.

"Sorry." Melanie flushed. "Didn't mean …"

Serena reached out and squeezed her hand. "Stop it. I'm glad. One less thing to have to think about. Promise. I mean it."

When Melanie had gone, Serena picked up the minutes of the last meeting and idly ran her eye down them. Another break from the past. This was for Anna. This was set up to make some sense out of such a cruel loss. She was about to throw the minutes into a drawer when the last item caught her eye. The committee had invited Mrs Brisley Jones to join them. She was proposed by Paula Van Stuckley and seconded by Miranda Hooper.

Slowly she tore the sheaf of papers one by one and then stuffed them into the waste bin. Where they all belonged, she thought. Every last one of them.

Chapter Eight

Serena waited in the drawing room, gazing unseeingly out over the garden square opposite. She stood well back from the window so that her presence went undetected. It was July and very hot. The square, protected by a circle of towering beech trees, was at its best. Crimson rhododendrons, blushing azaleas, creamy white roses in their prime — a cool retreat drawing one or two nannies with their charges into its leafy shade. An occasional breeze drifted through the open sash windows, stirring the white voile curtains into a gentle floating wave.

Louise and Harry were safe in the country with Melanie and Charles Westfield, driven there late the night before by Serena. The house was still, the room silent except for the steady tick of the clock. She had insisted on being alone. That way she didn't have to think about anyone else when she heard. One last time, that's all she now allowed herself — a brief few hours when she could have the luxury of caring only for herself, rather than for her children, her mother, her friends.

Her friends? She gave a slight shake of her head, a flicker of a smile. So few were there to worry about. Or ... Stephen. In her hand she clutched an uncustomary tumbler of whiskey.

Over the past few months she had lost far too much weight. She was no longer slender, but thin. Her severely cut black linen dress did her no favours. Her fair hair, fading highlights lifting its colour, pulled back from her face into a tortoiseshell clip curving into the nape of her neck, served merely to emphasize loss of sleep and excessive stress.

She glanced around at the clock. It was nearly midday. Andrew had promised to phone the minute he had a decision.

Her gaze travelled around the room, taking in the porcelain bowls crammed with old English roses, the portrait of a long-gone Carmichael above the mantelpiece. The needlepoint stool, the oval rosewood table, laden with evidence of a life that was waiting to be consigned to memory.

She paused to look at the faces of her children laughing out of silver-framed pictures, her parents on their anniversary, Stephen with the Prime Minister, both of them with the Prince of Wales at a charity dinner, another of them weekending with the present Chancellor at Dorney Wood, one as they laughed into the camera from the deck of the yacht leased for a cruise one summer.

She turned away before she reached the wedding photographs. Such a beautiful dress. Such a beautiful life.

Cautiously she leaned forward, risking detection, and with more hope than conviction, to see if the waiting photographers in the square below were showing any sign of flagging. Even though they were standing restlessly around, occasionally glancing up at the windows, they were clearly dug in. Every now and then a new arrival — not believing he wouldn't prosper where his colleagues had failed, and immune to the presence of the solitary policeman sent along to keep a wary eye on them — tried the intercom. She let it ring. The sound of laughter drifted up.

Serena's attention was suddenly caught by a bustle of activity as a black Jag inched its way around the square. The waiting pack closed in, flashbulbs exploded. Serena stiffened as she recognized the two figures emerging from the car. The last lingering absurd hope died in her. Of course it was absurd. But what else was left?

The first out of the car on the driver's side was the balding, familiar figure of Andrew Beresford. The second was Natalie Silverman wearing her habitual black suit.

Andrew glanced up at the window. Serena instinctively stepped back as Andrew disappeared into the melee of reporters, ushering Natalie ahead of him. She had given him a key so she would not have to be seen answering the door.

Serena was glad the waiting was over. She didn't have to be told the news. Andrew would have phoned if it had been different. She straightened her shoulders and faced the door. Without looking she fumbled to place the half-full glass on a table just behind her, but her hand was shaking and the tumbler fell to the floor, splintering glass on the stone surround of the fireplace, and whiskey on to the polished wood, staining the edge of the Aubusson carpet, just as Andrew opened the door.

"Sorry, Andrew," she said, looking up from where she was crouching, a wry smile catching the corners of her mouth. "Such a mess, isn't it?"

Andrew didn't have to tell Serena that it was over.

"How long?" she asked, handing him a tumbler of whiskey when she had finished clearing up the mess, and pouring another for herself. Natalie was already on the phone in the adjoining room. "How long to find somewhere else?"

Andrew rolled his drink between his hands. "No rush," he said carefully. "But if they get a sale it might be as well to have somewhere to go. At least start looking. Or at any rate have a contingency plan. Maybe your mother's? Relatives?"

Serena shook her head and stared past him at some private view only she could see. She half smiled. "I'm the only child of only children. So no relatives, only my mother. But I'm not running off to her. I'm going to manage on my own. Away from everyone."

Andrew glanced uneasily at her. "And that means what?"

She plucked at the neck of her dress. "I'm going to disappear. I mean it. Oh, not out of the country. I haven't the money or the inclination. I'm fed up, Andrew. Tired of watching people shrinking away in case I ask for help — which I won't — embarrassed that friends like Melanie, Charles and Emily urge me to live off them. Oh perhaps not that, but certainly to borrow. And," she hesitated, choosing her words carefully. "I want to prove something. That I can do it. I wasn't just a kept woman leeching off a rich husband."

"Where will you go?"

She shrugged. "Somewhere cheapish. Rent a house for a while, see what happens. Settle the children into schools that are paid for by the state. God, Stephen paid enough tax …" She stopped, looking confused. "Well, you know what I mean. I don't want to take any more, just learn to live on what

I'm entitled to, teach the children that it's a tough old world. I mean, how difficult can that be? Hundreds of women do it every day."

"Serena —" he began, but was stopped by the look on her face. It wasn't an expression he was used to seeing. Harder, less giving. Inside he doubted she knew what she was saying, but he reached over and squeezed her hand.

"You know where to find me," he told her. "Any time. You know that."

*

Serena's T-shirt was sticking to her back. Her legs ached and her linen skirt was crumpled. The relief of collapsing into the chair in front of Mr Stanley's desk, out of the sweltering heat of south London in August, was such bliss that at first she let him talk to her as though her request to find rented accommodation for a sum less than the national debt of Peru was about as reasonable as asking for snow in the Sahara.

"Four beds," he repeated, drumming his fingers on the table, clicking his way through lists scrolling up on the screen in front of him. He glanced at her. "Got to be rented?" he asked, hopefully. "Very nice one here, just came in, five beds, off-street parking, sale fell through this morning with one of our competitors. It'll be snapped up by the end of the afternoon."

"No, really, it's got to be rented," Serena insisted, in no doubt at all, having toured the area all day, why a competitor was so readily handing a sale over to a rival. "And not too big," she reminded him. "And I'm sure it's not impossible."

Mr Stanley gave a doubtful shake of blond spiky hair, blew out his cheeks and redoubled his efforts with his screen, darting up and down clicking the mouse like a castanet on speed.

He looked about fourteen. His jacket had been discarded and there were damp patches creeping down from his armpits. His tie was loosened, his sleeves rolled back to show thin pale arms adorned by a serious copy of a Rolex. When the phone rang he snapped a row of buttons in front of him, leaning dangerously back in his chair and swinging around to survey the thundering traffic outside as he spoke.

Serena waited patiently while he conducted a conversation in which the caller could not have been left in any doubt that Mr Stanley was an old hand at the selling game, and a big player to boot. His desk was little more than a top with two drawers suspended on one side, the surface taken up with a computer which he couldn't leave alone. On a narrow strip of wood perched at the front of his desk was written, "Darren Stanley, Sales Negotiator".

Tiredness, and not quite knowing how she had ended up in a dusty run-down area of London with this self-important boy making her wait, stopped her from laughing out loud at his grandness. Instead, after five minutes, she leaned forward and caught his attention, tapping her watch.

Mr Stanley's chair crashed back to earth. "I have a client with me," he hastily told his caller. "Let me transfer you to Contracts." He made it sound like a glass and chrome department on another floor of a building staffed with thrusting young executives. Instead a light flashed on one of the only two other desks in the tiny room and a bored looking girl put down a magazine saying:

"Contracts. Abigail speaking, how may I help you?"

Serena thought fleetingly of the smooth and courteous young man from the Knightsbridge firm Stradbrooke Properties who had arrived to assess her house. In a dark linen suit and discreet tie, he had murmured instructions to an assistant who had measured, checked and recorded their findings into a miniature tape recorder.

They had not troubled her for anything. And why should they? The house, and everything in it, was owned by the bank.

"It's not easy, four beds," Darren was saying to Serena, feeling less charmed with her after her interruption. "Popular area as well. Got MPs on the phone day and night, I have, begging me to find them something because it's within the division bell ... that's the alarm to tell them all to get back to vote ... Not an MP are you?" He peered at her as she told him she was familiar with the workings of MPs. "You look familiar."

Serena felt her heart beat double. She shook her head. "No. I'm ... no one. Just looking for a house."

Darren looked disappointed. Relief flooded through his client.

"Ah," his scrolling skidded to a halt. "What about Peckham?"

"Peckham?"

"Nice, six bedrooms, presented as bed-sits, easily converted."

"No." Serena interrupted with a patience she didn't possess. "I want," she pronounced each word carefully so there could be no misunderstanding, "a small family house in this area that I can move into that doesn't need masses done to it."

Enlightenment dawned on Darren's face. He nodded. "Got you," he grinned. "Husband not a DIY man, eh?"

"No," Serena smiled faintly, "I mean no husband. We're not living together."

It was true. She had rehearsed for just such a moment. She was not — please God — widowed, nor was she divorced or separated. Single mother wasn't right either.

"What do I put?" she had asked Andrew, laughing nervously when he had asked her to sign the papers accepting the court's decision about her future. "I feel dispossessed. No status." She couldn't bring herself to write "Missing" and certainly not "Wanted for questioning".

Andrew suggested separated but Serena refused. "That sounds as though I agreed to live apart. And I haven't." Her voice rose to a sob she struggled instantly to suppress. "I haven't agreed to anything, it's all been agreed for me. It isn't right," she whispered, blowing her nose fiercely. "Is it?"

Andrew gazed silently at her. Everything that could be said had been said. She was on her own. In the end she put "Married" and in brackets "Husband's whereabouts not known". He countersigned her signature without comment.

*

The press had, as Donald Trewless predicted, arrived back when the case had finally come to court. Even the police interest had revived with the hope that, seeing his family heading for eviction, Stephen Carmichael might turn himself in.

Draycott Mendes had relented enough to allow Serena to keep enough from the sale of the house to rent somewhere in London until she got back on her feet. They had also allowed her to keep essential items of furniture to start again somewhere else. It had always been a forlorn hope that she would be left with anything more than that, but Malcolm Brisley Jones, still clinging to his job, had personally intervened and urged the board to help Serena as much as they could.

They were bitter and angry men, but few had disliked Serena. Most had appreciated her warmth and genuine good nature. Now they were all united in their pity for her. Serena had taken the children to stay with her mother, while the house was looked over by a succession of people escorted by the Stradbrooke Properties representative.

It was, she said, for Louise and Harry's sake. But no one was fooled. Serena did not want to know who would be in her bedroom, whose children would be playing in the garden where LouLou and Harry should by rights be playing, who would be enjoying entertaining their friends in her dining room. Especially, she did not want to see someone else sitting in Stephen's study. The only room in the house left untouched.

Melanie told Charles, driving back from Serena's one night, that it was spooky the way Serena wouldn't let anyone into Stephen's office.

"Like a shrine. Almost as though he's dead."

Charles glanced sideways at his wife. "Maybe he is," he pointed out.

Melanie just shook her head. "Not him," she snorted. "Survival of the quickest was his motto. I'll be glad when she's out of there. Although," she paused, "God knows where she's going to end up."

Draycott Mendes had found a buyer almost immediately. Serena's instinctive eye for turning a grand house into a stylish but warm family home had been the subject of much envy. The fact that it was also the home of a wanted banker had encouraged rather than deflected interest.

"Why shouldn't it?" Serena demanded, when Natalie Silverman phoned to say a string of interested buyers were being assembled to see the property over three days to cause the minimum distress to Serena. "It's not as though Stephen murdered someone, is it?"

Staying with her mother also resolved at least one dilemma. Margot had urged Serena to come to her, but standing in the tiny kitchen of the cottage her mother had moved to after her father's death, in the village where Serena had grown up, she knew it was not what she wanted. What she wanted was her old life back again. But it had gone.

She now wanted anonymity, independence and a chance to disappear until Stephen came home. It was only later that Serena paused to wonder where that home would be.

The news that a buyer had been found was waiting for her on her return from her mother's. The client was an Indian diplomat who wanted to be installed by the end of the summer, in time for his children to be enrolled in English schools.

She crumpled the letter and stuffed it into the pocket of her jacket. Just for this moment, she told herself, this house is mine, and wondered why "Abandoned" or even "Deserted" — so much nearer the truth — was not acceptable on official forms. Or even, "Kept Woman"?

The fuss created by Mrs Owen had begun to fade. Other news, other disasters and new scandals had relegated it to just another cutting in the fat Carmichael file. If that deceitful and cunning woman could see me now, she thought, trudging from house to car, car to estate agent.

"Kept Woman" had rankled. But what else had she been? No income to call her own, relying totally on Stephen, it had never occurred to her to be independent. There had been no need. She could see now it had been a mistake. But who could blame her? She had lived no differently to her friends, or to Stephen's colleagues' wives. But in the end, none of it was hers or Stephen's. How could it have been, when the courts had only a month prior decided it could all be taken because it all belonged to Dray-cott Mendes?

*

It was the beginning of August. Louise and Harry had been despatched to stay with Jasmine in Lucca for two weeks while Serena went house hunting. At first Louise had refused to go, not relishing the prospect of two weeks with a grandmother she found boring, but promptly relented when she discovered that for the first time in their lives she and Harry would be flying alone, to be met by Minnie at Pisa.

Even Harry, who thankfully did not share Louise's disdain for their odd grandmother, was excited once he had been assured that Serena would stay with them until she could hand them over to the air stewardess accompanying minors, and that she in turn wouldn't leave him until his grandmother had been located.

It took a great deal of effort for Serena not to sound terrified at allowing her children to leave her. But Margot needed a break, and while Melanie had begged to be allowed to take them and Serena to Majorca with them, Serena had refused. They'd done enough. She was not an easy person to be around and she was sure there was a hint of relief in Melanie when she finally accepted they would go without her.

She missed Stephen. Missed his smell, his presence, his strength. She missed everything about him. Trying to concentrate on another subject lasted as long as it took to give a rational response, but her mind was elsewhere. She also missed sex.

"The only thing I can do something about," she muttered to herself, as she lay alone shuddering in the dark, embarrassed at her furtiveness, physically relieved but emotionally lonelier than ever. No lean warm body to curl against and to drift into sleep tangled up in someone's arms. No one to laugh softly into the dark at a shared joke. God, she missed him so much.

She could not believe that he didn't miss her too, or that he could not find some way of contacting her. But she no longer woke expecting to find him in the shower or to come in late after she had gone to bed. She dreamed about it. Sometimes the need for him was so overwhelming, she believed she could hear him moving around, and there were times — of which only she was aware and of which in calmer moments she felt ashamed and treacherous — when she hated him so much she couldn't breathe.

Jasmine had been gruff deflecting Serena's thanks. She was, after all, just glad to be able to help in some way, although the idea of entertaining two distraught children — with little to distract them but beautiful scenery and the occasional trip into Lucca, a forty-minute drive away — was causing her some misgivings.

But there you are, she sighed, as she shooed the dogs back into the yard and set off. The deed was done, they were on their way. Her only consolation was that she was helping her son's children — although they might not believe it — and they were unlikely to end up murdering each other, even if they never spoke to each other again.

Jasmine glanced at the dashboard of her car as she eased her way on to the motorway. Eleven o'clock. She was in good time, they weren't arriving until after midday. A shimmering wave of heat hung over the road as she put her foot down, signs for Pisa flashing past. In her head she mulled over several schemes that might appeal to them. Maybe a day in Florence, that was only an hour or so away. It would be a long day but they could do it. She began to feel excited.

"Too long on your own, that's your trouble," she scolded herself. "Making too much of it, you'll only end up disappointed. They're probably only interested in computer games and rock stars." She laughed self-consciously at her stupidity. Wait and see, she cautioned herself. Mind you, she mused as the sign for the airport turnoff flashed past, and forgetting that she had decided to play it by ear, they might be very hungry when they arrive. Airline food was dreadful. Perhaps they'd like to stop in Lucca for lunch. After all, they had two weeks. And none of them was in a hurry to go anywhere.

*

Four hours after leaving the small airless office and armed with the best that Mr Stanley could come up with, Serena trod up the path to a mid-terrace Victorian house which the photocopied sheet boasted had off-street parking. A brown windowless van was parked in front of the living room window, a child's bike was propped by a tin dustbin and two black bin liners were shoved roughly inside the porch.

The doorbell whirred as she waited on the cracked doorstep. At least inside it can't be any worse, she consoled herself. After a decent interval she rang again, stepping back to see if there were any signs of life.

They must be in. Darren Stanley had phoned to say she was on her way. But there was no answer. Slowly she walked down the path and at the gate stopped to check the address. Today she had seen seven houses. Six had been hopeless. Too big, too run down, too expensive or in streets where she felt unsafe just parking the car. And this one she couldn't even get into.

She was wearing the wrong shoes, she knew that now, but at nine this morning it had not occurred to her that at three o'clock she would still be walking in ever widening circles in an area across the river she had rarely passed, through let alone walked in.

The cream linen loafers, ideal for strolling from the car to the restaurant, or the length of time it took to walk from Harrods to Harvey Nichols, had not been bought the previous summer with house hunting in mind. The dust from the streets rose up as lorries rumbled by. The heat of the pavements seeped through to the thin soles of her shoes.

The sun was now directly overhead. This time last year she had been lying by a pool at their villa at Cap Ferrat, watching LouLou flirt with the Italian boy from next door, Harry and Chrissie splashing noisily under her lazy gaze. Stephen ... well, Stephen was disappearing back to London.

Serena pushed her sunglasses into her hair and wiped the perspiration from around her eyes with her knuckles. It didn't do any good to think about these things, but no matter how hard she tried, she always came back to it.

It no longer mattered to her who, if anyone, was watching as she slumped on to the edge of a brick wall protruding from under an overgrown hedge. Being watched had become part of her life.

Slowly she lifted one foot on to her knee, easing her shoe off, absently massaging her bare foot, while she thought about what to do next. The file of papers she held in her hand was now showing signs of fatigue. She looked at it with distaste. The reasons why she had chosen this small pocket of London were hard to remember now she was here. Dimly she recalled Melanie saying it was one of those areas that was easy to reach — but who would be coming to see her? She looked up and down the faded street and thought of Andrew advising her to look in an area that was considered upwardly mobile rather than crashing in defeat.

She had accepted their advice although she knew they were reluctant to encourage her, and in truth had done so because she hadn't a clue where to start. Her spirits rose when the sheets of house descriptions started to arrive. They all said the same thing. Much sought after, improving area. That's a good start. "Let's all improve together," she muttered, ticking her way down the list.

Serena slipped her shoes back on again and stood up. Her car was parked at the end of the street. She would try one more house. Just one, and then go home. There must be something in this area that was a reasonable size for her and the children, where they could start to live again, lost in a maze of streets, living alongside people who didn't know them, couldn't judge them.

It was surprising how quickly she had begun to recognize which streets were worth her attention, and which would terrify her to set foot in. She even knew the small pockets of affluence, a few carefully chosen streets favoured by those like the army of MPs quoted by estate agents as a selling point, but depressing Serena by the minute when she thought of living near someone like Richard Van Stuckley.

She turned her car into the main road and drove two blocks until she came to Foster Street. If she had seen this road first, with its cracked pavements and air of neglect, she would have walked away in horror. As it had been a day spent acquainting herself with streets lined with rusting abandoned cars, or prettier flat-fronted Regency houses that were beyond her reach, or roads where seedy hotels interrupted rows of dishevelled houses where the residents eyed her with suspicion, her thinking had switched from impossible to maybe.

She parked her car and began to walk slowly up the narrow road with its tired trees, flanked on either side by uniformly dull houses in red brick. Attempts at staving off age and infirmity varied from the valiant, with brightly painted front doors, to the vandalized, with plasterboard where a window should be.

Number forty-two was towards the far end where the road curved around out of sight and became Dunton Road. Serena consulted her notes. No. This was it all right. The door was painted blue, the knocker was hanging off, and she could see the frames on the sash windows needed replacing. Silently she gazed up at the net-curtained windows, fighting a desire to turn and run.

Stephen. Oh bloody Stephen. Her gaze drifted from the worn-out brick-work. She noticed the minuscule area between the road and the door. A willow tree occupied almost its entire space. Garden, she sighed. So much for the front garden. Utterly hopeless.

A small breeze rustled through the still air. Serena pushed her hair out of her eyes and gazed despairingly at the fronds on the tree swaying unevenly, lifting the trailing leaves to reveal a circle of smooth brown stones border-ing it in which some pansies were struggling to be seen through a tangle of weeds.

Serena stood very still and for a long while just stared at the patch of garden. She had to live somewhere. If the flowers could do it, maybe she could. In spite of herself, she smiled, giving her head a small shake. How could she tell anyone that she had settled on a house in such a road because she was at the end of her wits, but a small willow tree and a clump of flowers refusing to be cowed had singled out this unpromising house as her future home?

She looked back down the street and wondered how anyone could tell whether this road was going up in the world, as Darren Stanley had insisted, or plummeting as its sagging appearance suggested. There was only one way to find out.

With a deep breath, she walked purposefully up the path and rang the bell.

Chapter Nine

"It is *not* smaller than Harry's, it is just a different shape. Look, I'll show you."

Serena moved impatiently away from the door and began to pace the length of the oblong-shaped room, now her daughter's new bedroom, which overlooked the garden where a grey slatted fence and two gnarled apple trees separated it from an identical house backing on to theirs. A black lean-to shed was propped against one side of a loosely boarded fence. Around the perimeter someone had attempted to fashion flower beds to relieve the slab of brown turf that filled the small space in the centre, but there was no evidence that any flowers were waiting to burst into bloom in the spring — or indeed at any time. It was a view that seriously challenged Mr Stanley's description of a well stocked, mature garden in this four-bedroom, three-reception, early Victorian terrace house, in a highly favoured residential street near all amenities.

A few leaves swirled around in the back yard, disturbed by a gusting wind that was rattling two loose planks of the fence against each other. A cat pushed its nose through the gap, shooting through to safety as a howl of indignation erupted from behind, followed by a large thump as the black pointed nose and ears of an Alsatian dog tried the impossible feat of following through the narrow gap.

"Sov-*rin*," screeched a voice from the back door of the next house. "Gettorf that bleedin' fence. Wotchoo think you are? A bleedin' race'orse? Sov-rin, I'm telling you. Bradlee? What's that tyre doin' in my garden? If I've told you once, I've told you a bleedin' thousand times … Oh my God, look what that bloody dog's done now. Well, I'm not clearing it up."

Upstairs in the house next door two of the new occupants were also at war, oblivious to the view; the neighbours or the ambitions of the Alsatian tearing away at the fragile fence that divided their two gardens.

Louise leaned against the wall, one foot tucked up behind her, scuffing the brown flowered wallpaper with the heel of her shoe. Her arms were folded tightly around her waist, and she was glaring sullenly out through the window. She wouldn't look at Serena, who was struggling to control an overwhelming impulse to shake her.

"There. Four feet longer than Harry's but just one foot narrower. Exactly the same overall. Lou, stop that. That wallpaper's got to make do for now. Lou, are you listening? Darling, please. I'm exhausted. This is not forever, just until Daddy comes home."

She stopped, quailed by the furious flash in Louise's eyes. Stephen's eyes. The anger died in her. Such a tough little face, so angry with the world, and who could blame her?

Serena wanted to hug Louise and tell her it was going to be all right, but they both knew that it wasn't. Nearly a year after Stephen's disappearance it sounded ludicrous. Her shoulders sagged. She pushed her hands into the pockets of her jeans and stared down at Louise's bed, piled high with a duvet, sheets and pillows, waiting to be made up. Louise had been allowed to help choose the fabric ordered from Jane Churchill when the house in Belvoir Square was being redesigned by the very fashionable Darton Coombe. This time there was no choice.

Somewhere in a box downstairs the curtains that matched the buttermilk and blue pattern were folded. That they wouldn't fit the new house in Foster Street hadn't occurred to Serena when she had taken them down, but *somebody* must be able to tell her who to get to resize them. Certainly not Darton, who would be in trauma if he could see where his much-valued client was now living.

With hindsight she knew she should not have been so insistent that her mother stayed in Wiltshire and Melanie in St John's Wood rather than help her move, telling them both to visit when she was settled. She had truly believed it was the right thing to do but her more honest self, which she rarely consulted these days, said it was to avoid pity. And besides, she thought defiantly, that isn't strictly true. I'm doing it for them. I'm just protecting them from all this. They'll be upset for me, for the kids. And I don't want any more upset. No more grief. I have had grief, she told herself. I am the expert. When it looks better — when I've got it organized. Then they can come. Then they will see that it isn't so bad.

Her mother, Melanie and Melanie's housekeeper had volunteered to pitch in, and all worked tirelessly the day before packing and wrapping, discarding and dumping. But after they left and her mother had been dropped at Paddington by Melanie, Serena could not face going to bed. Her bed. The bed she had shared with Stephen had been sold. Not because Draycott Mendes had wanted the money or insisted on it, but because it simply would not fit into the room that was to be hers in Foster Street.

She had been sleeping in Chrissie's room, to be near to the children, near to Harry who was taking longer than Louise to adjust to a new school.

Today her day had not started early exactly, it was more a continuation of the night before. At the time she had welcomed it. Watching the clock creeping around to the hour when she would finally have to face up to Foster Street.

She gazed around Louise's new room. Until her daughter had stormed downstairs to ask why Harry was getting a better room, she had been doing rather well. No disabling panic, no lurching stomach at the sight of boxes one after the other containing all that was left of her old life disappearing through the front door, not even a tear as she turned the car out of the square following the van.

"All I need is a cock linnet," she muttered. "And indeed my home is locked in it. Oh, sorry, nothing darling," she said to Harry, squashed into the back clutching his computer which he had refused to entrust to anyone else's care. "Just a silly song."

It was not her car, of course. That had gone. This one she'd hired for a few days. There wasn't going to be a car by the end of the week. She'd decided that too was an unnecessary expense. What she found odd was that this new parsimony no longer caused her any pain. Just relief. Blessed, sweet relief that nothing more could be taken from her. If she didn't have it, they couldn't take it. It was so simple. And it didn't stop there. In her head she now traded losses for gains. If she didn't ask, she didn't owe. If she could have only bits of what she once had, she would have none of it at all.

At night she reviewed the small silent mountains, scaled each day, savouring her triumphs over the defeats. She would take nothing, to avoid pity. Retreat rather than risk rejection. She chose to move away from everyone who knew her, where gossip would not follow her. She would live where the little money she had would be enough to feed the three of them and keep a roof over their head. They would catch their breath, learn to live and wait, and learn to live with the waiting. The children would go to schools where they would learn about life and how to live in a tough world.

There were moments when she was astonished to find herself feverishly anxious to get going, impatient to put space between her old life and the one that lay ahead. She saw Louise and Harry valiantly coming to terms with a less cosseted life, her own replaced with the dignity that comes from anonymity. These twin ambitions became her lifeline when reality threatened to sink her into a distress that obliterated reason. Margot had been aghast at the idea. Minnie less so. Both had offered to find the money somehow to keep the children at their present schools. For once, Melanie had not even offered. There had been no point, and besides, Charles had thought it a bad idea.

"Where will it end?" he asked gently, fond of Serena but tired of her problems that had carved so severely into his own life. He wanted Melanie back. Her consuming and daily concern had become Serena. He wanted her concern to be for him, not her best friend. He wanted her to fuss over him like she used to. He wanted an evening talking about what the chairman had said and what he had said back that was invariably clever and insightful and Melanie would be so approving and ask him about lunch and the sorry plight of his colleagues who were getting it all wrong.

Charles sighed. Part of him was genuinely sorry that Serena would no longer be a routine part of their lives, but the other part, the part that he didn't examine too closely, was relieved that she was finally leaving and Melanie would stop feeling so responsible for her. This, he knew, was Melanie's fault. Serena, to give her her due, had never asked for financial help after that first time, and even then it had been Melanie who had forced the issue.

In many ways it would have been easier for them all if she was prepared to take money. At least Melanie would have solved some of the problems in a trice, freeing them to lead a normal life. He was tired of discussing Serena, tired of loyal gestures when they dined with their other friends. Only last week, he had been forced to take a stand over *Babyways* when Melanie, in an act of solidarity to her beleaguered friend, had wanted to resign.

"And what will that do?" he had asked earnestly. "At least if you're there you show you have nothing to be ashamed of in acknowledging Serena as a friend. And you don't want them to think you've chosen her over them."

"But I have," cried Melanie, blowing her nose hard. "I just thought if I made this ... this, gesture, if you like, it would make those stupid bitches like Miranda and Paula realise how despicable they're being. When you think how loyal Serena was to Paula ... I could scream."

"But it won't, will it?" He tried to keep the impatience from his voice. "Help, I mean. Paula's furious with Richard but she's more furious with Serena because she *knew*. The idea that she might be grateful to her is ludicrous. If anything, it's worse than ever. And besides, think how badly Serena would feel if she found out you'd resigned over her. She'd hate it."

He could see that Melanie was only half listening. He took a deep breath. "And I think," he said evenly. "She's suffered enough, don't you? Really, old thing, far better all round if we don't give her any more upsets, eh?"

Melanie looked up at him, shocked. "Oh God, I hadn't thought of it like that. You're right, of course, you're right. How awful." She leaned over and patted his hand, smiling affectionately. "Bless you, darling. Now why didn't Serena get someone as thoughtful as you, instead of that bastard?"

Charles blushed and disclaimed. He knew he'd got what he wanted, but for the rest of the evening he felt cross with Serena for making him feel so guilty.

With the exception of Melanie, Margot was no longer interested in her daughter's friends, but like Minnie — with whom she had struck up an uneasy alliance — she wanted the children to suffer as little as possible.

"And where does it end?" Serena asked her mother. "I keep LouLou at Collingham House on a scholarship, but then what? Do I make her suffer even more by allowing her to accept generosity she's not able to return, not able to keep up with everything she once took for granted? The holidays, the ponies — oh, you know what I mean. It would be too cruel."

To Minnie she said: "You are kind beyond belief. I'm perfectly sure it's what Stephen would want, but," she studied her reflection in the mirror over the phone and then turned away, not able to stop the treachery, or the bitterness. "But I can't afford what he wants any more. As a matter of fact, we all know now, I never could."

*

Spring had given way to a sultry summer and autumn to the first signs of winter, with unpleasant gusts of wind whipping up piles of leaves into the gutter in Foster Street. A steady drizzle was turning them into a brown mulch as Serena and her children had finally moved to their new rented home.

Ten months after she had lazily kissed Stephen goodbye as he disappeared down the stairs on what should have been a routine day, she was embarking on a new life. The children had started at their new schools two months before, Serena driving them each day there and back across the river.

Ten months since she had felt him, touched him, talked to him. Almost a year learning how to manage without him. She was worn out with missing him.

About a month after Harry had started at Dunton Road Juniors, the head, Jack Billington, a comfortable man in his late thirties with his own large brood of children at home, had called her in. He spoke to her of a child she barely recognized. His lack of social skills, his commitment, and cultural orientation were covered until Serena was convinced he had muddled up her son with another child from another country.

God knows it was perfectly possible. His office was an open house to a stream of children, each of whom was given a robust, discouraging welcome and short change if they loitered. How could he tell which was Harry? Serena gazed blankly at him as he ploughed his way through a language created in a soulless office staffed by disciples of political correctness, that they themselves had yet to address itself to the demons besetting a bereft nine-year-old. Poor boy, being plucked from the gentle nurturing of an expensive school and plunged into one that asked for nothing more than survival of those who seemed willing to learn.

Jack Billington had done his best to reassure her that they understood, but that Harry could not command all his attention and needed Serena to soothe his fears and be a bit more robust. Serena felt faint. More? She had nothing left to give. She hardly heard him as he openly applauded her decision to be realistic where her children's education was concerned. Privately he thought it strange that someone as well connected as Mrs Carmichael had not found the means to keep them at their schools.

She had politely listened to everything he had to say, but he wondered how much she had absorbed. He noticed she twisted her wedding ring, sliding it on and off her finger in a movement that suggested it was too big. But then he wasn't to know just how much weight she'd lost or that she had taken to stroking it in moments of great stress, like hearing that Harry was suffering. Encourage him to invite other lads home, see them at weekends, he had suggested. But who? She had already brought the subject up with Harry, but he just resolutely shook his head. She had hoped so much that after his visit to Jasmine a new confidence might make it easier for Harry not to be so afraid of the world.

Lucca had been a surprising success; even Louise had come back with no greater complaint than that Harry was sad, positively *sad*, the way he wanted to keep painting. But with no one to witness her doing anything more glamorous than eating out on her grandmother's terrace in the evening, or walking a mile to a tiny restaurant in the little hamlet of Carleagia for pasta and panna cotta and — she reported with a sly look at Serena — accompanied by a glass of red wine, she had been more entertained than she thought it cool to admit.

"Harry hated it, but I quite liked it," she announced airily, describing her introduction to the produce of the local vineyard. "It had a pleasant, um

..."

"Bouquet?" Serena supplied helpfully, wondering what miracle had prompted Jasmine to gauge her granddaughter's urge for a grown-up life so correctly.

"Yes, that's it. Bouquet. That's what I said."

"No, you didn't," Harry piped up. "You just pretended. Minnie had to finish it for you."

"She did not," Louise shouted, adding grandly: "We had a whole carafe."

"No, we didn't," Harry retorted gleefully, for once standing up to Louise. "Minnie and Gioglio —"

"Who?" Serena asked.

"Gioglio. Minnie's friend. He owns the restaurant. He's cool. He finished it."

"What would you know?" jeered Louise. "You're so sad."

Serena smiled as Louise disappeared to unpack and she settled down to study Harry's efforts at water-colours, carefully rolled into a cardboard tube supplied by Minnie. Minnie, after all that — who would have thought it? No grandma or granny, either. They called her Minnie.

Why she thought such lifted spirits would survive the move, she now couldn't say. It was November. Two months since Louise had started at St Saviour's, a girls' school a short bus ride away, and Harry at Dunton Road Juniors which was a five-minute walk from the house.

They had finally been given the keys to Foster Street by the letting agents on behalf of a Greek businessman who owned several properties in the area, only after he had been satisfied that Serena would be able to afford the rent. Serena met him only once which the letting agents said was unusual. Normally he cared only that he got his money and showed no interest on who inhabited his run-down house. On this occasion he insisted on meeting Mrs Carmichael herself. No one was fooled at his sudden zeal for checking his tenants, He knew who she was, but in return Mrs Carmichael insisted that he repaired the windows and replaced the locks before she took over.

So much to get used to. She wasn't at all sure how long she could go on comforting the children. Like now with Louise, who was being revoltingly selfish. She wanted comfort herself. But not from her children. A mental picture of Harry with his arms around her, Louise stroking her hair while she sobbed, flashed frighteningly before her.

*

Serena began to gather up discarded bin liners littering the room which that morning had contained Louise's CDs and magazines and started to fold them carefully to give her an excuse to stay, while she tried to think of something to say that would comfort both of them. The raking voice of their new neighbour soared through the open window beseeching her children to take the dog out before he crapped all over the garden again. Impatiently Serena banged the window shut, making Mrs Plaxton with her frizzy blond hair, too short skirt for her plump legs and shapeless T-shirt glance up and wave. Serena turned away. Mrs Plaxton had already introduced herself hot on the heels of Cheryl Tosney who lived directly opposite. Cheryl had very quickly worked out exactly who Serena was, and was delighted to see someone so infamous reduced to Foster Street, and equally, if conflictingly, excited that property prices might now soar. Negative equity ruled Cheryl's life and that of her second husband who, she told Serena, was a pillock.

Betty Plaxton, with her three terrifying children and her ferocious dog, Sovereign, was unimpressed with Serena's association with a man on the run. Since both her brothers had done time and a distant cousin was in Wandsworth for receiving, she horrified Serena by her suggestion that they were sisters under the skin.

"Bloody blokes," she announced cheerfully, catching Serena as she staggered up the path loaded down with the contents of her car. "All the bloody same. Not Les." She jerked a thumb towards the house. "His back stops him from getting into trouble — and me as well," she shrieked. "Three's enough I said. Mind you," she confided. "I've got to watch him. He'd still be a devil if he could — I said to him, 'Les, face it, getting lucky for you isn't pulling a woman any more, it's the bleedin' lottery.'"

Serena nodded in amazement at the outpouring of such intimacies as

Betty Plaxton screamed with laughter at her wit.

"Tell you what, though," Betty paused and glanced surreptitiously across the street. "Watch her," she mouthed indicating Cheryl Tosney's house. "She tried to pull my Les. Believe that?"

"Bet," a voice bellowed from within. "It's nearly twelve. What you gassin' about?"

Betty stopped and gave a squeal, dropping her cigarette on the pavement, grinding it in with the ball of her foot. "Oh my God, is that the time? Work calls and I've got to get me glad rags on. Nice meeting you. Pop in if you need anything. Take us as you find us," she called, disappearing into her house.

Serena turned back into the room where Louise was still in a massive sulk. In truth she hardly knew where to begin. Two laundry boxes packed with clothes marked Louise blocked the landing. In the corner a crumpled blue jersey and skirt — all that her new school demanded in the way of uniform — lay tangled in a pile of clothes that could not be crammed into the wardrobe. I am not ready for this, Serena told herself. None of us are. She impulsively and fiercely folded her arms around Louise's stiff little body. There was no response.

"I'll make a cup of tea." Serena pretended not to notice that her attempts at making up were being resisted. Instead she kissed Louise's hair and released her. "And then we'll have another think. What about switching to the spare room, next to mine? Or hey, what about my room? Would you like that?"

Louise shook her head. "No thanks," she yawned. "I suppose this will do. They're all crap."

"*Louise,*" Serena said wrathfully. "Don't speak like that."

"Sorr-ee," Louise replied airily. "Anyway, where's the phone?"

Serena watched as she clumped down the stairs. After a while she heard her ask for someone called Daffy. She tried not to listen, but in this house, privacy was at a premium.

Louise stopped talking as Serena squeezed past her in the hallway.

"My mother," she heard her explain. "Yeah, cool. Come round, it's a right doss house."

Serena wheeled round, a protest already springing to her lips, but Louise had turned her back to avoid her. She briefly closed her eyes and counted to ten before pushing open the door to the living room.

*

For someone who had lost everything, she had an extraordinarily vast amount of stuff to unpack. Tea chests and cardboard cases were piled on the floor. Serena had asked the removal men to put the beds in the right rooms and the few pieces of furniture that she had hung on to into the living room. The Georgian rent table, the chiffonier and the grandfather clock that had once belonged to her grandmother sat in this narrow room that ran the length of the house like disapproving old retainers forced to consort with the kitchen staff. At least the house is warm, she consoled herself, crossing the narrow passageway and down two steps into the kitchen where Harry was sitting munching biscuits and watching a portable television perched on top of the fridge.

Two plastic bags full of food bought from the supermarket had already been raided by Harry and biscuit crumbs were now congealing in a sticky trail of juice across the draining board.

"OK, darling?" Serena asked, hoping he would be too absorbed in his television programme to notice it had been several hours before a proper meal had been put before him.

He nodded without taking his eyes from the screen. The lead for the electric kettle was hanging out of a box of food that had come with them. She plugged it in, found a mug and unearthed a box of tea bags. A rock group blared from the television, bringing Louise in from the hall to hang over the table swaying her bottom in time to the raucous beat.

It had been a long day with only a few small reprieves. The scalding water plunged on to the tea bag and she extracted the carton of milk she had deposited in the fridge as soon as they arrived, splashing some in.

Off the kitchen was a small room, described by the imaginative Mr Stanley as a breakfast room stroke study. It was covered in cracked blue and cream lino and a brown rug that on closer inspection turned out to be pink.

A cream blind hung unsteadily from the window. A blast of cold air greeted her as she inspected it for somewhere to sit.

"Mu-um," screamed Harry and Louise. "It's freezing."

Hurriedly she closed the door but the noise from the television finally drove her to seek the sanctuary of the only other room available to her. She moved some boxes from a small velvet chair, sat down and pulled a coat over her knees.

Surveying the room crammed with furniture, a few porcelain pieces that had been gifts on birthdays and anniversaries and some paintings, she was amazed that she had anything at all. At times the impulse to break everything or tear it apart had been overwhelming. In a minute she would think about supper. But just five minutes to herself. That's all she asked.

Through the walls she could hear a low rumble and a distant voice could be heard raised in fury.

"Bradlee Plaxton. Get back in here, or I'll break ya' bloody neck."

Chapter Ten

"Can Harry come out to play?"

Serena choked on her coffee and wheeled round at the sound of a voice in her empty kitchen. The cup she was holding clattered on to the Formica surface of the table. Behind her stood two small children gazing blankly at her, one as plump as the other was thin. The girl was about ten, her small snub-nosed companion a couple of years younger. Behind them a large Alsatian, straining and panting on a short plaited lead held by the girl, was digging his hefty haunches in the doorway, refusing to budge. Serena pressed her hand to her chest to steady her breath.

"Harry?" Serena repeated as the girl, in paisley leggings, boots with tassels and a black leather jerkin, her straw-coloured hair hanging lankly across her shoulders, struggled with the dog who was resisting all attempts to get him inside.

"He's ill," Serena snapped. "God, Alana," she went on crossly. "You nearly gave me a heart attack. How did you get in?"

"Door's open, innit?" Alana Plaxton said. The middle child and only daughter of Betty and Les shot Serena a look full of scorn, pushed her too long fringe out of her eyes, and finally hauled the panting animal into the kitchen. Serena eyed the black pointed nose, the lolling, wet tongue hanging out between wide jaws displaying a challenging set of incisors, but was far too polite to ask Alana to leave it just where it was.

To her shame she had to admit that she was a little afraid of the rough and disorderly Plaxtons. She knew Harry was scared stiff of Ellis, but rather awed by the masterful Alana. Louise had already got off to a bad start with the eldest son, Bradley, who had infuriated her by bawling, "Oi tart" on the first day she had moved in. To Serena's horror Louise, a veteran of two months at her new school, St Saviours', screamed back: "You sad git." Bradley had nothing in his armoury of insults other than to waggle his middle finger at her.

"Oi, El," Alana called to the small boy who had darted ahead of her into the room and was calmly flicking through the channels on the television. "Leave that, I like that Jeremy whatsist. He gets real pervs on."

Serena clapped her hand to her head and watched helplessly as the two of them contributed to the chaos already at work in her kitchen. A pile of washing up as well as a stack of ironing that stared accusingly at her from a basket in the corner was left untouched. The swing lid of the waste bin strained to contain the evidence of the fast-food that had replaced her own attempts at supper the night before. Empty cartons smeared in tomato sauce, milk-shake tubs and the remains of the apple pie that Louise had insisted on having and then rejected were clearly visible.

Stuffed among the litter piled next to the sink was another letter sent by Harry's headmaster, Jack Billington, asking her to please make an appointment to see him. Towards the end of his second term, Harry appeared to be getting worse rather than better.

Finding the will to tackle it all had failed her. A black scrunch ribbon held her hair back off her face, stray strands tucked carelessly behind her ears. She wore no make-up and although it was a fine spring day outside and the kitchen warm she had been sitting hunched over the table in a thick black sweater that she had bought from Oxfam, her legs encased in the bottom half of a pale grey track suit which she had decided was more appropriate for her new position in the social order. Each day she wore something belonging to Stephen. A scarf, a sweater, pyjamas. Today it was a pair of thick skiing socks.

Margot had rung just after breakfast to say she was on her way, refusing to be put off any more. Harry was upstairs in bed waiting to see if the stomach ache he complained of as they were leaving for school that morning was leading anywhere. It was already twenty past two and in an hour's time she would have to leave to meet Louise from the bus. Before the Plaxtons had barged in she was deliberating whether to take Harry as well. There was a brisk wind but the fresh air might buck him up. After all, he wasn't really ill. They both knew it. But they both also knew that while one couldn't face another day without a friend to shield him from the taunting glee of those who fed on timidity, the other had no energy to deal with the anxiety of leaving him where he would be bullied.

The arrival of two forceful children in the middle of the afternoon finally felled her patience along with the wit to ask why they were in her house when they should have been in school. Serena listened in disbelief to the roar of activity and noise from a screaming and delighted audience blaring from the television. She reached over and snapped it off. Ellis, who she had long since realized had a behaviour disorder on a worrying scale, promptly snapped it on again.

"Oi," he said unabashed. "I woz watchin' that."

Serena had spent the morning negotiating the crowded aisles of the local supermarket, having chosen a trolley with wheels that wanted to go anywhere except in the direction it was being pushed. She had then had to deal with an officious woman from the DSS who had been sent to check Serena's request for financial assistance. She was consequently left with nothing remotely adequate to deal with such defiance. No one had ever behaved like the Plaxtons in her presence. No one had forced themselves on her, ignored her or reduced her to a helpless observer in her own life.

The DSS visit, like all those nowadays from people interested only in keeping Serena and her family under their gaze, or who were concerned only that she did not get or take anything beyond that which the state provided for penniless women, was unannounced and hard on her heels as she arrived home.

For ten minutes Mrs Cottenham from the DSS had roamed the house ferreting out disposable assets that might not have been declared when Serena, on her mother's instructions, had applied for assistance. Serena followed behind, curiously indifferent to the scrutiny her few possessions were subjected to. It no longer offended her. She had come to expect it.

"Nothing of value, is there?" the woman asked, unscrewing the top of a pen. She was standing next to the chiffonier which at auction would have attracted bids of around three or four thousand pounds and just in front of the Georgian rent table which had belonged to Serena's grandfather and could have fetched a greater sum.

"Only sentimental value," Serena hedged. "Only to me."

Mrs Cottenham shot her a suspicious look. "Meaning?"

"Meaning, some pieces of furniture that belonged to my grandfather — saved me having to buy more when we came here," she added quickly, recognizing the dangerous water she was wading into. Mrs Cottenham tapped her pen against her teeth.

"Hmm," she grunted. "Got receipts, anything like that?"

"No. The furniture isn't new."

"Oh, that's all right then."

Satisfied, Mrs Cottenham with her intimidating clipboard sat heavily down on a chair in the kitchen and proceeded to lecture Serena on what she was and was not entitled to and the penalties to be incurred for false claims which to Serena seemed mild compared with the deprivations she had already endured. Finally she rose to leave, busily tucking notebooks, pens and diaries into her bag, splaying a series of leaflets on the table that would guide Serena through the regulations governing her entitlement to assistance, pointing out that it was Serena's responsibility to keep them informed of her whereabouts and not the other way around. She snapped her bag shut with a shrug when Serena politely refused to consider a job while her children needed her.

"And besides," Serena pointed out. "What would I do? I have no training for anything and no time to train. Cleft stick, you see."

She too rose as she spoke, perfectly polite, inches taller than her visitor; she moved to hold open the door indicating with a small smile that as far as she was concerned the interview was over.

Mrs Cottenham's cheeks flushed. She was being dismissed. "Thank you for coming." Serena held out her hand. "Most kind," she added as Mrs Cottenham inched past her.

"Yes, well. Good. You know where to find me," she muttered as she walked down the path.

Serena closed the door quietly behind her and returned to the kitchen not having understood a word that had been said to her, and without the inclination to read the bossy looking leaflets that had been left on the table.

*

Harry had remained in bed while she had been at the supermarket, ordered to stay there where he would be safe. She hated leaving him but today the alternatives she had come to rely on were not attractive. Cheryl Tosney across the road would have been over like a shot. Bored and idle, Cheryl had developed an uncomfortable fascination with Serena and her few possessions but, as she was also a fund of local knowledge ranging from the state of Betty Plaxton's marriage ("Name only," she mouthed disdainfully) to the pub where the clerk at the DSS drank ("Knocking shop, that's what it is, and he's no better"), she had become useful.

She had stopped ushering Cheryl into the living room when she "popped over" on the slightest pretext and invited her to sit in the kitchen. It had taken Serena a few weeks to realize that, as a single mother and wife of a wanted man, such social niceties could be dispensed with. If Cheryl, with her over-made-up face framed by a cascade of sun-streaked blond hair and slavish devotion to gossip, had noticed this downgrading of her status she was far too entranced by the idea of Serena and her notoriety to take it to heart. Seemingly regardless of the fact that most of her questions were deflected or ignored, she chattered on. Rumour and household names jostled each other in a torrent of wild speculation and unshakeable belief in the tabloids' so-called facts, as she stood in Serena's kitchen sipping her mug of tea and flicking ash into the sink.

In the few months Serena had lived in Foster Street, she had grown to tolerate Cheryl, even allowing herself to be amused by her. Today however was one of the days when the prospect of Cheryl's incessant chatter did not amuse. It simply wasn't to be borne. Nothing was. Today was just for getting through.

The other option was to wait until Louise came back. But that was even less attractive. The smallest request was now regarded by Louise as an imposition of gargantuan proportions, an infringement of her rights as a child. Or as Louise had taken to saying: "Can't be arsed."

And now there was this unceremonious arrival of these two ghastly children who seemed to regard her kitchen as their own. At least Don Trewless and Mrs Cottenham used the front door. Even Cheryl usually called "coo-ee" as she hovered on the front step. But not the Plaxtons. The more direct route through a hole in their shared fence was their favoured mode of visiting.

"Ellis was bored," Alana told Serena firmly, not taking her eyes from the screen and ignoring Serena as she rushed to lock the door behind them. "We want to see Harry. We want to play with him."

"Well I'm sorry, Alana." Serena shot an anxious glance across at the hole in the fence to make sure no other members of the Plaxton clan had decided to pay her a visit. It took enormous effort to be pleasant. "It's very sweet of you to ask, but that's not possible. Harry had a wretched night —"

She stopped as Alana nudged Ellis, rolling her eyes as they began to giggle.

"And I'm extremely busy," Serena continued, warily eyeing Sovereign who was sniffing loudly at the skirting board. She resented the need to be polite to her neighbour's children who made no secret of the fact that her accent was an extremely good joke. "I'm expecting Harry's grandmother this evening, so why don't you run along and when Harry's better —"

Ellis, a small wiry eight-year-old with eyes like black buttons and shorn hair stiff with gel to make it stand up, ducked under Serena's arm and made for the door.

"He said I could have his computer," he whined. "If he's ill, he won't wannit, will he?"

"*Ellis,*" Serena called sharply and made a grab for him. She caught the back of his jeans as he reached for the door to the passage. "You really must do as I say, now Ellis, do stop that shouting … *Ellis,* please."

Ellis slung himself against the wall, shrinking away from Serena as though he was about to be hit. In the rush to go to her brother's aid Alana let go of Sovereign who promptly exploited his freedom by rising on his back legs to drink drunkenly from the bowl in the sink. Alana pushed Serena aside. "Don't touch my bruvver," she squealed. "He's only little. I'm telling my mum."

Serena's protest was lost in a terrified shriek as Sovereign — his thirst quenched — turned his attention to the chaos next to him and flattened Serena against the draining board. She lashed out wildly to grab the leash, but her flailing arm caught several half-full mugs and a couple of glasses, unwashed since breakfast, and sent them spinning to the floor. Crockery and glass shattered in a shower of cold coffee and Ribena as they hit the floor, spraying splashes up the walls and spitting brown spots on to cupboard doors. Diverted by a more interesting noise, Sovereign abandoned his captive, dropped on all fours and began pushing his long nose into the debris. Serena stared aghast at the two children glaring at her. Insolence was the word that sprang to mind as she gazed at their belligerent faces.

Her hands shook; she gripped the edge of the sink for support. "Alana," she breathed furiously. "Get that dog away. He'll cut himself. Ellis, *Ellis*, stop that noise."

To her relief but more to her surprise, they didn't argue. "And now," she said as Alana grabbed Sovereign and pulled his long snout away from the mess on the floor. "Please go *home*. *Go!* Do you understand?!" she screamed as they defiantly stood their ground. "Get out. *Get the fuck out of here.*"

"OK," said Alana, cheerfully responding to a language she understood, pulling open the door. "I'll come back later, shall I?"

Serena closed her eyes in disbelief as the door crashed behind her uninvited guests. Swearing at two children? She hadn't, had she? "Oh so what," she muttered. "They're not children, they're from hell." Or whatever hell it was that had landed her next to a family where MTV could be heard blaring through the walls long into the night, shoplifting was routine and discipline relied on screams and threats. She gave a weary sigh, turning to the sink. Was she any better than them now, screaming like that?

Automatically she ran water into a bowl, squeezed in some floor cleaner and bent down to deal with the mess. Gingerly she picked out the largest shards of china and glass and mopped up the sticky pool of liquid snaking across the floor with kitchen roll. Somewhere in the dim recesses of her mind she knew she should have found a pair of rubber gloves to protect her hands but the effort was too much.

If he is alive, she thought as she wiped the brown stains from the front of the green and cream cabinets, he must be thinking of me, he must be as scared as I am, missing us, lonely and lost. I won't believe he's dead. He's just waiting for the right moment to let me know. But what if he can't? Now we've moved. Who would tell him where we've gone?

But she knew that was a nonsense, her letters were being forwarded, the telephone company were diverting her calls; but those letters and phone calls were screened by the Fraud Office and that's why he couldn't.

These days she was more or less left to get on with her life. Don Trewless had dropped by shortly after she had moved in, no announcement, just a knock on the door. He had stayed for an hour, drinking coffee in this very kitchen. If anyone had seen them, he might have been an old friend. And in a way that is what he had become. She called him Don now. He called her Serena. Gone was the aggressive stance, the bitterness and hostility of those early days in Belvoir Square. It had been replaced by the resigned acceptance of two people forced to stay in each other's life, neither crossing the boundary of acquaintance into friendship, since neither trusted (or ever would) what the other would do should they discover Stephen's whereabouts. And how could it be any other way? She leaned back on her heels and absently re-wiped the surface she had just cleaned. If I close my eyes, and concentrate really hard, I will remember something. What was it Don had said? "Try and think. Something you took for granted. I want to help you as much as I want to find him."

"Mum?"

She opened her eyes and looked around. Harry stood in the doorway, a sweatshirt pulled over his pyjamas, his hair ruffled, his feet bare.

"Don't come in," she ordered, pulling herself to her feet, pouring the brown sludge collected in the basin down the sink. "I broke some cups."

Harry gazed at the basin and the floor mop. "Have they gone?" he asked.

"You mean those nightmares from next door? Yes, darling, they've gone. Ghastly, aren't they?"

"Ellis is horrible," he muttered, inching his way around the perimeter of the room towards the laundry basket. "He wants my computer. But I won't let him have it. Not Alana, though," he said, retrieving a pair of socks from its depths.

"Alana is a monster," Serena snapped. "And as for Ellis, the dog's got more wit than him."

"Not Alana," Harry said, staring anxiously at her. "She's OK. Actually I think she's my friend, only I'm not sure. Can she come and play later? Mum? Is that OK?"

Chapter Eleven

Margot was shocked. Clearing up the kitchen, demolishing the ironing, turning the volume down on the television was the easy part. And when — if — that plumber turned up, and the sink was unblocked, she would tackle the washing up.

Her eyes travelled around the dull kitchen taking in the cream and green cupboards, the blind on the window with ghastly grease stains which Margot had first thought was simply a shadow from outside, and a green and grey — no, not grey, on closer inspection Margot saw it was or had been blue — plastic mat. It served no purpose at all, being neither large enough to protect the lino underneath or small enough to fit under the door. Serena was certainly stuck for money, but surely she wasn't so poor that she could't replace the blind or find something more attractive for the floor. It reminded Margot of the elderly reclusive neighbour she had once known who had finally been removed to a home being in an advanced state of self-neglect.

She could deal with the advancing march of neglect so apparent in this house, but the paranoia that seemed to have gripped her daughter defeated her. Twice since Margot had arrived Serena had followed to prowl around the house, switching off lights, closing doors to keep the heat in. For no reason at all that was apparent to Margot, she would lift the phone and listen and then gently replace it. Occasionally she would check the front door, presumably to make sure it was locked. Louise, who had grown sullen and shockingly rude, had been ordered to stay in the kitchen and not use the other rooms, and who could blame her for complying when the rest of the house was freezing? That dreadful living room. She couldn't imagine why Serena had bothered forbidding them to go in there. What child would want to sit in that gloom? And surely to God, Serena wasn't serious about saving those dinner leftovers?

"She does it all the time," Louise yawned as Serena left them to check on Harry who had gone back to bed. "Can't think why. We never eat any of it."

"Well, I'm sure Mummy's right," Margot replied loyally. "I expect she wants to make, well ..." she trailed off lamely, not being able to work out anything more imaginative with cold baked beans than to put them on toast.

"Make what?" Louise flicked through the pages of *Loaded*.

"Well, lots of things," Margot said hurriedly. "Now tell me about school. What's happening?"

"Not a lot. Crap teachers."

"Louise," Margot shrieked. "You mustn't talk like that. I'm sure they're not."

"And I'm sure they are." Louise put the magazine down and leaned across the table to her grandmother, counting off on her fingers:

"Most of the kids bunk off ..."

"Bunk off?"

"That's right. You know, don't bother to turn up. The girls are sad — except Daphy, that's my friend. She's really called Daphinia and she's cool, but the boys are gross — not like the ones from Dunton High, they're awesome. The only thing worth eating at lunch is crisps and no one gives a toss if you're there or not."

"LouLou, that can't be true. Does Mummy know?"

"Mummy," mimicked Louise bitterly. "Doesn't give a toss either. She's lost it."

"Lost what?" Margot asked weakly. Dear God, not more bad news.

Louise tapped the side of her head. "Lights on, no one home."

Margot gazed at her granddaughter, bewildered. What lights, what was lost?

"I don't know what you're talking about, Louise," Margot said crossly. "And I wish you'd stop talking in riddles. I can see Mummy is under a lot of pressure — you all are. Now look, darling, why don't I just turn the heat on in the living room and you go and watch a DVD or something, yes?"

"Can't." Louise shoved her chair back, swung her legs, which were encased in thick black lace-up boots, on to the table and yawned.

Margot gave the sole of Louise's boot a sharp tap. "Feet, Louise. Not on the table. And I'm sure that's nonsense. Mummy won't mind, just while I'm here, if we use the other room."

"I mean, can't watch anything," Louise explained. "It was nicked."

Margot thought she was passing through a nightmare.

"Nicked? You mean, stolen? You were burgled? Oh my God. No one told me."

"No point," said Louise. "We were at Wisebuys — that supermarket down the road. I thought it was Bradley Plaxton, the dickhead next door, but they didn't take anything else so it can't have been. He would have taken Harry's computer because Ellis knows where we keep it. Well, nothing else unless you count that stone urn thing Melanie gave Mum for the porch as a moving in present. Mind you, that went on the first night we were here, so we can't count that as part of the DVD scam, can we?"

*

Melanie had warned Margot that she was in for a shock. Melanie had also said that the children were in a mess. Louise had gone native, she said, and who could blame her? How else was she to survive? And Harry absolutely cowed by it all. All that made-up illness.

"But is it?" Margot asked Melanie. They were talking on the phone before Margot had set off for London. They talked a lot, but Serena was not aware of it. Each noted her daily slide into a hollow that only she inhabited and each felt helpless to do anything that would pull her out of such a miserable place. Melanie because she didn't know how to now that Serena was in this alien world of assistance, social security and child welfare officers, and Margot because she knew one false step would alienate her from Serena. And that she could never have borne.

"Harry ill? Never," Melanie said firmly. "He just finds it easier to stay in bed than face the playground. And God, who can blame him, poor little chap. And while you're there, see if you can get her to see that man, what's his name? The headmaster chappie. Those children will be taken from her if she goes on like this much longer. She ignores all his letters. And of course, anything you need, money, contacts, whatever, just yell."

Margot had set off for London half hoping Melanie had exaggerated. After all, for weeks now, Serena had blocked her visits, just as she had Melanie's. Last time in desperation she had arrived unannounced to plead with Serena to reconsider and come and live with her, but she was met with a resistance that frightened her.

"You don't understand," Serena explained. "I have to go forward," she insisted earnestly. "Don't you see? If I come and live there it will be like going back, as though the last fifteen years never happened, and I will not," she emphasized each word almost as though her audience were larger than just her mother. "I will not deny Stephen. Ever."

"But, darling, you liked it at Christmas. It worked, didn't it? The children enjoyed themselves — well, as much as they could under the circumstances."

"But that's the whole point," Serena explained. "Christmas is a visit — they enjoyed it like they did when they went to Minnie's. It's not their home."

She could see for herself that Melanie had not overstated the case. Louise so full of rage, and no one to listen to her. And what was wrong with Harry? He looked perfectly well, but he just wouldn't get out of bed. And those clothes Serena was wearing. Where in the name of heaven had she found them?

"What's wrong with them?" Serena asked, as Margot tentatively asked where they had come from, passing Louise in the door and joining her mother in the kitchen. She glanced down at the track suit bottoms and the black sweater now carrying the fall-out from her tussle with Sovereign.

"What do you want me to wear?" she asked, ineffectually brushing at the short brown and silver hairs on her sleeves. "Chanel?"

Margot pursed her lips and fought back a desire to scream at her daughter to stop hoping. Where once she had skirted round Stephen, nursing ambivalent feelings for her ambitious son-in-law, she now hated him. The feeling shocked her, so savage was it in its intensity. She had stopped reassuring Serena that Stephen would never have deliberately landed her in this dreadful mess. She thought the words would choke her.

"Don't be silly, Serena," Margot sighed. "Of course not. It's just that I thought you might feel better if you wore something more, well, you."

Serena gazed steadily at her mother. "Of course they're not me. Me is packed away upstairs in boxes. My nest egg. There's a thrift shop in the High Street, they would buy them from me, if it came to it."

Margot mentally reviewed her daughter's wardrobe as it had once been. Who on earth, she wondered silently, would buy Armani or Chanel around here?

"But I'm not me," Serena was saying in an off-handed way, as if she was discussing the weather. "Not any more. I don't know who that other person could have been. Not caring that her husband had so many responsibilities, not noticing he was cracking under the pressure, letting all those people touch him for favours for their bloody charities — not one now to speak up for him. Oh God," she glanced at the kitchen clock. "Where's that bloody plumber?"

*

"It's like trying to get her to see that she should think of herself first — like on those aeroplanes," Margot whispered down the phone to Melanie next morning while Serena was closeted with a caller who had announced that she was from Social Services.

"What? What aeroplanes?" Melanie whispered back, forgetting that no one could hear her on the other side of London.

"Where they tell you to put on your own parachute — or is it lifejacket? Well it's one or the other — well you must put it on first otherwise you're useless to everyone around you."

At the other end of the phone at her house in St John's Wood, Melanie rolled her eyes. "Well, who's going to get that through to her? She just smiles and tells me not to worry. And you know where her make-up is don't you? All packed up in a box, stuffed under her bed, just like her clothes. You know, Margot, don't you think it's almost as if she is doing penance for something? The way she blames herself for his lordship's 'breakdown' and this is her way of atoning. Can't you make her see he was just an overbearing, self-absorbed crook? There was nothing she could have done. He was like it when she met him. Sorry, Margot," she mumbled. "Didn't mean to offend you, but it's true."

"I know, I know," Margot agreed, no longer prepared to defend Stephen. Such loyalty was not now a matter of integrity, it was pointless. And besides, she didn't want to.

"I expect you're right, but it's more as though she won't let go of the past. She keeps saying she wants to move forward, but it's my belief she can't."

"We've got to do something, we really have, or we'll all go nuts," Melanie went on. "But what?"

In the event neither of them was called upon to do anything. Jack Billington was not a man to be trifled with. In his last letter, unopened by Serena, he had warned her that he would ask the children's department to visit, if she didn't get in touch. Harry was not, *not*, he stressed, being bullied. Harry was refusing to join in. Quite a different matter.

Serena was unprepared for someone like Barbara Hill to call because she had ignored Jack Billington's letters. The sight of them exhausted her. If she opened them she would have to do something about the contents, whatever they were, and her energy had deserted her. And now here was this woman with her cream shirt, red jacket, her black-stockinged legs rounded off with a pair of neat black pumps, telling her that Harry was a problem.

Harry? A problem? Serena almost laughed. How wrong these people could be. If she'd said Louise, then yes. With her aggressive and unruly tongue, Louise was slowly outsmarting her, defeating her. Louise with her short black skirt, thick black tights and heavy shoes, screaming with laughter with her new best friend Daphinia whose only knowledge of her father was that he was from the Caribbean. Street-sharp Daphy, who glared at her feet, arms folded across her chest, if Serena appeared in Louise's bedroom when they were huddled together, had more control over Louise than she ever could.

Harry was home again for the third day running and Serena had been forced to admit, after this woman's gentle probing, that she had not thought it worthwhile to take him to a doctor. To add to her discomfort and her horror, Louise had arrived back at lunchtime claiming that there were no lessons that afternoon. She had brought Daphy with her who wore her afro hair in tight little plaits, livid green eyeshadow smeared across her lids. In every other way she was dressed identically to Louise.

Outside on Serena's wall a noisy group of boys who had accompanied Louise and Daphy home, and were hurling abuse at Bradley Plaxton and his friends. Serena could see from where she was sitting the tall imposing figure of Mr Mojani who lived across the street trying to remonstrate with them. Mr Mojani went to church every Wednesday and twice on Sunday and had forbidden his family to acknowledge Serena in any way once he had discovered she was the wife of a wanted man. Serena watched as he eventually gave up the unequal task and after finally admonishing them with a wagging finger walked majestically back across the road, past an abandoned car sitting squarely outside his pristine front door. He closed it firmly with all the dignity left to a man with a baying mob chanting behind him and tomato sauce smeared down his back.

Les Plaxton, however, was made of sterner stuff. Unable to watch the racing from Haydock with all that noise going on, he stormed out of his house, swinging wildly at the group blocking his path.

"You bloody well fuck off," he bawled, arms flailing as they laughed in his face and ran off. "Bastards," he yelled and cuffed Bradley across the back of the head to compensate for missing the others.

Barbara Hill, who had already spent an unfruitful half hour with Serena, winced as seconds later the front door to Serena's house slammed. She looked up as Louise came noisily into the room, slinging her school bag across a chair. She glanced briefly at her watch. Louise stopped when she realized her mother had a visitor.

"Louise, isn't it?" Barbara asked.

Louise nodded as Barbara Hill consulted her notebook. "St Saviour's? Your school, I mean. Is that right?"

Louise nodded again but more warily, shooting a glance at Serena who was wearing her familiar track suit, her hair held back by two clips. A ripple of uncertainty ran through Louise. Serena smiled faintly.

"Hello, darling." She made no attempt to get up. "I'll get you some soup or something in a minute. Miss Hill won't be much longer."

"Hmm," Barbara Hill frowned and continued to address Louise. "And the reason you're home at this time is — what?"

Daphy edged out of the room, but Louise stood her ground. "Felt like it," she answered defiantly.

"Lou, sweetheart," Serena protested.

Both ignored her. "Well, suppose you discuss it with your mother," Miss Hill persisted. "And try and feel like going back after you've had some lunch. And who's that with you?"

Louise blocked the doorway. "No one, I mean a friend. She's come to borrow my history notes."

"Well, that's a relief because for a moment I thought she might be bunking off. So she'll be going straight back to school as well, will she?"

A sullen look was all she got in return as Louise backed out of the room. Seconds later the front door slammed and through the window Barbara Hill saw the girls in a huddle with two of the boys who had drifted back, all of them glancing towards the house before they disappeared — she hoped back to school but she thought it more likely to be Dunton Road recreation ground. She wrote something in the margin of her notebook.

Throughout the exchange Serena had made no attempt to stop Louise or question her. Louise was expressly forbidden to walk up from the bus stop which was near the supermarket in the High Street. Serena, terrified of Louise being mugged or raped, had laid this one rule down.

Barbara Hill turned to Serena as Louise departed. "How often does she do that? St Saviour's doesn't have free afternoons or lessons, especially not at Louise's level. Have you never asked what she's doing?"

What Louise was doing? She was racing like a hoyden around Foster Street, crazy about every boy who passed the door, except for Bradley Plaxton, and incapable now of expressing herself in any other way except to say she was pissed off or couldn't be "arsed". That's what she was doing.

Serena witnessed the brutalisation of Louise like a woman watching a piano roll down a hill and not knowing how to stop it. Asking why she had bunked off school was a pointless question. Why ask a question to which you already know the answer? Louise hated the place. She was bored, her quick sharp mind blunted by lack of stimulation.

Far more pressing, but beyond her to find the courage to confront, was the stack of DVD's she had found in Louise's room that was way out of line with the five pounds each week that Serena was able to give her.

So she just nodded. "Of course I ask. I think she was just feeling a bit cornered, you know what they're like at this age. She would have gone back. I know Louise."

"Even so," Miss Hill refused to be side-tracked or fooled, "I think she needs a tighter hand."

Serena stared politely back, longing for her to go and take her justifiable criticism with her. Of course she needed a tighter hand. But whose?

Barbara Hill sighed and studied the notes she had made. She rested her elbows on her knees and dropped her head. Finally she looked up and said: "Don't you think, Mrs Carmichael, that you should at least go and see Mr Billington? You clearly need help and so does Harry. And Louise. I'm having trouble finding anything to say that would help your case ..."

"Case? What case?" Serena spoke sharply. "What are you talking about? I'm not a case."

"Oh, but you are," Barbara Hill contradicted her. "You most certainly are. You tell me you see none of your old friends, you have no close relatives apart from your mother — yes, I can see she is being very supportive, but who else is there when she goes back to her home? You have no work colleagues, no outside interests. I agree," she held up a hand to stop Serena from interrupting. "All of this is difficult for you. But it's a bleak picture and what I want is to prevent you becoming a family in which our intervention will be necessary. Jack Billington is not a man to overreact, God knows he's got enough to do, but I listen to him. And if he says he's concerned then I am too."

A sudden flash of Louise and Harry being taken from her rose up before

Serena's eyes. She half rose from her seat and then sank back with a small gesture of defeat.

"Look, Mrs Carmichael," Barbara Hill closed her notebook and put it on the table beside her, "I know what's happened to you, and I know what it must be like —"

Serena's eyes widened in disbelief. "You know?" she asked, her voice dangerously calm. "How could you know? That's all anyone ever says: 'they know how I feel'. You know, do you, the dull ache I feel here?" She pushed her fist into her chest. "Or," she said, raising her hands to her face, "the effort it takes to open my eyes each day?" She let her hands slide down her cheeks, pulling her eyes downwards. For a brief moment she looked skeletal, haunted.

"You know," she continued, staring into Miss Hill's eyes. "Do you, what it's like to imagine your husband dead or ill and not know for sure? You know, do you, that every night when I go to sleep, I dream he will be back, and I have to deal with waking up and knowing he isn't … I mean won't be? Oh God, I don't know. Tell me, Miss Hill. You know what that's like, do you?"

She rose to her feet and gripped the mantelpiece, looking sideways at Barbara Hill who simply sat and waited for her to finish.

"No," she said gently, "I don't know that. But I know that you're depressed. Depression leads to exhaustion and exhaustion leads to neglect and then it's easier to take refuge in the past. The past is funnily enough a very safe place to be. No nasty surprises, nothing to creep up on you."

"What are you?" Serena asked. "A counsellor? Is that what your job is?"

Barbara smiled. "No, thank God. I try and prevent the problems that most of *them* get rich on. No, I just see someone who won't or," she held up a hand as Serena opened her mouth to protest. "Can't help themselves. For whatever reason. Look, I can't tell you what to do, but I can tell you what will happen if you let these kids slide out of your sight. And that's what happening.

"You're not a daft woman, you're bright," she went on with what Serena thought was a touch of frustration in her voice, and she couldn't blame her. "I see women every day of my life who are as thick as shit and all I can do is try and get them to make sure their kids get to school each day. I see others who could run the country if they'd had the education, but they have nothing going for them, no social advantages, no money, lousy jobs — nothing to make their voice heard. And I just prop them up and hope for the best. But you …"

She sighed and shook her head, abandoning what she was going to say.

"What about me?" Serena turned to face her. "Don't I need propping up? Or," she gave a jerky little laugh. "Don't rich bitches count?"

Barbara looked amused. "What an odd thing to say. You're hardly rich and you don't seem to be a bitch — unless I've missed something here."

Serena grimaced. "I'm sorry, it's just, I wasn't prepared for how awful it would be. After … after Stephen left, I wanted to be responsible for myself. He'd always looked after everything. I thought if I went somewhere where no one knew us, started again, I would never again be dependent on anyone, but it isn't like that. Not a bit. You see," her voice faltered. "I didn't know just what a crushing — *weight* I would feel doing it on my own."

"Don't worry." Barbara interrupted. "I can see what's happening. You've had a body blow. You're right, I don't know how you feel, but I can see how it's affecting you. I have no idea if you can do anything about it because frankly I don't know what you were like before all this, but I do know that everyone has a choice in your situation."

She paused. Serena just nodded for her to go on.

"I don't have to spell it out for you, and frankly, I'm taking a risk here." She paused as Serena looked puzzled. "Well, perhaps not a risk. But it's there all the same every time I see someone who needs, might," she corrected, "need help. I mean I don't want you to start feeling defensive because I truly mean this when I say I just want to help."

Serena nodded. "Go on."

Barbara gave her a cautious look and then shrugged.

"Mrs Carmichael, you *can* do something. It's as simple as that. Look, I don't need your problems to deal with, I'm not looking for business, believe me, I'm not. And I don't think you want me hanging around you either.

147

While you rely on us for everything we have to check on you and you have to answer to us."

When Serena didn't answer, she gave an exasperated little shrug and tried again.

"Look, Mrs Carmichael — Serena — I don't know you well enough to know what you're like, but personally I would hate the intrusion, especially when there was another way around it."

"What do you mean, I can do something?" Serena turned on her. "You mean a job?"

"Maybe."

"And who looks after my children? I have no money, no one to turn to. The police tap my phone, my mail is checked and my children are bereft of a father."

"But they do have a mother. Didn't you — don't you count for anything in their life? Don't you think they need you more than ever?"

For a few seconds they stared at each other. Neither spoke. Eventually Barbara picked up her raincoat. "It's up to you. Now, shall I tell Mr Billington you'll be coming to see him — or not?"

"I don't know. Let me think … Let me just get today over with. Louise, you see …" She trailed off, staring at her hands, but she wasn't looking at the long, slender fingers or the plain gold band that was now too loose for her left hand. She was staring at something else.

Behind her Barbara Hill moved towards the door. "Look, call me." Like Mrs Cottenham before her, but a lot less officious, she placed a card on the table and a leaflet outlining the help available to lost women, and another pile of forms that would have to be filled in if she wanted to survive. Then she left.

Serena heard her speak briefly to Margot, who had emerged from the kitchen to let the visitor out. Serena heard her mother go upstairs to sit with Harry while he had lunch in bed.

For a long while Serena just sat and stared into space. This had to stop. These strangers just turning up, prying, peeling off the layers until they turned her life round to suit them. Forms, forms, forms. She lifted the latest batch and glanced resentfully at them. Her life reduced to an entry in all those boxes. "Maiden name, occupation, income, declare your life here," she muttered to herself.

You could do something. What thing? Without thinking, she began to tear the forms in half, and then into quarters, and then halved those again. When the paper was no more than confetti she reached over for a waste-paper basket and carefully scooped the pieces of paper into it, picking up the last bits that had clung stubbornly to the carpet. Then she carried them through into the kitchen and pressed them down on top of the rubbish in the swing bin. She walked across the kitchen and rooted in a cupboard until she found a pair of yellow rubber gloves. Heaving on both sides she wriggled the black bin liner loose, tied the top and took it through the hallway out on to the front porch and dumped it in the corner where the refuse collectors would remove it later in the week. Harry and Margot would be playing on Harry's computer. It would be another hour before Louise had to be met. She walked slowly down to the gate and gazed up and down the road.

Mrs Mojani shut her door sharply when she saw Serena. From next door she could hear the blare of the television as Les Plaxton attempted to drown out the competition from Bradley's computer, blaring out xbox games and God know's what else. For once she didn't recoil or hasten indoors. The sky was beginning to cloud over, the earlier spring breeze growing in strength, catching up old newspapers and slapping them against the wheels of cars, into open garden gates.

It was just how you looked at these things, she decided, sitting on the edge of the low wall. Foster Street had signalled the end. But what if it was just the beginning? Not forever. Just for now. What would Stephen want her to do? She tried to recall his voice, his smile, the impatient lift of a hand to push his hair back off his face, but it melted into a blur. She waited for the panic to hit her. But it didn't. She was too tired for even the familiar swell of fright to surge through her.

Large drops of rain began to plop on the pavement. She studied them until her shoulders were damp and Margot's voice brought her back into the present. She turned and walked back into the house. She would need an umbrella when she went to get Louise. She went up to see Harry and persuaded a reluctant Margot to return to Wiltshire and Harry to get dressed and walk with her to meet Louise from the bus stop.

Later she didn't miss the relieved look exchanged between her children as she bypassed the leftovers at supper and served up jacket potatoes filled with melting cheese and broccoli. Nor did she raise any objections when Louise took possession of the living room for the rest of the evening with Daphy and a boy wearing a baseball cap round the wrong way and a T-shirt emblazoned with "*Who Gives a F***?*" written on the back.

"What's wrong wiv your mum?" asked Daphy, on whom this unusual display of tolerance had not been lost, wrapping herself around the boy who was sprawled on the sofa.

"Don't know." Louise shrugged. "She must be going down with something. She hasn't even mentioned about today, you know, bunking off."

"Blimey." Daphy giggled. "Must be love. I 'spect she's got a fancy bloke what turns up when you're at school. My mum does. She thinks I don't know."

Louise stiffened. "No. Not my mum. She's not like that. She's …" Louise faltered. "She just thinks about my dad. All the time. She doesn't do anything else. Oh bugger it, Daph. You know I hate *Coldplay*. Can't you put something else on?"

Chapter Twelve

"You'll like Alex. At least, Harry will. He's great with kids. Not like me. He got the real thing. I got Dunton Road Juniors."

Serena smiled politely as the man in front of her chuckled at what was clearly a well-honed family joke. She took the card he held out. "I'm sure your brother wouldn't see it like that."

"No?" Jack Billington grinned. "Maybe you're right. And of course, I've got more hair. See him anyway. You don't have to go back if you don't want to, but ..." He looked at her, his head on one side, summing her up, she supposed. "But, I think you will."

"Who knows?" she agreed, lightly glancing at the card. "Alexander Billington" it said in thin black script. "Family Therapist." There followed an address and two phone numbers. "But," she placed the card in the pocket at the back of her handbag. "There's the small matter of money. Actually," she gave him a faintly embarrassed look, "I don't have any at all, so this might all be pointless. I have no idea what child psychologists cost."

"Family," he corrected. "He treats the whole family. And it won't cost you anything."

"Nothing?" Her eyes widened. "Goodness, who would have thought it? Who does he work for?"

"Well, he does have a private practice, but he does NHS work as well. You'll have to be referred to him but there shouldn't be a problem — Barbara Hill will send a note to your GP saying she recommends some sessions for Harry. She'll suggest Alex. He's a total bore on some subjects but I'll give him this. He knows his stuff."

Jack Billington leaned back in his chair, swivelling gently around as he spoke. Harry had returned to school the day before and arrived home with a note for Serena to say the head would see her the following morning. The interview had been brief and less of an ordeal than Serena had imagined. It occurred to her that she hadn't actually agreed to see anyone, but Barbara Hill had guessed, correctly, that Serena would not ignore Harry's headmaster for a third time.

So here she was, swept along by a man who saw Harry as a problem, urging her to see someone who might ease the child through his fear of going to school and even help him come to terms with losing his father.

"He's missing his father," she said stiffly. "But he hasn't lost him. That sounds as though he's dead."

Jack Billington shrugged. "I didn't mean it to sound that way," he said carefully. "But we both agree that there is a loss in Harry's life that needs addressing." He paused and twiddled a pen thoughtfully between his thumb and index finger. "We both know," he said gently, "that Harry's depressed. That's tough for a child. But he is."

She could feel the tears welling up in her eyes. She swallowed hard and nodded. She had expected a ticking off. In fact, she had been ready for it. She had rehearsed what she would say in defence of her poor child but in the event none of it had been necessary.

"Forgive me," she began. "For being so, well, so reluctant to talk to you. It's just that I needed to get so much sorted out. I just didn't — well, don't want actually — for Harry to be regarded as a problem." She hooked the air either side of the word. "If I hadn't been in such shock myself then it wouldn't have come to this, but then it wouldn't have happened, would it? I mean if I hadn't been in shock."

She knew she was sounding incoherent. She couldn't help herself. She could hear her voice babbling on. "It all escalates doesn't it? If you're not careful, after a bit no one stops to look at what caused the problem, they just see the effect. I think Harry's had enough to deal with. He's only ten. You hear about these things, you know, a handy label for a child who doesn't fit in."

"But also an opportunity to find out why, surely?" the head said mildly, appearing not to notice her stammering efforts to explain. "Harry comes from a different background to most of these children, but," he added gently. "He wasn't fitting in terribly well at his other school, was he?" He dropped forward in his chair, frowning over a page in the slim buff file lying open on his desk. Serena recognized the logo on the paper he was studying and the familiar scrawl of Harry's former headmaster.

He gave her a level look. Her shoulders dropped. "No," she sighed. "You're right. But it didn't seem to matter so much then. He didn't have to cope with all — all this," she indicated a vague area with her hands that encompassed more eloquently than words the noisy, stale-smelling school, the aggression, the size. More than anything she knew it was the overwhelming, echoing size of the place that had annihilated what little courage Harry possessed.

"No, that's true," Jack Billington agreed. "But have you ever thought, that — well, I wouldn't say it was a blessing in disguise, you don't need this kind of blessing — that Harry might have needed help in the long run? Don't you think that — well, OK, it isn't the ideal way to identify a problem, but now that we have, something can be done?"

An honest voice told her he was right. Money had subdued rather than confronted and solved a problem within Harry. She knew Harry's problems had been exacerbated, not created, by his new life. Harry was — always had been — a timid child, looking anxiously to Serena to take the weight from him, and she had been so willing to do it. She still was.

"Don't you think we all have problems that we don't have to worry about, unless life takes a sudden twist?" she demanded. "No one knows how they'll behave until they're tested. Anything," she went on, knowing she was beginning to sound wild, not understanding why her natural reserve had deserted her, but the rush of relief was overwhelming as the loneliness and fear of the past year poured from her. Things she had kept from her mother, from Melanie, suddenly became a matter of urgency to convey to a stranger.

"Death, divorce," she went on, casting round for more examples. "And you. You could lose your job and you have no idea what it would be like until you have to watch your self-respect vanish, suffer your friends pitying you. Wait until you're tested and then see how much you've ignored about yourself, because you haven't needed to confront it. Might never have had to. How do you *know?*

"Harry had his safety net taken away, that's all. It's not his fault. It's other people's fault. It's *my* fault." Her voice broke on a sob. She stopped, aghast, raising one hand to briefly cover her eyes. "I'm sorry," she whispered. "Ignore me. This is not like me. I'm not — I mean, this isn't your problem."

"But it is," he said and, quietly reaching into a drawer to his left, he pulled out a box of tissues and held them out to her. "And I don't want to ignore you. If I did I wouldn't have asked to see you. Harry is not your exclusive problem, while he's here he's mine as well. I don't need problems, I have enough. There's a queue of them waiting outside that door right this minute and only nine out of ten I can contain. That's why I grab hold of the ones I think might respond, might take advantage of a solution if one is offered. I think you will."

Serena blew her nose. "Yes." She tried to smile, trying to recover and let the dignity that had deserted her find its way to the surface. "Yes, I expect I will. You've been very kind."

She felt ridiculous. Her hair was falling in her face, she wore no make-up. The jacket that had once fitted her to perfection hung loosely on her now that she had lost so much weight. But it was important to her that she seemed in control. And here she was flailing wildly around with no evidence that she even understood a word. Jack Billington must be used to such scenes, she decided. He had made no attempt to do anything other than let her talk and make an idiot of herself.

"Nonsense," he said. "I'm being practical. I want an easy life — which is a bit elusive these days." He looked at the clock over his door and began to rise to his feet. Serena followed suit.

"Let's agree, then, that you'll see Alex and I'll do my best to get Harry to join in more. Yes?"

She nodded. He held open the door. Outside a line of children were waiting to see him. The noise did not abate as he appeared in the doorway. Unlike Serena, he didn't even wince, just raised his voice several decibels.

She looked at the brown wool jacket, check shirt and wool tie and saw a decent man with a decent degree who spoke roughly and without sentiment to the children in his care, but who clearly believed they were worth his time.

"You, you and you," he roared, pointing at three boys attempting to wrestle each other to the ground. "You were meant to be here before the bell, not after it. You were warned. Grounded at break for a week. Don't argue. Go. NOW."

Serena saw that one of the children was Ellis Plaxton, who poked his tongue out when he saw who was with the head before starting to scuttle away.

"*Plaxton*," Jack Billington reached out and grabbed Ellis by the scruff of his neck and hauled him back. "Stick your tongue out again and I will Sellotape it to the wall for a week. Now apologize. I mean now, Plaxton, not next month."

"She 'ates me," Ellis whined. "She tried to 'it me."

Serena gasped and blushed. "Ellis," she protested. "I didn't. You know I didn't." She turned in embarrassment to Jack Billington. "He lives next door, he wanted to see Harry who — wasn't feeling well, and I just tried to stop him."

"Well, you were lucky, Ellis." Jack turned to the child. "Mrs Carmichael only tried. I would have succeeded. Now hoppit."

"No, you wouldn't. I could fix you," was Ellis' parting shot before he swaggered off down the corridor, kicking an imaginary football.

"Little sod," muttered Jack, watching Ellis punch the air as he slipped a shot past an imaginary Italian goalkeeper.

"You must believe me," Serena began earnestly. "I only grabbed his waistband ..."

"Don't," Jack soothed. "He doesn't understand anything else. Neighbours, eh? We used to have Bradley here. I prefer Ellis," he finished grimly. "Now I believe you have an appointment to make and I've got to try and persuade the staff to stick to coffee and not hit the gin or — worse — the inmates."

*

Faced with a bored clerk, it did not take Serena many minutes to establish that, while she was adept at organizing a charity lunch for dozens of rich women with the influence to pull a celebrity to grace it at a moment's notice, none of these virtues seemed to be regarded as advantageous for any of the jobs on offer at the Wilberforce Street branch of the Job Centre. The psychological leap was perhaps harder to achieve than the cultural one when she examined what was available.

"You're not making it easy for me, Mrs Carmichael," the young woman said carefully. "You don't want to work full-time or at nights. You want to be home during the holidays and half term."

"I have to," Serena declared. "I wouldn't dare let my children stay on their own or walk home alone. Have you seen what's going on out there? I had no idea. I thought the area was — well, you know, well, not exactly Mayfair, but relatively safe. I would never have rented the house if I had known — not with two children. I mean, the road isn't terrific as it is, but it's right in the middle of a terrible area that I would never have considered. Do you know it? Near the Camberwick estate? You can't walk ten yards without someone asking you for money — and muggers ... A lady — a widow, a sweet woman — lives across the road, had her handbag wrenched from her just waiting at the bus stop. The one where my daughter gets off the bus. Would you let a child walk home on their own through all of that?"

The clerk looked over her glasses at Serena who was clutching her handbag and leaning across the desk. The woman was a nervous wreck.

She sighed. "Probably not. But I get people jobs, I don't clean up the streets. Now, where were we? Oh yes. Lottery time."

"Lottery time?"

"Of course. Landing a part-time job. What every working mother wants, but I'm afraid it isn't easy round here. Hang on, what about this? Elan Car Hire, they want a part-time telephonist. You've got a good voice."

A flash of irritation crossed the girl's face as Serena quickly shook her head. "Why ever not? What's wrong with it?"

"Nothing," Serena said. "It's just that I think my neighbour works there and I don't think that would be a good idea."

"No?"

"No," Serena agreed. God, Betty Plaxton worked for Elan, a mini-cab company in the High Street. Sometimes Serena would see her being dropped off by one of the drivers at the end of her shift. Cheryl, after one of her extended visits, would wink knowingly at Serena as they both witnessed Betty alighting from a car and leaning in to say something to the driver. A loud crack of laughter followed.

"Cheek-ee," they heard Betty retort with a giggle before she sashayed up her path, ignoring Cheryl completely but greeting Serena with a cheery wave.

"Car's not the only thing for rent, if you ask me," Cheryl sniffed as Betty disappeared into her house in a cloud of cheap perfume.

No. Elan was not to be considered.

"What about this?" the girl persisted. "Ward orderly at St Wilhemina's."

"But I know nothing about nursing."

The girl laughed. "That isn't what's required. They need someone to help give the patients lunch, tidy up a bit, generally help. No nursing involved. And your form says you've worked for a hospital. Talk to them about hours, but they generally want someone from either eight till two or two till eight. Couldn't you get someone to meet your kids from school — or take them?"

*

A week later, Serena presented herself to sign on at St Wilhemina's. She took the bus as far as Camberwell Green and then walked. Cheryl Tosney had embraced the chance to inveigle herself even further into Serena's life which left Serena feeling both relieved — at least she could take this job — and apprehensive, because Cheryl was not who she would ever have envisaged employing to care for her children. In fact it was Cheryl who had suggested it when Serena had mentioned she was looking for someone to help. Someone who wouldn't want a fortune, someone who could be at her house in time for her to leave.

"You know it makes sense," Cheryl insisted. "I could even pop over in my jimjams — well, not to walk Harry to school," she amended hastily.

"And holidays, think how easy it would be — and," she said warming to her theme. "If they've got a little cold or something and don't want to go, well, what could be easier? Besides, I could do with the extra," she added, surveying herself in the mirror in Serena's kitchen. "My highlights need doing something rotten."

"What about Kevin?" Serena asked, overwhelmed by Cheryl's rapid expansion of her role. "Won't he mind you abandoning him every morning so early?"

Cheryl screamed with laughter. "Mind? He wouldn't notice if an Alien army invaded before midday. No, do him good. Any road, I can't always be there to wait on him. No, Kevin won't say a word. Believe me."

Promptly at seven-thirty, fully made up and wearing one of her extensive wardrobe of leggings with high heels, Cheryl left her house and minced across to Serena's where Louise, half dressed, yawning and absorbed in breakfast television, barely acknowledged her.

"This is good of you, Cheryl," Serena said, frowning at Louise. "If you don't know where anything is, Louise will show you, won't you, Lou? Louise?"

"Mmm?" Louise dragged her eyes from the set. "What? Oh yeah, sure."

Serena smiled apologetically. "She's not at her best at this time. And Harry. Darling? Cheryl will walk you right to school and I'll be waiting outside when you come out, plenty of time before we have to go to —" She stopped, not wanting Cheryl to know that she and Harry would be having their first appointment with Alex Billington after school. "Now have you got everything, your lunch box is on the fridge, oh and ..."

"Now, now, Serena," Cheryl interposed, ushering her towards the door. "You just get off. Me and Harry will be just fine. Go on, off you go."

Serena looked uncertainly at the children. Louise was indifferent, Harry apprehensive. But it was only for an hour and then Cheryl would walk to the bus stop with Louise to make sure she was safely on her way, and Dunton Road Juniors was only a five-minute walk. Louise had objected to this chaperonage, but on this point Serena was immovable. The area left her nervous in spite of the fact that half the families in Foster Street were law-abiding and respectable, if financially pressed, as opposed to some nearby streets where whole terraces were known to the police and clearly not short of funds. Each morning she and Harry walked Louise to the bus stop before walking all the way back to Dunton Road Juniors. In the afternoon, Serena collected Harry and they both walked to meet Louise.

She hugged them both and then, grabbing her coat, absurdly near to tears, she fled out of the house and walked in the crisp early morning air to the bus stop in the main road.

St Wilhemina's was located in the centre of an erratic collection of Victorian buildings about a ten-minute walk from the bus stop. The end of the road was bounded on one side by a row of terrace houses and on the other by a small, dilapidated factory and garages. These were the property of the hospital but lay silent and disused. Plans for screening units, specialist units, even — daringly — a private wing, proposed by a management whose ambitions outstripped their business skills, now gathered dust with little hope of ever being implemented.

A wide curving black asphalt drive, with a sign announcing that visitors to St Wilhemina's should park in adjacent roads, led past boiler rooms and the hospital laundry, and opened up into a bleak square from which a series of paths dissected the grounds. These disappeared into a labyrinth of old buildings that looked ready for demolition but which local residents were fighting to keep open. Ahead lay the main entrance with a reserved space for ambulances outside. A glass and brick extension to the left added to the grey Victorian building with a greater regard for economy than design. A galaxy of signs pointing to X-ray, Outpatients, Maternity, Accident and Emergency and a long list of wards with depressing names were listed on an adjoining board.

A couple of nurses dressed in thick black stockings and navy woollen coats to keep out the sharp wind were coming off or going on duty. Their wide yawns could have indicated either. An ambulance swept past. Serena paused and watched as the back doors were swung open. A doctor accompanied by a nurse emerged from the building. The occupant was eased on to a stretcher, his pulse already being taken as the group, followed by an elderly woman who had been travelling in the ambulance and was now trying to hold on to his hand, whisked through the double doors and disappeared.

Serena had to quell an overwhelming desire to turn and run. Only a sharp rebuke kept her facing in the same direction. This way, she lectured herself, you stay outside the system. This way you don't have to answer any more questions. But the money's a pittance, her practical side reminded her.

It's freedom, she told herself.

A man pushing a hospital trolley piled high with white laundry bags trundled his way past her, shooting her a curious glance. She hurried on.

This is nonsense, she told herself, pulling up her coat collar. And it's not forever. Just a few meals a day. I can manage that. After all, it's just like working for the Wendy only it's NHS. They can't help the look of the place and I can be home by three. Just how difficult can it be?

She adjusted the strap of her bag and walked up a narrow ramp and into the hospital, following the signs that led her to the Maud Frierley ward for geriatric patients and Sister Mary Burton. It was ten to eight. Just time to phone home and see if everything was OK.

*

She had brought with her, as requested, a white cotton overall. But she was wearing all the wrong clothes under it. What had seemed appropriate at seven this morning before she had become more intimately acquainted with life on Frierley was hopelessly wrong. She had carefully extracted from the boxes stored away in the empty spare room a plain black skirt bought two years before in Bond Street and a white silk shirt, an impulse buy in Saks when she and Melanie had gone on a shopping spree to New York. Over it she wore a black Ralph Lauren waistcoat.

She looked quietly efficient. She looked — for a woman about to serve breakfast to a ward full of human frailty with wandering wits and in most cases no longer aware of bodily functions — ridiculous. She thought of Paula wearing her white designer coat to those meetings of *Babyways* and blushed.

Sister Burton clearly thought that, of the three new recruits allotted to her overstretched nursing staff, the other two being a stout black woman called Nonie who referred to Sister Burton as Missus, and a curly-haired young Australian looking for extra cash to fund the next leg of her journey round the world, Serena Carmichael was the most pointless.

By nine-thirty, Serena Carmichael, grimly emptying the first of fourteen bedpans, agreed with her.

Chapter Thirteen

Serena leaned against the tiled wall of the sluice room and eased her shoes off. Nonie and the Australian girl, Becky, were pushing soiled bed-linen into huge cotton bags and then handing them to Serena who secured the necks with yellow tape before hurling them into a wooden trolley parked just outside the door. "Property of St Wilhemina's, Do Not Remove" was picked out in white on the side, ready to be trundled away by a porter to the laundry room down by the hospital gates.

"As though anyone would want the bloody thing," Becky grunted. "You'll never get them on again," she warned, indicating Serena's discarded shoes.

"Not sure that I want to," Serena replied, massaging one bare foot against the other. Under her blue and white striped overall, she could feel a thin trickle of sweat running down between her breasts. Her neck and forehead were damp. Every available window on the floor had been flung open to contend with the heat of a warm June day, but the sluice room window had jammed years before and no one knew how to release it or the right person to summon to try. Such a task was not in Serena's job description but she had made an effort earlier in the week, when the first heat of summer had begun to take effect, to open it. She had been stopped by an outraged Sister Burton who caught her balanced on a chair, Becky holding it steady, while she eased the rusting lock from its moorings with a kitchen knife.

"Out, out, out," Sister Burton gasped, pointing to the corridor. "Who gave you permission to damage hospital property? No, not a word, back on the ward. Too hot, indeed. You don't hear the patients complaining, do you? And they are my only consideration. Now back to work."

It was unanswerable. The patients, as they all well knew, were beyond complaining. If she considered their well-being at all, it was in terms of an annual budget to which Sister Burton adhered with the zeal of a woman whose own life savings were in danger of being plundered.

Certainly it was not spelt out in the appointment letter, sent to Serena after her interview, that bagging up laundry was on the agenda either, but since there appeared to be no one else to do it and there were rows of helpless patients waiting for clean laundry and hospital gowns, she simply got on with it. Becky, on the other hand, complained unceasingly and to no effect, and Nonie's contempt for the patients in their charge was almost as wearing as Sister Burton's tyrannical disposition.

In fact very little of what Serena was doing was what she had expected. She had been told she would be helping on the ward, but no one had prepared her for the sheer drudgery of what she was asked to do or the risk involved in a great deal of it. On the second day on the ward, one of the harassed nurses, joining in the rush to aid an elderly man who appeared to have gone into cardiac arrest, had pushed the medication trolley at her and told her to get on with it.

"Just the paracetamol, you dummy," the nurse hissed at her as Serena started to protest. "Even you can do that, surely to God?"

Uneasily she started to work her way through the list, glancing furtively at the thin, severe figure of Sister Burton in her dark blue overall, black elastic belt and starched white nylon cuffs covering the short sleeves of her tunic who was berating a junior nurse for allowing a visitor to enter the ward out of hours.

"What a cow," the nurse muttered, rejoining Serena half way through the round. "You think she'd welcome a visitor, wouldn't you? No one ever comes to see the poor sods. But she's afraid someone might see what goes on here and complain. God knows who cares enough. I'm off at the end of the week."

"Where are you going?" Serena asked, handing her the list she had completed so far.

"Saudi," the girl said, dropping pills into small plastic containers. "Two-year contract. Make a fortune and then jack the whole lot in. You should try it. Oh, you've got kids though, haven't you? Shame. Oh God, there goes Mr Haworth. Grab him, will you?"

No one had mentioned either that Maud Frierley was — against all Government guidelines — a mixed ward where dignity was a disposable commodity and where two or three elderly male patients were inclined to remove their pyjamas at a whim and go for a walk, their sagging flesh and shrivelled bodies causing either hysteria or mirth depending on who apprehended them before they reached whatever destination — usually forgotten — they had in mind when they left their bed.

"Just as well most of the women haven't a clue what day it is," Becky muttered, helping Serena to get him back into his pyjamas. "I'm going to ask for a pillow to be put over my face if I ever end up in a place like this."

Serena just nodded. Too shocked to say anything. That had been two months ago. Shock had receded to be replaced by quiet rage and eventually rage had been transcended by the need to just get through the hours on the ward. Gone too were the smart clothes, replaced by cotton shirts and skirts and flat shoes or, like today, nothing but her bra and pants under the nylon overall. But even they could not eliminate the ache in her feet after five hours without an opportunity to sit down.

Sister Burton allowed her staff fifteen minutes per shift to recover and get a second wind. Serena had discovered that this was not enforceable and hardly ever materialized. If she was with a patient when it was time for her break — and this was the case on most days — her break could only begin when the patient had been dealt with. On this Sister Burton was immovable. She no longer bothered to ask.

"I'm amazed they haven't asked us to wash the bloody stuff as well," Becky grumbled over her shoulder to Serena massaging her aching feet. She held out a huge white cotton bag, shaking it impatiently as Nonie slowly lifted each item separately and even more slowly shovelled it into the bag.

"Nonie, for Christ's sake, get a bloody move on. Stuff this for a game of soldiers. I'm going to resign. I mean, I feel sorry for the poor bastards, but I'm not putting up with that sadistic cow telling me what to do any more. I thought this might be interesting, you know, to put on my CV when I get home. But Jeezus, not this."

Serena listened patiently, knowing Becky was right. But her own plans did not include a world trip. Hers were more basic.

"I don't know why you haven't told her to shut her face, Serena, the way she talks to you." Becky was still moaning on. "I mean anyone with a brain bigger than a Pot Noodle can see that it wouldn't harm getting some of the poor sods up to the table to have a meal, instead of pinning them to their beds all day. *No-neee!* That's the wrong bag. Oh God, give it here, I'll do it myself."

Serena pushed her foot back into her shoe, recognizing now the signs of the daily altercations between her two immediate colleagues.

"No, give it to me." She reached out and took the bag from Nonie.

"Nonie, why don't you swap with me," Serena suggested to the indignant woman who had pushed her face into Becky's ready for a heated exchange. She dragged the full trolley into the corridor and pulled an empty one into its place.

"She give me grief, Missus give me grief, I don't need no more grief," Nonie announced, glaring at Becky.

"Oh get a life, you stupid twat," Becky retorted, turning away.

"You call me names? You rude pig." Nonie began to tremble with rage, stabbing her finger at Becky's chest.

"We're all tired." Serena grabbed the agitated Nonie and pushed her gently towards the door, shooting a warning glance at Becky to quit while she was ahead.

Serena had been on Frierley now for nearly two months. Two months of washing incontinent or feeble-minded patients, emptying bedpans or soothing wandering wits had been easy compared with dealing with the heartless Sister Burton. Any sign of compassion towards her patients was taken as a poor reflection on her management skills and, as Serena knew to her cost, any suggestion as to how they might improve the lot of the abandoned generation lying mostly immobile in their high and hard hospital beds as a threat to her authority.

"Sit them at the table? AT THE TABLE?" Sister Burton could not have sounded more incredulous if Serena had suggested taking the entire ward to lunch at the Ritz.

"Oh, so suddenly you're an expert, are you? Four weeks and you think you can do this better than anyone else? My God, where do they find people like you? What the hell do you know about managing a ward like this?"

Serena attempted a mild protest but Sister Burton wasn't listening. "If I thought getting these patients up and over to a table to eat lunch would contribute to the smooth running of my ward," she stormed at Serena. "I would do it. But it won't. Understand? To do that I need another pair of hands and I haven't the money for that. Got that?"

"But it's only a question of two or three patients at the most," Serena tried to point out. "Mrs Ambleton for instance, and Mr Haworth. The rest of course I can see are not up to it, but it would only take me a few minutes …"

"A FEW MINUTES? *A few minutes?*" breathed Sister Burton. Serena saw the veins on either side of her temples visibly throbbing. "If you've got a few minutes to spare, my dear, I'd like to know why? Clearly you haven't nearly enough to do."

"I'm so sorry," Serena said quietly. "I just thought …"

"Then don't," Sister Burton snapped. "For heaven's sake, get a move on. Mr Merrow will be doing his round in an hour and I want this ward looking like the Hilton. Got that? And take these down to Records," she added, thrusting a pile of buff folders into her arms, "if you've got so much time on your hands."

"Yes, Sister, of course," Serena replied, retrieving the ones that had spilled on to the floor, ignoring the sarcasm. Only another two hours to go and then she would be out of here. She walked down three flights of stairs at the end of the corridor, past X-ray where she smiled hello to the receptionist, through Outpatients, until she reached an open hatch next to a door marked Records.

"Hi," she said through the hatch to a girl in a white coat and horn-rimmed glasses with her hair smoothed back from her face, sitting at a nearby desk.

"Serena." The girl got up and came over to relieve her of the stack of buff folders. "So you haven't put Sister Burton in traction yet?"

"Give me time," Serena laughed. "She's not quite up to speed today. She's too busy preparing for the great man's visit. How's life?"

Stacey Barclay gave a rueful shrug. She was, Serena decided, a remarkable looking girl, quite beautiful in fact, with coffee-coloured skin stretched smoothly over high cheekbones, long slender legs, tall enough to make her carefully chosen tailored jackets and skirts look a great deal more expensive than they were. She'd been at the hospital for a year, moving south to be with her boyfriend, leaving behind a well-paid and secure job in the local council not to mention a close-knit and shocked family.

It was an odd friendship but one that Serena had come to enjoy. Her real name was Eustacia, which she hated, but she loved her boyfriend who was, she said proudly, both good-looking and capricious. It was an odd word to use to describe a man, thought Serena, but days of walking to the bus stop after work with Stacey had made her decide that he was in need of a good shaking, and capricious wasn't such a bad choice after all.

"Wait for me when you get off and I'll walk down to the bus with you. Tell you on the way," Stacey whispered, seeing her boss approaching.

Serena gave her a wave and turned to make her way back to Frierley. She was looking forward to finishing her shift. Melanie was coming over later for a drink and Alex Billington had offered to drop Harry back on his way home, after their session. No hurry. A chance to talk to Louise.

As Serena arrived back a lone nurse, who looked about twenty and almost dead on her feet, was consulting a list of patients. Sister Burton was ensconced in her office. Becky and Nonie were swishing wet mops down the ward.

"Shall I start with Edith?" Serena asked the nurse as she came up behind her.

"Oh Serena," the nurse looked up with relief. "Thanks. I'm glad it's you, I just couldn't take another morning with bloody Nonie, she's so rough with them, they get upset and then we have to sedate them."

"Shame we can't sedate her," Serena smiled, walking round to the other side of Edith Ambleton's bed. "Anyway, she's far too busy baiting Becky to have time for the patients. Hi, Edith." She smiled down into the vacant eyes, pressing the thin hand lying across the blanket. "How does a luxury bath sound to you?"

As she began to turn Edith on her side, Serena glanced down towards the end of the ward. There she could see Nonie cackling contentedly with the porter who had come to fetch the laundry. Mr Haworth for once left his bed wearing both top and bottom of his pyjamas and walked no further than the ward door. On the other side of the glass partition that separated Sarah Burton's kingdom from the rest of the ward, Serena could see Becky talking heatedly. She had resigned. You could tell. Serena wondered why she didn't follow Becky's example. But before the thought had time to be given proper consideration, she knew why.

Frierley Ward had made her realize, as nothing else had done quite so forcibly in the last eighteen months, that unless she helped herself no one would. In spite of her sheltered life and pampered marriage, there was a strong sense of dignity about Serena, which was what had unsettled Sarah Burton. She wasn't used to an uncomplaining staff, or one who made her feel so threatened.

A strength of character that had always been there but had never been allowed to flourish had finally been given some freedom. A stoicism that had never been tested, not really, not until now, was making itself felt. The pay was poor and after tax and fares and paying Cheryl there was little left over in spite of the small amount she claimed from Income Support. But it bought her freedom. Freedom from every facet of her life being scrutinized and decisions made for her. What there was in her paypacket was hers, not a free handout from the state. And with it came the return of a modicum of control. This, she glanced around the ward, wouldn't be for ever, she knew that. She was already scouring the papers for another job, but meanwhile it was one she was able to do. She was learning as well. That couldn't be bad.

She looked down and smiled.

"Here we go, Edith," she said cheerfully to the skeletal figure curled into the foetal position in the bed. "And then I'll help you into a clean nightie. Let me know if you feel uncomfortable, won't you?"

Edith Ambleton, nearly ninety, with no immediate family and so stricken with bronchitis she had been removed by a health visitor from her flat where she had lived for nearly fifty years. She knew she would never go home and prayed every night not to wake up. She lifted a feeble hand and returned Serena's clasp. Claire glanced across at Serena in surprise. She had never seen Edith smile before.

At noon, Robert Merrow marched on to the ward followed by a young registrar. Sister Burton had been waiting in the doorway, a list of patients at the ready. He swept past, taking the list without stopping. The other two fell into line behind him. Claire leapt forward as Sister Burton snapped her fingers and pointed to a space behind her.

Serena was successfully spooning cereal into a patient's slack mouth when she saw Sister Burton's signal to her to stop while the great man consulted his notes.

"Would you mind if I continued?" Serena asked quietly. "This is the first time she's eaten for two days."

Sister Burton's refusal was drowned by Robert Merrow's agreement. "Certainly, certainly. Good sign," he nodded. "Nothing much more to be done, really. Carry on, nurse."

"Oh, but I'm not a nurse," she began, but stopped, partly because Sister Burton glared at her but mostly because Robert Merrow was staring intently at Serena, puzzled. He opened his mouth as though he were about to say something, and then changed his mind. Serena hastily turned her head away. She would not deny who she was, but nor did she want anyone to identify her. When she turned back Robert Merrow had already moved on and the old lady's mouth was opening like a small sparrow waiting for the next mouthful of food.

*

"Why do you do it?" Melanie asked, noting approvingly that, by the way Serena had re-arranged her living room, the lamps that had once adorned her drawing room in Belvoir Square now cast a warm, welcoming glow across the length of the room. The curtains looped back with taffeta ribbon softened the squareness of the windows and a glass vase stuffed with sunflowers provided a burst of colour against the plain walls.

Serena stretched her legs out and crossed her ankles, resting her coffee cup on her chest.

"Because it suits me, I'm here for the kids in the evening, and it won't be forever. Nothing is, you know that, don't you?"

She was looking better, Melanie noted with relief. The dreadful track suit had been replaced by a thin cotton sweater over narrow blue jeans. Her blond hair, now much longer and piled loosely into a knot on top of her head, was no longer highlighted and her make-up was confined to a splash of lipstick, but the improvement was noticeable.

About time too, Melanie thought grimly. It was a year and a half since it all happened and she talked about this Alex quite a lot.

Serena gave her a withering look. "He's terrific with Harry. And that's it. I mean it."

"Well, no harm in asking," Melanie smiled.

"You forget I'm still married," Serena pointed out quietly.

Melanie winced. Perhaps not so much progress after all. "So what's he doing for Harry?" Melanie sipped her coffee. "Does Louise see him?"

"A lot, and no," Serena replied, briefly addressing both questions. "He says I'm not to force it. In time she'll agree. But meanwhile Harry sees him once a week and they talk about all kinds of things."

"Like what?"

"Oh … you know, what Harry likes doing. I expect about me and Louise."

"Don't you sit in on the sessions?"

Serena glanced at her. "Well, at first I did. But then Alex thought Harry might respond more if I wasn't there. I expect he tells him I'm an ogre."

"Nonsense," Melanie snorted. "Harry? He adores you. What does he say about Stephen?"

Serena placed her cup carefully back on to the saucer and then leaned back, linking her hands behind her head.

"I don't know. Truly. I don't ask and Alex doesn't tell me. I'm not sure they've even got to that yet."

"Heavens!" Melanie's eyes widened. "I suppose he knows what he's doing."

"Yes. Absolutely. I have complete faith in him," Serena replied. "Well," she hesitated. "As much as I'll ever have in anyone, ever again. But he's kind and — well, not gentle precisely, more understanding, if you see what I mean. You don't have to spell it out for him. He doesn't say idiot things like 'I know how you feel.'"

"What does he say then?"

"He says, 'How *does* it feel? What do *you* think, why do *you* suppose?'"

"I see," Melanie said doubtfully. "So he doesn't give you any advice at all?"

"Me specifically? Not really. But then I haven't asked for any."

That wasn't strictly true. She saw no reason to tell Melanie that while Harry was waiting with the receptionist the first time she had met Alex, she had burst into tears and sobbed all over him.

"It's so stupid." She had struggled to keep her voice steady as he passed her a box of tissues. Her tears had turned to a watery chuckle as she took them. He looked startled. "It's just that your brother had to do the same," she explained.

"Essential equipment for both of us," he grinned. "And there's nothing stupid about crying. It can be very healing."

"But you don't understand," she said. "It's just that for the first time someone isn't telling me to fill in a bloody form or pushing me around but listening, actually *hearing* what I'm saying, and instead of being cheerful, here I am sobbing. It's kindness, you see. I'm so unused to it these days that it just bloody slays me."

Instead now, she said to Melanie: "So how's life? Charles?"

"Well," Melanie began, seeing that she was unlikely to get any more out of Serena — she was so secretive these days — "the dreadful Paula has fallen out with Miranda over who was to choose the celebrity for the next ball. Miranda says she's more or less asked the Duchess — provided she's not in the States — and Paula says she'd already put a request in for Princess Anne. The rest of us are staying out of it. But George is angling away for his knighthood and wants someone political. Incidentally, Malcolm's practically orgasmic over his picture at Rupert's wedding in the paper last month, he's asked for a copy. The vanity of the man. He asked about you, by the way. So did Meryl Holt. She, um," Melanie glanced uncertainly at Serena, "she asked if you'd like to have lunch some time?"

"Maybe." Serena smiled faintly. "I'll take a rain check on it."

Melanie left an hour later, pleased to have seen Serena, with plenty to report to Charles that would soothe both their minds. But she could not rid herself of the feeling that Serena was not so much interested in all their old friends, but simply humouring her need to tell her about them. She knew lunch with Meryl was unlikely to take place. She turned her car over Westminster Bridge and drove thoughtfully along Birdcage Walk, past the Palace, feeling a little surge of relief mixed with guilt at leaving Serena behind, back on familiar territory as she approached Knightsbridge, where she stopped off before heading home.

In Foster Street, Serena was closing the house up for the night. For once, Louise was in bed at a reasonable hour — no homework done but at least she had agreed to see Alex at some time. Harry was asleep. She sat in the silent kitchen sipping a cup of coffee.

Poor Melanie, she mused. Dear, loyal Melanie. What was it she had said about Paula? Serena paused and looked frowningly into the middle distance. What *was* it? She gave up. Whatever it was hadn't interested her. In fact she hadn't been interested in any of them. And as for Malcolm, who was still clinging to his job as chairman of Draycott Mendes. Serena had seen the picture Melanie mentioned. But unlike Melanie she had not been annoyed, just amused at the expression on his face. So pleased with himself. So puffed up.

I'm surprised he wasn't angling to marry Rupert instead of the bride, she thought drily to herself. She placed her cup in the sink and wrote a couple of reminders on the new message-board next to the fridge.

"Ring Alex," she wrote. So much to tell him, she mused as she switched the lights off.

Chapter Fourteen

The fact that Alex Billington had known what it was like to see his own family break up and be separated from his children most of the week was, Serena decided, in his favour rather than something to cast doubt on his ability to mend broken lives.

Looking back she wasn't at all sure why she thought he would be judgemental in spite of what Jack Billington had said of him. Successful, well-regarded. Maybe, she decided, watching him show Harry the fish in the aquarium in the window of the consulting rooms, she had been unprepared for his solicitous welcome. She had got used to being harshly judged by total strangers prying into her life.

For a while, apart from shaking hands with Harry and ruffling his hair, Alex Billington said very little to him, instead engaging Serena in quite ordinary small talk until — she wasn't sure how it happened — she found herself flicking absently through the pages of a magazine in a small ante-room, occasionally glancing at her watch or the door behind which Harry had agreed to explain the complexities of his latest computer game to Alex.

He was, she guessed, somewhere in his late thirties although it was hard to be absolutely sure. Older than his brother and built on more slender lines. His fair hair was receding but he wore quite youthful clothes, baggy cotton trousers, a denim shirt under a cotton jacket that she recognized as the designer item it was. And he was slim. She noticed his hands: slender, bony fingers with a signet ring on his left hand where a wedding ring might have been. His manner was gentle and he seemed to be familiar with nearly all one hundred and twenty-seven schools of behaviour therapy. Jungian was, however, his favourite.

"Not mother's fault," he explained cheerfully. "Unlike Freud who can't point the finger fast enough."

"Well, by all means, let's go with Jung," Serena said. "I've always thought he had a better handle on our dreams than Freud."

He groaned. "Don't tell me, you're an expert?"

"Dream on," she laughed. "Mild interest. I never finished my degree."

"In what?"

"English," she answered briefly. "Look, Mr Billington."

"Alex," he said. "Please."

"Well, Alex," she hesitated, choosing her words carefully. "In all seriousness I know what you believe in, mother's not being to blame, but I wouldn't want to duck out of it altogether."

She fiddled with the strap of her bag. He gestured for her to go on. "I mean what if I am? To blame, I mean. I'm not stupid — it's possible, isn't it? I mean, if we're going to be realistic, it probably is me that's Harry's problem. But all I ask is that you must be honest with me. And that's OK too." She knew she was sounding melodramatic. "You mustn't worry because I've tried to prepare myself for it."

"My dear girl," he said quietly. "You mustn't beat yourself up like this."

It was then that she horrified herself by bursting into tears. Swollen, convulsive sobs shook her which she made worse by trying to suppress them. Throughout months of answering questions about Stephen, facing the world's press, desperate for news of him, she had not cried in front of anyone except Margot and Melanie. Not in her whole life had she cried in front of a stranger. But the tears were for Harry.

She tried telling him, but he just spoke soothingly over her, urging her to cry all she needed to when all she wanted was to stop. Poor, broken little Harry who had done nothing to deserve the demons invading his life, and she was getting the sympathy.

"And are you also prepared for being blameless?" Alex asked gently, as she pulled a handful of tissues from the box he extended. "If you've got used to blaming yourself for whatever it is Harry finds difficult to deal with, you won't be helping me.

"You see," he said, patting her hand, "I think Harry's ability to be more forceful is there, it just needs a bit of encouragement to make itself felt. It's inside all of us you know — it's just that we sometimes let the less forceful side of our nature take up too much of our time, especially when so many negative things are just waiting to eat away at us."

Serena blew her nose. Alex removed the box of tissues. "And you know you may only be guilty of being a caring mother."

His kindness was meant to reassure her but she felt embarrassed by it because he thought the tears were for herself and she had expected him to understand they were for Harry. She thought he would tell her to pull herself together. But he didn't, and she wondered why. It sounded so wet. Instead she smiled gratefully at him. True, he could not possibly know the anguish of a sudden and shocking separation from someone you trusted with your soul, as she had done, or what Harry and Louise had gone through, but he didn't pretend to either.

At least his children, Spencer, he told her, who was eleven, and Sydonie who was nine, could call him up just to talk, secure in the knowledge that they would be staying with him every other weekend and any time they wanted to descend on him, even if that was midweek. Which they often did. Alex said it was because he and his ex-wife encouraged their children to be with them and never to feel they had to make appointments to see their own parents. Even though his wife had remarried and he had a relationship with an artist called Alice who stayed at weekends, the children, he told her firmly, came first.

"I normally see my other patients at my home," he told her, by which she knew he meant his private patients. "So it works quite well."

She knew without seeing it that Alex's house would be different to the sparsely furnished, square room she had become used to visiting at the medical centre just around the corner from Foster Street — its boring appearance relieved only by a gallery of children's drawings pinned to cork boards, a couple of green plants and some bright red cushions on the two easy chairs either side of a small coffee table piled with magazines and children's books. It was not Serena's idea of a relaxing room, but then she wasn't being asked to relax. Just Harry. She tried not to mind that Harry was being treated in such uninspiring surroundings.

It was because of Louise that she found herself taking the bus to Clapham just after nine-thirty the following Saturday morning to discover for herself how Alex lived in private. The letter signed S. Maxfield posted the day before was curt and asked if Serena would come to the school on a matter of urgency.

"What's this about, Lou?" she asked.

Louise shrugged. "What?"

"This letter." Serena battled not to shout at her. "Your," she glanced at the letter to see who it was from, "head of year wants to see me."

Louise gave an indifferent shrug, but Serena's suspicions were aroused.

"Darling, let me have it. Why have they posted this? Why didn't they give it to you to bring home? No nasty surprises, Lou. What is it? Homework? No? Oh, Lou, not bunking off?"

"What would you know about bunking off?" Louise retorted rudely, tying her school jumper around her waist.

"*Lou*, that is no way to speak to me …"

"No? *No?* Then how do you want me to speak to you?" Louise suddenly flared up, wrenching open the door as she spoke. "You don't speak to me at all. You talk to Harry. Oh lovely goodie two shoes Harry. Everyone loves Harry …"

"Louise, stop it." Serena tried to calm her down. "Of course I care about you …"

"No, you don't. I've got the curse and have you asked how I feel? No."

"Lou, it must just have come on." Serena too had started to shout. "How can I know unless you tell me …"

"I don't *want* to tell you. Go and see the bloody woman. See if I care."

"*Louise.*" Serena ran after her. But Louise was too quick and was out of the front door and down the path before Serena could reach her.

Betty Plaxton was standing on her doorstep watching, sharp-eyed, as Serena gazed distractedly after her daughter. She rolled her eyes at Serena. "Little sods," she called across the hedge. "What's Madam been up to, then? Boyfriends?" She started to laugh.

"All them bleedin' 'ormones. I said to Les, I said, they're like rabbits on 'eat, round here. Oh Gawd," she screamed, as she felt a shove in her back and fell forward off the step. "*Ellis*. You still here? Get a move on, you dummy."

With that she bounced back into her house leaving Serena gazing help-lessly after Louise who was no longer to be seen. Hormones indeed. But that wasn't it. Three months ago, when a pale-faced Louise had waylaid her in her bedroom and told her something was happening and Serena had cuddled her and marvelled at her wonderful grown-up daughter, she might have believed it. But not now. Now, there was something else. Letting Serena get near to her had been a momentary respite in Louise's sustained campaign of resentment.

Boyfriends? Maybe that was it. Oh God. It probably was. Louise was never without a boy on the phone or hanging around the gate. A terrible fear exploded in the pit of her stomach. What ... oh God, no. What was she thinking of?

Not Louise. Louise knew the facts of life. What Serena had told her when she was eleven had been well supplemented, she knew that, by giggling conversations with Daphy and the problem pages of the teen mag-azines that she had found in her room. She wouldn't? Hadn't. Impossible.

There was, however, enough truth in Louise's outburst to make Serena squirm. It was true that of late Harry had been her prime concern, but Louise was so difficult to talk to. Off-hand, impatient, dismissive. All day on the ward she vowed that when she got home she would sit Louise down and really talk to her, change things.

She would make sure Louise understood the consequences of sex. Or lack of it, she thought wryly. She even practised a few opening sentences so that Louise would see she was not a sad person at all, and each was dis-missed because she sounded, as Louise would have said, like a nerd.

Eight, nine, ten, she mouthed silently and then suddenly paused in the process of counting sheets going to the laundry. Maybe that was it? Her own sex life was such a solitary business she had not thought that her grow-ing daughter, with no history to deal with, no experience — she fervently hoped — to guide her might be a fraction more interested than her mother in dealing with the waves of need and longing that Serena had once taken for granted and with such pleasure and now dealt with perfunctorily and briefly.

And Stephen? Did he still need her as much as she needed him? She gave herself a shake. "Eleven, twelve," she said aloud, and then, dropping the last one into a wicker trolley, picked up a list next to her, ticked a box marked twenty-four single sheets with more attention than it really deserved.

"Getting like the inmates," Claire the young nurse giggled, coming up behind her.

"Getting? I think I've overtaken them," she grinned back.

"Well, at least you keep your knickers on, not like Mr Haworth. Sorry, Serena. Off you go. His pyjamas are on his bed, but he isn't."

"Oh God, not again. Where this time? Oh no, not the canteen."

*

"It's her age," Alex had said reassuringly when he phoned her about Harry's appointment cancellation. She hadn't meant to pour it out to him, especially not on the phone. But he seemed to draw it out of her, getting past her defences.

"You're right. You read about it all the time. I'll let you know. Thanks, Alex. It isn't your problem — Louise, I mean."

"Nonsense," he said cheerfully. "Anytime, I can help, Serena. You know I will. Why don't you bring Harry to the house on Saturday morning. Ten o'clock?"

At ten past four she was shown into the interview room at St Saviour's and confronted by Louise's year teacher who did not share Alex's optimism that age was Louise's problem.

"She's a bright, sharp-witted girl who has a good future, but she is wasting it by using this school to beat up the world," said the brisk woman who sat behind a cluttered desk groaning with buff folders and schoolbooks. She spoke brusquely with no preamble, checking a report in front of her.

"No homework submitted for over a month, bunking off lessons, insolence to her teachers and yesterday, which is why I've asked to see you," she said, closing the folder and clasping her hands together on top of it. "She was part of a gang of girls who pushed a teacher flat on her face."

Serena gasped. "Oh my God. Why? Is she all right?"

"Shaken and a bit bruised. And you had no idea about this?"

"No. None." Serena gripped her hands into a fist in her jacket pockets. Whatever next? No warning from Louise, and yet she knew. Absolutely knew what it was about. All that screaming. A rush of relief swept through her that it was not after all sex or boyfriends, followed immediately by a dreadful sense of shame that she felt such relief when a woman had been injured.

"We don't tolerate violence on any level, Mrs Carmichael."

"Of course not, but surely it was an accident?" Serena interrupted, rallying her wits just enough to defend Louise but not enough to impress the woman in front of her. Violence? Louise? Dear God.

The teacher, Mrs Maxfield, looked about forty. Her neat navy skirt and short-sleeved white silk blouse added to her air of quiet authority. She shook her head impatiently. Her day had started with an aggressive parent suggesting she went back to Africa when she had never set foot outside Europe in her life, and threatening to blind her if she picked on his daughter one more time. It had continued with talking to Social Services about truants and in the afternoon to child care officers over two suspected cases of child abuse. By four o'clock on a hot sultry afternoon, she was clearly in no mood to be sympathetic to a mother who didn't even know why she had been summoned to see her.

"It was not an accident. It was deliberate. I don't believe Louise instigated it, but she didn't stop it or step back from it."

"I can't believe this." Serena shook her head. "Louise is headstrong and unhappy — believe me, I'm her mother, I can see she is. But for heaven's sake, the child is only thirteen and she's come through so much. Surely you can understand that?"

"I can understand. But I don't condone. And she is nearer fourteen than thirteen. Mrs Carmichael, I am very aware of Louise's background and I am not attempting to under-play the shock of it, but I can tell you there are children in this school who have suffered much more serious deprivation than Louise — oh yes they have — and they don't resort to this. This is an official warning, Mrs Carmichael."

"What does that mean?"

"It means one more step out of line and we will suspend her from school."

"And you can do that?"

Mrs Maxfield challenged her with a level look. "Oh yes," she said softly. "We can do it. You may well decide to oppose it, but that is your right. But then the board will become involved and so too will the Local Education Authority. You might even have friends in the press — sorry," she paused, flushing faintly. "I didn't mean that."

Serena gritted her teeth and waved the apology aside.

"And in the end you might win. But Louise will lose, whatever the outcome, unless this is stamped on right now. You do understand what I'm saying."

"What can I do?" Serena asked, not bothering with a debate that was going to be fruitless. She had long since stopped believing she had any rights. Briefly she considered legal advice and then she thought of Alex. Alex would know what to do.

In all of this, it wasn't until she had left the office with Mrs Maxfield's advice that she should get Louise in order, stop her from thinking she could break life's rules and get away with it, that she realized she had not once felt sorry for Louise. Just frightened for her. She was to be grounded at all free periods for a week; the entire group would be made to apologize publicly to the teacher concerned and they were to clear the school grounds of all litter until half term.

Alex was inclined to take a more serious view of Louise's unrepentant stance, as described to him by Serena, than the actual crime. Mrs Maxfield, he explained, had got it right. Beating up the world was what Louise was doing. Only he said it was Louise's own world that she most resented.

"I know Susie Maxfield," he said, pouring a mug of coffee for Serena and leading the way into the pink and green conservatory that led off his kitchen. "She's one of the more sane ones down there," he said, referring to St Saviour's. "Her manner is a little abrupt, but then she's not running Roedean is she?" He smiled down at her. Serena was tall, but he still towered over here. "Here," he said, standing back and indicating with his coffee mug a couple of wicker chairs. "Sit over here. It's such a stunning day, isn't it?"

Serena relaxed against a pile of cushions in one chair while he settled himself into its twin on the other side of an open door that led on to a small oasis of a garden. A gentle summer breeze moved the heads of a bank of tulips in tubs on the narrow paved terrace that ran the length of the house.

Beyond was a perfectly manicured lawn stretching down to an apple tree. Overhead, the soft whirr of a fan sent a cooling shaft of air through her hair. The scent of jasmine drifted in, the telephone rang but Alex indicated that the machine would pick it up. From the drawing room at the front of the house she could hear the faint strains of a Chopin piano concerto coming from a sound system that was invisible, but perfect.

Harry was engrossed in unravelling a computer game on Alex's son's computer which, Alex had assured Harry, Spencer wouldn't mind in the least. She had to remind herself this was a professional visit.

"No, Susie is a good egg," Alex explained, cradling his mug in both hands, one leg flung over the arm of his chair. "She's just seen it all, and of course we've often had long talks about what's really causing their discipline problems."

"Poor housing, unemployment, single mothers?" Serena suggested.

"Um, maybe. But I think it's more complex than that."

It registered briefly that it didn't come more complicated than not having a roof over your head or a job, but then she could see what Alex meant. Louise had always been a rebel and Harry had never been anything other than timid.

"So what does she mean Louise is using school to beat up the world?"

"I think," he coughed, throwing a self-conscious grin at Serena, "Susie's quoting me, to be honest. Louise won't face the real problem probably because in the middle of all that anger and frustration she needs you and wants you to tell her what to do next. And when you don't, she takes it out on the nearest whipping boy. School."

Serena stiffened. "And you're saying that I am Louise's problem?"

He groaned, reaching out his hand to briefly grip hers. "No, of course not. Absolutely not. I'm saying the reverse. You're most likely to be Louise's solution. Only it might not seem like it at the moment."

She stared doubtfully at him. She the solution to a child who slammed doors in her face and screamed her hatred of her?

"I wish I could get Louise to talk to you," she said, letting her head drop back on to the cushions. "But she won't. Won't talk to anyone, I mean. Except Daphy and some boy called Damon who wears his baseball cap back to front and has three earrings in one ear and calls LouLou 'Babe'."

She shuddered theatrically, more to lighten the moment which had suddenly begun to feel like a betrayal of Louise.

Alex chuckled. "Give her time. Meanwhile Harry, I'm pleased to say, is much more relaxed. Who is Stacey, by the way? He likes her."

"Stacey? Oh, she's a dear. She works at the hospital — in the Records department. Mid-twenties, pretty. She's got a ghastly boyfriend who treats her badly but she takes all the blame for everything he does. She comes over for supper when he's away — which is often — and Harry was smitten when she knew all about a computer game he's hooked on. And besides," she glanced across at him, "I haven't made many friends since I moved here and it's nice to have someone to talk to who doesn't care about what's happened to all of us. You know, starting again."

He looked thoughtfully out across the garden. "Talking of which," he said, not turning his head. "I was going to ask if you would like to come to supper one evening?"

For some reason her stomach fluttered uncomfortably. Her eyes widened in astonishment. "How kind," she began, a little flustered. "But I don't think I could. I mean," she said, feeling suddenly and irrationally quite shy. "Not yet, I don't think I'm ready for …"

"For what? Supper with someone who enjoys talking to you?"

Serena felt her throat constrict. She who had accepted with grace invitations from half the British Cabinet and a clutch of European bankers was now stammering like a teenager at being asked out.

Panic gripped her. She no longer felt safe. Alice. She suddenly recalled there was Alice to consider. The yet to be met Alice who had shared, if not his life, but certainly his weekends for the last three years. Dear God, was her judgement so flawed? Was no man to be trusted?

"Alex, it's most kind of you, but I couldn't," she swallowed hard. "I mean Alice ..."

"Alice?"

"Yes, Alice. You must think of her."

There was a slight pause before he said, "Of course I think of her. I meant Alice and I would like you to come to supper."

"Yes, of course you did." Serena thought she would keel over with embarrassment. "I just meant," she began to ramble rapidly, "I just meant Alice might not want a stranger foisted on her, that's all."

"Nonsense," he said easily. "I'll get her to call you."

*

On the bus going home, two things had to be considered. The first and most obvious being that she had made a first-class fool of herself, and the overwhelming desire to sit with a brown paper bag over her head was not practical. Deprived of such solace, she turned to what would she have done if Alice had not existed and there was only Alex to consider.

For a wild moment she had been going to say yes. The vision of looking pretty and feminine and being flirted with and — oh God, who was she kidding? — to have sex that would exhaust her with its passion and engulf her with its ferocity had, for a brief moment, made her feel dizzy. I mean, she said to herself, while agreeing out loud with Harry that it had been an ace morning, if I had said yes — and I wanted, absolutely wanted, to say yes — what harm would there have been? Who would have suffered?

Everyone, said her common sense. Alice would have been betrayed and she herself would have been compromised. And could Alex have gone on treating Harry? Probably not. And Alex himself? Absurd. She had mistaken concern for attraction. That's all it was. Now stop beating yourself up, she told herself sternly.

She looked down at the flat-fronted shops sliding past. Saturday morning shoppers pushed slowly along the crowded pavement running into congested knots as pedestrians converging from different directions tried to ease their way around pavement stalls. Ranks of T-shirts hung from the canvas awnings of stalls piled high with shoes, crockery and such essentials as cheap T-shirts and DVD's.

There had been a time when she feared empty hours and her own company, but right at this moment she longed so much for a field to walk in, a country lane to stride down. She felt bereft. Involuntarily she closed her eyes and thought of Belvoir Square with its tall, towering trees and the cool interior of the kitchen leading to the sunny terrace and Kensington High Street waiting just around the corner in a world that she understood and still thought of as home. Where Harry and Louise were cared for by a solicitous Chrissie and the only concern Louise raised was covert alterations to her school uniform. Harry had ceased chattering and was resting his mouth against the metal bar on the seat in front. Automatically she reached out, easing him back, pushing his hair out of his eyes, half surprised and half pleased that he jerked his body in an impatient gesture to move her away.

Outside McDonald's the bus slowed to manoeuvre its way past a parked car. Idly she watched as the glass doors swung in and out disgorging groups of teenagers and small children. It took her a few seconds to register the couple pushing through the crowd gathered around the door. She stiffened, straining across Harry to follow their progress as they disappeared into the crowd.

There was no mistake. It was Louise draped around the boy with the three earrings who called her "Babe" and wore his baseball cap the wrong way round. The boy she had described to Alex. Louise, who had been told not to leave the house until they returned, was giggling up into his face, wearing a tight pink jumper that ended inches above the waistband of a pair of black jeans that imprisoned her legs and thick clumpy shoes. None of these things, Serena thought frantically, were Louise's. Or at least not that she recalled. From the distance of the top deck of the bus it was impossible to be sure, but Serena could have sworn it was make-up and not nature that had ringed her daughter's eyes in black circles.

She half rose out of her seat and then slumped back. By the time she reached the pavement, Louise would have disappeared and the bus was already gathering speed. All she could do was hope that Louise would be careful and come home soon. Sex suddenly lost its allure. It was a fiend waiting to spoil her daughter and wreck her life.

Alex's house had mobilized the familiar pang of longing. Alex himself had stirred feelings best left where they were. Harry nudged her to start getting off the bus as the stop nearest to Foster Street approached. And then, she thought going first down the stairs, Harry clattering after her, there was Stephen. Stephen who was still her husband, Stephen who she still yearned for. How could Alex, until he had disrupted that private and protected world known only to Serena, have known what a powerful effect a simple, if misleading, invitation would have on her?

He was a good, kind — and yes, attractive man. But that was all he could be. And she didn't need a man to lean on, not now. She'd come too far for that. It was the treacherous seduction of sex, not Alex, that had distorted her feelings. Having arrived at that conclusion, she felt almost lightheaded with relief. The bus creaked to a halt at the corner of the High Street. Anxiously she looked back down the road, knowing there was no hope of seeing Louise but trying not to imagine what she might be up to.

They crossed the main road, holding hands, darting to the centre and then across again to the supermarket where Harry pushed the trolley, occasionally scooting it along with one foot. The checkout was crowded. She longed for a cup of tea. One of the mothers at Harry's school was in the next line and called out hello. Serena couldn't remember her name, but Harry came to the rescue. "Hello, Mrs Matthews," he said politely.

"Lucky you," Mrs Matthews called over, pointing to Harry. "Mine are transfixed in front of the telly. On a day like this as well. Goin' to the car boot sale up Dunton Road?"

"I'm not sure I'll get back home, let alone go out again after this lot," Serena grimaced, indicating the loaded trolley. She had a quick vision of a pile of ironing to be reduced, sheets to be changed, the kitchen to be cleaned.

"Know the feelin'." Mrs Matthews rolled her eyes.

For once Serena was relieved to turn into Foster Street out of the incessant grumble of traffic, away from the clouds of dust thrown up by lorries. Harry had volunteered to carry one of the bags, but the other three were pulling her arms heavily downwards.

Slowly they walked up the road, past Bradley and his friends shoving each other on and off the pavement, knowing better now than to acknowledge him unless he was alone; this prevented a torrent of abuse being hurled at them to impress his mates. Across the road, Cheryl was leaning on her gate gossiping to one of their neighbours. She waved a hand at Serena who smiled and nodded back.

Outside their house, Les Plaxton's sagging jeans and a soiled vest parting company with each other to reveal an expanse of white flabby flesh was all that could be seen of him buried underneath the bonnet of his car, Betty leaning against it holding a spanner.

"Ere, S'rena," she bawled as they approached. "Where do all the old cars that are rusting and ready for the knacker's yard go? He buys them," she shrieked, not pausing for an answer.

Serena smiled sympathetically and turned into her gate. Alana and Ellis were weaving about the pavement on their skateboards.

"'Lo Harry," Alana called. "Wanna go?"

Harry hesitated, looking quickly at Serena. The last thing she wanted, already worried stiff about Louise, was Harry playing in the street. But she was no proof against the eager look on his face.

"Can I, Mum?" he whispered. "Just here, no further."

The refusal had sprung to her lips and as quickly faded. Alex had said let go just a little. Alex again.

"Of course." She grinned back at him. "I might even watch once I've dumped all this shopping."

He dashed off and she turned into the house. Who would have thought it, she pondered, putting the shopping away. This time last year Harry would have been in the country riding his pony, or … she stopped and gazed into the distance. It wasn't last year, was it? It was the year before. Nearly two years. Absently she began to wonder what would Melanie be doing, Paula, Miranda. What would she have been doing? Well, not lugging four carrier bags of shopping along Kensington High Street, that was for sure.

She frowned, trying to remember what it had all been like. But she couldn't. The vision of her driving down the M4 was easy to conjure up, but the feeling of being protected, cosseted, eluded her. She banged the cupboards shut and switched the kettle on. Later she would call Melanie — she hadn't spoken to her this week — and then she remembered, Melanie was in New York with Charles. How odd to have forgotten.

The seamless way her life had drifted from that one to this troubled her. So much so that she couldn't now recall when one had stopped haunting her and the other had taken over. Or, at least, the importance of it all. She took her coffee and wandered into the living room and glanced out at Harry speeding past, held up by Alana. No sign of Louise. If she hadn't turned up by two she would ring Daphy's mother and ask for that boy's number. Surely his parents would know where he was? But then why should they? She didn't know where her daughter was.

At times like this she felt Stephen's absence more acutely. Not there to turn to, to take the burden from her. But then, a more honest voice reminded her, there were times when it wasn't just wondering what Melanie was doing, or Paula. Or what she would have been doing at the cottage. It was a fact, and no escaping from it, that these days she had trouble recalling what it was like being with Stephen.

And where the hell was Louise?

*

Just after four, Louise came home. Serena had spent the last two hours making every pact known with God that if he would just keep Louise safe, she would pay more attention to her wayward daughter, not nag her, try to understand. The relief of seeing her saunter down the path tossing her hair, pausing only to exchange insults with Bradley, was short-lived. Fury that she had caused her so much anguish soared but in the end relief and Alex's admonition to try and keep calm, to see Louise's resentment and rebellion as a way of getting her attention, won. After all she had certainly got that.

As Louise turned her key in the lock Serena hastily dashed across the hall into the kitchen and was standing by the sink calmly drying a lone cup when the door opened.

"So, there you are," Serena exclaimed, putting the cup away. "I saw you coming out of McDonald's but that was hours ago."

A wary look crept into Louise's face as she stood in the doorway, hands dug into the pockets of her jeans.

"Did you? What big eyes you've got. Taken to spying now, have you?"

Relief dissolved. The pact shattered. "Louise," she breathed furiously, slapping down the tea cloth on the draining board. "If you are rude to me once more, I will really let you see just how tough life can be. You flatter yourself if you think anyone would want to spy on you. You weren't hard to spot with … Damon, is it? Why didn't you tell me you were going out?"

"I didn't know I was, until after you'd gone. Why?" Louise retorted sulkily. "What's wrong with that? Why should you mind? You were out."

Serena rested her hands on the kitchen table and leaned towards Louise. "Mind that you went out? No. Mind that you didn't have the courtesy to tell me? Yes. Don't do it again. Clear?"

"Maybe," Louise said defiantly, pushing herself off the door-frame. "What if I do? You didn't ask me if it was OK for you to disappear with Harry for the whole morning. I haven't made a fuss."

She reached into a bowl and took an apple. Serena took a deep breath. "And nor am I. I am making a 'fuss', as you put it, because I was worried about you. You at least knew where I'd gone. You don't need to be rude, Louise. You know perfectly well that I didn't have much of a choice about this morning's appointment — and I asked you to come, remember?"

"No thanks." Louise gave an exaggerated shudder. "I'm not into being treated like a nutcase."

"Nutcase? *Nutcase?*" Serena halted incredulously. "That's a charming way to describe something as normal as Harry not having your confidence, your ability to make friends. What a lucky girl you are, Louise Carmichael, to have everything without trying that Harry so longs to have. Nutcase indeed. And don't slam the door, do you hear?"

Chapter Fifteen

On Tuesday afternoon, the DSS office was crowded and slow-moving. Serena collected a ticket allocating her place to be seen. There was a spare seat in one of the rows about three back from the front. It was away from the only gust of fresh air by the door, but it was better than standing. Serena pushed her way through until she reached it, stepping over a motley crowd of people who gave her no more than a cursory glance or else grumbled loudly that she was disturbing them.

Clutching her bag she wriggled into a seat wedged between a plump woman with rolls of fat cascading from her chin who periodically dabbed at the beads of perspiration collecting in the folds with a fistful of tissues, and a man wearing an anorak with a fur-trimmed hood, although it was a particularly hot summer's day. It wasn't until she was seated that she became aware of the jerky little movements he was making, grabbing the air with his thumb and index finger, snapping at invisible irritants and then carefully wiping his hand front and back on the knee of his trousers before starting again.

Oh great, she sighed, praying he wouldn't attempt anything more ambitious that would involve her. The smell of stale sweat was overpowering. Bossy notices glared from every wall except the one where three cubicles, separated from each other by a free-standing partition, dealt with the business of doling out or refusing money to the rows of people waiting in turn in the airless room.

Serena glanced around for somewhere else to sit. Three rows behind her she noticed Mrs Mojani who, when she caught Serena's gaze, hastily buried her face in a book. Poor woman, Serena thought, turning back. What was there to be ashamed of? They were all in the same boat. And she was not ashamed, she reminded herself. She was very angry and too tired to stand.

In her hand she clutched a letter which was as impersonal as the power it wielded. A wonderful start to the week, she thought bitterly. Louise had spent the whole of Sunday sulking, leaving her room only for meals. Serena didn't know whether to be amused or irritated that, no matter how big their rows, Louise's appetite remained unimpaired. The wonderful thing about her daughter, she decided, and there were, she reminded herself, some good things, was the ease with which she switched from seething resentment to forgetting she was at war with the world. The sight of Daphy and Damon hovering at the gate at ten to eight on Monday morning had transformed her from a vixen to a lamb. Serena watched her go, head down, giggling with her best friend, as she slowly opened the post.

Among the multi-choice reasons for sending the letter in the first place, two of the boxes ticked were those that pointed out that now she was employed she had to declare her earnings, and secondly, the amount she was earning might forfeit her right to Income Support. They were also cross that she hadn't informed them of the change in her circumstances. They had also ticked the severe penalties to be levied for such deception. Serena read it through twice and waited for the usual fear and anxiety to hit the roof of her mouth. Instead anger that some faceless bureaucrat had tried to frighten her blazed through her. It wasn't until she was on the bus going to St Wilhemina's that she felt a small stab of surprise that for once her first instinct had not been to race to the phone to call her mother or plunge into a panic that there was no one to tell her what to do next.

At first she was tempted to screw the letter up and hurl it into the waste bin, but experience told her that it would only result in a house call and endless questions to be addressed that would necessitate another unwelcome intruder into the house. So it was that later that morning she approached Sarah Burton to ask if she would mind if she left an hour early next day. Even the ill-tempered nurse had lost the power to disturb her for more than it took to move on to the next task.

"It's some personal business I have to attend to and I'll make the time up," Serena assured her.

"Make it up?" cried Sister Burton. "When? That's what I'd like to know.

Tonight? Tomorrow? I can't run a ward on this kind of casual basis. I'm sorry, but you'll have to try and arrange your private life in your own time. You're not here much as it is. No weekends, you had a week off at half term. And you want more time off? What next?" Her voice was almost a shriek. "A sabbatical?"

"Sister, I am being as reasonable as I can," Serena persisted, wondering why she hadn't, as Claire had advised, just phoned in sick and taken the whole day off. "I'll stay for a couple of hours longer the next day if you like."

"Reasonable isn't the word I would have used," Sister Burton retorted, two familiar red spots appearing on her cheeks.

It was at this point that Robert Merrow happened to come on to the ward, and smiled in a rather familiar way at Serena which was not lost on Sister Burton.

"I'm sure — Serena, isn't it? — will make the time up somehow, won't you — Serena? Now, Sister," he said, guiding Sister Burton up the ward. "What's the problem with Edith Ambleton? And, Sister," he paused, adding gently. "I think you might not have noticed but Mr Haworth is trying to climb into bed with Mrs Gantry."

As he pushed Sarah Burton ahead of him, he turned and gave Serena a wink. In spite of herself, she half laughed. Perhaps he wasn't so brusque as she had thought. Probably mid forties, she decided, watching him flick over a patient's chart. Not particularly tall, slightly balding, but he wore a Rolex and his shoes were almost certainly Gucci. Claire said he only did the NHS work because he was obliged to and without it no one would give him a knighthood. She thought of George Kincaid. Only too true, she reflected, beginning to stack up the lunch trays.

As it was, Serena only just made it before the office shut for the day the following afternoon. Anxiously she glanced at the clock as the hot dusty afternoon dragged on. Cheryl Tosney had agreed to pick up Harry and Louise and stay with them until six-thirty when Serena would be home. Stacey was going to babysit. She just hoped she would be out of here by three-thirty and back at the hospital by four to make up the two hours she had taken off. If nothing untoward happened, she could be home, feed Louise and Harry and just have time to get ready. Tonight she was going to Alex's house for dinner.

The first two dates she had fudged when Alice called, thankful she couldn't see the flushed cheeks and the screwed-up eyes clutching the phone when she realized who it was. Alice sounded pleasant, rather vague, but, she assured Serena, she was looking forward to meeting her. In the end, it was more embarrassing to keep refusing than to accept and she had given in. Eight o'clock, Alice had said. Informal. They would dine on the terrace if the weather held.

You couldn't count going to dinner at Melanie's, she told herself, realizing with a start that it was the first time she would be going out alone since Stephen had disappeared. Taking Harry and Louise with her to supper at Melanie's was not the same thing, nor strolling up to a small family-run Italian trattoria over the bridge in Pimlico that Stacey had taken them to, all squashed into her tiny Metro.

This was different.

She was going to go by bus and order a taxi to bring her back. That was the easy part. Harder to decide was what to wear. Black, she thought finally. There was the linen, sleeveless dress she had bought from Harvey Nichols three years ago. She glanced down at her straight skirt and pulled it away from her hips. Where had it all gone? No hips at all now. The dress might not be as sleek on her as it once had been, but being black it might not notice quite so much either. And maybe just a pair of earrings. The amber and jet ones her mother had given her on her twenty-first and which had escaped the bounty hunters employed by Draycott Mendes.

There was also Jasmine to call, with some dates for Harry and Louise to go to Lucca. God bless Minnie, she thought fervently. Nearly three weeks this time — although Louise had kicked up a terrible fuss at the prospect. But at least she could keep the money coming in. Then two weeks staying with Margot — or maybe Margot would come up? She must suggest it. At least that would placate Lou. And she would take a couple of weeks herself. It would just work. She knew better now after last summer's nightmare attempts at scheduling, relying on her mother, Minnie and Melanie, no supporting Chrissie, or the children's friends, or even that treacherous Mrs Owen to look to, that any two consecutive days that worked out as planned was an unlooked-for bonus.

The noise of the last two clients hurling abuse at the clerk behind the counter stopped any further reverie. Four-letter words spun in the air, threats were delivered with wild abandon and nothing was achieved.

How stupid, she thought. Can't they see that screaming gets you nowhere? It just gets everyone's back up. At three-thirty, determined to disguise any hint of fury, she was summoned. The crowd had thinned considerably and Serena had tactfully averted her gaze when Mrs Mojani's number had been called and she rose to her feet.

"Yes, that's right," the young man yawned. "You're now earning over the limit set to qualify for family assistance, so we have to stop payments. Have you brought your book with you?"

"No, I haven't," Serena replied politely, wrapping her arms around her bag in a protective gesture. What a prat. "Now," she said pleasantly, and she hoped sympathetically, "I appreciate it is not your fault personally, after all you don't make the rules, but, really, is it sensible to penalize me like this when I am earning so little? Wouldn't you have thought they would be *pleased* that someone is trying to stand on their own two feet? It's not as though I'm asking for a fortune either. If you take that away, I'll be forced to take another job and then what happens to my children?"

"That's not my department." He sounded bored and glanced at his watch. "Do you want me to arrange for you to see someone in the children's department?" he asked, tapping the end of his pencil on the desk. "No? Then I can't help you."

"Now look," she started again, determined to remain calm; after all, she had seen the result of hysteria. "You must see it will cost you more if I stay home and draw all the benefits I'm entitled to. Excuse me," she stopped him as he called out the name of the next client. "I don't think you can have understood, I haven't quite finished. Sorry," she turned with a smile to address the man hovering behind her waiting to take her seat. "I won't be a minute."

The man shuffled back, half raising his hand in a good-natured salute. The clerk stared stonily at her.

"Look," she tried again, moving two forms in front of him. "This," she said pointing to the first column, "is what I earn. This is the difference between that and what I need to live on that you give me. This is what it will cost you if I stay home. Now, does that make any sense to you?"

"It doesn't have to. Mrs ..." he glanced down at his pad, "Carmichael. I don't have a hot line to the minister who makes up this fairy story of a benefit system. My job is to catch the cheats."

"Cheats," she repeated, quietly sitting back in her chair, itching to slap him. "Is that really your job, Mr ..." She leaned forward to study the name on his lapel. "Mr Ormstrode. Surely your primary function is to ensure that those who are entitled to income support get it. I appreciate of course that it's more exciting to tell your friends about the villains you've clocked up for the day, and one knows from government figures that abuse of the system is widespread, but really would it not gain you more co-operation if you didn't immediately jump to such distressing conclusions about everyone who comes before you?

"Most people here, myself included, have better things to do — like working — than to try and learn the intricacies of 'working the system', I think you call it. Now, let's start again, shall we, and assume I am not out to cheat you?"

He let her finish and then without taking his eyes from her face pulled the paperwork lying between them to his side of the counter. No one, and certainly not someone like her, was going to tell him what his job was. Just because she could speak well, and didn't raise her voice. Bloody Duchess time, that's what this was. That she had repeated something uncomfortably like his department head had pointed out to him only that very day had not endeared her to him one bit. He stifled a yawn and began tapping out some sums on a calculator next to his elbow.

"As a matter of fact," he said, smiling triumphantly at her. "Far from restoring your benefit, just glancing at these figures, we might have to reclaim some of the benefit you've been enjoying."

"Reclaim it? You can't be serious?"

But he was. Serena gazed helplessly across the narrow counter. The whole interview had taken less than ten minutes. You couldn't win.

"So do you want me to tell the children's department?" he repeated.

"No."

He looked past her and called the number for the next client. "Oh, and don't forget to return your book," he said, making no attempt to disguise his glee at yet another small victory.

"Of course." She smiled brightly back at him. "And I'll pop a copy of the history of the Spanish Inquisition in with it. I bet you'll be sorry you missed it."

"The what?" He looked blank. "Here, what do you mean?"

Serena ignored him. She pushed the chair back, yawned, gathered up the paperwork between them and stood up. Whatever else she did, she was going to keep Harry and Louise out of their clutches.

"Oi, I'm talking to you," he bellowed, as she sauntered down the centre of the room and out into the street. Common sense told her that now that Alex was on her side, she could no longer be considered a failure, but common sense was no longer the reliable tool it once was. Common sense had dictated that if she tried to be honest and reasonable, she would be dealt with in a similar manner. But it was not true. Common sense had told her that Stephen would turn up somewhere, sometime, to explain everything. But he hadn't.

Which was worse? She debated, as she headed for the bus stop. Being protected by him — because surely that was the only reason he hadn't contacted her, to keep her free from further stress (and indeed, Don Trewless had dropped by only last week) — or having her heart broken because he hadn't tried to? She glanced back and saw the bus she needed to take her to St Wilhemina's rumbling along the High Street. She broke into a run and as she swung herself aboard the platform she did what she had grown used to doing. Put it to the back of her mind. If her money was being cut, she would have to make a real effort to get another job, one that paid more.

This was hopeless.

She wasn't surprised that Sarah Burton had piled up the chores when she got back. But she was surprised to see Edith's bed empty.

"Tests," Sarah Burton said briefly. "She might be going home."

"Home? Edith? But how?" Serena's gaze swivelled around the ward. "She has no one."

"Will you just do as you are told," Sister Burton snapped. By six, when Serena was due to go off duty, Edith was still not back on the ward.

"Tell her I'll see her tomorrow," Serena whispered to Claire, the nurse on duty, as she raced to get her jacket.

The rush hour was in full swing as Serena half walked, half ran down the drive to the entrance. She was never going to make it. A car inched past her and she stepped back on to the dry grass verge to let it pass.

"Can I give you a lift?" a voice called from the driver's side. Serena halted and glanced back. Robert Merrow was leaning out of the window, dark glasses shielding his eyes, the cuffs of his shirt rolled back, his tie loosened. She hesitated and walked slowly back.

"It's kind of you, but I live the other way from town. But thank you anyway."

She prepared to step back, expecting him to drive on. But he didn't. "I know where you live," he called to her. "Otherwise I wouldn't have offered you a lift. Besides, I want to talk to you."

"Me?"

"Yes, you. Be a good girl, will you?" he added plaintively. "I don't want to set tongues wagging, so just hop in. You can always hop out again if you don't like what I suggest."

Serena looked around. He was right. Curious eyes were already taking in the scene of a senior consultant in a Jag fraternizing with a ward orderly. In the end it was time, or the lack of it, rather than busy tongues, which decided her. She swung herself into the passenger seat and he drove off.

"You're Serena Carmichael, aren't you?" he said almost immediately, not taking his eyes off the road. "Stephen Carmichael's wife."

Serena sat very still, staring straight ahead.

"Can't imagine what you're doing in a dump like this," he went on, unperturbed by her silence. "Surely some of your friends could have helped out?"

"Mr Merrow," she began carefully, wondering what the form was for jumping from a moving car. "It's kind of you to give me a lift but my reasons for working here, like my life, are my own private affair. I appreciate it might look odd, but believe me, it is one of the saner things that I have had to deal with in the last year or so."

"Why didn't you change your name? Anyone could find you if they wanted to. I spotted the connection almost straight away."

"Why should I?" she asked politely. "I've done nothing wrong. I'm not ashamed of my name. It's my life that's changed. Not me. Besides, if I had changed it and someone," she paused, letting the significance of what she was saying sink in. "Had recognized me, the inference would be that I had something to hide. All I wanted was to disappear and not have to keep explaining myself. There is a difference. All the choices were mine. Besides, it's unlikely that anyone on Maud Frierley would know me or make the connection, it would only be someone who moved in the same circles I once did."

"Mmm, I know," he said, turning the car into the crawling traffic leading from Camberwell to Kennington. "I made some enquiries. I know George Kinkaid ..."

She turned to face him, her eyes wide with horror. "You didn't tell him, did you?"

"Don't be silly. Anyway, I thought you just said it didn't concern you?"

"I said it was easier if no one recognized me without having to lie about who I was. No one asks me, so I don't have to lie. Of course I'm concerned. I don't want my privacy invaded ever again. I don't know you terribly well, but I hope you don't feel it necessary to tell anyone at the hospital, but then I can't stop you if you want to."

"Good heavens, no. I won't say anything. Besides, I want you on my side, not running a mile."

"Your side?"

"Uh huh. Tell me something. Why did you take this job? Why not something more, well, upmarket?"

Serena sighed. "So easy for you to say that. Who would give me a job where the gossip wouldn't have been dreadful? Besides, I have no real qualifications, I can't work five days a week all day because of the children, but I had to start somewhere. Anyway, I don't think the job is a bad one, just hopelessly paid."

"And how long do you plan to do it?"

"Well, funny you should say that," she said. "I really will have to get something else — it's finding something that isn't full-time."

"What about four mornings and one full day? Thing is," he said, acknowledging a bus driver who had let him in. "I run a private practice just off Harley Street, dealing in nutrition and digestive problems, and I need a good receptionist. Someone who's discreet and has some experience of medical life. I need someone who looks good, conducts herself well and isn't fazed by difficult patients — the rich ones are the trickiest — and is used to dealing with them. Good money too," he added, mentioning a sum that was three times her salary at St Wilhemina's. "Thought you might consider it."

Chapter Sixteen

Alice didn't so much move around the table as drift. A gentle touch on the arm here, a hand lingering just a fraction too long on a shoulder there. Sometimes she bent to whisper something in an ear, a shared private moment that had the recipient laughing appreciatively up into her face.

She looked like what she was; an artist. Serena knew from conversations with Alex that Alice, who was thirty-six, had lived for ten years with a fellow artist until three years before when she had met Alex, and had no children of her own but adored his two. Her russet curly hair fanned out in a halo of frizzy curls, the front of which was restrained into thin little plaits holding her hair back from a face that reminded Sarah of a silent-movie queen with its pencilled-in eyebrows, and hooded lids over startlingly blue eyes.

Alice was stunning to look at but after less than an hour in her company Serena decided she was also tiresome. Then she felt terrible because she wasn't at all sure if this impatience with a woman she had barely met was rooted in the fact that Alex was tied to her. After a moment or two reflecting on this, noting the trailing chiffon sleeves of Alice's deeply feminine dress catch on Alex's hand as she consulted him on a small domestic matter which concerned just the two of them, she decided it was an unbiased view. After all, she didn't want Alex for herself, not at all. For a brief absurd moment Serena had thought Alex was attracted to her, and what troubled her now was that if he was, what did that say about her if someone as affected as Alice had become his partner? She wondered gloomily what his ex-wife was like.

Three other couples, the director of an art gallery whose wife, a designer, was abroad, and Serena made up the rest. If they knew her history — and she was convinced they did by the way they hastily looked away if she happened to glance in their direction — they were too polite to mention it.

Alex introduced her as someone he had met through his work, which was perfectly true, if a little misleading. She was, however, grateful that he hadn't been too specific even though she knew his professional interest in Harry precluded revealing it. For herself she didn't mind what they knew about her, or indeed thought, she was beyond such concerns. In any case it was a bit late now, having occupied column inches and television footage for so long, to expect no recall of her face or her story. These days anyone who asked a question that was too intrusive was deflected politely, but so pleasantly, that few left her company aware they had been firmly diverted from getting an answer to their question.

It wasn't just her present circumstances that made it second nature to her to encourage people to talk about themselves, but a legacy of both Margot — who had instilled into her from childhood that socially it was her duty to make other people feel interesting — and marriage to Stephen, when she had endeared herself to his friends and colleagues by making them feel what they had to say was of enormous importance. Somehow with Alice she couldn't find it in her to encourage such a notion, nor did it seem at all necessary.

As she listened to the art gallery owner bemoan the lack of subsidies offered by this philistine of a government, she noticed Alex keeping a protective eye on her and felt touched by his concern. When the opportunity presented itself, she smiled across at him to let him see she was fine.

The weather had held, so they moved into the garden from the conservatory where she had sat with Alex on that memorable Saturday and from where they were gathered for drinks as soon as Alice cried gaily: "Well, not exactly Ambrosial, but you will forgive — long day, more thrown together than prepared, I'm afraid."

Alex sat at one end of the glass-topped cane table, Alice — when she sat at all — at the other.

"Serena, do sit here, next to Gordon, and Tricia, here next to Alex." Alice went on in this way until everyone was seated, Serena at the opposite end of the table to Alex and between two male guests who seemed to be as amused by their hostess as Serena was unsettled.

Alice reminded her of Malcolm Brisley Jones's young second wife who thrived on the power that being Malcolm's wife brought her. All these people appeared to be friends of Alex's rather than hers. Two at least had been in his life since Cambridge and knew his first wife, the other was head of a private health group where Alex was a consultant. None of this fazed Alice who encouraged an intimacy with all of them based on what appeared to be solely a shared affection for Alex. Serena found it hard to equate this frivolous woman with the paintings of hers that she had seen in Alex's study. Elaborate swathes of fearless colour had nothing to do with this dippy display of helpless femininity.

Discreet lighting threw a subtle glow across the small terrace, glass globes protected candles from the occasional warm gust of wind scented with the sweet smell of mimosa and jasmine. Bleached wicker chairs with blue and green cushions lined each side of the long table over which a matching canopy deflected the curiosity of night moths. It reminded Serena of Paula's, on a less magnificent scale. So much for "informal", she noted, taking in the gold necklace and jangle of bangles of one, the midnight-blue silk strapless gown of another and the shocking pink silk bustier and black satin skirt of the third. I wonder, she thought ruefully, what they select when black tie is required.

Throughout dinner, they were constantly being called on to reassure Alice that the meal was delicious. First she invited them, with a small frown, to consider if they didn't think she had not put *quite* enough teriyaki sauce in the vegetables which accompanied the roast salmon, and later, would the pecan streusel cheesecake have benefited from less cream? All this drew a chorus of protest from everyone, Serena dutifully joining in, since the meal was perfect.

There was a vagueness about Alice that was at first quite amusing but after a while appeared horribly contrived. A ripple of laughter greeted most of her anecdotes, all of which seemed designed to reinforce the view that her charm arose from a natural unworldliness that age and success had not dimmed.

"Got frightfully lost on the tube." She gave a peal of laughter which made everyone look in her direction. "I thought that blue line was going to take me all the way to Earl's Court but it turned out to be a smudge of paint on that map thingy next to where you buy, you know," she flapped her fingers across her mouth in a little helpless gesture. "You know, *tickets*, that's it. But it was all right because this awfully sweet little man who said he was from Romania was lost too, so we joined forces … Oh dear, what have I said? Why are you all laughing?"

Alex smiled indulgently. Serena hoped her smile hid her wish that the Romanian had lost Alice completely. Later when the conversation, mostly of people and times of which she had no knowledge, left her feeling stifled, she was ashamed to realize that what she missed was being amused, made to laugh, by the very people whom Alex's friends could only discuss. She didn't want to speculate on the private lives of a clutch of household names whose wives she knew and some of whom she had liked. Nor did she want to be so forcibly reminded of the life she no longer inhabited by people who exaggerated their knowledge of it. On balance she thought she preferred Cheryl Tosney's unabashed curiosity.

"D'yer know him?" Cheryl would ask, flicking through the pages of *Hello!* showing Paula inviting its readers into her country retreat and putting paid to those ridiculous rumours about her marriage. "Gawd, what's he see in her?"

Tempted though she was, Serena would smile and say: "Not really, but they've been together a long time. Cheryl, I meant to ask you, have the dustmen changed their day for collecting?" And the moment would pass.

The evening was winding down, the conversation at the other end of the table slightly drunk. Alice's hair had come loose from the little plaits that held her tossed red hair in place. Her face was flushed. So too were the other women who must, Serena decided, be regretting the constricting dresses and jewellery on such a warm night.

The man next to her, whose wife was abroad, and who had been content to describe his entire career to Serena for the past hour, recalled his duty to a fellow guest and said, "Alex says you're a volunteer at St Wilhemina's."

Serena took a sip of coffee, glancing in surprise at Alex who knew she was not. "Actually I work there. I help on the geriatric ward. Really it isn't that interesting. Anyway, I've just accepted another job, so I'm looking forward to that."

"A new job, Serena?" Alex's voice came down the table. "When did this happen?"

Alice glanced quickly from one to the other. "How exciting," she said. "Do tell all, Serena. No, wait, I must sit down. I don't want to miss a word."

"Oh please," Serena said quickly. "Too boring for everyone. Nothing special."

"Nonsense." Alex rose to his feet, holding his wine glass, and came to perch on a low stone wall just behind her chair so that she had to swivel round to face him, her knees just inches from his. "It's wonderful news. I know you disliked the job you were doing."

Serena paused. Disliked? No, she had never disliked it. All kinds of things had left her feeling frustrated and angry at a system that could push frail and dependent women like Edith back to a home where they would have even less support, but not dislike. Robert had told her about Edith in the car going home.

"She won't be back," he had revealed. "They need the bed. Besides, it's my fault."

"Yours?" Serena repeated, startled.

"Mmm. I shouldn't have taken such good care of her. She's improved more than they thought which means she can't stay."

"That's dreadful," Serena protested. "Poor Edith. She has no one, just some ghastly daughter-in-law who only lives three streets away and never comes to see her."

"Well, now she'll have to, won't she?" he said brusquely. "Probably done Edith a good turn in the end. Now, what about this job?"

The money was good, too good to ignore. She couldn't ignore it. Harry and Louise needed a better life.

"Just give me enough time to sort out how I'm going to organise my children," she said. "And of course tell Sister Burton."

"Oh, no need to tell her," he yelped in fright. "I'll still have to face her after stealing one of her staff."

Serena smiled briefly. "Believe me, she won't mind. I'm not her favourite person."

He gave her an odd look. "You know, it might seem that way to you, but has it ever occurred to you that it isn't that she dislikes you? No, I can see it hasn't. I think — know, in fact — her problem with you, which is why I noticed you before I knew who you were, is that you look and often sound like you should be running the ward, not her. She's simply frightened of you and the way you get things done without being told."

Serena laughed nearly all the way home at the very idea. In many ways it had been her salvation and she was grateful for that. But dislike her job? Oddly enough, no.

"So? Tell me?" Alex said encouragingly, squeezing her hand.

It was a warm, friendly gesture, but at that precise moment, with Alice gazing intently at them, a fraction too disturbing for her comfort. "Nothing much to tell," she assured him, sliding her hand from under his. "One of the consultants wants me to work for him at his practice in Harley Street. Running the office, overseeing patients, that kind of thing."

"But that's wonderful," he enthused. "Why didn't you tell me?"

All eyes were on them. Everyone except Alice's were waiting expectantly for further enlightenment. Hers were watchful.

"Well, I only heard this afternoon and I was seeing you — I mean both of you —" she glanced up at Alice who was standing behind one of her guests on the other side of the table, taking in this exchange. "This evening."

Serena felt a stab of annoyance that she had been forced to justify herself to someone who had no rights over her at all, even more that she had to include a woman she barely knew to protect her from a non-existent threat.

"I still have to work out the details; I mean the children have to be catered for. It isn't absolutely settled."

He was still sitting near to her even though she had clearly come to the end of the explanation. "I'll keep you posted," she promised. To her relief there was a ring at the doorbell.

"That'll be my cab," she said, rising quickly. "Alice, that was a wonderful evening. Thank you both so much."

Alex rose to his feet. "I'll see you out."

"Me too," said Alice, pushing the coffee jug into the hands of the nearest rather startled guest. She walked quickly round the table after Alex and Serena. It was only when she was halfway home that Serena realized that Alice had not so much drifted but run after them.

*

Cheryl said she rather liked the idea of working a few more hours. "Just the one full day, is it?"

"All the other days he has hospital rounds, surgery, that kind of thing. The point is, Cheryl, I won't need to ask you to do it right through the holidays because they'll be going to my mother-in-law in Italy for a bit and my mother is going to stay for a couple of weeks and he's said I can take the two weeks before they go back to school as holiday. I think he'll be away."

Cheryl waved all this aside. "No sweat." She shook her head. "Let's all aim for September and then I can get myself sorted out. Here," she giggled. "Do us all a bit of good, you working for someone who understands diets. That one I did from that magazine was useless. Didn't lose an ounce."

"Well, actually, I think he deals more with balanced diets for people with health problems," Serena explained as tactfully as she could. "And besides," she added manfully. "You don't need to diet, Cheryl. You're in very good shape."

Cheryl beamed. "Think so?" She twisted round to look at her backside in the mirror. "Could do with an inch or two off here," she said slapping her bottom. "But it could be worse. Do you diet or anything, Serena?"

If she had the time there were plenty of things Serena would do but dieting was not one of them. However, she had found it easier to imply that her interest in the subjects closest to Cheryl's heart, all to be found in the pages of a weekly magazine, matched hers. After all, Cheryl meant well and she had been a godsend to Serena.

"No time. Eat on the run at the hospital. You must let me know your secrets sometime."

"Me? Secrets?" Cheryl chortled. "I should avoid cocoa. Right, let's say, soon as the holidays finish, we'll give it a whirl."

Stacey came round that evening with a bottle of wine to celebrate. "Wish it was me," she sighed. "But Barry wouldn't hear of me working in the West End. He likes me to be there when he gets in."

Serena said nothing. At first she'd tried to encourage her to stand up to the overbearing Barry, but knew it was useless. Stacey was in awe of him and, Serena suspected, frightened of him. Once he had been waiting outside when Stacey left Foster Street and had just stood silently on the pavement, holding the car door open. Briefly he jerked his head towards the front seat and Stacey had not even waved to Serena and Harry standing in the open front door.

"Well, let's see how I get on," Serena said, topping up their glasses. "Tell you what, on my first pay day we'll go out to celebrate."

"You're on," Stacey laughed. "Here." She reached into her bag and pulled out a book on computer games. "I found this for Harry. It was in that shop on the corner of the High Street. How's the lovely Louise?"

Serena just grimaced. "Sulking. She's not too thrilled about going to Lucca on Sunday, but Minnie says at this age they're easily diverted. At least she says Stephen —" She stopped, glancing quickly at Stacey.

"Take it easy," Stacey said. "Hey, Minnie's right. Fourteen isn't forever."

"I know, it just seems like it," Serena replied. She leaned back in her chair. "By the way," she said, her eyes closed. "If you find out where Edith is, let me know, will you?"

*

The Carlyle Clinic where Robert Merrow had his practice was just off Harley Street in a tall red-brick house with a brass plate next to an important-looking brass knocker on a black panelled door. The clinic occupied the whole of the ground floor, a calm oasis of pastel colours, plush carpets and fresh flowers. A long, wide, carpeted corridor ran the length of the house with rooms leading off from one side.

At the front, in a room overlooking the street, thick grey carpets, pink and blue armchairs with plump cushions and deep seats were arranged in small groups around low tables with English, French and American glossy fashion magazines fanned out around bowls of roses. Here patients waited for their turn to see Robert Merrow. His room was an even larger version of the waiting room without the number of armchairs. Ice-pink shot-silk curtains were pinned in swooping loops across the windows, pulled back with gold tassels curled around brass claw-shaped hinges.

Robert Merrow did not sit behind a desk to talk to his clients. He invited them with a graceful gesture of his hand to sit on one of the two well-upholstered velvet sofas placed opposite each other either side of an Adam fireplace. Robert would sit next to them on whichever one his client chose.

The reception area where Serena was to work reeked of luxury and reminded her of a discreet but fashionable hotel rather than the first stop in a medical establishment. This did not surprise her. None of it did. She had just forgotten how absurd it all was. George Kincaid's consulting rooms were built on similar lines, but the state-of-the-art technology at the Carlyle Clinic, built into blond, limewashed surrounds with concealed lighting, made her blink. Robert Merrow assured her she would be used to it in a day and left it to his secretary to show Serena what to do.

His staff, including Serena, numbered four people. Two nurses, one who worked in the dispensary and the other whose prime function seemed to be to shuttle patients from the waiting room to Robert Merrow's office. A part-time secretary who dealt with his correspondence announced herself as Jill. She eyed Serena critically and just rolled her eyes when she heard she had never come into contact with a computer on this scale, let alone felt equipped to operate one.

"Never mind." She sounded resigned. "You'll learn. It's hardly NASA." Serena's job was to keep the patients happy, make and confirm appointments, keep track of their notes and to make sure that at the end of each morning Robert had updated the files on his computer.

"And play agony aunt to the ones who don't think their treatment is working and keep them from nagging Robert. He hates it."

"Goodness." Serena opened her eyes wide in surprise. "I'll do my best.

Poor things. It must be so frustrating if their treatment is lengthy."

Jill raised an eyebrow and looked amused. "Yes, well. C'mon, first patients will be here in half an hour. Now you turn the whole system on here, OK?"

It was also Serena's job to despatch samples to various laboratories in the area for testing, which puzzled her since there was a fully equipped, if small, lab on the premises.

"All the samples go to labs for testing. Nothing's done here," explained Jill, when Serena queried this. "Suits me. I only want to work part time and that would mean more work. Bit like you, really. Besides," she lowered her voice, glancing quickly across the hall in case Robert appeared. "It's all for show, keeps the patients happy if they see test-tubes all over the shop."

It took Serena less than a day to realize two things. The first she could deal with, which was that she would be bored witless with so little to do and with such patients to deal with. Her second concern and the one that disturbed her were the patients themselves.

Poor things indeed. A parade of stick-thin women passed through the clinic each day with no evidence of any kind that their problem was any greater than a desire to remain that way. Robert Merrow appeared to agree. And not just thin women. Rotund businessmen who took their medication to the next expensive restaurant, sad middle-aged women fighting the effects of gravity, and others who were so obese it was not Robert Merrow they needed with his pills and injections but a half-way decent doctor who would provide a very different kind of help. Serena wondered why no one had thought that anorexia might be the problem assailing one or two of them.

Her first sight of Cindy Moreton scared the life out of her. Cindy was quite beautiful, exquisitely made up, with green eyes and a sweep of blond hair falling over one shoulder.

"I need to see Robert again this week," she told Serena when she emerged from his consulting room. "I've got to go away on Friday. I'd like to see him Wednesday."

"Of course," Serena said, turning to tap into the computer. The girl was stunning and nervous. "I'm afraid Wednesday is rather full," she told her.

"Would Thursday be all right, he seems to have a free —"

"I said Wednesday, you idiot. If I'd wanted Thursday I'd have said so."

Serena waited for a moment, keeping her eyes on the screen, gritting her teeth. "If you'd like to wait a moment, I'll ask Mr Merrow if he can fit you in, but it looks very booked to me. Would you mind taking a seat in the waiting room and I'll find out."

It was then that Serena saw Cindy's wrists. Her bag had been resting on the counter. She turned to take it and the sleeves of her jacket fell back, revealing a skeletal arm that made her hand with its bony fingers appear too large to be part of such a limb.

"What's the matter? Why are you staring?" she demanded, pushing her sleeves over her hands.

"I'm sorry. I wasn't staring. I'll be with you in a minute." Instead of phoning through to Robert, Serena waited until he was free and then asked the nurse to hold the next patient for a couple of minutes.

"It's a girl called Cindy Moreton. She's rather agitated, wants to see you on Wednesday, but you're full."

"Oh, just be firm with her," he said easily, tapping in his notes from his last patient. "She's a spoilt brat."

Serena hesitated. Robert glanced up. "Anything else?"

"Well, only that she seems incredibly thin and … and as I said agitated. I just wonder if there might be something else wrong with her."

Robert put his pen down and surveyed her. "If there is, I'll soon find out. Now, be a good girl and just get the next patient sent in."

"Yes of course, only —"

He stopped her. "Serena," he said softly, "I am not Sister Burton. I never raise my voice, but neither do I repeat my instructions. Next patient, OK?"

She nodded. Cindy was waiting for her.

"Mr Merrow said he can only see you on Thursday, I'm afraid. Either that or perhaps you could wait until you come back from your trip?"

Cindy bit her lip, glaring at Serena.

"Oh fuck him. Fuck the lot of you," Cindy muttered, and stormed out.

It wasn't until she was due to go to lunch that Serena saw the dispensary open for the first time. Bridget, who wore a black cardigan over her white overall and a small disposable white cap perched on her overpermed grey hair, presided over the white-tiled room where patients duly reported after a session with Robert. Serena was left with no doubt about the nature of Robert's real business. Stacked on a table at the back of the room, just out of sight of the patients whose view through the hatch was restricted to lines of glass cabinets filled with apothecary jars, were rows of plastic containers filled with brightly coloured tablets, like Smarties without the chocolate. Mauve, green, white, yellow and some bright red ones were shovelled into plastic phials as each patient presented their new prescription.

"Oh my dear," Bridget crooned to a patient called Teri Courtney who looked vaguely familiar to Serena. "You're doing so well. A little slipback this week, but do stick to the diet. Delicious in many ways. Think chicken with a drizzle of lemon juice or limes. Have you thought of limes? Oh positively gourmet, sliced and added to smoked salmon. See you next week. Oh, Mr Conway. You have been naughty." She wagged a motherly finger at a plump man who could have been anything from thirty to fifty such was his size, who looked abashed but unrepentant at his failure to stick to the diet sheet he had been given.

"Never mind," Bridget comforted him. "Mr Merrow has increased the dose so you now take a white tablet before breakfast and lunch, and a green one before six. Not after, you don't want an uncomfortable night, now do you? Would you like me to repeat that? Right, one white …"

On the third morning, after a sleepless night, Serena waited until Jill walked into her small office just off the reception area and followed her in.

"I just wondered if any of the patients had genuine problems," she explained. Jill just laughed.

"Oh, don't worry, he knows what he's doing."

"It's not that," Serena said quietly, not wanting to alert the practice nurse standing in reception who was packing up urine samples for despatch to a laboratory. "It can't be right."

"Course it is," Jill said cheerfully, a pile of post wedged under her chin as she sorted through another bundle. "Perfectly legal."

"But look at this," Serena interrupted. "File after file marked GP not to be informed. How can that be right?"

Jill sighed. "Oh dear. Well, they're all over twenty-one and he doesn't just dole out pills. I mean he takes blood and urine tests and checks their blood pressure, they're quite safe."

"Dear God. Doesn't he understand this is just exacerbating the problem?" Serena whispered urgently.

Jill walked past her and closed the door to her small office and leaned against it. "Now listen to me," she said firmly, "Mr Merrow sees plenty of patients who aren't here just to lose weight."

"Not many," Serena retorted.

"Well, they're not as numerous as the other kind, I grant you. But there is nothing illegal about what's going on."

"No, I know that, but it's just that he's encouraging some damaged people who need help, not pills."

"You don't know what they need. You're not a doctor. Serena, I know what you're thinking, but believe me you're wasting your sympathy. Look at these people. Do you really think if Robert said, 'Go on a diet, exercise,' they would? Do you think if they could afford to have it sucked out or flattened out, they would be here? Course not. Look at Teri Courtney — surely you remember her? She had that song out, years ago, you know the one ..." Jill, giggling, began singing the words and the line-dance that had made Teri Courtney the heroine of the Costa Brava for a whole summer twenty years before with the one song she had only ever recorded.

Serena clapped her hand to her head. "I'd never have recognized her. What's she doing now — and here?"

"The now is that some lunatic has put it into her head that she should make a comeback and the here is that she is convinced that it's her weight that's stopping it. Try telling her that at nearly fifty it's her age, not her weight, that's the problem, and who do you think she'll believe? At least she can do something about her weight. Forget it. If it wasn't Robert it would be someone else. They know what they're doing, believe me."

"I wish I knew what I was doing," Serena muttered, walking back to reception. "Let alone them. Oh God, what a mess."

Chapter Seventeen

The afternoon wore on with the steady procession of those Serena had come to refer to as the usual suspects.

Brian Conway rolled in with a lascivious wink at Serena who studiously avoided his outstretched clammy hand. According to Jill he had enjoyed expense-account lunches for so long he was beginning to believe that his sales figures were diminishing in direct proportion to his expanding girth. All of which he thought could be reversed if he lost weight.

"Here," he said to Serena, brandishing a brochure in her face. "You should try this. Solo agency. Great place, but those babes like their guys to be a bit lean, know what I mean? You'd do well there. Come with me if you like."

"How kind," she murmured, hearing Jill choking behind her. "However, I have a partner," she lied. "He'd be a bit cross if I suddenly went, er ... solo."

Brian Conway chortled and waddled away to the dispensary. Jill rolled her eyes theatrically. "He tried to pull Cindy Moreton once," she giggled. "Can you imagine that celery stick with that tub of lard?"

"Pull Cindy Moreton?" Serena snapped. "He couldn't pull a hair from his head, revolting little man."

At five Madeleine Selway appeared, shyly presenting herself at reception. Serena's heart went out to the middle-aged woman who had confided in her that her husband was furious with her for gaining weight and now, on this hot summer afternoon, she looked ill and tired.

"The 'change' you see," she confessed, her cheeks going pink, moisture standing out on her upper lip. She dabbed at her forehead with a tissue. Serena glanced at her in alarm. She certainly looked faint.

"Let me get you some iced water." Serena moved around from reception and led Madeleine to a quiet, cool corner away from the waiting room and pressed her into a comfortable wicker chair before going to fetch the water. When she came back Madeleine was looking a little better and she sipped the water gratefully.

"Much better," she smiled, handing the glass back to Serena. Serena glanced quickly round to make sure no one was waiting to book in. Robert was ensconced with Brian Conway and that would take another ten minutes.

"Mrs Selway," she began. "This is nothing to do with me. But why are you doing this? You look fine to me — better than fine. You look a very normal weight. Do you honestly think this is doing you any good?"

It was a risk, but she couldn't let it continue. Madeleine closed her eyes briefly. Serena gave an inward sigh of relief. She hadn't told her to mind her own business or threatened to tell Robert.

"No. Probably not. But you see it's not as easy as you think."

To Serena's horror, large tears welled up in the older woman's eyes. "Mrs Selway, please, what is it? You mustn't cry." Serena took her hand and squeezed it.

"Sorry, dear, it's just that I blame myself. I let myself go, so easy bringing up the children, so busy, we forget, don't we, to look after ourselves — well, you've obviously been a great deal more sensible, haven't you?"

"That's not true," Serena contradicted her. "I'm like this because ... because all the women in my family have been built on lean lines."

"Lucky you. Even your mother?"

"Even my mother," Serena assured her, picturing the slender Margot who ate like an ox but equally walked her dogs for miles each day.

Madeleine sighed. "It's difficult for Colin when appearances count so much. And to be honest, I'm doing it for myself as well. I hate going to those dinners — well, not many now, I admit. I duck out of them. But only because I can't bear seeing all those other women looking so together."

"What? All of them?" Serena asked.

"Well, perhaps just the ones married to Colin's colleagues," she conceded ruefully. "Anyway, the good news is I've only got another pound or two to go and then I'll have reached my target and Robert says he'll put me on a maintenance plan. Now," she patted Serena's hand. "Let me just toddle off to the little girls' room and I'll be fine. Oh look, there's Robert waiting for me. I'll just be a moment." She smiled past Serena and gave a little flicker of her fingers to Dr Merrow who was looking curiously at the scene in front of him.

Serena rose hastily to her feet. "She was feeling a little faint," she explained, hoping the truth wasn't too evident.

"You should have fetched Jessie," he said, referring to his nurse. "That's her job. Send Mrs Selway in when she emerges, will you?"

After she had shown Madeleine into Robert's room, Serena walked slowly back to reception. What could Robert possibly have deduced from seeing her give water to a starving woman? And that's what it was. Colin Selway, eh? Ghastly little man. She remembered meeting him once, and the woman hanging off his arm had not been Madeleine.

All the way home, she wrestled with giving in her notice. The Carlyle Clinic was not for her. Unfortunately the money was. The sight of the bills plopping through the door no longer sent panic waves into the roof of her mouth, she was saving little by little for the down payment on a small car and the children had both had birthday presents that had even made Louise forget she was a cool dude and show signs of pleasure. Just until the end of the summer, she decided as she joined the crowd pushing its way towards the escalator. Then she would get something else to do.

*

It was odd coming home to an empty house. The children had left the day before to stay with Minnie in Lucca while Margot had hung on to her wits and humour just long enough to wave them off with a hug and a silent cheer before hastening to stay with her cousin, Isabel, where she lived in a remote village north of Inverary to recover.

Two weeks in charge of her grandchildren while Serena had been at work had cured Margot of any desire to have them live with her. Not Harry, of course. God knows whether that psychologist was helping, but he was still as timid as ever. Well, not perhaps timid, but not showing any sign of making friends. In her day they didn't have such things as psychologists. Wars were fought, scenes of carnage witnessed and loved ones lost without a counsellor on hand to deal with the fall-out. Poor Harry, she just hoped he wasn't made to feel a problem by being treated like one. Louise, she reflected with a grim smile, was quite the opposite. The stuff of nightmares, that one, and no mistake Stephen to a tee. Not that you could say that to Serena beyond remarking on physical similarities. But all the signs were there.

The vision of Serena's horror when she discovered the tattoo on Louise's thigh and the triumph on Louise's face who had deliberately — yes, deliberately, of that Margot was sure — let her rant before she confessed it was only a transfer, the rose in front of her. She suppressed a shudder. No. Louise was certainly not to be borne for more than short periods at a time. She didn't envy Jasmine the next two weeks one little bit.

Sitting in the comfort of the train speeding her north, four weeks in Scotland ahead of her, her eyes closed, half dozing, half just letting her mind wander, Margot realized that for the first time in months the awful fluttering feeling in her chest every time she left Serena and the children was no longer there. If Serena had not been displaying signs of moving on Margot would have felt less sanguine about leaving her. As it was, this new job, and the fact that she was going out just a little more, was enough to make her cautiously confident that Stephen did not dominate Serena's life in quite the same way. On the other hand, Alex Billington appeared to be playing a more significant role in her life than just Harry's therapist.

At least Serena's reliance on his judgement made it look that way. "Alex says" was quite a feature of her conversation. Admittedly nearly always in connection with the children, particularly Harry, but some very satisfactory relationships, Margot reflected, had started out with less. When she casually mentioned it, Serena had just raised an eyebrow at her and said he had been a great support to her.

As the train slowed and began to ease its way into York, Margot opened her eyes and looked out of the window. Jostling crowds pushed their way off the train, while new passengers boarded, heaving suitcases and bags in front of them, searching for somewhere to sit. Margot settled herself contentedly back into her seat and rummaged in her bag for her book. Now where had she got up to? She found her place and started to read. Bliss. After a moment she lifted her eyes from the page and gazed thoughtfully at the huddle of houses and buildings as the old city gave way to open fields and distant rolling meadows, the train gathering speed on the next leg of its journey. Who knows, she sighed, resting her book on her lap, who knows what will happen next?

*

Serena threw her bag on the kitchen table with the post she had just scooped off the mat, eased her shoes off and flicked the switch on the kettle. Yawning, she reached over to the answer machine. There were two messages. Her mother to say she had arrived safely with Isabel and the second from Alex saying he would call later.

She frowned as the machine whirred back to the start, pleased that Margot was not around to hear it and jump to annoying conclusions. The post was routine. A card from Melanie in the Loire Valley, a letter from Andrew Beresford inviting her to the annual summer garden party that his company threw. She wouldn't go. But it was nice of him to ask. She tossed them into a small wicker basket to one side, and sifted quickly through the rest of the post. Bills, circulars, nothing of interest. There never was, but she never stopped hoping.

The sun was still hard up against the back wall of the house. Serena unlocked the kitchen door and took her coffee outside to sit in one of the canvas chairs, safe in the knowledge that the Plaxtons had gone to Benidorm, taking the dreadful Bradley with them. Cautiously she peered over the wall for signs of Sovereign. It wouldn't be beyond Betty to leave him in the garden relying on a friend or neighbour to feed him. But there was no sign of him.

She breathed out and settled herself in the canvas chair, swinging her bare legs on to the low table. She lifted her face to the sun and contemplated a day in which a middle-aged woman had broken down in tears because she wasn't losing weight fast enough, and the wearing scene with Cindy who had arrived back from a modelling assignment demanding to see Robert instantly. In the midst of this reflection, the heat, the journey on a packed tube and a crowded bus all had their inevitable effect, and she drifted off to sleep while the sun crept over the roof.

The distant rap of the door knocker roused her from a muddled dream in which Robert Merrow was giving her a lift to the DSS where Melanie was waiting, wearing a fur coat and holding Harry's hand. All of them were trying to cross the road which was empty, but for reasons she understood in her dream, none of them could do it.

She stumbled from her chair at the insistent knocking and ran barefoot to the front door.

"Stacey," she exclaimed, pushing her hair out of her eyes. "I dozed off in the garden. And to think I tease my mother for the very same thing. Lovely to see —" she halted. "Stacey? What's wrong? Stacey, tell me, what is it?"

Reaching out she pulled the weeping girl into the hall and closed the door. Stacey sank against the wall, tears pouring down her face. Serena grabbed hold of her, trying to support her, half lifting, half carrying her into the sitting room. A livid bruise was beginning to make its presence known just under Stacey's chin and her shirt was torn where a button was missing. Serena didn't have to be told. That bloody man she was living with.

"Don't move," she ordered and ran back to the kitchen. Armed with a basin of water and pulling a bottle of witch hazel and some cotton wool from the cupboard, she rejoined Stacey who was crouched on the floor next to the sofa, her head buried in the cushions.

"What did he do?" Serena asked, abruptly pulling the remains of a bottle of brandy from the cupboard and pouring some into a glass. "Here, drink this. Go on."

"Oh Christ, Serena." Stacey choked as the brandy hit the back of her throat. "I said I wanted to go back to my parents for a bit. Just to think, you know, and he went berserk. It was my fault. I shouldn't have sprung it on him ..."

"Oh for God's sake," Serena muttered, soaking some cotton wool with witch hazel. "Stacey, my poor girl, you don't thump someone because they've taken you by surprise unless they're burgling your home. Sit still, this will help."

Stacey winced as Serena leaned over her and pressed the cold lotion against her bruised face. "I mean, he's thirty, not three."

It was hopeless. Stacey just wept, clutching the damp pad to her sore face, reproaching herself for her clumsiness until Serena could bear it no longer.

"Stacey," she gently admonished her. "I'm not doing you any favours if I agree with you. He's a pig. No man should hit a woman. Ever. Where is he?" She rose to her feet. "I'll speak to him."

Stacey tried to get up, her face a mask of horror, reaching out to grab Serena's arm. "No. Please. No. Promise me. *Promise me*, you won't?"

"How can I?" Serena demanded. "You're in a terrible state. You can't go back there. He'll do it again. You know he will. Stacey," she dropped to her knees in front of her. "Stay here," she urged. "Just for a few days, the children are away. It won't be any trouble."

Stacey closed her eyes, still weeping softly, and shook her head. Even as she gazed helplessly at her, Serena knew she was wasting her breath.

An hour later she watched Stacey, calmer, but still visibly distressed, turn her car in a three-point turn in the narrow road and roar away. Back to the man who needed her more than she needed him but had tampered so successfully with the scales of responsibility that an innocent woman would be begging him to forgive her.

Afterwards she knew that if Stacey had not left her feeling so frustrated and angry she would probably not have agreed to supper with Alex. But she did.

"You need someone to talk to," he sympathized. "A bit of one-to-one for yourself. I'll pick you up in half an hour. Don't argue." And then he added after a short pause, "Please?"

*

They went to an Italian restaurant in Fulham where Alex was obviously a favoured client. At first she thought the owners might jump to the same conclusions as her mother, and she asked Alex quite clearly how Alice was so that he would know she was regarding this meeting as a mercy mission on his part and that the owners — should they be familiar with Alice —

would know that she knew about her and it was all above board.

By the time they handed her a menu she felt mugged with effort and not at all certain it had been necessary. Alex studied the menu. "I think," he said, not lifting his eyes from the task. "You'll find the oysters particularly good. And Alice is fine. On a course at the moment. Sent her love."

"How kind." She smiled back and began to study the menu. "Yes, the oysters sound wonderful."

"Good." He handed the menu back to a hovering waiter and ordered for both of them, including an excellent wine. And Alice knew. It made her feel comfortable, while the thought of Alice did not.

"And now," Alex turned back to her. "Tell me about Stacey and why you're feeling so involved."

"Not so much involved as rather helpless at helping. You're so wonderful like that, so skilled that I've learned not to offer advice as glibly as I might once have done."

He disclaimed but she refused to accept it. It had all been so long since she had been entertained in a half way decent restaurant and this was more, much more than halfway, she felt almost euphoric and something of the woman she had once been began to surface.

She made him laugh, teased him and debated the merits of Jung over Freud with enough credibility to engage his interest and in turn told him, with a groan, about the dilemma she faced each day with Robert Merrow and Louise's latest attempt to paralyse her good intentions to be a tolerant mother. By the time they left to go home, Serena felt so relaxed she had forgotten her initial qualms, delighted that they shared so many views on so many things which had nothing to do with Stacey.

Outside Foster Street he got out and came round to open the door for her. "Do come in for a moment," she suggested warmly. "I'm sure I can manage to make you coffee after that wonderful meal."

Alex glanced at his watch. "Why not?" he smiled, following her in. "As a matter of fact I wanted to ask you something." She looked sharply at him in surprise.

"About Harry," he explained.

"Harry?" She paused with her key in the lock. "Is he all right?"

"Fine," he soothed. "I was thinking about suggesting someone else he might see instead of me."

Her heart sank. More change. "Of course," she said. "Let me get the coffee and you can tell me why."

When she returned he was sitting on the sofa, legs crossed, one arm stretched along the back. "Let me," he offered, rising to take the tray from her. She sat at the other end of the sofa and poured his coffee.

"And why do you want to change Harry to someone else?" she asked handing him the cup.

"Two reasons. One, I think he has moved on sufficiently to join a colleague of mine. I hadn't planned to suggest it just yet, it's earlier than I would ideally like. But I think it's best. Wonderful girl, Pauline Somers. Harry's a great kid and I think he has made real progress. What I would like him to do now is to join a small group of children who paint. He loves it, I think he must take after his grandmother."

"Painting?"

"Uh-huh." He reached over and placed his cup on the small table. "Harry's interests are not, I think, perhaps those that you and Stephen envisaged for him. He finds expression in other ways."

Serena remembered Jasmine saying Harry had a good, unusually good, eye for colour.

"Well, fine," she smiled. "You frightened me for a moment. I thought you meant he had real problems. No, that's good. I'm delighted. But he will still see you, won't he?"

He leaned forward, his elbows on his knees, his hands clasped. "Not in that way. No. I think," he spoke slowly, carefully. "I'm not the best person for him any more."

"Oh rubbish," she cried, putting her own cup down. "You've been wonderful. Harry goes to school now so much more easily. He couldn't have done that without you."

"Thank you, but I don't think you understand."

"Understand what?"

He looked sideways at her. The room felt very still. "Understand what?" she repeated.

"Understand that I cannot treat a child when I'm interested almost — no," he gave a light laugh. "Much more interested than is good for me, in his mother."

"Oh God, I'm sorry, Alex. I knew I shouldn't have burdened you with all that stuff about Stacey, all my problems." Even as she said it she knew she was making one last attempt to stop him saying what she knew she couldn't prevent.

"Stop it, Serena," he said abruptly. "You know perfectly well what I mean. You've known for a long time. Don't say you haven't. I don't feel safe around you any more. I'm not sure I ever did."

She looked down at her hands, the slim band of gold, the unvarnished nails, and frowned.

"Why didn't you tell me this in the restaurant?" she asked, not understanding why hearing — Alex was so right — what she had known for so long had now caught her unawares.

"Because I thought I could do it," he told her with a rueful smile. "I thought I could cheat fate by not telling you. But the need to tell you defeated me. Once you know something, if you're one-dimensional — as I am where my feelings are concerned — I feel the weight of it and I feel the relationship is unfair. I'm not a complex character at all. Nothing so interesting. I'm sorry, Serena, this is hell for you."

"No. No." She closed her eyes briefly. "Not hell. How could it be hell to be told by someone like you that they're attracted to you? The hell is what it alters, not the feelings."

He laughed. "Goodness, I feel very threatened. You're a psychologist at heart. And need it be hell?" He couldn't keep the hope from his voice.

"Possibly not. You're right," she sighed. "I thought I was ready for this moment, but I'm not. Odd that. Reality is much clumsier, isn't it? No fluent, elegant speeches. No clever rationalizing. No answers that will make any sense."

He hadn't asked her how she felt, whether she felt as drawn to him. He just let her talk, not taking his eyes from her face. Not attempting to touch her. Somewhere in the flattering shield he had thrown around her, she felt locked in rather than protected. But she also knew that it was a long time since she had felt emotionally aroused. And she loved the feeling. She felt suspended from judgement and conscience, removed from making a decision she knew was right but didn't want to make.

When he moved to sit beside her, she didn't stop him. Nor when he leaned forward and looked at her for a long moment before kissing her very gently. She felt a small explosion of shock at an intimacy she had not known for so long and, without thinking, she clung to it.

He pushed her carefully backwards, his hand sliding her skirt towards her hips, and she shut her eyes and let him, feeling his body ease over her to cover her own, propelling her gently down into a swirling dark well that almost disabled her senses, but not her mind.

"Alice." She began to push him away. "Alice," she reminded him breathlessly as his mouth slid down her neck. "Alice has to be considered. And," she added slightly more urgently, "and Stephen. You've forgotten. I'm married. There's Stephen."

"I haven't forgotten about him," he whispered, lifting his head, trying not to see the panic that now filled her eyes. "I just want *you* to."

"I can't," she whispered back. "I can't do this. Not yet. No, please, I mean it. Forgive me."

She struggled to sit up, pushing him away, straightening her dress that was half off. She couldn't look at him.

"Please don't feel bad about this," she mumbled, grabbing at stray strands of hair, attempting to pin them back. "My fault entirely. Not yours."

He said nothing, just leaned back, one hand covering his eyes, the other stretched along the back of the sofa.

"No," he said wearily. "My fault. I was dishonest with everyone. Alice, you, myself. I told you I was one-dimensional." He smiled briefly. "The trouble is, falling in love at my age hurts twice as much because it's twice as hopeless. We don't come uncluttered, do we? And you're right," he reached out and caught her hand. "It's what it alters that's the real damage."

Chapter Eighteen

As a grey early morning light began to signal the end of a very long night, Serena rose and made herself a cup of tea. Foster Street was silent, curtains tightly drawn. It was just after five. She pulled the blind up in her kitchen and stared out at the still garden. A cat making his balletic way along the dividing fence between Serena and the Plaxtons, returning from his nightly trawl through the gardens and dustbins of more interesting houses than his own, froze as Serena appeared in the window and nose-dived in one athletic movement into the scrub that was the Plaxtons' kingdom.

The effect I have on everyone, she grimaced, turning away.

What had she started? What a fool. Why, when she was beginning to make sense of life, did she have to plunge it back into chaos? Later as she hung on to a strap on the tube taking her to work, hollow-eyed from lack of sleep, Serena winced at her own behaviour.

Alex had left shortly afterwards, calmly insisting that his was the blame for rushing her. She had been vulnerable, while he had been — was — too besotted to think clearly. She had of course protested, but in vain. He seemed determined to shield her from her own behaviour.

And what behaviour, she grimaced. Her conscience struggled against sense. One moment agreeing with him, the next feeling utterly cowardly that she had taken refuge in such chivalry. Of course he wasn't entirely responsible for what had happened. Her own conduct did not bear close examination. At her age, to behave as though the crown jewels were at stake was absurd. Sex was sex, surely to God? It did not commit you to anything. But even as she said it, she knew she didn't believe it. At her age too, she thought bitterly, to behave like a stupid teenager, ignoring the consequences of the signals she had been throwing out.

"No, not signals, bloody great explosive charges," she muttered.

She had not charmed him, she had flirted. Convincing herself she was simply being the perfect guest, she had instead confused a man who she knew, *absolutely* knew, wanted little encouragement to see if his feelings were returned. If she had been anywhere else but on the packed Northern Line heading for Goodge Street, hanging on to a strap that swayed and jolted, she would have buried her face in her hands with shame. A declaration, an acknowledgement that she was desirable, had been her subconscious goal. And even that, she thought grimly, had not been buried that deep. It was a test of her power and Alex had been the experiment to prove she could still arouse such strong passions.

This in itself was odd. Stephen had been a considerate lover, even at times a passionate one, but not since those early days, when the mere sight of him reduced her to a storm of emotions that could not rationally be called love, had she been disturbed by anything more ardent than simply knowing, quietly, uneventfully, that she was loved. And she had been, hadn't she? Was still, wasn't she?

In this miserable and self-flagellating mood which part of her knew was nonsense, but the other part, the part that wanted to be punished for her stupidity, triumphing, she arrived at the door of the Carlyle Clinic. Jill was already there, bustling between Robert's office and her own cubby hole off the reception area.

"Oh dear, bad night?" She paused, registering Serena's unmade-up face and hollow eyes.

"Mm." Serena pulled a face. "Something I ate, I think. Much better now. Anything special today?"

Easily deflected, Jill shook her head. "Oh, yes, nearly forgot. Stacey rang you about ten minutes ago and Alex Billington just before you walked in."

Serena's stomach crunched. She would have to call him sometime. There was Harry to consider. Armed with a strong black coffee, she activated the answer machine for overnight cancellations and messages. Among those were the familiar voices of Cindy Moreton and Teri Courtney who both needed urgent appointments and a slightly more hesitant one from Madeleine Selway who asked if Serena could ring her back.

227

There was just time to slap on some mascara, slick a lipgloss over her mouth and call Stacey.

"It's fine," Stacey said brightly. Too brightly. She raced on. "Barry's really sorry and I am too … no, listen … for dragging you into it. I can see what it looked like. But he really is going to make an effort and I'm going to delay seeing my folks until September so that we can have some real time putting all this behind us. Hey, listen, must go. Your friend Edith, by the way, is now in a home in Sussex. There's a letter here for you. I think it's from her. I'll drop it round if you like."

"Edith? Heavens. She must have got someone to write it. Fine. Come straight from work, I need an early night."

There was a pause. "Well, not tonight if you don't mind, Serena, I promised Barry I'd cook a special meal … you know."

"Of course," Serena said. "Listen, drop it in the post, I'll get it in the morning. Fine. Promise. Talk soon."

Then she checked Madeleine's number and called her.

"Thank you, my dear." Madeleine's voice sounded tired. "I'm just calling to cancel my appointment. Actually all of them."

Serena gave a start of pleasure. "Oh I'm so glad," she spoke quietly. "I'm sure it's for the best."

Madeleine's weary voice interrupted. "No, you don't understand. It's just that …" Her voice broke. Serena strained to hear her.

"Mrs Selway … Madeleine … what's wrong? Are you all right?"

"I will be. It's just that Colin told me he wants a divorce. Last night." She gave a brittle laugh. "Just when I'd reached my target weight as well."

Serena's eyes widened in dismay. "Oh, Madeleine. I'm so sorry. Is there anything I can do? Have you got someone with you?"

"Yes, yes, my daughter. She's on her way. Going to see her father first at the office, but it won't do any good."

Jill whistled softly when Serena told her. "Well, what do you know. The strange thing is," Jill pointed out, "that if she'd walked out on him years ago she wouldn't have looked so dreadful. She'll bloom now. I know I did when my ex told me. Bombshell, it was. Never expected it. You don't, do you?"

She stopped, looking awkwardly at Serena. "Oh, you know what I mean, don't you?"

Serena just nodded. She understood what shock did to your weight, but she didn't understand about blooming. But then she hadn't been unhappily married, just living in fantasy land.

Robert Merrow simply shrugged when Serena told him what had happened. "Now she'll lose weight anyway," he remarked casually.

"You mean because of the shock?"

"Mmm. Odd that, isn't it? All he had to do to get her to shape up was leave her. Could have saved him a fortune too."

A small ripple of disgust went through her. Quietly she picked up the files from his desk from the first patient and left him.

"Serena," he called after her. "Meant to say ... good a moment as any. It's not a wonderful idea to get personally involved with any of the patients. I thought you knew that."

She stopped and turned back. "Personally involved?" she asked politely. Dear God, had Madeleine said something after all? "I'm afraid I don't know what you mean."

He raised an eyebrow. "No? I thought you might have guessed. Brian Conway. Says you're ..." he glanced down at his notes "— a right 'go-er'. None of my business, but it's sensible, however unintentionally, not to give out the wrong signals, especially to male clients."

Serena walked back and leaned across his desk.

"Robert," she spoke icily and directly into his face, "I would rather go out with a man wearing a frock and clutching an axe than walk to the end of the street with a man like Brian Conway. In fact, almost any man who comes into this building. Have I made myself clear?"

Robert Merrow narrowed his eyes and looked at her, his head on one side. "Perfectly, my dear. And have I?"

Their eyes locked. She was about to ask if he understood integrity, but then the bills and the children flashed into her head.

"As crystal," she said with studied courtesy. "Is there anything else?"

He shook his head, already immersed in a report she had handed him.

At lunchtime she walked up to Regent's Park and sat on the grass hugging her knees. Then she folded her jacket into a makeshift pillow and stretched out. The sun beat down, making her drowsy. She'd had no sleep that she could recall, and a tiresome morning. Phoning Alex hung over her and she knew that if she got that out of the way she would feel better. What stopped her was not knowing how he would react. It filled her with dread. So badly had she turned out as a judge of human behaviour, who was she to even hazard a guess at how he would respond? And Alice. There her conscience was clear. She at least had reminded him about his loyalty to Alice. And then a thought struck her. Not once had she asked him about his feelings for Alice until the moment when she had stopped him, and not once had he referred to them.

Or Stephen. His existence had been ignored. She rolled over on to her side, curled tightly into herself. No, not ignored. Just forgotten. Just for a perfectly human moment.

*

By the time she had allowed Cindy Moreton to browbeat her into asking Robert to see her without an appointment, Serena's head was in the grip of a pounding headache. Cindy had been prepared to wait even though there were three clients for Robert to see before he got to her.

From her vantage point in reception, Serena could see the emaciated girl flicking through magazines. She was wearing a knitted cotton sweater with long sleeves and in spite of the heat of the afternoon, a silk chiffon scarf was wound loosely around her neck.

"Why does he let her come here?" Serena asked Jill, exasperated that clues to Cindy's condition were flashing like neon signs and still no one did anything.

Jill shrugged. "You worry too much. I've said that to you before. People have got to be responsible for themselves."

When she next looked up she was surprised to see Cindy was gone. Not for a moment did she think she had thought twice about what she was doing. More likely gone to feed her meter.

The last patient had just gone in. "Jill," Serena called, "I'm just going to get something for my head. Won't be more than a minute."

Jill waved her hand in acknowledgement as Serena headed for the cloakroom. As she opened the door, she heard a gasp and saw Cindy Moreton standing by one of the two sinks. Both women gazed in horror at each other. Cindy because she had clearly not expected to be interrupted; Serena at the sight of Cindy's ribs painfully stretching through blue-veined skin, the ball and socket that kept her arms in place barely concealed. She was also inhaling deeply on what looked like an asthma inhaler.

"Dear God," Serena whispered, closing the door and leaning with her back against it. "Cindy, for Christ's sake, you need help. Stop that."

Cindy grabbed her sweater from the armchair where she had flung it and stuffed the asthma inhaler into her open bag. "I don't," she breathed. "Get out of my way. I'll have you fired. What are you doing in here?"

Serena ignored her. "Stop this," she begged. "If you don't I'm going to ring that agency and make them get help for you."

"How dare you?" Cindy cried, hugging the sweater to her. "Get out. Get out. And I do have asthma."

Instead Serena slipped the catch across the door to prevent anyone else coming in. "This could be the biggest favour anyone's ever done for you," she spoke rapidly, knowing in a very few minutes Robert's patient would be out and notes for the next one would have to be taken in.

"I'll give you a chance to do it yourself but, believe me, I'm going to check. I don't want to see you here again. If you do I'll make sure you never work as a model for anyone. Do you understand?"

"It's my metabolism, you interfering cow," Cindy panted, trying to struggle back into her sweater. "I'm like this —"

"Oh please," Serena stormed back. "Do I look stupid? You have a hyped-up metabolism and you need bloody pills to make it faster? You're sucking away on an asthma inhaler?"

Cindy looked shocked. "Look," Serena went on. "I've only got a few minutes. I'm going to go back to reception and tell Robert you cancelled. Then tomorrow I'm going to call your agency —"

"Do that. Do what you like. There's nothing wrong with me. Nothing.

231

Do you understand?"

Serena just shook her head. "Yes. I understand you have a problem. I don't know what's causing it. I know you think you've got a weight problem —"

It was as far as she got. Cindy threw herself against Serena, pulling her away from the door screaming, "Let me out. Let me out of here."

From outside Serena heard a rustle and then a banging on the door. "What's going on in there?" Bridget called out in alarm. Then came Robert Merrow's furious voice joining in, "What's happening? What the hell's going on?"

Serena sagged against the doorframe. Cindy had stopped shouting and was now gazing fearfully at her. Slowly Serena slid the bolt back and opened it. Outside a small group had gathered, including two patients who had been drawn along in the wake of the crocodile of people who had rushed down to the cloakroom.

"I'm out of here," Cindy muttered, and pushed through them. The group looked after her and then back at Serena who stood with folded arms, waiting for Robert to erupt.

"My office, Serena. Now," he said curtly. "Jill, please see my patient out and look after reception."

Inside Robert's office, Serena waited calmly for what she knew was inevitable.

"Before you say anything, Robert," she began calmly, "let me just say this. Cindy Moreton is anorexic and using a prescribed drug to encourage her condition. Her presence here cannot be helpful."

"I will be the judge of that," he breathed furiously. "What do you think you're doing telling me — a doctor — how to treat my patients?"

"Then treat them. Don't abuse them," she said icily. "It's OK," she held up a hand to stop him. "I resign. Do you want me to stay until you get someone else or shall I go now?"

*

I wonder, Serena asked herself as she let herself out of the Carlyle Clinic half an hour later, if there is something about you that courts disaster? She hoisted her bag more firmly on to her shoulder and began to walk slowly towards the station.

The panic would rise later. Later when she had had a sleep and could think clearly, when she had called Alex and got that out of the way. Briefly she considered calling her mother and as swiftly dismissed it. What could she do anyway? Melanie was at her cottage in France. Stacey? At another time, but this was not it.

The most obvious candidate was Alex. And she had ruled him out. Dear me, she mused as she reached the end of Wimpole Street, you do nothing to help yourself, do you?

She paused to let a black GTi convertible turn the corner before crossing. But instead of driving on, it pulled up next to her.

"Serena," a voice called from the driver's seat. Serena looked round, puzzled. "Serena, get in," called Cindy, pushing back her dark glasses so that Serena would recognize her.

Serena's eyes widened. "Get in? You have to be kidding."

"Please," Cindy called. "I'm sorry. I only want to help. You got fired, didn't you?"

"Oh, thanks a lot," Serena called back. "Now you've told the whole street."

Cindy clapped a hand over her mouth. "Oh God, Oh please. Just get in. I want to say sorry. I want to help."

An interested little group of pedestrians had now halted, watching this exchange. Oh what the hell, thought Serena, and got in. Cindy shot off before Serena could even pull her seat belt on.

"Where are we going?" she shouted above the noise of the traffic and the roar of the wind as they sped towards Marble Arch.

"Friend of mine. I rang him just now. I guessed Robert would throw you out ..."

"For what it's worth," Serena yelled, "I resigned. And I still think you're in trouble."

"Oh shut up," Cindy shrieked. "Do you want a job or not? I know who you are, Robert told me."

"Great," Serena sighed. "What else did he tell you?"

"Oh, that you were being all cool and stuff and wouldn't let anyone help. Personally I think you're mad. You could be a model."

Serena tried not to laugh. "Maybe a few years ago, but I don't fancy posing with Hoovers and rubber gloves. See enough of those at home. Listen, I meant what I said."

"And I meant what *I said*. I do feel bad about you losing your job. Frankly, my problems — if I have any and I'm not saying I have — are my own. But I don't want anyone to lose a job over me. And I want you off my case."

"OK," Serena agreed, now wanting nothing more than to never see anyone connected with Robert Merrow ever again and to sleep for a week. "But I don't need any help getting a job. I'll get by. Now if you could just drop me by the next tube."

"Don't you want to meet this guy?"

"No. I don't want to meet anyone. I want to go home."

"He's called Ed Stein. He owns Frobisher's. He's been very good to me and I know he'll help."

"Frobisher's being what?"

"Frobisher's? You don't know Frobisher's?"

Serena looked at Cindy's amazed profile. "You mean Frobisher's, the club? Businessmen?"

Cindy looked relieved. "That's the one."

"And this Ed Fine."

"Stein."

"Sorry, Stein, owns it?"

"Well, he's chief executive — same thing. He turned it around when it was going really badly. Waiting list for membership is about five years now —"

"Stop. I can get a tube from here," Serena interrupted. "Thanks, Cindy, but no thanks. Listen, good luck. I won't ring your agency, but you should think about what I said. If nothing else, lose the inhaler."

"And you don't want to meet Ed? He's expecting us."

Serena slammed the door of the car and leaned over to get her bag from the back seat. "I'll do it another time. Take care."

By the time she reached home she had decided to call Alex and get it out of the way. He was out, not expected back until later.

"Please tell him I called," Serena asked. "I'll call again."

Just as well, she decided. The only message was from Jasmine in Lucca, saying the children were fine and she was going to take them to stay with a friend near the coast until the weekend.

"More for them to do," she explained. "Call me if you'd rather I didn't. They both send their love."

The second message was from Ed Stein, or rather from his secretary. He wanted Serena to call. She stared, perplexed, at the machine. And then rang the number and asked for him.

He came on the line almost immediately. It was a deep voice, classless, direct. "Just wanted to thank you for looking out for Cindy."

"Oh please, don't mention it. I wish she'd get help. Perhaps as you seem to know her you could do something?"

"Good God, not me. I run clubs not clinics."

"I see," Serena replied coldly. "For a moment there I thought you sounded concerned."

She heard him laugh. "I am. But I don't run charities or therapy groups."

"Or clinics. Just clubs," she added drily.

"Don't panic. Her father's an old friend of mine. He's in the US. I told Cindy if she agreed to go over there and stay with him, I wouldn't get heavy."

"And is she going?"

"God knows. I've arranged the ticket. She's here with me tonight — under guard — and she's on the early morning flight to New York. Happy?"

"Well, thanks for calling, Mr Stein. I'm relieved to know Cindy's in such careful hands."

"Hold on. What about you? Cindy said you got fired."

"I resigned."

"OK, resigned over it. Stop being so touchy. You need a job, I have one on offer. Think about it. Call me in the morning if you want to talk about it. Great salary."

She tried to remain unmoved when he mentioned how much.

"I'll do that, Mr Stein. Goodbye."

She waited for him to acknowledge her but the phone was already dead. Rude sod, she decided, replacing the receiver and making her way upstairs. She stripped off her crumpled clothes and stood under the shower for ten minutes. Later she pulled on a pair of cotton trousers and a white cotton shirt and wandered aimlessly around the kitchen, knowing she should eat but failing to find the idea tempting. The doorbell went just as she finished eating an apple, trying not to let panic set in. She hoped it wasn't Cheryl, who had temporarily run out of excuses to pop over. Not when she had just summoned up the courage to call Alex again, this time on his home number.

Alex stood on the doorstep, or rather leaned against the frame. Serena swallowed and instinctively pushed her wet hair out of her face.

"Hi," he said gently. "I think we should get this out of the way, don't you?"

Chapter Nineteen

Serena stepped back and Alex walked past her into the hall. "Kitchen?" he asked, turning back to look at her. She nodded. The idea of the sitting room was not attractive to either of them.

"Drink?" she offered.

He smiled. "Coffee."

While she pulled cups and coffee from the cupboard and made a fuss of being busy, Alex stared out of the window on to the garden.

"Pretty," he remarked, turning back as she began pouring.

"Well, liveable with," she countered. "Especially after I built the Sov'rin-proof rockery — you can't imagine the excitement of sharing your quality time with a dog who can't tell the difference between you and a juicy bone."

He laughed. "You're amazing," he said softly. He pulled out a chair and sat at the table, not taking his eyes from her.

She stiffened. "Alex. You must listen to me. I'm not. I'm feeling pretty ashamed of myself ..."

"No." He reached out a hand and placed it over hers. "I'm the idiot. Rushing you like that, not thinking through what would happen. No, please, just listen to me, although God knows you have no reason to want to."

It was remarkable the way he shielded her. Not wanting any of it to be her fault. Alice was very lucky. Well, maybe that's not how she would see it.

Alex was talking quietly but earnestly. "We can't," he was saying. "Pretend it didn't happen, any more than we can pretend I'm not quite, quite smitten with you." He gave a shaky laugh. "But we can do something about what happens next."

"We can?" she asked doubtfully, sliding her hand from under his.

He moved his own hand to cradle the coffee in front of him. "Of course. We only have to accept what's happened and not pretend it didn't.

I can't disappear out of your life any more than you can disappear out of mine. Because it isn't about you and me, is it? Or at least not just you and me."

"It isn't?" She felt so tired she just let him speak. He was making it easy. Just the mere fact they were talking so calmly was having the effect she had been craving all day, the need for someone to lift the weight from her. Odd that it should be Alex.

"No. It's about Harry and Alice and Stephen as well," he told her.

She dropped her head and nodded miserably.

"What is it?" he asked gently, bending his head to try and see her face.

"Stephen." She was abrupt. "Stephen stopped me." She lifted her eyes to look at him. "Stephen's unresolved. Alex, the truth is, if he walked in now I would fall at his feet."

A flicker of surprise, rather than pain, crossed his face. "You would?"

"Is that so surprising? We hadn't quarrelled. Our marriage was fine. He just had some kind of breakdown — which I agree I should have spotted, but I didn't and I can't keep going over and over it. Part of me says I will forgive him for leaving me in the way he did, because I failed him in the first place."

Alex leaned back in his chair and studied the wall above her head. Then he looked back at her.

"Failed him?" he mused. "I'm sorry. You never speak about him. What you felt for him seemed to me to be anger and disappointment, but not guilt."

"Yes, of course, all those things," she almost snapped back at him. "But the guilt, the guilt is the worst."

She pushed back her chair and stood up, not quite knowing where to stand or even how to stand, gesturing with her arms. She stuffed her hands into the pockets of her trousers and leaned against the sink.

"Don't you see? If you love someone, you love them full stop. I wish to God I didn't. But I knew last night, Stephen is still part of me. Oh God, Alex, I'm sorry. If I didn't feel all this ..." She groped for the right word. "This anguish about him, believe me last night I would have been a pushover."

"Well," he spoke lightly. "That's something I suppose. I hope not anyone, just me?"

Serena winced. "Give me a break, will you?"

He looked steadily at her. "That hasn't exactly answered my question, but I have a suggestion."

"What's that? I don't accept dinner invitations under false pretences?"

"I don't think you did. And remember, I have to deal with my feelings for Alice."

Alice. Of course. She must stop forgetting about Alice. "And what do you feel for her?"

He frowned, absently pushing his cup in small circles. "I thought I had that worked out. But that's clearly not the case. You know, Serena, we must both lack something in our lives to have moved so quickly, to have felt so drawn to each other. Oh, don't panic, I'm not suggesting we explore that together."

She breathed out. He went on: "I just don't think we should let that need spoil a relationship I value and — and one I hope you do too. You see, I'm sure I can put how I feel in perspective. But not if I only have our last meeting to go on. You see, Serena, I'm now asking you to help me. Could you do that?"

It was hard to decide whether she could or not. He didn't sound at all bitter or resentful. She thought he was remarkable and yes, she did value him. The question she had to decide was, how much. Because she was beginning to feel she had overreacted, and relieved that Harry wouldn't be affected, she finally agreed she could at least try.

Relief flooded his face. "Look," he went on eagerly, standing up and moving around the table to where she was standing and taking both her hands, "I know you're tired but let's have a quick dinner together. Now. I bet you haven't eaten all day. That place just across the river. I'll have you back by ten. Scout's honour."

And he did. During dinner Alex did most of the talking and she was content to listen. Perhaps because she was tired, she didn't want to tell him she no longer had a job or that come the morrow she would be job hunting. Nor did she tell him about the offer from Ed Stein. Not because she didn't want to, but it was only later after he had dropped her home, kissed her gently on the cheek and watched her go in alone that she remembered that the chief executive of Frobisher's had phoned and there was a job of sorts on offer.

*

At the end of the week she phoned Frobisher's. The job would probably be gone but it was worth a try. After a couple of minutes her call was put through not to Ed Stein but a man called Mike Griffith. Patiently she repeated her name and explained why she was calling.

"Mr Stein rang me about it on Tuesday," she finished.

"Tuesday? But it's Friday."

"I know," she agreed. "I wasn't sure I was in a position to discuss it until now. But of course if you've already filled it —"

"Hold on. I just want to check something."

In front of her on the kitchen table were the application forms for three employment agencies, none of whom held out much hope given her restricted availability, and a notepad in which were scrawled the details of the twenty or so jobs that had caught her eye in the *Standard*. Either she didn't match up to what they needed or the hours and days were hopeless for her.

"Can you come in today?" Mike Griffith came back on the line. "I've got a window at four."

Frobisher's was tucked away between a restaurant and a firm of solicitors on the edge of Soho. Easy to find once you knew where to look, it was in the middle of a terrace of Queen Anne houses, the former residence of a tea planter who had made his fortune in the East Indies and from whom the club derived its name.

At four on a Friday afternoon, the club was almost deserted. The lobby was gloomy so it took Serena's eyes a minute or two to make the adjustment from the bright white light in the street to the shadowy interior. The porter, a grey-haired man wearing a navy jacket with thin gold braid on the sleeves and pocket, took his time about letting Mike Griffith know she was there.

She was wearing a cream sleeveless dress with a matching short-sleeved jacket which was not exactly this year's but classic enough to escape detection from discerning eyes that knew about these things. It was what she hoped was appropriate for a gentleman's club which she vaguely knew from its reputation was remarkably discreet about members bringing companions with them. As she waited the lift opened and two young women strolled out. She followed their progress as they crossed the lobby and stepped out into the sunshine. A skirt with a slit and fetish high heels might be more in keeping with this club, she thought ruefully.

Anyway, she decided, with a not entirely sinking heart, the chances were that whatever effort she had made would be wasted. She had, after all, not exactly raced to be considered. And what was the job anyway? Gloomily she surveyed herself in a large mirror hanging over the empty fireplace to one side of the room. Probably something quite ghastly.

On one side of the reception area, a solid oak door was firmly closed and marked private. On the other the double doors were open. Through these she could make out groups of armchairs and tables, small gold shaded lamps on each, weighty dark blue silk curtains over half pulled blinds shielding the room from the sunlight that flooded through from the floor-to-ceiling windows at the far end. Ahead of her a wide staircase led to the next four floors, blue carpeted and highly polished. A small service lift was tucked around a corner for those guests who preferred to reserve their energy for what, Serena decided glancing around, the club had to offer above ground level. A ripple of misgiving ran through her.

A thin corridor led away to one side of the stairs into the interior of the house. Serena was peering along this when she heard herself called, trying to recall which terrible nightclub in New York she and Stephen had found themselves in and the inventiveness of their excuses when they had left less than half an hour after they had arrived. Sometimes, she recalled ruefully, you could never tell with Wall Street bankers. Or ones from the square mile, either she admitted with a small ache.

"Mr Griffith will be with you in a moment," intoned the porter. "He's with someone. Perhaps you'd like to take a seat."

241

He indicated one of two velvet armchairs filling the alcove by the stairs, another gold coloured lamp standing on the low table in front of them. While she waited she considered just what the job must entail for her to justify such a generous salary. A thought struck her. Good God, she panicked. Not that, surely?

There was no time to further consider the thorny question of her virtue. A surprisingly brisk-looking woman in her middle years, dressed in a cool tailored linen dress, appeared from the door marked private.

"Come with me, Mr Griffith will see you now."

Mike Griffith was, she judged, in his forties. He was very tanned with bags under his eyes, the sleeves of his pink shirt rolled up. As she came in he rose from behind a scroll-topped leather desk and extended a hand.

"Thanks for coming in at such short notice. I'm sure you understand I need to get this out of the way. We have another candidate for the job but when you phoned we held off telling her. Now have you done anything like his before?"

Serena blinked. "I'm dreadfully sorry," she said. "I'm afraid I'm not quite sure what the job is. I heard about it in rather unusual circumstances."

Mike clapped a hand against his brow. "I knew it. Ed told you at a dinner party. No? OK, the races? No?" He screwed up his face, mentally ticking off other possibilities. "Opera? Catford?"

Serena tried not to laugh. "No. None of them. I'm afraid I've never met him at all. It was a … um … a friend of his who told him about me. I'd just left a job I was in and she was keen for me to see him."

"Can't keep up with the man," muttered Mike. "I thought the way he spoke about you, he knew you. Must have misunderstood. Let's start again. The job is broadly speaking a club executive."

Executive? Good grief.

"The hours are the tricky bit. Six until two each night, no weekends. But the salary reflects the unsociable hours. We have what Ed calls High Maintenance members. No rock stars but a few film producers. Industry, medicine, politics. That's our bag. Waiting list is closed until someone pops his clogs. We need someone to know who they are, keep them happy and discreetly make sure they behave themselves. Frobishers' is perhaps a little more enlightened than some other clubs but we still don't want them misbehaving, drawing attention to the place. Press being nosy, that kind of thing."

"Press?"

"Oh yes. We have a policy of not speaking to them at all, and our vetting system for members' guests is very thorough. No tabloid hacks slipping in. Happened once and the member was barred immediately."

She took a deep breath. "Then I don't think you'll want me."

"And that would be why?"

"If Mr Stein said he knew me, I suspect it's because he knew my husband, or at least of him. Stephen Carmichael. He's missing. Every now and then a tabloid contacts me through my solicitor to see if I want to talk. I never do, of course, but the point is you have no way of knowing that, do you?"

He gave a soft whistle. "Banker chap? Good God. Funnily enough I wasn't thinking of that kind of attention. More the fall-out from irate wives discovering who they're dining with. Well, it's up to you."

"Perhaps you should ask Mr Stein," she suggested, gathering up her bag. "I'm afraid I don't come with a clean track record in that sense."

He gave her a sympathetic smile. "No, I understand. Tough for you."

"Besides I'm not sure about the hours." She stood up. "I have children to consider."

He agreed to phone her later that evening and she made her way back home, suddenly wanting the job very much. The money would mean a car, maybe even a small holiday somewhere. Away from Foster Street, just her and the children. In fact, when she considered it, if she had someone to stay overnight with the children, the hours were perfect. During the holidays and half-term she could be with them during the day, and for most of the time she was working they would be doing homework and going to bed. Well, at least Harry would. Louise was less predictable. Far less.

In many ways Louise was a typical fourteen-year-old, crazy about boys, rock music and clothes, but there were moments when she forgot to be rebellious and when her charm, Stephen's charm, shone through. She longed to give Louise something that would make her happy. Bribery, of course, but she had been deprived of so much. Alex would not approve but then he didn't know her. Not really.

By the time she reached home, Stacey had left a message to say she would call round later and one of the agencies had called back to say they had something she might be interested in. Too late to call them now, she would do it on Monday morning.

Alex had gone to Heathrow to collect Alice and to take her to dinner. He was, he had told Serena, going to try and reinvent his relationship with her. Too fond of her to cease seeing her altogether, he said with an honesty she thought admirable, but knowing his feelings for Serena must temper that.

She begged him not to tell Alice about her. "Why?" she demanded. "Why hurt her with something that we both agree was a mistake? Why burden her with it just to make us — you — feel better?"

He had looked shocked. "Give me some credit," he protested. "I just meant to tell her that I feel undecided. How do I know that it wasn't there anyway, not being sure, and not just because I met you?"

At least Alex was to be relied on, she told herself, kicking off her shoes and peeling off her tights. No job though.

*

Ed Stein called her at ten that evening. Stacey had gone, leaving behind a moving little note from Edith in which she thanked Serena for her flowers and to let her know she was as well as could be expected and if ever Serena was passing, to please drop in. Serena glanced at the address. A nursing home in Hove. The letter had been written by a volunteer who Edith had said was called Carol. There was no explanation about how she came to be there. Edith seemed to assume Serena knew. Even Stacey couldn't discover what or who had moved the frail old lady from Maud Frierley back to her tiny house in Camberwell and then to Holewood Nursing Home on the coast. Still, better than Maud Frierley, she supposed. She paused. Anything was better than going backwards. That was so easy. For the first time in a long time she had pushed aside the brown envelopes that were clearly bills without opening them, the familiar lurch of fright not rippling her stomach.

For a moment when Ed Stein announced himself, she couldn't register what he wanted.

"What's the matter with you?" he asked mildly. "I hear you were a bit of a tragedy queen with poor Mike."

"Tragedy queen?" she asked blankly. "Bilge. I was being honest. I thought that was the right thing to do. Tragedy queen indeed."

"That's better," he said approvingly. "Can't get along with weeping willows. Might as well start as we mean to go on."

"Go on," she repeated. "Go on with what? And I'm not a weeping willow either."

"No, I can hear that. Mike must have had a touch of the sun. He said you were cut glass and roses."

Dear heaven. "For goodness' sake," she said impatiently. "What on earth are you talking about? You sound like a demented gardener, not a club owner. I'm nothing of the sort."

"No. I've just said that. What's the matter with you? I'm agreeing with you. Bloody women. Now do you want this job or not?"

Serena had never ground her teeth in her life. It was an interesting feeling. "Mr Stein," she said calmly. "You have a most novel way of hiring staff. And, now let me see, how can I break this to you? I'm afraid I won't be one of them."

"Difficult too," she heard him sigh. "Course you will. Mike says you sound terrific. And I know you look terrific. Just what we need. You can't go on letting that old man of yours rule your life. I doubt as many people as you imagine still think about it. Frankly, I couldn't give a sod. No offence, but I've got other things to concern me."

In two and a half years, no one had spoken to her like that about Stephen or intruded so clumsily into her private life.

"Mr Stein." Her voice was dangerously polite and icy. "Do you have a pen handy? Good. Now pick it up and draw a line through my name. That way," she continued, "you will have no difficulty in recalling that I do not want to hear from you again."

Just in case, she pushed her finger on the cut-off button and then slammed the phone down. Afterwards she wasn't at all sure that the noise she heard as she cut him off wasn't the sound of someone laughing.

*

With no children to worry about, Serena slept late on Saturday morning. Minnie had asked to keep them until the following Saturday and while this had infuriated Louise, who claimed she would miss a party crucial to her whole future happiness, Serena was now grateful that she hadn't succumbed to her rage and let her come home. It gave her another week to find a job before they came back. Since there was nothing she could do about it until Monday and the weather was still holding, she decided to take a train to the coast, walk along a beach somewhere and come back later in the evening. There was no point in ringing Stacey to see if she wanted to join her; the dreadful Barry would have her firmly under his eye.

Even Melanie, had she been around, would not have been keen or able to. The children would have been carted off to the country. On reflection, she realized that she wasn't seeing quite so much of Melanie. Inevitable really, she decided. When they had both been on committees together, sharing the same friends, the same school run, their lives had been seamless.

She gave herself a shake. Melanie would be horrified to think Serena felt neglected. And nor did she. Nothing stayed the same.

In the end she decided that she would go to Hove and see Edith. Once the children were back she would find it difficult to get down there. And once she had a job, it would be impossible. The thought of her unemployed status mobilized panic waves to the roof of her mouth. Get out of here, she told herself sternly. Cheap day return is an investment, not a waste.

At Hove station she asked directions to the Holewood Nursing Home. It was on the other side of the town, inland from the coast. Serena glanced at her watch. It was just after one o'clock, she would see Edith and then go for a stroll on the beach before getting the six o'clock train back.

The bus dropped her at the end of Holewood Hill. Opposite there was a small row of shops. Serena scanned them for the one she was looking for and emerged a few minutes later with a tub of ice cream. Large detached

Victorian houses, some screened from the road by high laurel bushes, others, now turned into flats judging by the assorted cars and bikes that lined the gravel drives, posed grandly if a little shabbily along each side.

Holewood was nearly at the top of the hill, set back from the road and reached by a long curving gravel drive softened by rhododendron bushes and well-tended flower beds. Serena was quite surprised at the obvious attention given to the place. So used was she to seeing Edith in bleak surroundings, she was not prepared for a modest but cared-for home.

Edith, she was told by a surprised Matron, was in the loggia at the back, dozing off. Serena promised she wouldn't stay long.

"Relative?" asked Matron, showing her the way.

"No. Friend. I helped nurse her in hospital. I was just concerned about her. I've brought her some ice cream. Would you mind if she had some while I was here? I can help her."

"No, of course not. Look, do you know her daughter-in-law? The one who arranged for her to come here?"

Serena shook her head. "No. All I know is that after her son died, Edith fell out with her."

"Hmm. Well, she never visits. Social Services arranged for Edith to come here. She was born here, you know. Her family moved to London when she was a tot, but I gather that until she was too ill to move she used to love coming to Hove."

"Who's paying for this?" Serena asked.

"Edith. Only I'm not sure she realizes," Matron said. "I shouldn't be telling you this, of course, but I am concerned. Her daughter-in-law has sold the house but she says Edith incurred a lot of debts so there's enough to last for two or three more months but after that ..." Her voice trailed off, accompanied by a meaningful lift of the eyebrows.

"But Edith's house must have underwritten the fees for longer than that," Serena said, puzzled. "What debts? We never heard any of that while she was with us — I'm sure we would have done."

"You'd have thought so," Matron agreed, leading her through a clean but sparsely furnished lounge full of slumbering figures. "Still, none of my business. Look, there she is."

She pushed open a door into a long narrow room, warm, too warm, on such a hot day. "Hello, Edith." Matron bent over the sleeping figure. "You've got a visitor. I'll send someone along with a spoon and a napkin," she murmured to Serena.

Serena crouched down by the hunched figure in the wing chair. Edith slowly opened her eyes and gazed at Serena for a long while.

"It's me, Serena."

The weak eyes fixed on Serena's face. Then with a tiny flutter she tried to raise a hand. "Hello, dear," she said in a whispery thin voice. "I was expecting you."

Serena reached behind and pulled a chair up to Edith's. Thank heavens she'd made the effort.

"Of course I'm here. And with some ice cream. I thought you'd like some."

"Oh nice. Can you help me a bit, dear? Don't want to spoil my ballgown." She gave a rasping laugh which turned into a cough.

"Of course," Serena said and, tucking the napkin one of the helpers had delivered into Edith's collar, began to feed her.

"How are you, dear?" Edith asked faintly, having satisfied her need for the ice cream Serena knew she loved. "Still at Willie's?"

"No," Serena grinned, replacing the lid on the tub. "Just pop this back to Matron to put in the fridge."

When she came back, Edith was looking sleepy again. "Matter of fact I'm looking for a job. Nearly got one in Frobisher's, but the owner and I didn't hit it off."

"Oh?" Edith cackled softly to herself. "That Eddie Stein did well, didn't he?"

Serena sat back. "Sorry, Edith, do you know him?"

"Know him, dear? Not really. Knew his grandma. Then they all went off to Australia and then ... I forget, dear. Came back I think. Lily showed me a newspaper cutting about him. Doing ever so well, he was. Good to Lily. Naughty though, he was. Can't remember why."

All this way to hear about Ed Stein. Serena glanced at Edith who, having finished her ice cream and the longest conversation she'd probably had in weeks, was dozing off again.

Serena leaned over and kissed her on the cheek. "I'll come again, Edith," she promised. But Edith was already asleep.

On the way out, she stopped by Matron's office. "Look, there's nothing I can do financially, but will you let me know what happens to her? I'll try and get down again. Here," Serena scribbled her name and address on a scrap of paper. "Keep it in her file."

On Monday morning, she knew she would never have even entertained Mike Griffith's rather exasperated call if Edith hadn't mentioned how good Ed Stein had been to his grandmother. Or perhaps more truthfully because the agency job had been impossible.

"Thanks, Mr Griffith," she said. "When would you like me to start?"

There are, she decided, better reasons for taking a job than hearing the boss had been good to his granny. But it was a start, she decided a week later, once again pushing open the heavy oak door to Frobisher's. And it wasn't a step backwards.

Chapter Twenty

Ed Stein was responsible for the success of several clubs in New York and was on the board of as many companies again. In Frobisher's, all red plush and low lights as it had been when Ed had taken it over, the décor not changed in over a century, with a membership fee that made a Fabergé egg look cheap and clients who privately thought the staff came with the price — and indeed some of them had — was however the flagship of his business empire and the one for which he was best known in England.

To those who had since been admitted as members it was an exclusive businessman's club where they could go to entertain their guests and enjoy conversation with their own kind. To those denied admittance, it was a morally bankrupt and socially ruinous pit for anyone discovered to be going through its doors.

"Not worth the risk," said one of its critics whose application had been rejected. "Applying for membership, I mean. You don't see people like that at Balmoral for the weekend. And the bar is like a bordello."

"You risked it," his companion pointed out. Unlike his friend, who had inherited a fortune, he had become a self-made millionaire before he was thirty-five. He did not mention, out of respect for his friend's already wounded pride, that inherited titles and wealth were low on the list of those invited to join its ranks. Nor did he mention that he had been invited to become a shareholder as well as a member and had himself only recently been a guest at Windsor.

"I went because Jonny Cooper insisted," his friend retorted defensively. "I had a drink, that's all. Couldn't wait to get out of the place. Ed Stein's a shit," growled the luckless candidate, ignoring the teasing. "Who'd want to be seen with him anyway, or in his scabby club? I know someone who met his ex-wife at a dinner party in New York and she practically had to be stretchered out at the mention of his name."

"Which may account for the fact that women can only come in as guests."

"Or employees. High class tarts, the lot of them."

Such were the rumours about how membership was achieved and the even richer versions of what happened behind closed doors, never proven but worth repeating, that, by the time Serena was recruited as a club executive (in reality a rather superior kind of receptionist), it had closed its list to new members for the foreseeable future.

Ed Stein had returned to England from New York five years before to resurrect it from a fading gentleman's club — run with a disastrous combination of unrealistic hope allied with hopeless management — to a replica of the one he had brought to life on the Upper East Side almost ten years before where he made his business name. There was no point, he had decided when invited by a consortium of English nobility to bring his expertise to their failing venture, in trying to make it compete with long-established clubs like the Cavalry or Carlton. The pedigree was no longer there.

"Frobisher's will become a businessman's club," he announced to a hushed committee meeting in the faded gentility of the old boardroom. A ripple of unease went round the table. "It will make rich men of you all."

"Businessmen?" ventured one of his audience uncertainly. "You mean offering facilities to existing members who may want to conduct business affairs from here?"

He thought Ed Stein was about to laugh but it must have been the way he was lighting his cigar.

"Not quite. Look." He opened a folder in front of him. "There's no room for growth. You've locked yourselves in. The rent is money down a black hole. We should buy the lease from Frobisher Holdings."

"Buy the lease?" exclaimed several voices in unison. "What with? And they won't sell."

Ed continued. "They'll sell. Frobisher Holdings have over-expanded. If they're to keep their hand in textiles, which is where their money has always been, they need to shore up that leaking plant of theirs in Halifax. They're trying to reschedule their loans right now. The money will be a godsend. Prime site, central London. Then we've got an investment to build on."

"Why have they never suggested it then?" asked an heir to a baronetcy. He looked round with a raised eyebrow and a small smirk at his chums.

"Because unlike you they've looked at the books and they don't know where you'll get the cash, so they haven't bothered. They'll sell. We'll raise the money in other ways. I'm coming to that. Then we can expand. The guys next door don't need the two floors over that law firm and we do."

"They won't —"

"I think you'll find they will. It's draining them. Overambitious. A couple of good cases and they thought they need a new address. Should have stayed in Clapham. I need that space for a casino and a couple of private dining rooms. And all these folk." He consulted his list, oblivious to their growing discomfort. "Membership consultant — what the hell is that? — accountants, lawyers and the rest of them will be dispensed with, gracefully and gratefully. They"re all on retainers that are never used, except for the accountant. I think we can work out for ourselves how to get members. We'll ask for tenders for lawyers, and hire our own finance director who will work from here.

"Now," he turned to another folder. If he was aware that he was being regarded with horror, he made no sign of it.

"Membership fees have remained the same for seven years and even then a lot of them don't pay up on time. Some," he flicked his eye down the list. "Have never paid at all. If there is a point to running a charity for a bunch of guys who want to fall asleep all afternoon, then I can think of worthier recipients. If this isn't your intention, we will be inviting all these gentlemen to re-apply for membership at a rate that reflects what Frobisher's is to become and what it will offer. Let's see then how much they care about preserving its image."

"And where are you going to get the money for all this?" asked the baronet, aware that some of his support was already on the wane at the prospect of making money.

"Shareholders. They can invest in this club. No one turns down the chance of making money — and enjoying it while they do it."

He stacked the folders together while they digested the idea of strangers having a say in Frobisher's. When they had met him in New York he had warned them what might be at stake. Afraid they would lose his skills, they doubled their offer. Now he knew they would be trawling through the contract looking for a get-out. There wasn't one. Without looking he handed the files over his shoulder to a young woman who had been sitting just behind him taking notes.

"That's it for now, gentlemen. My proposal, including a draft of the prospectus brochure, will be before you in a month."

Then he left, followed by the secretary and two assistants who had sat discreetly behind him throughout the meeting. After he had gone a babble of voices broke out. Some visibly excited by the vision Ed had drawn of a rich investment. The rest, to do exactly as he had expected.

"What can you expect?" said one, gazing disdainfully at the initial report Ed had supplied them with. "The man has no roots, so how can he expect to understand what our members need?"

"I think he does understand," intervened a calm thin young man who had welcomed Ed Stein's approach.

"Understand? He understands making a buck, but what is he? East End lad made good. Probably got racketeers as friends. That's how he's made his pile."

"May I remind you, Simon," the thin young man sighed. "Your family got their pile from pillaging farmers in the Middle Ages, so we'll leave racketeers out of this. We had him checked. Shoplifting when he was a kid in the East End is about his limit. Knocked off the occasional car. We're not talking Krays here. Besides, the whole family went to Australia when he was fourteen — yes, I agree, probably to stop him ending up in Dartmoor — and the first time he's lived back in England is when we got him over here. I'd say he's the East End kid made very good. And, incidentally, I'm not averse to making money."

Those who had visualized a discreet and elegantly furnished club, whose name they would be happy to drop socially, resigned when they saw what

Ed Stein had in mind.

"Your choice, gentlemen," he shrugged at a stormy board meeting. "I'm not forcing my decisions on you, I'm telling you some facts of life."

"The facts, Mr Stein," one said coldly. "Are that without us you wouldn't be here. You're turning this club, this highly regarded and respectable club, into a circus. I knew it was a mistake. You don't understand about people like us."

Ed blew a cloud of cigar smoke slowly down the table. "No I don't," he returned pleasantly. "You see, I was led to believe I would be dealing with gentlemen and businessmen. Frankly, I think mine is the time that's being wasted."

The speaker, whose title derived from a long line of baronets, all of whom had distinguished themselves as diplomats or soldiers, while his reputation depended on mentions in social columns, flushed angrily.

"You know perfectly well what I mean. There are certain rules, codes of behaviour ... You would make us a laughing stock, no one would want to be associated with us."

"Seems to me they haven't exactly been knocking themselves out to get into bed with you as it is." Ed grinned cheerfully at the blustering man opposite him.

The rest, uneasily aware that money was to be made, buried their misgivings, did as he bade and begged him to be chairman and chief executive of the newly formed company, and lived to be glad they did. Frobisher's flourished. And so did they.

Ed operated on a need to know basis, but in Mike Griffith he had a lieutenant who was loyal. He had known him since they both turned up in New York twenty years before in need of jobs and inspiration. Mike was the only one who had access to him at all times.

His staff had grown used to his habit of keeping unpredictable hours and making unpredictable plans. These he announced in a conversational manner as though they were all his equals and in on his thoughts, when they knew — some to their cost — that they were not.

At the top of the narrow house, his business life was directed from a suite of offices. These were only ever deserted in the small hours before dawn, after Ed had left for the night if he was in the club, and before his secretary and various assistants arrived at nine the next morning. Only a handful of people were asked to make the journey in his private lift to consult him. It did not take Serena long to work out that she was not one of them.

*

Between them, Mike Griffith and Tipper the barman made Ed Stein's lifestyle known to her.

Serena was relieved that she was not required to report to Ed. The club executives — as Mike seriously called the half-dozen young women who were employed throughout the club — were usually on duty by seven and were not, as Serena had assumed, out of work actresses or models. One was a medical student, two were teachers and a fourth had been an advertising executive who had been made redundant and found she made just as much at Frobisher's in one week as she had in a month in her previous existence in Charlotte Street.

Like Serena, they reported to Mike Griffith, who Serena decided was gay in spite of his bloke-ish approach and the crude jokes he made about the girls working there. Between them, the hand-picked, immaculately groomed team made an evening in the casino on the third floor or the library across the hall from the casino a pleasant interlude for the members and their guests. Particularly if the member had no guest.

Serena's role was settled between her and Mike Griffith who told her that Ed's insistence that she got the job was because he didn't like to be turned down and preferred to remain on equal terms with the world.

"A favour is a favour, and I gather you did that stupid god-daughter of his …"

"God-daughter? Cindy? I didn't realize that. Explains a lot," she said, her eyes widening.

"Well, that and the fact that everyone's got to look attractive."

It was not the job or the place that Serena would have chosen. But she couldn't afford the luxury of choice and it was, she reflected, a great deal more honest than Robert Merrow's. It was also a chance, small, but there all the same, to get out of Foster Street and into something half way decent before Stephen came back. The hope of this happening never left her. She also wanted him to be proud of her, not ashamed that she couldn't manage and to find them all on the bread-line.

She paused in this reverie. Proud of her? Of course. But even as she said it she knew it was more important to her that she was proud of herself. A little piece of her had begun to understand why he had done what he did. Pride. His confidence, she could now see, had been merely a screen to hide his resentment. He had never quite been accepted into the ranks of those he longed to recognise his worth. Rupert glided in effortlessly, with no thought of earning his place. Stephen had watched his easy rise to the top purely on his name, and had been too proud to say it hurt.

She gave herself a shake.

Even Cheryl was fine when she heard she would no longer be needed during the day. "I'll have to get someone who is free to stay overnight," Serena explained. "I'm so sorry, Cheryl."

"Well, that's no problem," Cheryl beamed. "I'll do it. Easy peasy. I'll just slip over as you leave and I'll be back in time for his nibs' breakfast. Much easier than getting in someone who has to get to know the kiddies."

Not for the first time did she have to ask Cheryl about the effect this nocturnal existence would have on the indolent Kevin who had not, in the entire two years Serena had lived in Foster Street, done a day's work that she could recall. He made Les Plaxton look industrious.

Cheryl waved an indifferent hand in the general direction of where she thought Kevin's position in front of the television would be.

"Meals," she said. "That's what he lives for. That and bloody Sky Sport. Leave him to me. At least your two watch *Eastenders*. That spare room of yours will do me fine. You won't even know I've gone in the morning. I might even get my cleaning job back, up Whitehall, so it suits me to be gone early."

Weakly, Serena gave in. Curiously enough, Louise and Harry, back a day or two later from Lucca, took the news philosophically. Minnie, she decided, had an amazingly calming effect on them. They could even speak some Italian and Harry's paintings had been really extremely good. Alex was so right. Later when he dropped round for a drink she would show him, and tell him about her new job. She had only heard briefly from him to say that he and Alice had talked.

"So," she said as the children sat in the kitchen, tanned and full of their weekend at Minnie's friends who had a pool, and the cool day they'd spent in Florence and the one in Pisa. "It won't be forever." Harry listened intently and Louise, one eye on the television and the other on a copy of a magazine Serena wasn't entirely certain she should be reading, just yawned.

"Just until Daddy is better enough to come back and then all this will stop."

Louise turned round slowly, pity etched in her face. "Daddy come back? You know he won't," she said calmly. "How can he after dipping his fingers in the till?"

Without thinking Serena, trembling with rage, rose and grabbed Louise's magazine from her hands. She ripped it across then rammed it into the bin. Behind her Louise was mimicking her by calmly tearing up *The Times*.

"That's where I read it." She glared at Serena, tipping it in after her shredded magazine. "Not in my mag. They'd think he was a right lad. You're so stupid you can't see that, can you? Daddy would never have let us live in a street like this —"

She got no further. Serena heard herself begin to shout. It sounded like someone else. Not her at all. Harry started to cry.

"You ghastly, revolting child," Serena half sobbed. "Do you think I've done this to you deliberately? Do you? Do you think I'm enjoying working in these scrubby jobs, worried sick about you both, about what's going to happen to us? And what have you done, Louise, while I've been doing it? I'll tell you. You have wallowed in self pity. You have been disloyal and treacherous."

Louise's eyes were dark and horrified. She seemed to shrink into the wall. But Serena couldn't stop. "Don't think I don't know what you say about me to your so-called friends. But you have a roof over your head which *I*

257

put there, not your father. Instead of being ashamed of me you should be deeply ashamed of yourself. Sorry, Harry, sorry, darling. Come here."

Harry rushed over to her and grabbed her round the waist, staring horrified into Serena's stormy face as though to make sure this was his mother. Louise stood petrified against the wall, the silence that fell broken only by Serena's attempts to soothe Harry.

She took a deep breath, holding the child as much for the comfort it gave her as for his sake. Eventually she pushed her hair out of her eyes. A more rational sense was returning.

"I'm sorry, Louise," she finally said. "I shouldn't have shouted. I'm tired. Forgive me."

A sob broke from Louise who suddenly ran across the room and flung her arms around Serena's neck. "I'm sorry, Mum," she wept. "I didn't mean it. Don't be angry with me. I just say these things and I don't know why because I just feel worse after and I say them because they're all gathered here," she pushed her fist into her chest, "and I want them to stop."

"Oh darling, don't ..." Serena was crying and Harry joined in. "Don't. It'll be all right. I promise you, promise you. You've been through so much. Don't think I don't understand. Harry?" she gulped over Louise's head. "Be a darling. Get LouLou a drink, will you?"

She sat down again, drawing Louise on to her knee, stroking her hair, rocking her until she was able to speak without the awful convulsive sobs that racked her thin body.

"C'mon," she finally said, as Louise rested her head against Serena's shoulder. "I think we all need a treat. Let's go out to supper."

Louise lifted her head. "I can't." She blew her nose on a tissue that Serena handed to her. "I've promised Daphy she could come over and copy my Nirvana tapes."

Serena swallowed hard. "Of course. We'll do it another time. Harry," she smiled at his disappointed little face. "Why don't we walk down and bring some hamburgers back for all of us?"

"Cool, Mum," Louise said. "I'll phone Daphy. Will you get one for her too?"

*

She had argued with Mike for a better salary than that on offer so that she could afford the extra money to pay Cheryl, and was surprised and suspicious when the word came back that Ed Stein had agreed.

"I bet," she had told Stacey over supper. "The present incumbent already gets more. I suppose I ought to thank him when I see him."

In fact, she had been at Frobisher's for nearly a month before she actually met him, by which time she had discovered that the previous incumbent had indeed been paid a great deal more and she revised the level of her gratitude accordingly.

Once or twice she had seen Ed Stein stride through the lobby just as she was arriving at six, but he was usually with a group of people en route to another appointment. He had also, she learned on the grapevine, been in the States and was said to have been having trouble with his latest companion, of whom much was gossiped and little was seen.

Each night Serena changed in the staff room into a short black dress, swept her hair into a coil, slipped on some simple gold hoop earrings and black suede high heels. With a quick glance in the mirror she emerged to start checking which guests would be in that evening. Her job, she decided, was not tottering on the brink of tacky. It was undoubtedly so. Thankfully she was spared the indignity of being stationed in the front entrance and saw no one until they appeared on the first-floor lobby where there was a bar to one side and a dining room to the other.

She glanced in as she passed and waved to Tipper who was on duty. She had struck up an instant friendship with him, seeing in the sad eyes and deliberately flippant manner a rather lost soul. Each night she had taken to sharing a cab home with him and had grown fond of this young Irishman with close-cropped hair and a skeletal appearance. His partner, he told Serena, had abandoned him after five years to live with someone else in Italy. He looked older but he was not even thirty.

"Gay of course," she told Melanie, who had been hard put not to appear shocked when she heard what Serena was now doing. "But sad. He's trying to get over it. That's why he left Dublin and came here. I've asked him over for Sunday lunch."

"Have you?" Melanie had asked faintly. "How kind of you."

Tipper beckoned her over. "You look fab." He admired her dress. "Just as well, I've heard himself's in this evening."

"Himself?"

"Ed Stein, you eejit. Back from the States. The girlfriend's playing him up so he's going to be in a right old dander."

Serena giggled. "Tipper. How do you know these things? And why don't I ever hear this gossip? By the way, are you still coming on Sunday? Wonderful. Whoops. Here goes. Good evening, Sir Lewis." She smiled at a dumpling of a man heaving himself up the narrow steps. "Lovely to see you. I've arranged orchids for your guest — Miss Atkins, isn't it? — and I'll bring her over to you myself. Now let me organize a drink for you."

She moved away to greet the next arrival. "Mr But — Buttermere," she remembered quickly. "We've been expecting you. We have two messages for you. Your secretary called and asked if you could call your wife. She's left your mother in-law's and is on her way to Edinburgh. And your secretary will bring the papers over that you wanted."

"Perhaps you could arrange for her to have dinner," Mr Buttermere murmured. "So conscientious. It will be a treat for her."

"Lucky girl," Serena smiled back. Creep, she muttered in her head as he turned to go into the bar.

Halfway through the evening, when the dining room was full, Serena was able to relax for a few minutes before the rush of guests who, having dined elsewhere, would start to arrive. She slipped downstairs to phone the children.

Cheryl said Harry was already asleep and Louise was in her room with her headphones on.

"No, don't disturb her," Serena said quickly. "Tell her I phoned and I'll see her in the morning."

"Enjoyin' yourself?" Cheryl asked with a giggle.

"Well, it's not so bad," Serena replied, glancing up at the clock. Nearly eleven. Only another three hours.

"So how many do you have to entertain, if you get my meaning, of an evening?"

"Sorry?" Serena asked. "I'd hardly call it entertaining."

"Well, not if my Kevin was a client. Bloody hard work," Cheryl replied. "Dull as well, if you know what I mean?"

Since her Kevin was unlikely to be a client and he couldn't be any duller than some of those in the club, Serena said, "You'd be surprised. Must go."

It was worth it, she reminded herself, fighting a pang of longing to be home with the children. You live in Foster Street, not Belvoir Square. It won't be for long. She turned to go back upstairs and automatically stood aside to let a guest go ahead of her.

"You decided to stay then?" a voice said chattily beside her. She looked up into Ed Stein's face.

"Heavens!" She was taken aback. "How do you do? Yes, indeed I've decided to stay. I always do what I say I will."

"Glad someone round here does." He paused on the steps and looked her over appreciatively. Serena wanted to wrap her arms protectively around herself.

"Busy tonight?"

"Tonight? Busy?" She stared at him. "Yes, of course. Tonight. It will be. Jonny Cooper is coming in with some friends to celebrate his birthday and his father, Viscount Charlsworth —"

"I know who his father is," he interrupted. "No one important."

They had reached the first floor. Serena expected him to walk ahead and take the lift to his own suite. Instead he strolled over to the library, greeted two or three people sitting there and seemed content to be entertained for a while.

She signalled to Tipper to send a waiter through while she checked the very detailed instructions Jonny Cooper's secretary had telephoned through for his birthday celebration. Mr Buttermere's secretary arrived as she replaced the phone and, with a smile she hoped was charming, Serena led her through to his table. As she left them to greet each other in a way that suggested they had more than dinner planned, she noted that she would never make it as a secretary if you were required to wear a skimpy dress, fake tan and dye your hair that colour and be nice to a man like Brian Buttermere, chairman of an electronics firm or not, with or without his penthouse in Manhattan. It must have been written all over her face as she turned around. Ed Stein was watching her and laughing.

"Come and talk to me," he suggested. "At least I won't try and pass you off as my secretary."

"Well, I can't really leave here," she began.

"No," he agreed, picking up the phone. "Mike, send someone up to cover for Serena for half an hour. No, nothing's wrong."

Tipper brought Ed a whiskey and Serena some iced water.

"And is it a raise you're after?" he mocked into her ear as he bent to put her glass in front of her. Ed, preoccupied with the pleasure he clearly derived from lighting a Davidoff cigar, ignored him.

"Back in the knife-box, Miss Sharp," she murmured, and turned her attention to Ed Stein.

His size was not all that was deceptive about him. He was a big man but it was his shoulders rather than his girth that gave this impression. What she found jarring was the glimpse of a gold watch-strap when the cuff of his clearly expensive and beautifully cut suit slipped back. She tried hard not to notice or wince at the cufflinks that were as big as they were obvious. Solid gold, she guessed. A signet ring adorned his left hand. Stephen would have been appalled at such taste. Ed's age was more difficult. Early forties, she guessed, not from the dark hair spliced with grey or the sharply cut suits, but from his eyes. She thought they looked bored.

"Why do you want this job?" he asked abruptly when they were alone. "It isn't your sort of thing, is it?"

Serena smoothed her skirt and sipped her drink. "No," she agreed, slightly taken aback at such a direct approach. "It isn't. However, I'm perfectly capable of doing it. And besides, I couldn't turn down a man who was kind to his granny."

"My what? My granny?"

"Yes," she continued, impassively. "I went to see an ... old friend of mine, Edith Ambleton. She knew her. Lily? Is that right? She said you were good to Lily. A man who is good to his grandmother can't be all —"

"All right, all right," he interrupted, "I think I know who you're talking about. But we hared off to Australia when I was fourteen. Not Lily. She wouldn't shift. Loved it here. Towards the end, every Sunday without fail, she would go to the graveyard on the edge of Camberwell and make sure her plot was waiting."

"And was it?" Serena asked.

He nodded. "How do you know, whatsername, Edith?"

She explained about the hospital and how it had led to Robert Merrow and then the sudden departure when she told him what was so wrong with the way he ran his business.

"You told him that, did you?" he asked when she'd finished. "But that isn't why you want this job, is it?"

He blew a halo of smoke from his cigar. Serena delicately flapped a hand in front of her face.

"Well, it sounded interesting and if nothing else I am trained in meeting people." She smiled at him. She had rehearsed her speech well.

"Gammon!" he retorted rudely. "Why couldn't one of your friends step in? Give you something more in line with …"

He paused. Serena waited. "A kept woman?" she suggested lightly.

"No," he said mildly. "A classy one."

Serena crossed her arms and legs. "I take it that's a compliment. The answer of course is that I didn't ask, they didn't offer and if they had I wouldn't have accepted. And I want this job, if you want the truth, because I need the money, because I want to buy my way out of the life I'm in and never again will I do it through anyone's efforts but my own. OK?"

For a long moment he just looked thoughtfully at her. "I'm surprised," he said, stubbing out his cigar.

"Why?" she asked, knowing he wasn't offended, surprised he wasn't. "That someone like me is prepared to work?"

"No. That Robert whatsisname didn't strangle you." He drained his whiskey and signalled for another.

"I have no intention of telling you how to run your club," she told him. "If that's what you think. Anyway, I wouldn't have said it was their health that was in danger here," she added.

"What would you say then?"

At that moment, Sir Lewis emerged from the dining room, a little unsteady on his feet, not enough to fall flat on his face, but enough to make it necessary for him to clutch his companion who, Serena hoped, was getting what she wanted out of the evening with such a man.

She turned back to Ed. "I must be getting back," she said pleasantly. "Thank you for the drink."

He made no attempt to detain her. "By the way, Serena," he called after her as she turned to go. "What were you going to say? What's in danger here, if not his health?" He nodded towards the departing Sir Lewis.

"Oh that's easy," she said, looking over her shoulder with a charming smile. "His integrity."

His eyes narrowed. "Mmm. Interesting. Just tell me, none of my business of course, but if it comes to that, what happened to yours?"

She paused briefly, her back to him. And then without looking back she walked down the stairs and out of the club.

Chapter Twenty-One

It wasn't until she was nearly at the corner of the street, furiously pushing her way through the late night crowds that swarmed the pavements that Serena realized she had no jacket, no money and her bag was still at the club.

Dear heaven. She glanced uneasily back in the direction of Frobisher's and bit her lip. Now what? It was late September and the evenings were already decidedly chilly. Out here on this dodgy street, her options were not promising. The doorway behind her led to a strip show; ahead of her a cinema promised to expose virgins to the mercy of the sexual desires of aliens.

She stood on the kerb, unsure of which way to go and being jostled on both sides, already regretting a scene she would have found absurd enacted by anyone else. Anyway, she thought, defensively, who was he to question anyone's integrity? The man paying her rent, of course, she answered herself gloomily.

"Damn," she muttered. "Oh bloody, fucking, damn,"

She sank against the wall and dropped her head, chafing her bare arms. Another job gone, she thought morosely. The job was fine, she was fine. Everything had been fine until he showed up. He was the problem. Maybe she could telephone Tipper from a call box, if there was one, get him to bring her things out to her. Maybe she could ...

"Looking for business, sweetheart?" A voice leered over her shoulder. She gave a stifled scream and sprang away from the wall.

"Oh my God," she yelped, backing away from a swarthy-looking man with greasy hair and a gold tooth who, just minutes earlier, had been guarding the doorway to the strip club. "Go away, you revolting little man. Do I look like I want a trick? Go away, *away*. Do you hear me?"

"Bugger off, sunshine." Ed was talking to the man who had accosted her. "And yes," he took Serena's arm and drew her away from the interested crowd who had gathered hearing her scream. "You do look dodgy, slouched against the wall like that. Oh, stop looking so outraged," he said. "C'mon back. I shouldn't have said that, but you shouldn't be so fucking rude."

"Me? Rude?"

"Yes. Rude. You wouldn't have said that to one of those sleazeballs who run the banks in this country, would you? Bit short on integrity there, if you don't mind me mentioning it. But it doesn't matter that you insult my business integrity, does it?"

She had, as it happened, begun to feel ashamed of how she had behaved, but the truth in what he was saying now had the opposite effect on her. Instead, she glanced either way and lowered her voice as she glared into his face.

"Mr Stein. Believe me, I'm sorry if you don't like the truth, but what do you expect me to say? That all my life I've been waiting to smile at men like Lewis whatsisname and not care that they're utterly vile? That I think it's the ultimate thrill to leave my children each evening just to flatter airheads with brains the size of a pea and 'For Rent' written across their forehead? You wanted honesty and you got it."

"So what's the difference between smiling at Lewis Bagley and people like Malcolm Brisley Jones? No, no don't take off again. You'll get picked up or mugged."

"Don't mention that man to me," she breathed, trying to shake off his hand and striding along the pavement. "That was for my ... Stephen's sake. And sometimes," she added, "for charity. What's so dishonest about that? And anyway, how do you know what I did?"

"Saw you one night at the opera." He blew a cloud of smoke from his cigar. It curled up into the night air. It seemed to interest him more than she did. "Some fundraising thing or other," he went on, looking down at her. "You were sitting next to him, charming the pants off him."

"If you mean I was being pleasant, what's wrong with that?"

"Well, if you want my opinion — and I can see that you don't but I'll tell you anyway — you look a great deal more honest standing in the reception at Frobisher's than you did that night. At least everyone knows why you're being nice to them. That stupid twat, Brisley Whatsis thought you meant it."

"No, he didn't," she said uncomfortably. "You know it's not the same thing."

"Isn't it? What's the difference, then? Go on, enlighten me. What is it?"

"One is a courteous social exchange and the other is …" She trailed off. "This is ridiculous. What does it matter? You shouldn't have said I had no integrity. That was insulting."

"I never said that. I simply asked what had happened to yours to allow yourself to be in the company of people you despise. I don't despise them."

"You should," she shot back.

"Why? They don't interest me. They're clients. That's all. Business."

"Not all business has to be swarming with such repellent customers."

"That's about as sensible as saying a butcher should only serve vegetarians. Stop prancing around on the moral high ground, Mrs Carmichael. Morality is only possible if everyone is moral," adding helpfully as she stared blankly back at him. "Jean Paul Sartre."

"I know that," she snapped, pretty sure that he didn't. She glanced sideways at him. "What was I supposed to say, then?"

He shrugged. "You might have said, 'Well, I can't afford integrity at the moment', like everyone else here I have to earn money. Or, even better, 'I certainly don't think being paid an honest wage to do an honest job is sacrificing my integrity.' Instead of which you stormed off."

Serena silently berated herself for creating such a scene. They had reached the steps leading up to the club entrance. She wasn't sure what to do next.

"I don't come after all my staff," he told her in a cheerful voice. "On the other hand, I can't remember that anyone's ever stalked off before, so that might be why."

She managed a weak smile. "You surprise me. Thank you, I can see you're trying to make it easy for me to return to work but we both know that's not possible."

He looked up into the sky. "Bloody women," he breathed. "We don't know that at all. We both know that at this moment we need each other. I can't be without a receptionist — and I don't want another one. I like seeing you when I come in — and you don't really want to go, do you?"

She threw him a startled look.

"Oh Christ." He walked round in a circle, his hands stuffed in his pockets, then came back and stood in front of her. "OK," he sighed. "I'm sorry. Truly, unbelievably, one hundred per cent kosher sorry. How's that?"

"Well, really," she said, flustered at such extravagance. "I mean, absolutely unnecessary. Clearly I need to apologise as well. For heaven's sake let go of my arm, people will think you're trying to pick me up."

"I take it that's a yes. Good. Now buck up. I'm late. Mike thinks you were feeling dodgy — that's what I told him — that you'd gone to get some fresh air. Just go back and say you're feeling better."

He was already walking towards his waiting car, the driver on the pavement holding open the door. He slid into the back seat while his driver hurried round to take his place behind the wheel. She watched while the maroon Bentley inched its way into the gap between the parked cars in the narrow street and then, gathering speed, swept past her as she stood on the steps. She half lifted her hand to wave, but Ed was already talking on the car phone and didn't notice. Quickly she lowered her arm, glancing hastily around to make sure her wasted gesture hadn't been noticed. Then she turned and walked into the club.

*

Unlike Cheryl, Alex didn't enjoy the idea of Serena working at Frobisher's. He frowned, listening carefully as she told him what it entailed. For some reason she was anxious that he approved and understood; but had she really wanted this, she knew, she would have confided in him before she accepted the job. His good opinion was necessary because he had been there for her and Harry was, in her view, so much better. And of course because he had made her feel needed.

"I'm just afraid you'll exhaust yourself," he explained, gently. "When people have been through traumatic experiences, fatigue is a natural result.

Not just physically but mentally as well. It takes longer than you imagine to mend as a whole person. I just want you to be careful."

She smiled and reached across the table to squeeze his hand. "I will. Of course I will. And it's not for ever. But I love your concern, it means a lot to me."

His face glowed with quiet pleasure. The small restaurant in Pimlico that Alex had decided was 'theirs' was nearly full and they couldn't be heard above the pleasant buzz of conversation. But still Alex lowered his voice to an intimate whisper. "Sometime," he took both of her hands in his. "We'll resolve everything. Without hurting anyone."

A small flicker of dismay crossed her face. Too late she remembered her resolve to avoid activating Alex's interest in her. Alice was still in his life, albeit removed from the central position she had once occupied. But still there. Alex couldn't find it in himself to hurt her by ending it. "All of us need time to adjust," he explained to Serena, who queried the wisdom of this.

"Of course," she agreed, reaching for her wine glass. "Now tell me, how was the conference?"

Cheryl, on the other hand — when she wasn't giggling girlishly at some private idea of her own about what happened at Frobisher's — took to grilling Serena about what was worn there and seemed disappointed that understated cocktail dresses were the order of the day.

"I mean what about when you have to entertain the customers, don't you have to, well, dress up a bit?" she asked, waggling her eyebrows.

"Well, they have their own guests." Serena piled laundry into the washing machine, trying to envisage Frobisher's awash with full evening dress. "I'm not required to entertain them. Except ..." She paused with an armful of Harry's T-shirts, recalling Jonny Cooper insisting she joined him for a drink when a girlfriend was late, and another occasion when a friend of Ed Stein's paused by the desk and asked her if she'd join him for dinner to balance out an all-male party. She had tried to refuse but he lifted her phone and called Ed ensconced in his office at the top of the building.

"Boss's orders," he said, replacing the phone. "Says Mike will have you covered. Just to let him know. C'mon."

With no alternative Serena moved after him. Mike just grunted when she explained.

Since the night when he had persuaded her to return to Frobisher's nearly a month before, she had seen little of Ed. Tipper said he was having an affair with a married woman who lived in New York which accounted for his frequent absences. Mike was more forthcoming.

"Stupid cow's putting the pressure on. The only reason she doesn't pitch up here is because he heads her off by going there, and her present husband wouldn't give her a penny if he found out."

"What difference would that make? Ed's not exactly a pauper is he?"

"True. But you're assuming he'll marry her. And there's no guarantee that he will. She's not stupid."

"Then why's he based here?" she asked.

Mike lifted his head from the list in front of him and chuckled. "He says it's because his tailor's here. Horniman's in Savile Row."

"Heavens." Serena laughed. "I've heard of stranger reasons."

"Could be true," Mike told her. "Lenny Horniman used to live next door to him when they were kids in Plaistow. He wouldn't go to anyone else. Course, Lenny's chairman of the company now, but he personally supervises when Ed goes in."

Ed had, however, taken to giving her a brief nod and a smile as he walked through the lobby en route to his office when he was there. During dinner, which she had to reluctantly admit had been more amusing and entertaining than she thought it would be, she had been sent a note from Ed. It read: "Thought you might be a bit lonely up there on the moral high ground, so relax and remember what Emerson said: 'Nothing is at last sacred but the integrity of your own mind.' And it's only dinner." It was signed with a flourishing E.

She gave a covert look around the table then screwed it up and quietly slipped it into her bag.

"Except," she now said to Cheryl. "If their guest is late or fails to turn up for whatever reason. You step in for a moment or two."

"You could be talking about my Kev," she shrieked as she departed to get her Kevin's lunch.

"What's she on about, Mum?" Louise asked, sitting at the table painting purple nail varnish on to her toes.

Serena shrugged. "Who knows with Cheryl? Lou, be a love, go and round up your laundry."

"Oh Mum," Louise wailed. "My toes'll smudge. I'll do it in a minute."

"Wretched child," Serena growled. "Don't worry, I'll do it myself."

Louise's room was a tip. With a sigh, Serena began picking her way through the chaos of discarded clothes, magazines, wet towels and the remains of last night's chicken nuggets that she and Daphy had shared when Daphy had stayed over. Automatically she began straightening the room, although she knew Alex would have said Louise should have been made to do it, with small penalties imposed for every day she failed to restore it to something approximating order. But then Alex didn't really understand the huge compensation quota that Serena carried around with her.

Whatever exchange she had with her children was confined briefly to the morning and two hours in the afternoon before she left to get to Frobisher's. They were short-changed enough as it was. The risk Alex described, that they would see her workload as the natural lot of a single working mother, was one she was prepared to take if it meant her time with them was reasonably harmonious. This mood lasted until she tried to pull Louise's bed aside to find any errant laundry and found it wouldn't budge. Kneeling down she craned her head to see what was causing the blockage. It appeared to be a long narrow box piled so high with Louise's possessions that it had wedged itself tight underneath the bed.

With a huge tug Serena pulled the box free and for a moment gazed uncomprehendingly at the contents as the top layer spilled over on to the floor. DVD's, and dozens of them. Too many to justify Louise's limited pocket money. She turned the first few over, which were still untouched in their boxes, and then with a sickening lurch of her stomach sat back on her heels.

Later she wondered why in moments of crisis she was incapable of rational thought or action. Her first instinct had been to storm downstairs and confront Louise with what was clearly a haul of, at best, black-market DVD's and, at worst, stolen goods.

She began to sift through the box. It made no sense. Hair combs still on their cardboard holders, cheap perfume, tights in their packets, scarves, T-shirts with heavy-metal slogans daubed across them still in polythene bags. One by one she lifted them out and then dropped them hastily back in the box. All were items that could be discreetly slipped into a pocket or a bag.

"My God," she whispered. "Oh my God."

Rapidly she reached out for a bin liner and poured the entire contents into it. Then she filled a second. After that she tore a blank sheet of paper from one of Louise's schoolbooks and, with a black Pentel, carefully printed in block letters a short note which she put inside the first sack. She left them both by the front door and went in search of Louise.

"Come with me," she ordered, standing against the door, holding it open. "No buts. Just come with me."

"But where?" Louise sulked. "I've got to meet Damon and Daphy."

"Listen to me." Serena kept her voice down for fear the Plaxtons might hear. "The people you are most likely to meet the way you're going on are child crime officers. You stupid, stupid little fool."

Louise stared back, her mouth slightly open. First she went red and then the familiar defiance began to creep into her face.

"You shouldn't be spying on me," she began. "It's not right —"

She got no further. Serena strode into the room, picked up the nail varnish and hurled it into the bin. "I'm only sorry I'm too fond a parent not to hand you over to the police," she retorted fiercely. "Now, get your jacket. We're going to that church in the High Street and we're going to give this lot to the Vicar. I've written an anonymous note saying I have no way of giving this stuff back and for him to give it to the police. And then we'll talk about this. I said your jacket, Lou. Right now."

Without a word Louise did as she was told. Harry was at his art class and would not need collecting for another hour. The twenty-minute journey on foot, each clutching a bin liner bulging with stolen property, to the church at the end of the High Street, was made in silence.

It was surreal. Me, she kept telling herself, a respectable woman. Well, as respectable as any woman could be with a husband on the run, a klepto-daughter and a job that is dubious to say the least, walking brazenly along the High Street with a sack of stolen goods. She just prayed Alex didn't drive past or that she wouldn't run into Betty Plaxton or Cheryl. Or worse, the Mojanis, who would have had every prejudice against her confirmed.

A handwritten sign saying "Please leave jumble in vestry" with a big blue arrow pointing around the corner was on the church door when they got there.

"Wait here," Serena ordered a silent Louise. She walked around to the side door, her feet crunching loudly on the gravel path, and cautiously pushed the door open. It led into a small vestibule which was piled high with boxes and bags, just like the ones she had dragged from the house. A notice read, *"Thank you for your donation. Mrs Priston and Mrs Anderson will be here between five and six if you wish to give them your donation personally. Otherwise we would be grateful if you would just leave it here."*

The inner door was closed. She twisted the handle but it was locked. "Hello," she called out just in case and waited. Silence. She glanced at her watch. Almost five. Just time. She went outside and hissed loudly to Louise.

"Buck up," she ordered, beckoning to her, looking around to make sure no one else was coming. "Lou, get a move on."

Louise came panting around the side of the church, lugging her plastic sack. "Throw them in there," Serena ordered, hurling her own sack on top of the others.

Louise did as she was bid and then, carefully closing the door after them, Serena pushed Louise ahead of her and they both half ran, half walked, back down the path. As they reached the corner, Serena signalled Louise to stop behind her as she cautiously peered round the edge of the grey stone building. No one was coming up the path. She grabbed Louise's arm and they scurried towards the gate, trying not to run. The trickle of passers-by gave them only a cursory glance as they emerged into the road.

It was only once they had put a reasonable distance between them and the church that Serena let out her breath, and not until they were both safely indoors again that she rounded on Louise.

".The truth, Louise," she demanded, peeling off her coat and throwing it across a chair. "It's too serious for anything else."

"They were given to me," Louise claimed.

Serena damped the ball of her hand to her forehead. "Oh stop it," she ordered. "Think. I've just become an accessory to a theft to keep you out of trouble, and you come up with that? Try again."

"OK," Louise mumbled. "Someone dumped them on Damon and he was petrified that his dad would go berserk if he found them."

"With good reason," Serena broke in grimly. "And you did what?"

"I said I'd keep them until he could find some way of getting them back to the shops or the lad who nicked them in the first place. That's the truth, Mum," she finished. "I didn't think you'd find them. I didn't mean to involve you."

Serena gazed silently back at Louise. How could she tell if it was the truth? There was no way except to hope that the basically decent child she was lurked beneath this street-wise being she had become.

"OK, Lou. I believe you. But next time, I won't bail you out. God knows what the Vicar will think when they go through the sacks, but don't tell anyone, not even Damon. Say when you looked they were gone. That I must have taken them to the dump. But don't tell him. The fewer people who know, the better."

"But he'll think you're really cool," Louise protested. "He won't tell."

Dear heaven, she'd finally got her daughter's admiration, and only because she'd behaved like a petty criminal herself.

"Certainly not," she told her firmly. "Damon might tell his parents and then I couldn't possibly — I mean, it Louise — I would not be able to lie. So far at least I've been spared that."

There followed a small tussle in which for once Serena emerged the winner. Louise was despatched to tidy up the rest of her room and Serena collapsed into a chair with a strong cup of coffee. When Mike phoned to ask if she would come into the club to have dinner that evening as a favour, she groaned with exhaustion.

"Dinner? You mean work?"

"No, I mean dinner. Ed's got some investors coming in from Paris. You speak French, don't you? Well, he's the only one who speaks it and he can't manage them all. I don't speak a word of the lingo. He said he'd make it worth your while."

Chapter Twenty-Two

Tipper came over to babysit. This was greeted with a cheer by Harry, who had found a soulmate with whom to indulge his passion for his latest craze, Fantasy Football. Nor was any serious objection raised by Louise who, Serena suspected, approved of Tipper once she discovered he preferred Nirvana to Damon's unremitting passion for rap. She was to come home from the party she was going to by cab, called for by Tipper at midnight.

The argument that erupted over this had been settled before Tipper's arrival, an uneasy compromise between Louise's demand that she come back on her own with Daphy and Damon in a cab they called when they felt the night's revelries offered no more, and Serena's view that she was not being unreasonable in monitoring activities and that eleven-thirty was not unjust. The discussion had lasted a relatively short time. After the afternoon's dramas, Louise was very aware that it was a miracle she was being allowed out at all and disappeared to her room without the customary bang of the door as she went.

"Is it the dessert you're after being?" Tipper teased, his crooning Irish accent laced with laughter as he stood in the doorway to see her off. Panic crossed her face. She dived back into the hallway and started tugging her black crepe dress down and the neckline up as the driver waited patiently by the car.

"You don't think I look like an old slapper, do you?" she asked anxiously.

"I don't think any man looking for a 'good time'," he rolled his eyes suggestively, "would choose you."

She gazed down at the dress, now three years old but still wearable, and tried to make the wide shoulder straps do more than cover a few inches of her shoulders. "You mean I look frumpy?" she demanded.

"I mean," he groaned, winding her velvet wrap around her shoulders and pushing her gently back down the path. "That you look just what Ed Stein ordered."

"I do? I mean, what do you mean? Tipper, stop it." But he'd already closed the door with a curious Harry staring up at him.

When Alex called round at ten he was taken aback when Tipper opened the door.

"Out?" he repeated. "But we arranged that I'd drop by for a drink. She never said anything about work."

"Well, you know what these career women are like," sighed Tipper, who felt a pang of sympathy at the disappointment on Alex's face. "Come on in. It's just me and Harry watching the footie. Madam's at a party."

Alex shuddered. "Thank you, Tipper, but I don't think that's quite my idea of a cultural evening. I'll leave you to it. Let Serena know I called." He turned and walked briskly down the path to his car parked at the kerb.

Tipper watched him go, trying to find in the restrained, well-dressed figure the passion, the energy that most women preferred. He was an odd choice for someone like Serena, but then, as he was fond of telling her, it was because he didn't understand women that he preferred men.

*

Serena had never been to the club at the weekend. Most members disappeared to their wives and homes in the country and it was usually relatively quiet, which is why she was never needed. Mondays were always hectic when they all returned, needing to unwind after the exhaustion of family life, followed by Thursdays and Fridays, building up their stamina to prepare for it.

She made her way up the broad stairs to reception and paused to have a quick word with Trish, whose turn it was to be on duty.

"Upstairs." Trish nodded towards the lift as Serena removed her wrap and handed it to her to be put away. "Wants a pow-wow before they all turn up." She leaned forward and whispered with a giggle. "See if you can see any whips. Pansy's convinced he's got a whip fetish."

"Heavens," Serena raised her eyebrows. "Well, if I see so much as a riding crop, you'll see two people haring out of here in minutes. And if you do," she chuckled. "Let the first one go — that'll be me."

"What?" Trish said. "Looking like that? You'll be lucky."

Tipper's words rattled uneasily in her head as she pressed the button on the elevator. Inside she tried to see her reflection in the dark oak-panelled lining and gave one last ineffectual tug at her skirt, suddenly wishing it was longer than knee length and that she'd worn lower heels than the three-inch satin ones that had been bought to match the dress. Suddenly, in a dress bought so long ago to please Stephen, who wanted his wife to look feminine and sexy, she wasn't so sure. By the time the doors slid noiselessly apart and she stepped out into a large, square, carpeted lobby, she had decided she looked like a tart. Hastily she rushed back into the lift and pressed the lobby button.

"Trish," she ran to reception hissing urgently, "lend me your combs. Yes, yours. I think I'd look better with it up."

Trish obligingly gave her the slides from her own hair. Serena raced for the powder room and whipped her hair which had been hanging loose around her neck up into a coil. She studied her reflection. Business-like and severe enough to detract from the dress. A condition, she thought grimly, as she once again rode up in the lift, that couldn't easily be applied to her state of mind. She really shouldn't be so influenced by what people said. She never had been before. She knew it was to do with Ed Stein, not wanting him to think that she couldn't cut it, annoyed with herself for caring if he did.

Ahead of her the double doors, firmly shut, were flanked on one side by what appeared to be a Turner over a French console table. On the other, a Stubbs by the look of it. Her eyes widened. There was no sign of life and no one seemed to have heard her. From behind the doors she heard the sound of male laughter. Her hand was already raised to knock when the door was opened by Mike, holding a tumbler of whiskey and wearing a dark silk suit.

"Serena." He greeted her warmly, took her arm and drew her in. "I wondered where you'd got to. You came out of the lift, and then went down again."

Christ, there must have been a security camera watching her. She blushed. "I forgot to tell Trish that, I ... that if anyone called, to say I was up here." She looked around uneasily. "Where's the monitor?"

"Under Ed's desk," he explained. "Looks like NASA under there. He's got buttons that activate every door and lift in the building without his moving an inch. And he knows who comes in and who leaves."

"Heavens," she said. She peered over at the timeless elegance of the roll-top antique desk and then at the man who'd dragged it into the twenty-first century. Stephen, she reflected, would have recoiled in horror at such a beautiful piece being sullied by technology.

"Ed's gizmo mad," Mike explained. "Good ot you to come at such short notice," he murmured, as a white-coated man appeared at his side. "What'll you have?"

"Oh, just orange for the moment." She smiled at the manservant. "Incidentally, why am I needed, I can't quite figure it out?"

"The Frogs suddenly announced they've got their fancy-bits with them. Mistresses," he added, when she said nothing. "I don't think Ed wanted to be outdone with his strife being in Manhattan."

"You don't mean he's told them I'm his?" she whispered, appalled.

Mike shrugged. "There's no telling what he's told them. But I don't think so. I think he just wants someone to deflect the women if they get in the way of business, or maybe just to even things up a bit."

Relief flooded her face. Mike laughed. "Oh, don't look so horrified. He's not that bad, surely?"

Serena shook her head. "No, not at all," she said politely, as he led her over to where Ed was standing.

She had been expecting something more functional, more business-like than this elegant drawing room. She gave a quick glance around as they made their way across the cream and blue patterned Aubusson carpet to where they were standing. The walls were lined with pictures, among them, she was sure, a Goya. The rest of the room was filled with eighteenth-century consoles and sofas. The conflict with the style he had chosen for the club was sharp indeed.

Ed was talking to Matthew Turner, the club's finance director. They both turned as she came up to them. Ed smiled.

"Bit rushed? Sorry about that." He was holding a fat cigar in one hand and the other was pushed into the pocket of his trousers, crumpling the line of his beautifully cut charcoal double-breasted jacket. He made no attempt to shake her hand or even, as Mike had done, touch her arm in greeting.

"It was no trouble," she replied. "Only I should warn you, my French is not absolutely accurate."

"Doesn't matter," he said, appraising her. "Mike says you translated for him the other night. Seemed to do the trick. Surprising lady, aren't you?"

She thought he was about to say something else, but changed his mind. "C'mon," he went on briskly. "Let's talk strategy."

Briefly, and mostly for Serena's sake, he gave an abbreviated account of why it was so important to look after the French. They were courting Ed to transform their club in Montmartre in the same way he had Frobisher's.

"Which is only interesting if in return Frobisher's get a slice of the action in France and the benefit of their members coming over here at weekends — special deals, that kind of thing. We need to fill up this club at weekends." He waved his cigar hand around. "If we do, we can then make it financially viable to think about a country branch to soak up those who disappear to the Shires on Saturday morning."

"Of Frobisher's?" Serena blurted out.

"Yes, Frobisher's," he agreed, knowing exactly what she meant. "More country club. Entertaining the neighbours and the weekend guests, that kind of thing."

"And where do I come in?" Serena asked.

"I wasn't expecting Zizi and Jeanne-Maire or whatever their names are to pitch up. Too many for me to handle since none of them speak English. And these two can't say good morning between them."

Mike and Matthew looked sheepish. Serena smiled sympathetically. "I think you might do worse than let them charm Zizi and Jeanne-Maire," she responded loyally. "I'm sure they'd prefer them to me."

Mike and Matthew laughed.

"I know what I'm doing," Ed growled, exhaling a blue cloud of smoke, his eyes narrowing. Serena put a hand to her neck. She wished he wouldn't do that. It made her feel uncomfortable rather than attractive.

"Who said I wanted to keep them happy?" Ed remarked mildly. "I just don't want them to make old Jules and Jim — what are they called?" He turned to Mike.

"Gilbert and Olivier," Mike reminded him.

"Well, whatever. I just don't want Gilbert and his mate to feel the need to rush off to f —" he paused, seeing Serena's wooden expression. "To entertain them," he corrected himself. "Before I get a few details on the table."

Serena stiffened. Her mouth went dry. A pang of disappointment went through her. "I'm sorry," she began coldly, Tipper's words rattling frantically around her head. "Just what do you mean? What are you suggesting I do?"

"Suggesting? Nothing. You just be yourself."

"You mean I er ... I'm nice to them," she emphasized the word.

Ed turned to find an ashtray and ground out his cigar. "Well, Serena, I hope we'll all be nice to them," he said conversationally. He turned and thrust the other hand in his pocket. "I just want you to be nice to them, but in French. I'm not a great judge of these things, but I would have thought with their bit of stuff sitting alongside them, you'll be perfectly safe from any ideas they might get. Not to mention knowing that old Mike here and Matthew or even me, come to that, are ready to step in should your charm overpower them. I just thought with you speaking French you'd be perfect for what I had in mind. You look terrific. Now, shall we go?"

He stood aside to let Serena go first and if it occurred to him that she'd suddenly gone pink, she hoped he would think it was a reaction to the compliment and not fury that she had misread the situation.

As they reached the entrance to the restaurant, where they were to meet their guests, Ed touched her arm. She looked up at him to find him grinning down at her. "I thought your hair looked nice down. After you."

Serena's French became a source of delight to the representatives of l'Hirondelle, the holding company of the leisure group who owned Les Cages, since it was the fractured element rather than the accuracy which they appeared to find entrancing. Ed, who spoke the language fluently, placed Serena between the president of the French company and its finance director, at a round table in the corner of the restaurant. Their companions sat either side of him. Expensively dressed, immaculately made up, jewellery from the exclusive shops that lined the Rue St Honoré. She recognized every item they wore and at a pinch could have priced them too.

At that moment she looked up and caught Ed's eye. To her they looked exactly what they were. Kept women. Dear God, had she ever looked that obvious?

"Gilbert," she turned to the man on her left, knowing Ed was listening to her: "*Dites-moi, cela fait si longtemps depuis que j'y étais, était le Grand Vefour toujours merveilleux?*"

When Serena excused herself to ring home, her side of the table was being noted for the element of competition that Gilbert and Olivier were engaged in for her attention. She had the oddest feeling Ed was annoyed with her.

She called from the bar to remind Tipper to check the taxi to collect Louise and shrieked when he reminded her about Alex.

"Oh God. Alex. I was so busy trying to get ready and get here on time, I absolutely forgot. Oh poor Alex. Ring him, Tip, will you? Tell him I'll call tomorrow. And Tip?" She turned away from the bar so that the two men sitting nearby wouldn't hear. "I know what you meant about being what Ed ordered. You're quite wrong. It's absolutely legit and above board."

Tipper shook with laughter. "If you say so, darling heart. Whoops. Must fly, a divine man is doing unspeakably delicious things to an alien force. Taxi's checked. I rang the party and spoke to Madam. Well, I just didn't want a hassle with someone telling me she wasn't there when the taxi arrived. No, Harry's asleep. Well, at least, he will be when the film's finished."

Serena replaced the phone and hesitated about ringing Alex herself. The decision was made for her when she glanced round to see Ed leading his guests to the elevator to go up to his quarters for coffee and brandy.

He looked up as she joined them, the group sitting comfortably in deep armchairs, and with no more than a cursory glance returned to what he was saying to the man next to him. Business or not, she was a mother first and too bad if he didn't like her leaving the table until he thought she should. The evening was going well. If they didn't ask him to perform the same miracle with their club in Montmartre she would be surprised.

By the time they had left it was after one. Serena felt exhausted and, having been kissed by all their guests, twice by Gilbert and Olivier, she was all but wiped out. Slowly stiffing a yawn, she turned back to collect her wrap from Trish while Ed and Mike went to see their guests to their cars. She felt tired but pleased with how things had gone. She couldn't believe that Ed would find fault with her contribution, in which she had managed to act as interpreter between Mike and Matthew and their guests, and persuaded the two Frenchmen to overcome their reluctance to at least try to speak English. Not to mention sidelining the women once they were upstairs so that the business end of the evening could be completed.

As the evening progressed, so too had her French and her wit. She was still smiling about a particularly funny remark Ed had made to Gilbert when she heard a gasp next to her. The lobby was fairly full with the evening beginning to wind down and other guests making their way to the front door, so it took her a minute or two to register the identity of the man in front of her.

"Good God." She gave a small step back.

"Serena," exclaimed George Kincaid. "What are you doing here?"

"Well, George," she battled for composure, "I could ask the same of you." Behind him a woman with red hair and a tight dress hovered. George turned and whispered something to her and she moved away with another couple. Serena did not recognize any of them.

"Well, some friends dragged me along," he blustered. "Odd sort of place. Not me, really. If you know what I mean."

Serena's mind was racing. If he was here as a guest he might never turn up again. She could bluff, say she was dining with friends. And then she stopped. Partly because George was looking so flustered himself but mostly because she had nothing to be ashamed about.

"I work here, George," she told him calmly. "Tonight was a business dinner."

His face went pale. "You *work* here?"

She nodded. "Of course. Why else would I be in this club at this time of night?"

"But why here?" He registered more horror than was necessary.

A flash of irritation went through her. "Why not? I have two children to raise and a home to maintain. I'm not exactly in a position to call on anyone else to finance all of that, am I?"

"But Melanie, surely ..."

Serena leaned against the wall. It had been a very long day. "Melanie was the only one, George, and you don't understand friendship — no, of course you don't, what am I saying? — if you think you should impose on your friends, but neither do you abandon them. That's why I'm here, George. What about you?"

George looked round and licked his lips. Hastily he grabbed Serena's arm and led her to a quiet corner. Out of the corner of her eye she saw Ed returning with Mike, but seeing her with George they walked on into the library.

"Serena," George was saying, "I'm sure you're aware of my membership."

"Your membership, George? No, I had no idea. I haven't seen you here before."

"No, well, I only pop in at weekends. To unwind, you know." He laughed a choking jovial laugh. "Need to de-stress, enjoy some good conversation."

"Good conversation? Here?" She almost laughed in his face. "Tell you what, George, let me know when that happens and I'll have it stopped. No one would come if that gets out."

His face hardened. Gone was the urbane and chic gynaecologist who all the mothers loved. In its place was a panic-stricken man with his reputation in her hands.

"Yes, yes, I know." A small line of moisture had gathered on his upper lip. Serena almost felt sorry for him. And would have, if George had once phoned her in two years, had championed her when the world closed its doors. If George had not conveniently forgotten her existence and the vast sums of money she had raised for his precious Wendover wing, she might have felt a stirring of pity for a man revered by the world as above reproach only to be found, humiliatingly, in a club that was everything they sneered at.

"Look, Serena, I would appreciate it if you forgot you ever saw me here. What do you say? I mean, we were always good friends."

"Remind me, George, when that was," she returned coldly.

"Well, you know how it is, Serena. You never called me. I just assumed you wanted to disappear."

"Oh *please.*" She could see the group of people he had been with waiting for him. "George, I'm here during the week, so it's unlikely I'll see you again. Let's pretend we never saw each other, OK. Now, I think your friends are waiting. Bye, George."

She turned and walked away, almost colliding with Ed who was watching her from the library doorway.

"Old friend?" he asked quietly.

She looked wearily up at him. "Sort of. Not any more. Ed, I think I'd like to go home now. Would that be all right?"

"Of course. I was just waiting for you. I'll drive you."

"No, please. That's fine," she protested. "If Mike could just arrange a car ..."

"Oh stuff it, Serena. You've done me a real favour. If bloody old Gilbert could have," he stopped and then smiled, "I mean, taken you with him, he would have done. Look," he spread his hands and smiled into her tired face. "No whips, no handcuffs. I'll even drive, so you'll be quite safe."

She blushed. Wasn't there anything he didn't know? "OK," she smiled back, tiredness triumphing over independence. "That would be most kind."

"Most kind," he mimicked. "C'mon, Mrs Carmichael. Home."

Chapter Twenty-Three

Cheryl Tosney saw Serena alight from the passenger seat of Ed's car well after two in the morning. The sight filled her with such envy she unconsciously gripped the net that stood between her and detection from the street.

From where she was on the other side of the road, Serena could see the eerie blue glow from the television in the front room of Cheryl's house where the hapless Kevin sat transfixed. A slight movement of the curtain in the room above made her eye travel up and quickly look away. For a moment she considered waving. But then pity more than irritation stopped her. Serena knew Cheryl's chief preoccupation was the comings and goings of the residents of Foster Street. Life with Kevin, it was clear to the slightest observer, was an emotional and intellectual wasteland. But she stayed, for whatever reason.

"More to spite him," Betty Plaxton retorted, after Cheryl had complained to Les about Bradley's hooligan life in the street. "He'd be thrilled if she buggered off."

"How do you know?" Serena asked, uncomfortably aware that she should not be prying into Cheryl's life.

Betty went pink. "Because I do, is all I'm saying," she replied firmly. "Must fly. Les'll think I've left home I've been out so long. Ta ra."

Serena wondered if Cheryl had not exaggerated after all, when she said Betty had been a bit too chummy with her Kevin. God, my girl, she admonished herself with a giggle. You're getting to be just like the neighbours.

Of late Cheryl had been quizzing Serena quite closely about Frobisher's. It must, Serena thought, be obvious by now that she was not going to get names out of her, but it was also clear Cheryl's interest in the clientele was increasing rather than diminishing. That she was now monitoring her arrival home was not surprising, just rather sad. Especially as she was probably unaware that the light from the landing in her house perfectly outlined her shadowy figure standing behind the net curtain.

Cheryl held her breath. The car alone had been worth the wait. Sleek, shiny, the embodiment of Cheryl's dream of what she would be riding around in when she won the lottery or when she finally made it as a model. Not a model who wore clothes and paraded along catwalks. More one who wore very little and draped herself across satin sheets or a bloke like a Chippendale. Then she would tell Kevin that her life was going to mean something. Then she could dress like Serena, meet men like that bloke ushering her out of the car.

She watched as Serena disappeared into the house, followed by the man. Only then did she step back and sink down on the divan with its pink satin pillows and padded satin headboard. Absently she smoothed the matching bed cover and anxiously bit her lip.

The photographs had not produced anything, even though the photographer she'd got to come round had told her that *Who's Next Door* would jump at the chance of using them. With this dangling in front of her, Cheryl had willingly disported herself on the bed for the man whose number she had found on a card in a shop window.

If there had been a moment of doubt before she laid out the flimsy minuscule negligee, unwrapped the suspender belt, basque and the leopard-print thong that she had hidden under the bed, it vanished in the beautiful dream she had of being featured as the star find in the next issue of the magazine that boasted it only ever used ordinary women. A feeling of exhilaration engulfed her, egged on by the crooning man behind the camera who encouraged her to greater feats of daring.

For an hour she writhed and turned on her own bed, legs splayed, holding her breasts like melons, her mouth opened in the way she had seen other models — as she now thought of herself — doing in an approximation of ecstasy. All the while the pleasing vision of telling Kevin that she had found a new life spurred her on. Kevin, who was so indifferent to her that he had believed her story about the carpenter coming to measure the bedroom for new cupboards, had remained in the room below while she embarked on the first stage of her new life.

But that had all been six weeks ago. The session had cost her a hundred quid, plus the accessories, and today a card had arrived from *Who's Next Door* turning her down. Cheryl almost wept with disappointment. Now she was also in debt. She eased herself up and glanced across the road and wondered if Serena could up the money a bit. Clearly she was doing all right.

*

On the drive home Ed neither needed nor wanted instructions on how to find his way so the area came as no surprise to him, just perhaps that Serena lived there.

"Used to know this area like the back of my hand," he remarked, as they crossed the river. "By the time I got back from New York it was nearly razed to the ground, new housing estates, one-way systems. Knocked the life out of it."

"What made you come back?" she asked. "New York sounds like it suited you."

He shrugged. "Nowhere is forever. My family — what's left of them — are in Melbourne. America is where I really started, nothing spectacular. I was sixteen last time I lived with my family, with a choice between joining my old man, running the dry-cleaner's he set up, or jumping ship. What would you have done?" He paused. "Exactly."

"So what did you do. In New York, I mean?"

"Really want to know?"

"Of course. You seem to me to have done remarkably well."

"You mean," he said, turning the car towards Kennington. "For a hooligan from Plaistow?"

"Plaistow, eh?" She gave a soft whistle. "You should have said. If I'd known you'd started life with such an advantage, I might have been less impressed."

"Advantage?"

"Absolutely. Nowhere to go but up. Nowhere to fall from."

For a moment he just drove in silence.

"Perhaps you're right," he said. "I've never thought of it like that."

Serena leaned her head back against the headrest. It was a long, long time since she had been so luxuriously chauffeured.

"Try it," she said. "I've discovered the bottom is a very safe place to be."

"Not for someone like you," he answered. "Not much gets past you."

"You mean I sound tough?" she asked, surprised.

"Maybe."

Serena was shocked. Tough? When did that happen? "Anyway," she gave herself a shake. "What happened in New York?"

"Well, I didn't go straight there. Bummed around Europe for a few years, worked in Monte Carlo where I learned to speak French, how to serve drinks and get big tips. Then I got involved with someone that I shouldn't have and when it got heavy I went to America."

She said nothing. Just waited for him to continue.

"God, you're odd," he chuckled. "Most women would have wanted to know about the affair."

"I don't know you well enough to ask," she replied. "And even then, I think it would be unwise to press you."

"Unwise?"

"Well," she said beginning to count on her fingers. "If it was someone you 'shouldn't have' then she was either married — in which case you will, of course, want to protect her name. Or she was underage, then you would do better not to tell me — being the mother of a fourteen-year-old. And if you just went off her, why embarrass her memory by telling anyone?"

"Do you always go on like this?" he asked mildly. The traffic lights halted him at Vauxhall Cross. He turned to look at her.

"When the occasion demands it," she replied primly. "Please go on. You had just left Monte Carlo. And the lights have changed."

"I had noticed," he returned politely, moving forward in the deserted street. "But thank you for drawing that to my attention. So, then I got to New York, I got a job in a bar, then I managed it. Then I moved to a club and then managed that and then the guys who owned it asked me to get the 'Eighty-One' up and running. And then this mob arrived from here and said come and get Frobisher's on its feet. And it was the right moment.

"Marriage broke up, I wanted to be home for a while. You know that feeling? You just need to get back to the point where it all started and see if you can do it all again without fucking it up."

Serena glanced at him. "Did it work?"

"Not sure. Maybe. Still working at it. Here we are, Foster Street. Which one? This it?" Ed asked, peering through the windscreen.

She nodded, watching his face to see his reaction to such a faded house. Not that he'd said anything, but she knew he knew she was used to a more affluent life. He said nothing, just grunted.

"I'll see you in," he insisted, walking round to hold the door as she stepped on to the pavement.

She didn't need an escort on such a short journey, but she was beginning to realize that Ed always did what he wanted. It was easier not to argue. At least Cheryl was being given enough to justify her lonely vigil at the window.

"Would you like a drink? Coffee?" she asked, as she put her key in the door, just praying that Tipper and Harry had not reduced the sitting room to a minefield of discarded cartons and DVD cases and praying even harder that Ed would decline.

"Why not?" he replied, dashing her hopes and stepping into the hall after her. They both paused. The sound of heated voices was coming from the sitting room. Serena moved quickly forward and opened the door.

"How can you say that?" Louise was shouting, standing in the centre of the room brandishing a copy of a music magazine.

"Because they're crap," Tipper retorted, lolling back in the armchair, clearly enjoying baiting the furious Louise.

"What on earth's going on?" Serena stopped them both, standing in the doorway. Together they wheeled round.

"Oh, just Tip thinking he's the world's expert on indie groups," Louise answered, casting a scathing look in Tipper's direction. "Anyone with half a brain knows Nirvana are brilliant."

"And what would you be knowing about Nirvana?" Tip jeered back. "Boy bands are about your level."

"Stop it. Tip, give her a break. And Louise, the Plaxtons will complain at the noise."

"*They'll* complain?" Louise dropped her voice. "Listen. Just listen." She indicated the wall that joined their house to the Plaxtons. "Hear us above the din Bradley's making? Fat chance. He was at the party, absolutely wankered, all of them."

"*Louise*," Serena rebuked her.

"Oh, you know what I mean. I knew they were going to be a pain, Betty and Les have gone off for the night."

From next door the faint strains of a rock group could be heard accompanied by Bradley and several friends roaring along with it.

Ed, standing just behind Serena whispered, "Friends of yours?"

"Friends, you choose," she pointed out, without turning her head. "You don't think, at this moment, I'd choose either of these two, do you?"

She moved aside so that Ed was now visible to them both. "Jesus," Tipper muttered, catching sight of his boss, scrambling to his feet. Louise stared curiously at him.

"You know Tipper of course," Serena said, trying not to laugh as Tipper put an armchair between himself and his employer.

"Evening, sir," he acknowledged, gripping the back of the chair.

"Tip." Ed nodded at him.

"Louise, this is Mr Stein who owns Frobisher's. He was kind enough to bring me home. Ed, this is my daughter Louise, who should be in bed."

"But who has been kind enough to wait up to make sure you're safely home," Ed extended a hand to a suspicious Louise. "And I don't blame you," he added, as she briefly shook it. "A night out might have gone right to her head." He nodded towards Serena. "My mother was just the same. Went berserk whenever we let her out."

Tip stared and Louise giggled. Serena let out her breath.

"Louise, as you're up would you start some coffee?" she asked. "I'll just check Harry. Tip, you've been an angel. Have you ordered a cab?"

"Right away," he said.

"Don't bother with that," Ed chimed in. "A quick cup of coffee and then I'll drop you. Somewhere near here, isn't it?"

Tip looked surprised. "Oval, sir," he grinned. "And that would be grand. Now I'll just give this misguided child a hand with the coffee."

"Well now, if you haven't hit the jackpot," Tipper whispered gleefully as they trooped into the hall. "And it's Ed now, is it?"

"Unless he's changed his name," she retorted, making for the stairs. "And what jackpot?"

"Don't come the innocent with me," he called back. "Oh, and your mother phoned. Call her tomorrow. She had a long talk with Harry."

Serena returned in a few moments to find Ed studying the backs of some of the CDs Louise had left lying around.

"Doesn't look like you, does she?" he remarked, with a nod towards the kitchen where Louise could be heard clattering cups on to a tray.

"No. She's totally Stephen. In every way. Harry looks more like me, I'm told."

"Hmm." He grunted. "Who the hell are *Suicidal Carpets*?" He peered at the label on the back of the plastic wallet.

She laughed. "Don't ask. They'll be history next week. Do sit down."

"Come to the opera with me," he said abruptly, sitting in a corner of the sofa. "Next week. *Rigoletto*. New production."

For an awful moment she thought her jaw had gone slack. She began to stammer. "Opera? With you? Well, I mean, I don't know. How kind. I'm not sure."

"Is that a yes? Christ, what's this?" He eased himself up and removed some of Harry's abandoned *Star Wars* figures. Serena, torn between laughter and nerves, rushed forward and removed them.

"I'm so sorry," she gulped. "I keep telling him to put them away."

"So that's on, is it?" he queried, handing her the last of the figures, peering sideways to see her face where she knelt throwing them all into a wicker basket next to the television.

She sat back on her knees and surveyed him. "Look. Ed. I know you might find this odd, but I would be delighted to come with you to the opera, if you weren't my employer."

"So that's settled then. I'm told the production is trendy. Saw *Così Fan Tutte* all done up in suits. Couldn't stand it. I like opera to look like opera, but I'm prepared to be pleasantly surprised."

"Ed," she protested. "Didn't you hear me? I said —"

"Yes I heard. You sounded ridiculous. Like some middle-aged spinster. Anyway, who's going to know, if you don't say anything? Of course, if you're so sensitive about being seen with me, I mean if I'm not up to your weight, just say so."

She looked at him, appalled, hoping her face was not revealing her inner self trying to come to terms with his gold bracelet. "Are you trying to insult me? As though I would ever think such a thing."

"There you are then." He gave a satisfied smile. "I can be as barmy as you, any day. Don't panic," he relented. "Got some guys in from New York. Thought you might perform the same miracle on them that you did on Gilbert."

"I would have thought," she replied icily, rising to her feet and furious that she had been made to look absurd, "that as English is their native tongue, trying to grasp the general drift of what they're saying shouldn't be too taxing."

"Obviously. But I don't say, 'tell me all about yourself'," he mimicked. "Like you do. It's sexy. Makes the hair on the back of my neck stand up."

Serena folded her arms around her waist and leaned against the fireplace. "I do not," she corrected him. "Ever use such a toe-curlingly embarrassing cliché."

"You see," he spread his hands, "I've got so much to learn. So that's all right then? Good. Anyway, it's work. That my coffee, Louise? Good girl. Now, Tip, my man, who do you fancy in the Cup?"

*

Alex was very understanding about her forgetfulness. "Poor you," he sympathized. "As though you don't do enough for them as it is. Was it very ghastly?"

It was no secret that Alex disliked the idea of Serena working in Frobisher's and was only persuaded it was for the best when Serena pointed out that it might mean she could afford to rent something or even — she hardly dare say it — get a mortgage on a small house, somewhere else.

"No," she replied truthfully. "Actually it was quite interesting. I was glad to be able to help. Feel a bit wrecked today, though."

"Then let me take you for a restorative drink this evening," Alex promptly suggested. "Otherwise I won't see you until next weekend. You work every night, remember?"

A surge of guilt swept through her. Every night except Wednesday of this week, when she was going to the opera. She didn't want to have to explain because she wasn't sure herself why she was going, she just knew that the shaming idea that getting dressed up, feeling human, going somewhere she once took for granted but now had become a longed-for treat, had felled her resistance to the idea of being seen with her boss and just hoped the gold cufflinks with their miniature clock faces would be replaced with something else.

"Oh Alex, I'd love to," she said, "but I won't be able to get someone to sit with Harry and Louise has already said she's spending the evening with Daphy."

There was a small pause. She knew she should say come here, come and have a drink here with me. But her energy deserted her. Ed and Tipper had left at nearly three and she was roused by Harry at nine to go with him to watch a charity bungee jump from Chelsea Bridge. When Alex phoned she was wading through the ironing, with the bathroom still to be tackled.

She pushed a hand through her hair. "Look," she said, "why don't we meet up next Saturday for lunch? Harry will be at his class and Louise will be glad to have me out of the way for an hour or two."

Even as she said it she knew she would be hard-pressed to find the time. Saturday was her only day off. The rest of the week she got through by snatching a couple of hours' sleep while the children were at school, topping up the shopping, collecting Harry from school and keeping track of Louise's disturbingly exotic friendships.

"I can't," he answered simply. "Alice, you see, she's feeling a little distraught. I owe it to her."

Why don't I feel sorry for her? Serena thought. Because I'm like Alex, can't make up my mind about what this relationship is, or because I don't like her as a woman?

Aloud she said warmly, "Of course you must. Alex, listen to me. Don't ruin a relationship with Alice because of mistaken feelings you think you might have for me."

"They're not mistaken." His voice sounded cross. "What I have to discover is what those feelings are. Quite different."

She was too tired for this and too busy. The pile of ironing was balanced on the kitchen table and she wanted to get back to it. She wanted to put it away, finish the bathroom, cook lunch — which had now turned into dinner it was so late — and then enjoy the soothing pleasure of knowing it was done with only a bath and a warm bed to gather her up.

With a shock of pleasurable surprise, she knew that, slowly but undoubtedly, she had become a complete member of the working mothers' club. Even the exhaustion was like a badge of honour. And she had earned it alone. Honesty compelled her at that moment to acknowledge that Alex had played a major part in that achievement. Where would Harry have been without him? Where would her confidence have been if he hadn't shown her she was still a desirable if unavailable woman?

"I'm sorry," she sighed into the phone. "I'm just grumpy because I'm shattered. And of course I understand about Alice. Look, why don't you let me see how the rest of the day pans out —"

He stopped her. "You're the nicest person in the world and I won't let you. I'm just being horribly selfish. In fact I'll drive round to Jack's for supper and let him remind me."

Immediately she disagreed, knowing that his brother who had a large brood of his own to contend with would have no time to tell him any such thing, but it was with relief. Next Sunday, she had insisted he came to lunch, and wondered why when she replaced the phone, having resolved the situation, she still felt guilty.

*

It was obvious to Margot that Serena had changed. The mild days of autumn had plunged more quickly than usual into a sharp frost and with it a flu epidemic had caught Margot as one of its first victims. The result was that she felt quite low for a few weeks and so spoke more often on the telephone. She refused to have Serena and the children anywhere near her and resisted all attempts made by Serena for her to come and stay with them.

"No thank you, dear," she said, "I'm fine. Isabel is going to come and stay for a while, so you needn't worry. Harry says you went out to dinner last night."

"Work," Serena told her briefly. "They needed someone who spoke French. Hardly entertaining, but not dull. Surprisingly."

Her mother sounded disappointed. "I thought it might be Alex," she said, "but Harry said it was your boss. Poor you."

It occurred to Serena that her mother and Alex would adore each other. They held exactly the same view of Serena's job. To Margot, knowing how it would alarm her, Serena had diluted the sharper facts of her working life and in conversations distracted her from probing too closely by updating her on her grandchildren, the letter she had from Minnie and what Melanie had said last time she called. Even the Tosneys and the Plaxtons were a source of interest to Margot, who pretended to be shocked. Serena knew however that the details were routinely relayed to Cousin Isabel in their long monthly letters to each other.

"Uproar next door," she told Margot, glad to be able to divert her away from Frobisher's. "Bradley was hauled off for stolen radios and they found drugs on him — cannabis, according to Betty. Ecstasy according to the police."

"Oh my goodness. Don't let him near LouLou or Harry, will you?" Margot begged. "He sounds dangerous. They all do."

"Well, Alana isn't so bad. She hasn't got any gentleness in her life so she doesn't know how else to behave except with this awful aggression. In a way she's been good for Harry and she's different when she's here on her own with him. Less," she groped for the word. "Less defensive. Yes, that's it. She starts from the point that she's going to be told off, but if you sound friendly and welcoming, she's quite different."

"You make her sound like that brute of a dog," Margot shuddered.

Serena frowned. "You're probably right. But that's how Betty talks to them. All the time. As for Bradley, he's too frightened of Louise to step across the threshold and Ellis is never here now he's enrolled in his karate class.

"Bradley's on probation and Betty's incandescent. Says he's been framed. Honestly, Ma, she sounded like James Cagney's mother in that film where he's polished everyone off, bodies everywhere, and he's holding a smoking gun and she's screaming, 'My son is innocent.'" Serena mimicked the old movie star so accurately that Margot chuckled.

"Everyone else is to blame. Can't possibly be something Bradley himself thought up."

Margot said nothing. The idea of saying to Serena: "that's how you sounded about Stephen," was too cruel. Besides, Margot was just thankful that the subject was rarely raised any more. Serena was so involved in her new life.

Margot was happy to be diverted, but she was conscious of the fact that, unlike her previous two jobs, Serena spoke lightly of this one. But at least they could now go for days, weeks even, without mentioning Stephen. And why should they? What was there left to say? The confidence was what Margot noticed. The harder edge to her daughter's views, the brisker, less expectant tone was not lost on her.

Serena replaced the phone, satisfied that her mother's recovery from flu was progressing well and uneasily aware that while mimicking Betty she had simply been echoing her own defence of Stephen.

As she walked back to the kitchen she glanced through to see Harry and Louise, for once curled up side by side on the sofa watching an afternoon movie on television. The house was warm, she was coping. No longer did they watch her every move, fearful of the woman she had become unravelling in front of their young eyes. For a while she stood watching them. Then she took the ironing upstairs and put it away, she finished the bathroom and then came back down to start dinner. Tough? If they only knew. Knew how near to tears she sometimes was, but had learned to control it. How could they know the times she gazed at posters of Ireland, finding herself wondering in that soft misty moment before sleep claimed her what it would be like if she had to live there.

From time to time she hovered on the brink of telling Alex, knowing it would not faze him and that he would envelop her with sympathy and understanding. But she no longer wanted that from him, or anyone. As for Ed, there is, she told herself whilst slicing carrots and mushrooms, a safety net in appearing equal to anything in his presence. It was not the wisest course of action to be going with him to the opera, she knew that. She knew it would not look good at Frobisher's if it got out, if — she paused and looked out of the window — if a day would ever come when she didn't once, not once, think about Stephen.

Chapter Twenty-Four

Serena told Cheryl that she was going to be at the opera and then at supper with Ed and his guests, instead of at Frobisher's.

"I'll check in when we get to the restaurant, but you can get me here." She scribbled the number of the theatre, adding Ed's name. "He's got a box so he's easy to find. And we're having supper afterwards here." She added the number and stood up, handing the piece of paper to Cheryl.

"Night out?" Cheryl asked, reading the itinerary.

"No, work," Serena replied, checking her bag. "Nice work for once."

"Ooh, sounds promising," Cheryl giggled.

"Well, I like opera." Serena glanced briefly in the mirror in the hallway. It was the same dress she'd worn the other night but she'd added a jacket to take it down a bit. "I'll just tell the children I'm off."

She found Louise sprawled on her bed with earphones on and just kissed the top of her head.

"Homework," she mouthed.

"Done it," Louise called back above the din only she could hear.

Harry, controller in hand, was sitting on the floor in the living room flicking through Fantasy Football.

"Bye, darling." She stooped down to kiss him. "I'll call later. See you in the morning."

"Tell Tip I'm trying to buy Gareth Bale so we won't need Ronaldo." He barely looked at her as the mouse clicked across the screen.

"I might not see him tonight, sweetheart." She gazed fondly at him and the mention of his favourite footballers. "But I'll tell him tomorrow. I won't be at the club. Cheryl's got the numbers where I'll be."

"Ye-es!" Harry howled in delight as the screen flashed the successful purchase of the brilliant striker.

Serena looked thoughtfully at her small son punching the air. She put down her bag and coat and sat on the arm of the sofa.

"Harry," she said, ruffling his hair. "Would you like to go to a football match, a proper one?"

"You mean like Chelsea or Arsenal?" he asked, one eye still on his prized acquisition. "A proper, proper match? Who would I go with?" he asked nervously. "I don't know anyone who goes, except some of the boys in my class but they go with their dads or their brothers."

Serena remained expressionless. "Well, I'll take —" She stopped and amended. "I'll go with you. In fact we'll go on Saturday. I'll find out who's playing and at what ground and we'll go. It'll be good fun."

"Spurs are playing a home game," he volunteered, hesitantly. "We could go to that."

Serena looked blankly at him. "How do you know?"

"It's here." He grabbed the paper and showed her the fixtures on the sports page. "See? White Hart Lane. I read it all the time."

"Then that's dead easy," she said, a rush of remorse rising at herself for not seeing how much he had always wanted to go. Louise would have sulked and pleaded until she got what she wanted. Harry just waited to be noticed. "Spurs it is. Now I must fly. I'll be late."

Cheryl was already glued to *Jeremy Kyle* and Louise had clomped downstairs to join her. As Serena let herself out with a final goodbye, Cheryl rushed into the hall to see her go. Ed had arranged a car to collect Serena to take her to his house in Hans Crescent. To Serena's relief and Cheryl's disappointment, it was a routine dark saloon that the club used, but even so Cheryl watched it until it disappeared from view.

*

It was easy for Serena to spot the conflict of cultures in Ed's tall, redbrick house at the back of Harrods. There was the poor kid made good love of gadgets — doors opened, lights were generated by an unseeing hand — and the self-educated man's passion for fine books and works of art.

When the door was opened before she knocked and, now she thought of it, even before she had got out of the car, she saw this conflict at work. The butler, who wore a sober black suit, majestically inclined his head and led her to the library where Ed was waiting. He also had a broken nose and a nasal twang that suggested a former career as something less refined than a gentleman's gentleman in Knightsbridge.

"Mrs Carmichael," he intoned, stepping aside to let her pass.

The library, like the house, was a handsome business. Brass lamps stood on impressive claw-footed tables; leather Chesterfields and a velvet wing-chair lent a pleasing cultured air to a room she decided looked noble. A pleasantly welcoming fire licked yellow flames behind a leather military fender. The walls were lined with rosewood bookshelves, there was a series of equestrian prints hung together in a group that she recognized with a start of amazement. She didn't have to wonder if they were the originals.

It took, therefore, a great deal of discipline not to recoil in horror at the panel that slid up in the centre of one row of shelves as a computer thrust itself forward so that Ed could demonstrate how the house linked up to his office in New York and the penthouse suite at Frobisher's.

"Fascinating," she managed.

He had been in the act of pouring himself a drink when she came in and saw no reason to stop as he greeted her. "Terrific," he approved, taking in the jacket just shaped at the waist and flaring gently over her hips and the suede shoes with heels she felt safer in. Her hair was loose. For a moment she was fearful he might think she'd done it that way because he had said he liked it and not because she had decided that at least, if she couldn't change her clothes, she could change herself. But he made no comment and she relaxed.

"I'm sorry now I have to share you," he grinned. "Now let me get you a drink. Wally likes doing it, but he takes it all so seriously, you'd expire with thirst waiting for him to do it just right."

"You mean, the butler?" she asked. "Thank you. Just orange will do."

"Wally's great. Used to be in the ring."

"You surprise me," she murmured, taking her drink and sitting in one of the wing-chairs next to the fire. "How did he become a butler?"

Ed perched himself on the edge of the fire surround and rubbed his chin trying to recall. "He lived in the next street to me. His dad used to be a fairground pugilist, you know, 'win a pound, if you go a round,' and Wally was brought up to do the same. Trouble was he was useless and they practically went bankrupt when he took over the business. He spent more time flat on his back than a Curzon Street hooker. My Lil could have knocked him down just looking at him.

"Then Lenny — Lenny Horniman, he's a big noise in Savile Row now, I grew up with him — well, he called me one day and said he'd seen Wally coming out of a dosser's hostel, right mess he was. Anyway, he bundled him into his car, took him home, got him straightened out and discovered that all Wal had ever wanted to do was train to become a butler like his grandad — his mother's lot were in service."

"So you sent him to be trained?" Serena tried to guess the end of the story.

"No such thing," he said, reaching for one of his habitual cigars. "I wouldn't be that magnanimous. Not like Lenny. He paid for that. But once Wal was trained he had to have a job and poor old Wal couldn't get the accent right which meant no one would employ him. So Lil rang me who heard all about it from Wal's grandma — the things I did for that woman — and she told me she'd said Wal could work for me. So he's been here more or less ever since."

Serena was entranced. "And he doesn't mind that you and Lenny have done so well and he's now working for you?"

"Excuse me." Ed lowered his voice. "Wal is always giving me little tips on how to go on. He'll love you. Thinks riff-raff like me are no better than they should be. I'll show you."

He walked to one of the tables and picked up a small black phone. "Wal," he said. "Car in three minutes." He paused, listening. "OK, five."

Serena nearly choked.

"Don't, please," he begged, with mock weariness. "You can't imagine what I'll go through if I argue."

An image of the dreadful Mrs Owen and the daily need to accommodate her sense of her own importance flashed before her.

"I can. I did," she replied drily.

"Worth it?" He paused, looking at her over the rim of his glass.

"Probably not. Hindsight is wonderful, isn't it? Now can I just have some idea of the people I'm, er ... interpreting for tonight?"

"Tonight? Oh yes, tonight. I should have got you to order the car. Can't imagine Wal arguing with you. Right, tonight."

Ed's guests were surprisingly nice. Equally surprising to Serena was that they didn't appear to be on anything but the closest terms with him and if business was in the air, it was, she thought, remarkably well hidden. Her recollection of similar outings with Stephen was that Americans did nothing but talk business, but maybe club people were different from Wall Street bankers.

There were two couples. Both from New York and eager to make Serena feel one of them. It was a disorientating experience since she had been expecting to help them relax, only to find they thought it was their responsibility to do that for her.

The women were especially nice to her. One, a striking blonde called Ceri, who she gathered was on several high-powered charity committees, said Serena was taller than she had imagined.

"Taller?" Serena asked, not understanding why her description would have been of interest before tonight.

"Sure, but then I suppose because Ed's so big, he thinks anything under six foot is a pygmy. Oh, Bernice," she gurgled to the other woman. "Do you recall Patti?" She turned with a roll of her eyes to where Bernice was sitting and Serena also politely turned. Serena was just in time to catch a warning glance flashing from Bernice to the outspoken Ceri.

"Oh, that was nothing," she dismissed the unknown Patti. "One of Ed's little flingettes who was at least six foot and he said it didn't last because she wasn't big enough. I think he was referring to her brain," she explained. "But it was after Willow," she went on, clearly mystified by Serena's interest in their host, which was at best polite. "I mean it was nothing. Willow," she repeated, as Serena continued to look blank, "as in Willow Stein."

"Oh, you mean Ed's ex-wife," Serena exclaimed. "I'm so sorry. You must forgive me, I had no idea what she was called. I'm not familiar with Ed's background to that extent. Well," she cast an uneasy look between them, wondering why they looked so relieved. "I mean you don't if you're working for someone, do you?"

"No, no. Of course not," they both chorused, with such eagerness that for a brief moment Serena was sure they were hiding something. But why? And why from her? After all, she told herself, it was not her place to mention that all she knew about Ed was that he had a mistress, but then they must know about her. In the end she decided they were being cautious in front of what was, after all, an employee.

Ed was a good host, attentive to everyone's needs including hers. As they were about to take their seats in Ed's box Serena took him aside and whispered anxiously was there anything she could do. She thought he looked offended.

"Why? What's wrong?" he asked, digging his hands in his pockets, a gesture she had come to recognize as defensive.

"Nothing. Heavens, nothing at all. That's the point. I don't think I'm earning my salary. There's really nothing for me to do, is there? I feel a bit of a fraud."

For a brief moment he just looked at her. Then he said, "Oh, you're earning it all right, Serena. Believe me. I'm not a charity. And you're not a fraud. Now enjoy yourself. I'm going to."

With that, he ushered her before him to her seat between his friends, Will and Barclay, who showed every sign of behaving as oddly as their wives.

It was a memorable evening. The performance left her near to tears and when the philandering Duke of Mantua finally sang *La donna è mobile* she turned impulsively to Ed as they stood to cheer the performance.

"Oh, that was stunning. Thank you for including me. I'm overwhelmed."

It wasn't until she was making her way through the lobby that it occurred to her that she had been included because she worked for him. She felt oddly disappointed, but the moment was brief. She froze as a more pressing problem presented itself. Immediately in front of Will were Paula and Richard Van Stuckley with a couple she thought looked familiar and another she knew well. At least she knew Miranda Hooper well. She was hanging on to the arm of a man last seen with his wife as far as Serena could recall. She could not avoid colliding with them.

"Heavens, Serena," Paula croaked, clearly horrified. Hemmed in on all sides, there was no escape for any of them. "Richard, it's Serena. How marvellous." She turned wildly round. "Miranda, it's Serena. What a surprise."

Somewhere behind her she heard Will exclaim, "Hey, you old dog. What are you doing here? Where's Meryl? Hey Ceri, look who's here."

In the commotion of greetings and squeals of recognition, several heads began to turn in the direction of the group converging on each other in the middle of the foyer. Serena dragged her gaze from the stupefied Van Stuckleys to the American couple they were with. Oh God, Meryl Holt.

Miranda was looking dazed. Her companion puzzled. Richard Van Stuckley, last seen by Serena nursing a bruised ego and with whiskey down his shirt, looked aghast. Only Serena looked composed.

Ed had returned and was now looking at Serena. Her heart hit her ribs. She had no choice. "Ed, this is Paula and Richard Van Stuckley and Miranda Hooper. Ed Stein," she indicated his presence. Paula nodded politely, Richard shook his hand briefly and then turned away whispering something in Paula's ear. Paula in turn threw a startled look at Ed and then, with a smile that turned Serena's stomach, she moved away. Miranda made no attempt to hang around. Humiliation swept over Serena. The crowd in the foyer made a hasty exit impossible. Behind her she saw a firedoor.

"Excuse me," she muttered to Ed. "I'll join you later. Forgive me. I'll get a cab to the restaurant."

She tried to move away but Ed stopped her, gripping her arm and murmuring, "You're going nowhere on your own. Stuckley's an appalling little shit. Tried to be a member. Wouldn't have him. Now, chin up. Smile. Here comes Meryl Holt. Lovely woman. Meryl," whom he caught in a bear hug. "Why haven't you left that no-hoper and run off with me?"

Instinctively, and because she was desperate to be told what to do, she did as she was bid. The second reason she had to stay put was Meryl.

"And you have hidden yourself too well." Meryl released herself from Ed's arms and kissed Serena. "Here," she said, refusing to catch her husband's eye. "Not the best moment to catch up. This is my number. Let's do lunch. Serena and I are old friends," she explained to Ed. "She and ... and," Meryl gave an uncertain look at Serena.

"Stephen." Serena threw a defiant look around.

"Yes, she and Stephen spent time with us out at East Hampton a few summers ago. Don't forget to call." She looked pointedly at Serena. "Ed. How many calls does a girl have to make to get a reply from you?"

Ryland and Ed greeted each other with what appeared to be genuine warmth. Following his wife's lead, he leaned across and kissed a shaken Serena on the cheek.

"Listen, you guys, must dash. Business. You know how it is."

It was only then that Serena knew she was shaking. She wanted to sit down before she fell down, just go home. And she would have done if Ed hadn't stopped her. Under cover of the Americans all exchanging plans to meet, he stood facing her, shielding her from any curious onlookers, looking away over her shoulder but close enough to prevent anyone moving her away from him.

"C'mon. Take it easy," he murmured, glancing at her. "It's over. That the first time you've seen them?"

She nodded, beginning to recover. "Stupid of me. One always thinks you're prepared. But you never are."

She gave him a weak smile. "I'm sorry. Forgive me. Now," she took a deep breath. "Would you like me to go with Ceri and Will in their car?"

He swore softly under his breath. "I would like Ceri and Will to take Bernice and Barclay out of my way. You don't need them, but you might need me for the next couple of hours."

She looked up, startled. "Please," she said quietly. "It won't be necessary. But you're awfully kind."

"Awfully kind," he mimicked. This time she just smiled at him. "All right," he said. "You know best. Let's move it."

*

Throughout dinner Serena struggled with one overriding emotion. Bumping into the dreadful Paula had dismayed her but it was not until she saw the look of disdain on their faces when she established Ed's identity that Serena wanted the earth to open and absorb her. At that moment Paula's very public snub had been delivered with a force that would be re-echoed in the telling of it to all her former friends.

She glanced across the table to where Ed was listening attentively to Ceri explaining why he should come back to live in New York, and felt misery rise up in her throat. The fact that she was working for Frobisher's may not have travelled back to her former world except as a rumour, but it would now be embellished as only Paula knew how, with myth transcending myth, assumption replacing facts.

It was a harsh but inevitable penalty, she berated herself, for allowing her judgement to be defeated — and so readily — by her weak-willed need to taste just once, her old life. At that moment she would have willingly traded any number of sublime productions of *Rigoletto*, or even dinner in the rarefied surroundings of the Savoy Grill, for a quiet uneventful dinner with Alex at the small trattoria in Pimlico. A rush of longing for his sane, calming presence swept over her. With Alex she felt safe. Here she did not. In Foster Street she could protect herself. Sitting here with just another kind of wealth with people she hardly knew was disabling. She wanted the security that came with Alex, sharing a glass of wine with Stacey, Sunday lunch while Tipper zapped through computer games with Harry. She wanted to organise taking her small son to football, listen to LouLou and Daphy giggling over boys.

Ed chose that moment to bring the evening to a close. It was done deftly by implanting the idea in Bernice's head that she was exhausted, and his guests apologized to him for not being able to stay the course. Serena felt almost giddy with relief. Outside they all parted company with kisses and hugs and invitations to lunch which swirled around her. And then they were gone. She was still smiling when she turned to Ed. It was the nearest she'd seen him come to scowling.

"Good heavens!" she exclaimed. "Didn't it go well? I thought it was terrific."

"Don't lie, Serena," he snapped. "You're transparent."

She stiffened. "Well, I'm sorry for what happened earlier, but truly —"

"Oh shut up," he interrupted. "I watched you. You were carrying it off until I pitched up and that's when you fell to pieces. Well let me tell you something, my girl. They're trash. All of them. And you still care what they think. Still care that you're seen with the right people. Yours is the tragedy, sweetheart. Not, as you seem to think, being seen with me."

"Don't be absurd," she replied calmly. "How could you think such a thing? Ed, everyone's watching. Don't shout."

"Shout? You call this shouting?" He lowered his voice. "I can do shouting. Want to hear?"

"Well I'll take a rain check on that experience," she answered hurriedly, fearful that in his present mood he might think a demonstration was called for. As she spoke she grabbed his arm and propelled him towards the waiting car. His driver was already on the pavement holding the door.

"You're mistaken," she spoke calmly as they approached the stationary vehicle. "My shame was Paula. That I ever knew such a vulgar person and one that I was forced to introduce my boss to is not up there with my happiest memories. Come on, get in."

He grabbed her arm and swung her round, searching her face. His voice held a note of suspicion. "No messing, Mrs Carmichael?"

She gave an exaggerated sigh and grinned at him. "No messing, Mr Stein," she mimicked. "Now buck up. In you get."

"After you," he argued.

"No. I'm getting a cab. I'm sure you won't mind me charging it. Stop arguing. Bob," she ignored Ed and turned to the driver, "Mr Stein's had a tough evening. Ask Wally to give him a brandy and put him to bed and if that doesn't work, tell him I suggest a sock in the jaw. Taxi!"

She ran to the black cab as it pulled up and clambered in. "Foster Street, Kennington," she ordered the driver, pulling the window down. "I'll check if I've still got a job in the morning," she called out to Ed, who was standing, hands stuffed in his pockets, on the pavement. She almost laughed.

"You know Ed," she added thoughtfully, as her driver waited for her to tell him to move and Ed came over to the cab. "You'd get a gold medal at the Olympics if they had such an event."

"What event?" he asked, resting one arm on the window ledge, the other on the roof.

"Jumping to conclusions. No contest."

He began to laugh. "Only from you."

"Me?"

"Uh huh. Who said you were working tonight? The guys thought you were my new date."

He leaned in and kissed her on the mouth, then he stepped back, banged the roof and the cab took off, sending Serena lurching back against the leather seat. She strained round to see him walking towards his car.

Chapter Twenty-Five

Serena let herself into a dark and silent house. Carefully she eased her key from the lock and paused to listen for sounds from above and then walked down the hall to the kitchen. A note from Harry lay on the table saying he'd double-checked and it was definitely OK for Saturday. Underneath it in Louise's distinctive bold script was a note to say Melanie had called and so too had a Mrs Harding. Mrs Harding? Serena frowned and then remembered. The matron at the home where Edith was a resident. Tomorrow she'd deal with that. She yawned. All she needed now was bed.

The journey had been sufficiently long to recover from both Ed's unexpected outburst and to restore her sense of humour. Ceri and Bernice's haste to emphasize Ed's affairs now made sense. Their husbands' gallant behaviour fell into place. In the dark of the cab, she had covered her face with her hands and silently rocked with laughter and embarrassment, wondering how she would ever face them again. Then she drew comfort from reminding herself that another meeting was unlikely since she was not going to allow it to happen again.

The phone rang as she was checking the back door and the side window. Hastily she picked it up so that the noise would not wake everyone upstairs.

"Bloody woman," came Ed's voice. "Just wanted to make sure you made it."

"Too kind," she murmured. "I take it I still have a job?"

She heard him laugh. "You don't deserve it."

"You don't deserve for me to stay," Serena pointed out. "Lying to the staff is not clever."

"I know. But you made it very obvious you wouldn't come if I hadn't changed it to work. And you must admit you enjoyed it, except for those prats."

She had to admit she did. "Your friends must think I'm mad," she told him. "They kept being tactful about your love life."

"What there is of it," he replied. "Anyway, they'll just think you're eccentric. It's how they view the English aristocracy."

"I'm not aristocracy," she pointed out.

"Your old man was a baronet, wasn't he?"

"Mm. But that doesn't mean I'm anything but at best upper-middle-class. And the way things are at the moment I must be a dreadful disappointment to them."

"How's that?"

"Well," she glanced round the kitchen and paused, seeing a jacket thrown across a chair that she didn't recognize. A man's jacket.

"Because I'm working class." She reached out and picked the jacket up. It was leather with a zip, quite worn. A strong smell of tobacco clung to it. Puzzled, she turned it around, holding it gingerly out in front of her, looking for clues.

"Ed," she broke off, "I must go. Thanks for this evening."

"If I'm honest in future, will you have dinner with me?"

"No." She didn't need to think about it. On the way home she had already decided. "No," she repeated it more gently. "I work for you. It wouldn't be sensible. I need a job, not complications."

"It doesn't have to be complicated. Come back here. I'll send the car for you. It's early. If you were at the club it would be at least another hour before you finished."

"Ed," she protested, "I'm going nowhere except bed."

"Well, there you are," he said. "You see, we have so much in common. That's where I'm going too. We could do it together."

She tried not to laugh and said severely, "I'm going on my own."

"That could be lonely," he pointed out.

"Not that lonely," Serena replied, primly.

"Oh well, worth a try. Bloody woman." The line went dead.

It was then Serena noticed the bottle of wine and the two glasses on the table. Her first instinct was that it must be Louise but her second, coming hard on its heels, knew that Louise would not leave evidence of drinking around. There'd already been one row over the stock of alcopops she had found in her school bag. Probably one of her friends who'd left it behind. That was it.

Yawning, she doused the lights and as quietly as she could mounted the stairs. Louise's room was next to hers, the door shut. Silently she pushed it open. A lozenge of light from the hallway fell on her sleeping daughter, one arm flung over her head, her earphones still clamped to her ears.

Serena tiptoed over to Louise and gently removed the headphone. Louise stirred in her sleep.

"Only me, darling," Serena whispered. "Back to sleep."

After that she crept up the next flight avoiding the stairs she knew would creak, to check Harry whose room was next to the tiny spare room where Cheryl slept when she stayed over. Satisfied all was as it should be, she retraced her steps to her own room next to Louise's. A comparatively early night for once. Not quite one o'clock.

At first she couldn't register what was going on. Light from the lamp just inside the door cut through the darkness of her bedroom as she reached out to switch it on. There was a gasp from the bed. Serena screamed and jumped back.

For one frozen moment no one moved. Serena's heart was tangled painfully against her ribs. She groped for the switch behind her and blinked as the overhead light flooded the room. Cheryl Tosney, wearing a bra so ornate and small her breasts were almost pressed against her chin, suspenders and one stocking, sat astride a body whose bare, hairy legs were all that were momentarily visible, his arms tied to the end of the bed with what appeared to be the matching stocking to the one Cheryl was wearing.

"What the hell are you doing?" Serena demanded furiously, recovering first. "Get out of my bed. Both of you."

"What you doing here?" Cheryl bleated breathlessly, trying to clamber off the prone figure of the man who was, as far as Serena was prepared to look at him, a total stranger.

"I live here," Serena reminded her. "Get dressed, Cheryl, and come downstairs. And you," she snapped at the bemused man now propped on one elbow. "Get dressed and get out before I call the police. You have two minutes exactly. Both of you."

"You mad or somefink?" the man shouted. "Barging in here."

Cheryl tried to quieten him. "She lives here," she hissed. "She doesn't usually get back until nearly three. Oh for god's sake, just go. Oh bugger off, you stupid git. Go, will you?"

Serena stood stonily by the front door as the ill-shaven and greasy-haired man came downstairs first, pulling a T-shirt over his head. Serena motioned to him that his jacket was hanging over the end of the stairs. She wouldn't touch it. Without a word he shrugged it on and looked Serena up and down.

"Can't get any yourself? That it?" he jeered.

"Get out," Serena breathed, pulling open the door. "If I see you even near my house, let alone in it, ever again, you'll be arrested."

With a sudden sharp jerk, he pulled the door from her hand and leered right into her face.

"And for what? Shagging your mate? Leave it out, you stupid slag."

Blind with rage, Serena wrenched the door from his grip. "Out. Now."

Behind her she heard Louise stumble down stairs.

"What is it, Mum?" she asked, rubbing her eyes. "What's going on?"

The man shrugged and walked away down the path.

"Nothing, darling," Serena assured her, trying to control her shaking voice. "Go back to bed, Lou. I'll come and see you when I've got rid of Cheryl."

"Rid of her?" Louise's eyes widened. "You're sacking her?"

"She should be grateful. My other option is to murder her."

They both looked up as Cheryl began to make her way downstairs. In her hand she clutched a carrier bag. Her demeanour was not that of a woman expecting to negotiate her future. Serena itched to slap her.

"Bed, Lou," Serena instructed, pressing her gently in the back.

Louise looked nervously from her mother to Cheryl. "I'd rather stay," she answered. "I don't want to leave you."

Serena squeezed her shoulder. "I'll be fine. Promise. I'll be up in a few minutes."

Reluctantly Louise pushed past the self-possessed Cheryl and disappeared.

"I'm so shocked, Cheryl," Serena began. "You of all people. I trusted you. What the hell do you think you were doing? If you're having an affair, that's your concern, but not in my house."

"Affair? Who's having an affair?" Cheryl gawped at her. "It's ... you know."

Serena returned her blank stare. "No, I don't know. Explain it."

"God, you don't need me to spell it out, do you? A client. Bit of business. OK, I wasn't expecting you home and another half-hour and he'd have been gone. No harm done."

Serena thought she was passing through a nightmare. She looked in bewilderment at the woman in front of her whom she had left in charge of her children. A shiver of fear went through her.

"No harm? My children in bed and you think there was no harm? A client? What do you mean, a client?"

Cheryl separated the strands of her fringe peering in the mirror. "Well, what else would he be? Give us a break," she said, indignation making her abandon the task. "Well, maybe not as rich as yours, but they pay about the same I 'spect."

Serena asked her to repeat what she had just said. "What do you mean, '*as rich as yours*'? Are you talking about me?"

"Course. Who else?" Cheryl looked surprised. "I'm sorry I started in your bed, but really I thought I was doing you a favour."

There was a beat missing. In a moment she would grasp what it was. At this moment, all she could do was grope her way through this bizarre conversation.

"Favour? What are you talking about? Start what?"

"Building up clients," Cheryl nodded at her. "You know." She wiggled her hips. "Look, I know this is jumping the gun a bit — and I am sorry about tonight, but everyone's got to start somewhere — but I thought with your contacts I might get in on it. Expand a bit. I mean we could cut each other in. Those guys at Frobisher's, they must give you cards, stuff like that. They must want extras, don't they? We could split the money. I mean I might not have your accent or stuff but in the sack what does it matter?"

Serena sat down heavily on the stairs, the back of her hand pressed against her mouth. On the game. That's what Cheryl thought she was. A tart.

"Cheryl," she began slowly, her voice shaking. "You've made a terrible mistake. I'm not on the game. Never have been, never would. It isn't necessary. It would never be necessary. I would starve in the gutter first. Am I getting through to you?"

Cheryl gazed at her in total disbelief. She gave a nervous laugh. "Not on the game? Get out of it. Listen, I won't put it about, you haven't got to worry about me. Not on the game? Do me a favour." She began to laugh at the absurdity of it until she noticed Serena's ghostly pallor and stopped. "I mean that's what Frobisher's is about, isn't it?" she faltered. "I know it is. I know someone who cleans there."

"Believe me, Cheryl, not where I'm concerned. Cheryl, have you any idea of the danger you put my children in tonight? Yourself? That man could have murdered you."

"What, that nutter?" Cheryl squealed with laughter. Serena thought she was going to faint. "He's a regular up the Feathers," she continued, naming the local pub. "He's got the bottle of a wet dishcloth. Performs like it too," she added, as though to herself.

It was enough. "Cheryl, please leave. I'll drop your money over tomorrow. You can't stay here any more. We ... we just have crossed wires. Now please go."

"Go?" Cheryl whispered. "Why? I'm only doing what you do."

"I've told you. I don't. And —"

Cheryl's mouth opened and closed. "You mean you won't help, is that it? You think I'm not up to it. That right?"

Serena dragged her fingers down her cheeks, looking helplessly at the over-made-up face, the streaked mascara. Finally she said, "Cheryl, I don't want to continue this conversation. I would never help you to … to do anything like this."

"What? Never?" Cheryl almost whispered, her face beginning to crumple. "No. I couldn't. You don't understand."

"Oh yes, I do, you jealous hag," Cheryl screamed. "You're a taker, that's what you are. What was it they called you? Kept woman? Bloody whore, more like." She gazed venomously at Serena; her eyes had narrowed, her arms were folded tightly across her chest. "I thought you would help me like I helped you. Know what I think?" She was almost sobbing, her dream of escape from Foster Street shattering around her. "I think you deserve everything that's happened to you, I hope you rot. You vicious bitch, with your big cars and flash blokes."

Serena's face was white with shock. She opened the door and said quietly, "Leave now, Cheryl. Now. Don't come back. You need help. But not the kind you think. Now go before I have to ask Kevin to come and get you."

With a strangled sob Cheryl pushed past her. Serena leaned weakly against the door.

*

At midday she called Mike and told him she was having problems on the home front.

"I'll try and get some cover but it isn't very likely. You may have to do without me tonight."

He grunted and told her to ring when she knew for sure. Serena replaced the phone on the wall and leaned against the sink. Who on earth could she get? Stacey was too locked in to her dreadful Barry to be free, Tip worked so he couldn't. It would take her mother at least a day to organize her life to fill the gap. And besides she wasn't at all sure she wanted Margot to know quite what she was doing.

Louise and Harry seemed indifferent to Cheryl's departure which in itself alarmed Serena since she had comforted herself that they got on.

"Never says anything," Harry told her.

"Watches television or reads a magazine," Louise reported. "Stupid old bag," she added, ignoring Serena's sharp rebuke. "Daphy said she was on the game."

"Well not here, she isn't," Serena replied grimly. "Not anymore."

She rang Melanie and cancelled seeing her at the weekend. "Send a recent photograph," Melanie sniffed, "I'm beginning to forget what you look like."

"Sorry, Melanie," Serena said. "Had a little local difficulty here."

Melanie screamed in horror when she heard. But strangely enough, Serena reflected, she seemed more anxious for Serena at hearing she had run into Paula and Miranda in the company of Ed.

"She'll make it bad if she can," Melanie was clearly worried. "Look. Don't worry. I'll make sure everyone knows it was business. I'll say it was something to do with a charity. Leave it to me."

Serena studied the toes of her shoes. All at once, she didn't feel comfortable with Melanie's offer. Once she might have done. Once, of course, it would have been unnecessary. A wave of loyalty to Ed swept over her.

"Don't worry, Mel," she told her. "I'm sure Ed won't hold it against me that I know the likes of Paula. Let her say what she likes. I've moved on from her, all of them."

There was a small silence. "If that's what you want, then of course."

"It is," Serena said. "Ed's been good to me. I'm more concerned that the dreadful Cheryl might try and wring a few quid out of the papers. We'll see. Listen, must go. Call you soon. Love to Charles."

It wasn't until well into the afternoon that she remembered the call from Mrs Harding at the nursing home. What she had to say was not unexpected. Edith would have to be moved.

"We'll fix something," Mrs Harding explained. "But you said you wanted to know."

"What happened?" Serena asked.

There was a short pause. "Hard to say. Her daughter-in-law says they've run out of money. Seems rather soon to me," Mrs Harding said pointedly.

"How long?"

"End of the month. Certainly by the New Year."

"I'll try and get down," Serena told her. "And I'll try and think of something."

Ed phoned at seven. "Thought you were going to do a bunk," he said when she explained. "And she just walked out, no explanation?"

Serena winced at her lie. "But I have to find someone else, Ed. I might need a day or two off. But I could take it as holiday. Rather sudden, but would you mind?"

"I mind that you think I'd be that small-minded. Take your time."

"I've also got to dash down to see Edith. That dreadful daughter-in-law of hers is having her chucked out of the nursing home by Christmas."

"Oh? Why?"

"Says there's no money left from the sale of the house. I can't believe it. I think Matron should get a bit heavy. Ask to see the books. I'll suggest it."

"Waste of time," Ed grunted. "She'll have spent it all. Let Mike know what you're doing."

He hadn't, she noticed, asked her to let *him* know.

In fact it was Stacey who came to the rescue. "Temporary," she explained, "just until you get someone permanent. My cousin needs somewhere to stay for the next three months. Give her dinner and breakfast and she'll babysit in return."

Serena squealed with relief. "Stace, you're a pal. When can I meet her?"

"She'll be down at the weekend, but I don't think she'll be able to start for a week. I'll phone her tonight. And Serena? Got time for me? I need sorting out."

"Come now," Serena suggested. "Come over and we'll have a cup of tea to celebrate."

A breathing space. That's all she needed. Just until she could get this mess under control. And if Ed argued she would insist it was regarded as part of her holiday. An unexpected holiday. Of sorts.

*

Saturday dawned cold and windy with a steady drizzle that didn't ease up all day. When she had first suggested a football match to Harry she had immediately regretted it. Lurid headlines leapt into her head. A mental vision of Harry being attacked by yobs sent her heart to her mouth. Maybe it wasn't the place to take a small boy, but Harry's disappointment would have

318

been beyond misery if she had failed him.

Now she was relieved to have something to do. If Louise had not gone to the cinema with Daphy and then to spend the evening with her, she might have hesitated. The violence of Cheryl's reaction had shaken her and haunted her all the next day. Panic seized her as she relived in her head the scenes from the night before. It was ridiculous, she told herself a dozen times. Cheryl was stupid, not mad. Deluded, not dangerous. But all the same she found herself hovering over the children, checking where they were.

To her relief and Harry's delight, Tipper, to whom she confided her plans of a football match, insisted on going with them. Somehow the idea of Tipper being with them transformed it in Harry's head to real lads' stuff. They caught the tube to Tottenham and then followed the crowd to the home end which Harry had told her was important so that they wouldn't get into any fights with the away supporters.

"Fight?" she asked, staring down at him. Her mild, reclusive son knew of such things? Over his head she said, "There won't be a fight, will there, Tip?"

"Well, there might. But I'm relying on you to behave yourself, Serena."

Harry was convulsed. "Ever since I moved to Foster Street," she looked haughtily ahead of her, "my life has become steadily more bizarre. Harry, don't let go of my hand," she squealed, catching sight of a sea of supporters, their faces daubed in blue and white stripes, chanting aggressively as they pushed their way through the turnstiles to the stand.

Harry was mesmerised by it all. The vast expanse of ground that rose up to meet them as they emerged from the stand entrance into the open air surpassed anything he had ever imagined. It was, for him, a dream. Even if each time a goal was scored or nearly scored his view was obliterated by the roaring wave of bodies in front of him, hurling themselves into the air, he didn't care.

On the way home Serena discovered she was hoarse from shouting. Harry was rapturously clutching the programme and a home strip that she had bought in the team shop. Tip said he was desperate for a pint and that he'd told them Spurs were useless. They reached Foster Street in exceptionally high spirits and by the time Alex phoned to see if she was free for dinner, she said her condition was that she had to be back in time to see *Match of the Day*.

*

In the end it wasn't until nearly five days later that she got down to Hove. She decided to go straight from seeing Harry into school, catching the bus to Victoria and then the train to Hove. Serena rang Mike and said she would be back at the club by Wednesday. Bella, Stacey's cousin, would be starting on Tuesday and, to everyone's relief, she seemed to fit in.

In two weeks it would be Christmas and this year Serena was confident it would be a better one for Harry and Louise than the last two. The unexpected extra days had been a godsend to allow her to shop and the bottom of her wardrobe was now hiding a stack of presents waiting to be wrapped. Louise was the only one to raise obstacles about going to her grandmother's for Christmas but this time Serena refused to budge. Having expected and prepared herself to deal with all Louise's objections, she demolished them following Alex's advice. They would be leaving after lunch on Christmas Eve to go down to Margot's, and would not be back until after the New Year when the club reopened.

Serena was aware that she was sinking into Ed's debt. To take time off so near to Christmas couldn't have been welcomed by anyone. In her bag she had a gift for Edith, a pair of bed socks and some slippers shaped like little boots. Maybe she should buy him something as a thank you. Maybe he would misconstrue it. Maybe, she looked thoughtfully at the keys in her hand, maybe she would forget the whole idea.

As she closed the door, she looked across and saw Cheryl coming out of her house. There was an awkward pause. Serena was loath to speak but neither did she want any continuing unpleasantness. In the five days since she had asked Cheryl to leave, they had not caught sight of each other. Serena had carefully avoided leaving the house during that time before checking Cheryl was nowhere in sight, and she guessed the other woman was doing the same.

320

In that same time Serena had come to bitterly regret her own actions. Wanting help, she had fallen into a trap that would never have even opened itself before. The luxury of choice had not been hers, but the danger she had exposed her children to left her shaking and sitting bolt upright in bed at two in the morning. Cheryl was a tragic case, but the blame had been Serena's for not checking her out, for not listening to Betty who had, in her own way, tried to warn her. Nor could she now trust Cheryl not to ring a newspaper and tell them — albeit a selective version — of what happened. What a good story, she thought grimly. "Disgraced Banker's Wife on the Game."

It was partly in the spirit of protecting herself and the children that she had decided a truce of some sort should be reached with the pitiful Cheryl, and almost as much because it suddenly came to her that perhaps Cheryl, too, wanted some kind of healing of the rift, but did not have the necessary social skills to achieve it. Serena bit her lip and took the initiative.

"Cheryl?" she called over and began to walk across the street. "Have you got a moment?"

Cheryl paused and turned. Her face seemed older.

"I just thought we should try and clear the air a bit," Serena began as she drew near. "I'm sorry we had such a misunderstanding."

"A what?" Cheryl snapped. "A misunderstanding? Don't think so, ducky, what's to mistake in you? Slut."

Serena shut her eyes in disbelief and then turned sharply away.

Cheryl spat on the ground between them. "Slag," she screamed, "I'll get you for what you did to me. You just see if I don't."

Serena kept walking. Her cheeks were burning. As she walked she tightened the belt on her raincoat, pulled the collar up and wrapped her scarf more firmly around her neck. She strode past a shocked Mrs Mojani, who hurriedly crossed the street to avoid contamination by either of those wanton women, past the curious stares of another neighbour hurling rubbish into a skip outside the door, and it was not until she turned the corner into the High Street that she sank down on the wall by the bus stop and gripped her bag in her lap.

A handful of people were already waiting but gave her no more than a cursory stare as she sat, her eyes fixed on the strip of pavement in front of her. When the bus to take her to Victoria swayed into view, the signal for the straggling queue to surge forward, it was all she could do to struggle to her feet and join them. Downstairs was full. She climbed upstairs as the bus took off, the movement making her reach instinctively for a handrail to guide her to a seat near the back.

At Victoria she bought a cheap day return to Hove. Then she crossed the concourse and bought a morning paper and a magazine. The train was already waiting at the platform. Serena walked towards the front and eventually settled into a crowded compartment for the hour's journey to the coast.

From Hove station she took the bus to the corner of Holewood Hill as she had in the summer. The wind was icily sharp, the day dull and overcast, the road deserted except for the solitary swish of tyres as a car passed. Thick ominous clouds hung over the sea, grey sullen waves swelled into a crescendo and crashed on to the shingle. For a few minutes Serena leaned against a wobbling railing staking out the narrow strip of pavement that acted as a kind of promenade between the stony expanse of the beach and the road. The wind flattened her hair, stinging her eyes. Oblivious to the icy blast rolling in off the sea, she stared out at the grey heaving mass and let the tears that had been threatening her for over an hour slide unchecked down her cheeks.

The journey to this point was beyond recollection. The embarrassing public abuse that had been hurled at her had left her stunned. Sitting miles away and an hour or so between them, she felt safer but no less distraught. Cheryl's rage had terrified her. She hadn't bargained for such an outpouring of venom. Inside she knew it was not to do with her. It couldn't be. The problem lay with Cheryl. She'd been merely the whipping-boy for thwarting the absurd and impossible dreams of a hopelessly inadequate woman. Perhaps you had to be born to it, she thought miserably, to withstand such violence. No matter how hard she tried she didn't fit in. Not anywhere. Ed thought she was tough, Melanie thought she was too proud for her own good and Cheryl Tosney that she was a tart. Only Alex guessed at and sympathized with the mountains she climbed each day, but even he didn't understand her fighting spirit. It was just that the fighting spirit kept being flattened.

For a few minutes she stood leaning against the rail, the fierceness of the wind calming her scattered wits. Eventually, the sound of a child squealing as his mother pushed him along in his buggy caught her attention and brought her back to the task in hand. Head down against a squalling rain, she turned and ran across the street to the small row of shops opposite. She bought two egg custard tarts and then made her way to the nursing home at the top of the hill.

*

"Mrs Carmichael?" She got to her feet as the matron came towards her. "Edith will be so pleased to see you."

Serena turned and picked up the small box containing the custard tarts. "I wanted to see you first. Just to see if there's any way I can help."

"With Edith? Oh, that's all settled." Matron beamed. "Some mistake with the accounting on her daughter-in-law's part. I was a bit unsure about giving Mr ..." she paused, frowning, "Mr Turner, that's it. About giving him the details — but he was most insistent and frankly if there was a chance that Edith didn't have to be moved, I'm not above bending the odd rule."

A weight lifted itself from Serena's shoulders. Ever since she had heard of Edith's plight she had been desperately trying to work out how she could help and she had worried for nothing.

"Who's Mr Turner?" she asked, as they made their way to the day room.

"Finance director for some company. Someone there knows the family I believe."

Serena halted. Turner? Matthew Turner. Ed's finance director. She began to smile.

Well, fancy that. Strange to think he had done just what Stephen would have done if she'd asked. What was a sum like that to Stephen? Or indeed Ed. Stephen would have been impatient with her for involving him, to be sure, but he would have signed a cheque and solved the problem, got it off his back. She smiled to herself. Ed had obviously paid up for Edith. His affection for his dead grandmother was clearly the reason for his generosity. As she approached Edith's wing-chair, Serena was pleased now that she had mentioned it to Ed. How awful if he had heard too late to help.

The visit was brief. Edith did not seem to know why Serena was there visiting, had trouble recalling her name. She did however eat half of one of the custard tarts and before she fell back to sleep asked Serena how her mother was and if she still worked for the bookie on the corner. Serena gazed affectionately down at the crumpled figure, her mouth half open, eyes closed, lost in another world at another time. Gently she wiped the crumbs from around her mouth, adjusted the rug and then left, kissing her lined cheek.

"It's all right, Mrs Carmichael," Matron told her, as Serena met her in the lobby. "She's such a fighter but she is ninety-two. You should try seeing her in the evening. Comes to life then and insists on watching *Wallander*."

They had reached the front door. "Rather you than me," Matron shivered, looking out at the gradually worsening weather. "You know," she paused in the act of opening the door, "it was an odd thing. For a few days she was very agitated and fretful when she heard about the money running out. That stupid daughter-in-law wrote to her and told her. Heartless. Quite heartless. And then when everything was settled and the solicitor had been to see her, she calmed down almost within the hour.

"Come and see her again." Matron pressed Serena's arm, opening the door. The wind gusted in. "She'll love her Christmas present. I'll make sure she gets it."

*

Serena decided to phone Ed rather than wait until she next saw him. Walking up Foster Street, the shoulders of her raincoat sopping from the driving rain, her hair hanging in damp tendrils, she kept a wary eye open for Cheryl but equally she was determined not to be intimidated about leaving and entering her own home. Out of the corner of her eye she was sure she saw Cheryl's door open and close again with a hasty slam. Oh well, she thought, at least I fit in with one group of neighbours. Those on whom Cheryl had vowed revenge.

Once she had shed her coat she called Ed's house. Wally answered and announced grandly that she had reached Mr Stein's residence.

"I've just been to see Edith," she said warmly when he came on the line. "You are a good person, Mr Stein. You've made an old lady very happy."

"Well, I hope it helped Edith as well," he joked. "Nothing to thank me for. Her daughter-in-law copped up the money."

There was a pause. "But surely Matthew … I mean why did he …?"

"Tsk, tsk, Serena," Ed chided her. "Practise what you preach. Don't jump to conclusions. I haven't paid a penny. Why should I? Edith has the money herself, it was just a question of unravelling her accounts. Thank me for that. Nothing else, I promise you."

A ripple of unease ran through her. A vision of a couple of heavies threatening the unknown daughter-in-law flashed before her. "Ed. What did you do?"

"Nothing. I got Matthew to hire a solicitor down in Hove for Edith, got him to explain to her daughter-in-law about fraud. Edith shouldn't have to sell her house to pay for that home and Fanny Adams, whatever her name is, has had her fingers prized from the deeds. Now Edith's savings are in a bank account set up in Edith's name administered by a solicitor and in a few days' time a direct debit to the nursing home will be in place."

"You mean you haven't paid the fees?" She was struggling between disappointment that he had not made such a generous gesture when he could afford it and acute embarrassment that she had clearly expected him to have done it. Not like Stephen at all. "Well, it was still good of you."

"Serena? Listen to me. That isn't the way things are done round here. I wouldn't help anyone rip off a poor old cow like Edith."

"Of course not," she protested feebly, "I just wanted Edith to be safe."

"That's great, fine. But just think how she would feel. A proud old lady like that having to rely on charity or a handout when she knew she had the money somewhere and no home to go back to. Edith might be a bit gaga but from what I can gather she's a stout old bird at heart and she would have been mortified to hear a near stranger had to support her. I'm not into that either."

"No, of course not," Serena agreed hastily, remembering what Mrs Harding had said. Edith had calmed down when she had been told how things stood. She felt deflated.

"When are you coming back?" Ed changed the subject abruptly. It was a habit of his she'd noticed.

"Day after tomorrow," she told him. "I've got some temporary cover — breathing space really."

"Well now you've got your breath back, come to the dogs with me. You'll enjoy it."

"The dogs? How brilliant ... I mean no. I meant what I said. I'm really sorry, Ed."

"Is this to do with your old man?"

She stiffened. "Yes, of course, how could it not be? But it's just as much to do with not going out with the boss."

There was a pause. "Two years, isn't it? Up to you, but I still think you'd get more out of a night at the dogs than being loyal to a bloke who dumped you in it. Don't get too trapped in the past, Mrs Carmichael. It's a safe place but bloody boring."

"Who said I was?" She tried to keep the anger out of her voice. "I have friends who I see, go out with."

"But no one who's interested in you for you?" He sounded sceptical. She should have been flattered.

Instead she was stung into saying, "Of course. I have a ..." she paused, "a kind of relationship with someone."

"A kind of? What kind is that?"

"Someone who understands, listens, helps me keep things in perspective ..."

"Sounds like a shrink," he laughed.

"He is," she replied stonily.

"Oh Christ," he muttered. "Spare me. You don't need a shrink, Mrs Carmichael, you need ..."

There was a long pause.

"What?" she demanded.

"A night at the dogs," he said flatly. But she knew it wasn't what he had intended to say. She found herself blushing at what she guessed he'd really meant. "Let Mike know you're back tomorrow."

She replaced the phone and leaned her head against the wall. Today was not a good day. Her hair was stuck to her head from the rain, she wore no make-up, and most of all she had begun to think a night out at the dogs sounded like fun. She rang Alex.

"Alex," she said miserably, "I'm in need of a friend."

Chapter Twenty-Six

At Alex's suggestion they had supper at his house. "You can't talk properly with Guigo asking if every last lettuce leaf is perfection," he pointed out, referring to the maître d' at the restaurant they favoured.

She hesitated. "It's all right," he said, reading her thoughts. "Alice and I have agreed not to see each other. Not for a while. It seemed only, well, sensible. God, I sound boring, don't I?"

He didn't. To Serena he sounded like a haven of sanity after the last few days. Alex calmed her, made her feel she was in control. He made sense of decisions, rationalized arguments. The destabilizing effect of Ed was not one she enjoyed. She could see this was something a lot of women may have found exciting, but she didn't. She could not, as she did with Alex, tell him about Cheryl or ask him why he thought Louise veered exasperatingly from a wayward teenager to one who cared about her mother's safety that night. Nor could she say exactly why not, except she knew she was safer if Ed thought she was what he had decided she was.

"You could never sound boring," she told Alex fondly. "Not to me. I'm sorry about Alice."

It would have been folly to have pretended she was entirely divorced from influencing their decision to split up, for which she felt a pang of guilt. However, something in Alex's voice told her the end result of such a protracted analysis of his relationship with Alice went deeper than just her being the sole distraction. She wasn't surprised. What he had in common with the affected, deeply irritating Alice had always puzzled her.

"Sounds like we both need a shoulder," she said.

"How about I blow a whistle and we swap over at halftime," he joked. "Now that you're a soccer fan?"

He was, she decided, replacing the phone, awfully sweet.

On reflection she was not surprised that she had ended the evening in bed with him. There was a limit, she told herself as they slid breathlessly on to Alex's bed, to what the human spirit could endure in isolation. There was also the fact that she had become very bored with her own lovemaking, and a glass or three of a very good Chablis had told her getting sex out of the way with Alex was an exceptionally good idea.

"I absolutely hadn't planned this," Alex murmured into her hair, as the dinner he had so carefully prepared cooled and congealed in the dining room below. He shifted his weight so that he could look down at her. Her eyes were closed and she was breathing evenly, drowsy with relief and a sense of freedom.

"Nor me," she answered, sleepily. "It wouldn't have happened if we had."

"Nothing ever does," he laughed, softly kissing her. "I am so happy. So amazingly happy. We must," he added with such earnestness she managed to open one eye to gauge the seriousness of what he was saying. "Take this slowly. At this moment I just want to rush you to the nearest registry office and marry you, but life isn't that simple."

Serena's eyes flew open. "Especially as I'm still married," she pointed out, alarmed at the speed with which he was progressing their relationship, the first stirring of sobriety beginning to make itself felt.

Alex rolled off her and gazed at the ceiling. "Of course," he said, "for a moment I forgot. How do you feel about — Stephen?"

Stephen. In four weeks it would be exactly two years since she had seen him, spoken to him, slept with him. Not a word, a sign. Not for a moment had she ceased to believe he was alive. Somewhere. Even Don Trewless, who had turned up a few weeks back after a long gap, believed that too. She wasn't surprised that he knew where she was working or who for.

It was hard to assemble her feelings about Stephen, now that Alex had asked her. The guilt she had for so long believed would be part of such an act was strangely absent. For a long while she had never believed she would feel anything but treacherous if she had slept with someone else.

She shook her head. "I don't know," she finally answered, truthfully. "I know I should be feeling something but I don't. It's like I'm two people.

The Serena that loved him, adored him really, and this other person of whom he knows nothing."

"Oh my darling," Alex whispered. "It's a start. That's so good."

"Is it?" she asked doubtfully. She turned her head and looked at his face smiling contentedly at her from the pillow next to hers. For him, the solution was falling into place. But she knew for her the puzzle was just starting.

"Alex," she asked quickly, "would you mind if I didn't talk about Stephen? I'm not sure how I feel about it. I need to, as Louise would say, I need to get a fix on it." She smiled a little anxiously. "You do understand, don't you?"

At once his face filled with concern. "My precious, of course. Take all the time you want."

For some reason his understanding response didn't help. A small knot of apprehension tugged away in her head. "You know what, Alex?"

"Yes, my precious?" he answered with such tenderness, smoothing her hair from her face, she felt unnerved.

"I think we could salvage some of that dinner, don't you?"

*

The children were asleep. Bella, Stacey's cousin, was installed in the spare room. Serena sat curled up in an armchair clutching a cushion against her chest, looking out at the deserted street below. The rain that had eased off as Alex brought her home had revived, along with a gusting wind which moved the branches of the tree outside across the street lamp, sending odd shadows across the room.

Where did she start, or rather what had she started? If she could have turned the clock back she would, but she couldn't. She had slept with him and now she couldn't understand why she felt so empty about it all. Where was the rollercoaster of emotion that was meant to accompany the start of an affair, the sense of well-being, the moment she would pinpoint for ever as when she had turned the corner? If she had regretted instantly what she had done, then she could have understood. But she hadn't. Regret had seeped slowly into her reasoning once she was alone.

It was, she told herself repeatedly, just sex, not the dismantling of the

Bank of England. Craving warmth and closeness she had responded with little resistance to Alex's tentative opening gestures and had been grateful that he was a thoughtful lover, not rushing her, not expecting anything sophisticated. He was after all only the third man she had ever slept with in her whole life and on her next birthday she would be thirty-six. Thank God that it had been Alex and not someone like Ed, who would have been impatient with her qualms after the event and been, she was sure, a great deal more demanding sexually. But not Alex, who had listened and counselled in spite of being the person most easily affected by what she felt. All she knew as she turned from the window and contemplated her neatly made and empty bed was that what had taken place this evening with Alex had been unconnected in her head with Stephen.

She glanced at her wrist-watch. It was just after three. It was unlikely she would get any sleep, but it would be a great deal warmer in bed. She slipped off her dressing gown, reached into the bedside drawer for a pair of socks, wriggled into them and slid under the covers. In minutes she was asleep, Stephen's old tennis socks warming her feet.

*

Christmas at Margot's was as happy as they could make it for the children. They stayed until New Year's Day and then travelled back to London for Serena to resume work the next day. It was quite amazing, she decided as she drove along, how the children just accepted the fact that they now had a car again. Not the plushest car in the world, but a sturdy estate car that she had bought the Saturday before, second-hand from a garage in Stockwell, with Tipper acting as her adviser.

Life was improving; she was getting there. Provided, of course, she thought grimly, she could prevent Bradley and his friends from removing essential items like the wheels while it was parked in the street. And of course the dreadful Cheryl who might wreak revenge with a spray of paint or graffiti.

For the first few days, Serena had anxiously checked that neither of her tiresome neighbours had vandalized a car for which she had worked long and hard.

"Bradley doesn't want the tyres," Louise told her scornfully, watching her return from yet another surveillance.

"Radio, tapes. That's what he's after. Tell you what," she giggled, "put all those old Kylie tapes in there. Or better still, those compilation ones Gran gave you. Yuck. What a scream watching him try to flog those."

Serena wasn't listening, she had already streaked into the road to remove the radio from the dashboard and bring it indoors.

She had sent a Christmas card to Ed with a pleasant message and in return she had received a basket of plump winter roses, entwined with tartan ribbon and foliage. The note merely thanked her for all her help during the year and was signed with a scrawled signature. Melanie raised her eyebrows when she saw the display, recognizing the hand of the florist who had become the best kept secret in London.

"Who's advising him?" she whistled appreciatively.

"Why should he need advice?" Serena replied, placing the basket in the centre of the sitting room. "He left school at fourteen and is now a millionaire with an ex-wife who becomes catatonic at the sound of his name, even though they've been divorced for five years. God knows what the woman he's having an affair with is like. Married, apparently — but he's not," she stopped and amended hastily, not wishing Melanie to know how she suspected, "I mean I don't think he's faithful to her. And he's blunt to the point of rudeness.

"He's got a box at the opera and one at the dogs. His home is filled with first editions but if you suggest he's well read, he disclaims and says quite the reverse, he just reads a lot. On his walls, I swear, although naturally I didn't march over and study them closely, he has a Millais and a Tissot and, because he loves a joke, a Sadler. He has the worst taste in cufflinks of any man I've ever seen as well as the most horrifying habit of vandalizing exquisite furniture to accommodate his passion for technology. And he can quote anything you name from Abelard to Zen and have room to argue why Millwall would have been a great team if he'd only been let loose on them. Someone advising him?" She shook her head. "No. I somehow don't think he needs advice."

"Heavens." Melanie looked sharply at Serena. "Well," she picked up her bag, preparing to go, a number of interesting ideas in place to occupy her journey home, "on present evidence it seems like *he's* also a very well-kept secret."

Serena looked at the flowers and then back at Melanie. "Seems like it," she agreed. "So, what day are you off to Mexico? Wonderful that Charles got the time off, isn't it?"

Alex had presented her with a silk scarf from Liberty and some perfume which he had guessed she would like. She gave him a handmade wooden picture-frame which sent him into such raptures she enquired solemnly if he had found gold in the back.

*

January gave way to a mild February and a stormy March. Ed had spent the greater part of that time in New York. From time to time he strode through the club and nodded a greeting to her. Once or twice she thought of waylaying him to try and engage him in a friendly conversation, but the opportunity didn't seem to present itself. Maybe it will, she consoled herself, watching him in deep conversation with Mike in the library. But only if you create it, she pointed out to herself.

"Goodness," she said lightly as he emerged. "We hardly see you here. You seem so busy."

He paused and then came over to where she was checking messages for the evening. "Les Cages re-opens in the summer so I expect I'll be seeing a lot of Paris in the next few weeks. The 'Eighty One' needed a kick in the butt which is why I had to be there these last few weeks. Frobisher's is the one place I don't have to concern myself with. Mike knows what he's doing."

"Well, that must be a relief," replied Serena, oddly pleased that it was work and not his mistress that had kept him so long in New York.

"How's your kind-of relationship going?" He wasn't looking at her, but at the bar Tipper was pretending not to notice the unique attention Serena was getting from the man whose appearances among them since Christmas could be counted on one hand.

Since the kind-of relationship had turned into a sexual one and one in which she felt torn between suffocating at Alex's attentions and enjoying being so wanted, she gave an evasive answer.

"Going, I think is the answer to that."

"And that would mean what?" he asked. "Going as in grinding to a halt or going as in getting up to speed?"

"Going well," she held his gaze defiantly, although for the life of her she couldn't imagine why it was suddenly so necessary for him to know she was having a sex life.

"Hmm," was all he said. She was the first to drop her gaze. He glanced at his watch. "OK, Mike," he called over to where the general manager was clearly impatient to be off. "I'm out of here."

Chapter Twenty-Seven

By the beginning of May, Serena was tentatively mulling over the possibility that this time she might go with the children to Lucca. It was Jasmine who had urged her to think about it. Perhaps it was because Louise, at nearly fifteen, might prove too much for their kind but ageing grandmother on her own — and with good reason, since Louise had sulked for a week when Serena refused point blank to consider her going away alone with Daphy. This news, relayed in their now monthly phone call, might have encouraged Jasmine to want her along for moral support. On the other hand their relationship, she had to admit, was more relaxed and warmer since Stephen had disappeared and it could be that after two years Jasmine wanted to see her as much for herself as from a sense of duty.

Their lives in Foster Street had settled into a routine that worked after a fashion. Bella had managed to switch her course so that she could stay in London until the end of the summer, which suited all of them, especially since it meant they saw more of Stacey who Serena could see was trying to loosen the grip the dreadful Barry had on her.

Serena continued to work at Frobisher's, continued to save and continued to hope that within a year or two she would be out of Foster Street and not working at night. The job was not to be knocked. It paid well and during the crucial times the children had needed her she had been around, but it was not and never had been intended to last forever. Just to get her back on her feet. However, the idea of where that was shrouded in doubt and indecision. Where was this place now where happiness and security had been snatched from her and what was there for her to go back to?

There had been a time when she first moved to Foster Street when she physically ached as much for the sight and touch of Stephen as the comfort and pleasure that she had taken for granted living in Belvoir Square. Of late when she had tested herself she had found that sense of longing hard to reach. Recalling it was the easy part. The carefully groomed, tree-lined square; the knowledge that Mrs Owen and dear Chrissie would lift from her expensively clad shoulders the necessity to think beyond who they were entertaining or dining with that evening. The garden at the cottage at her favourite time on a summer evening, long shadows falling across a perfectly manicured lawn, roses climbing the wall that had been built when George III was on the throne, the sound of Louise's pony clattering back into the stable yard, Harry splashing noisily in the pool. And Stephen. She frowned. So rarely there and now not at all. So easy to recall, less easy to understand why it was the feeling of happiness that had once been her constant companion that eluded her.

Walking through Soho's bustling streets towards Frobisher's one early summer evening, she wrestled with this conundrum and by the time she had pushed open the door and climbed the stairs to reception, she was no nearer to knowing why the thought of going back no longer appealed to her. And it wasn't because at the end of the road Stephen would be waiting. It was perhaps because she could no longer recall what she had been like. A stranger stared back at her down the path that had brought her here. That woman was the result of a comfortable life. The one striding along in flat shoes, a linen skirt and plain white T-shirt, about to change into a cocktail dress, pile her hair on top and slip into high heels didn't know her.

Even the job lacked the edge she had noticed in her first few weeks when Ed had nearly always been around. Now she hardly saw him. Since the beginning of March he had been in Paris and New York. Tipper heard from one of his many sources that Ed's affair had left her husband and moved into his Park Avenue duplex. Mike said it was crap and that Willow Stein would have had the building torched if Eve had so much as pitched up on the sidewalk.

"Willow and Eve?" Mike yelped, looking at her in horror. "Do me a favour. Willow blames Eve for the speed with which Ed applied for the divorce and Eve thinks it's because of Willow that Ed won't marry her."

"And is that true?" In spite of herself Serena could not help being curious.

Mike shrugged. "Could be. Ed doesn't go out of his way to offend Willow. In as much as he can feel guilty about any woman, he feels it about her."

"Why? Because he cheated on her?" she asked, smiling a greeting at two regular members walking into the bar.

Mike shook his head. "Don't think so. Willow's not exactly Snow White herself. He told me once he should never have married, they were OK while they lived together."

"Put pressure on him, did she?"

"God no. It was the other way round. There's a lot of the working-class lad still in Ed, you know. He thought it was the right thing to do. Marry, have kids. All that stuff. That's why Willow goes into orbit if he even looks as though he might be happy. She didn't mind the marriage bit, it's just that she didn't want any kids and it was only after they married that she realized he was serious and he realized so was she.

"Also she wanted to live in LA where all her friends are, and Ed hates the place. So there she was stuck in New York with all those artists and writers he gets off on and he was hardly there."

"And that's what broke them up?"

"That and the fact that he found her in bed with some low life from LA that she had shipped in while she thought he was in Chicago."

"And he feels guilty about her?" Serena asked, amazed.

Mike nodded. "Weird or what? Says he left her alone too much. Business got in the way. So he filed for divorce, got her a house in Brentwood, didn't argue about the alimony and she says he ruined her life. Bloody women."

Serena laughed. He sounded just like Ed.

She couldn't say why, because he didn't add to her comfort, but Serena missed not having Ed around. All she knew was that when he was present, teasing her or being blunt, she felt the club worked. A buzz lifted the whole evening. Tipper agreed and then gave her a sly look.

"Now if I were a betting man, I'd say you weren't so cool about him as you make out." He ducked as she threw a napkin across the bar at him and strolled out with a toss of her hair to greet some late arrivals.

Harry would be leaving Dunton Road at the end of the term to start at the secondary school a mile away in September. Louise was already creating about the pressure of GCSEs. In this Bella had been a godsend, talking Louise through texts she was either bored with or couldn't penetrate, and getting her to concentrate in a way that had evaded all Serena's attempts at focusing her mind on something other than Damon.

Every Sunday Tipper would turn up for lunch, which Serena cooked, and afterwards if the weather was reasonable they would all troop off to Battersea Park where Harry would practise roller-blading. On these occasions they would often be joined by Alex if he wasn't seeing his own children. At first, it had caused Serena some disquiet that whereas his children had been allowed to stay over with Alex and encouraged to enjoy a relationship with Alice while they were together, Lorrayne, Alex's ex-wife, had made it dear that she was not prepared to extend the same goodwill to Serena until she understood what her relationship with Alex was.

Curiously Alex had bowed to her demands. "She has a point," he explained, "I don't want them confused."

"Alex," she stopped him as they lay in bed at his house and turned to face him. "Is this anything to do with who I am? I mean, being Stephen's wife?"

He pulled himself up in the bed. "My precious, absolutely not. It's more to do with the fact —" He paused and threw his head back as though considering how best to put what he wanted to say. "It's more to do with Alice. Lorrayne liked her. Still does. In fact," he looked a little self conscious, "I met Alice through Lorrayne. The children already knew her. So you see, it worked so well for everyone. They all thought she was perfect for me. And maybe if I hadn't been so in need of *someone* after Lorrayne, it might not have happened, and if you hadn't come along and made me question the relationship I had with her, it might have gone on. And now," he smiled down at her. "I'll never know, will I?"

She said nothing, just squeezed his arm. Of the two, Lorrayne or Alice, she thought she preferred Alice, and since her own feelings had remained unresolved she conceded that Lorrayne might just have a point. If it had been Stephen, she would not have wanted Harry and Louise exposed to a series of lady friends, each of whom they would be pressured to like. If she wished for anything, however, it was that Louise would be more polite to Alex. Harry treated him with the ease of an old friend, which of course to Harry he was, but Louise found him tame and boring. Just like Stephen, she thought wryly, demanding and needing excitement and exciting people around her. As a result she couldn't bring herself to attempt to alter that view. They would both need time. And so would she.

It was odd, she thought, how her life had reshaped and settled into this pattern. Accepting what had once horrified her, shrewder about how to handle her daughter's almost daily attempts to challenge the rules she laid down. For instance, Louise had consented to come on one of their outings, but only if Damon came too, knowing that would signal her relationship had moved on to something special. Serena told her it was a lovely idea and gripped her nails inside her clenched fists out of sight in her pockets.

Damon no longer made Serena uneasy. Not that she would trust his re-actions strutting around the streets with his loud mates who seemed to rely on pushing, shoving and insults as the proper social intercourse with the world. But with Louise he was calmer, more in awe of her, she suspected. Better to have him under her eye than try and stop it — she was uneasily aware that it was not beyond Louise to see him secretly. Alex said Louise was just being tribal when she told him. Wanting a boyfriend, rather than Damon in particular. For once Serena spoke sharply to him and told him it was likely her daughter was just being awkward and she was besotted with the lad.

Margot now stayed in Wiltshire to attend parish council meetings, of which she had just accepted the chair, to enjoy her friends and her garden and the fact that her daughter was a phone calls were.

In fact, if it wasn't for the realisation that Stacey was increasingly a prob-lem, Serena would have been content. Even Bella, who was Stacey's closest friend as well as her cousin, had taken to falling into silent disapproval whenever Stacey embarked on what she should do with her life. By which she meant her life with Barry.

*

Cheryl had waited a long time but her revenge when it came was vicious. The shock for Serena came more from having believed the danger from another embarrassing assault from Cheryl had passed, and that life had started to take on an air of normality.

The car had remained intact, windows unbroken. Graffiti had not been daubed on her door, and the neighbours who were friendly remained so. The sight of Cheryl scurrying to close her door if she caught sight of Serena became familiar. Betty Plaxton, to whom the entire scene had been recounted by another neighbour, to her credit — or maybe, as Serena suspected, because she had never thought her word had been doubted — refrained from pointing out that she had been right all along.

And then Cheryl struck. It had to be her. No one else who knew Serena would have accused her of neglecting her children and living off immoral earnings, not to mention being Ed Stein's paid mistress. The Plaxtons would go nowhere near authorities of any description, not with Bradley still on probation, and no one else in the street cared enough about her to bother. Even the Mojanis had stopped crossing the street when they saw her coming.

It came through Ed.

"Boss wants to see you," Mike told her as they arrived one evening, giving her an odd look. "Upstairs."

"Ed? I didn't know he was here." She began to take off her jacket. She paused. "Upstairs? You mean," she pointed with her finger to the penthouse, "upstairs?"

"Uh huh," he nodded. "Won't say. Buck up, get changed. Said he needed to see you."

Ed was waiting in the drawing room. He looked fit and tanned and Serena thought he had lost a little weight.

"Nice to see you." She greeted him with genuine warmth. For a moment she thought he looked surprised. And serious.

"And you. Although what I want to see you about isn't entirely pleasant." The smile on her mouth faded. "Not pleasant?" she faltered. "Ed, don't

... I mean, am I being fired?"

She tried to keep her voice light, careless even.

"Not by me. Have a seat. Drink?"

She shook her head.

"Here. It came this morning."

From inside the top drawer of a small bureau he removed a letter and handed it to her. A faint smell of cheap perfume wafted from it. It was marked personal and private, typed and postmarked in Whitehall. She wrinkled her nose and removed the single sheet of paper. She read it through and then glanced up at Ed. Her face was pale, her hands shaking. In her entire life she had never felt so mortified or dirty. Her only relief was that she was sitting, she felt so sick.

"I see," she said, handing the letter back to him, absently wiping her hands on her skirt. "Living on immoral earnings, apparently ... leaving the children all night on their own. And I do," she nearly choked on the word, "*business* while they're in the house. It's wicked," she gulped painfully.

"It's from a nutter," he said. "Sent it to the fraud office as well. They came over to see me. This morning."

"Oh God," she looked stricken. "Why haven't they called me?"

"Because," he said exasperated. "They know what you're up to, you know that. You told me you're still monitored. They know you're working here. If you were on the game or leaving the kids, they'd know first. If the kids were abused, they'd know that too. Doesn't Harry go to that quack? There you are then. It was me, they wanted to check out. Not you. Any excuse. And this gave it to them."

"Ed, I'm so sorry," she whispered. "All I ever do is bring trouble with me." Her voice began to crack. "And it's not true. You know that, don't you?"

"Give me a break," Ed replied calmly.

"No. I know you don't believe the other stuff. But the bit that says I know where Stephen is and what he's done with the money? Look, I know I'm under surveillance most of the time now. Their interest is Stephen, not me. I mean what possible reason could he have for surfacing, other than me or the children in trouble."

"No reason at all." Ed said lightly tossing back his drink.

"And you're now caught up in it. No one gets away with anything around me. And it's truly, truly wicked. And it's Cheryl." To her horror she found herself on the verge of tears. Rage of course. She rose hurriedly to her feet. She mustn't cry. *Must not.*

Ed rose, guided her to a sofa and pushed her on to it. He handed her a glass of brandy. "Go on. Drink it. No hysterics," he commanded, squeezing her hand. "And who the hell is Cheryl?"

Serena explained. "Jeezus," he whistled softly. "You mean the sight of my car put all this crap into her head? Why didn't you tell me?" he asked shortly. "You just said the help had left. You never mentioned the rest."

She shook her head. "Not something you tell your boss."

"Oh stop that shit, will you?" He stood up abruptly, running a hand through his hair. "You know bloody well it's not like that. What do you take me for? Some groping old bastard that comes on to the best-looking women and gets nasty if they turn him down?

"Oh, forget it," he growled, as she began to protest. "Let's sort this load of rubbish out first. What do you want to do about the old bag from over the road? Sue?"

She shook her head. "No. God no. Less attention the better. Ed? Listen to me. You don't need the kind of trouble I bring with me. I'll resign of course."

"Leave?" he cut across her. "Why? Because some vicious old hag tells a pack of lies? Strewth, give me strength. I thought you were above all that."

"Don't, Ed," she spoke wearily. "Don't make me feel worse than I do now. I'm not a wimp but I'm not up to a fight with anyone. Especially not you."

"Oh for Christ's sake," he muttered, sitting down heavily on the edge of the desk. "Why would I do that? There's no helping you, is there?"

"But there is," she pointed out. "Help me by making it easy for me. I don't want to leave. The money's good, it's got me back on my feet, I'll always be grateful to you, always. But I know what will happen next and I've got to think of the children. If it were just me, it would be different. But it isn't. I come as part of a package. You see, I know, just *know*, she'll go to a tabloid. It's on the cards. I'm surprised she hasn't already."

"But they must know where you live, what you do."

Serena gave him a weak smile. "You'd think so, wouldn't you? But when I refused to talk and kept myself to myself — you know, few friends, low profile — they moved on. One day someone will be going through some cuttings and a bored features editor will say, 'Hey, why don't we follow her up,' for no better reason than they need to fill a space, and I'll be back in the news for a while. I remember what Don Trewless told me."

He looked questioningly at her.

"My guy," she gave a wry smile. "The one assigned to the case. Drops by to see me every now and then. Anyway, he said they'll never go away, ever. On a slow day, I could fill a column. And then there's the big picture still to be got."

He looked steadily at her. She could see he didn't need to be told.

"Stephen?" He ground out his cigar. "You don't believe that will happen, do you?"

She turned away and placed the glass on a small table next to her. "You know, a little while ago I would have said undoubtedly. He's not dead. I know that. But if he was going to be back I think it would have happened by now. One day," she spoke softly, more to herself, "one day I will see him again, but it will be because I've found him, not the other way around. That's what I think. Odd, isn't it, I've never told anyone that, not even …" She was about to say Alex. She changed it to: "Don Trewless."

He was standing with his back to her. "Not even the shrink," guessing shrewdly what she had left out.

She shook her head. "No. Not even Alex."

"Don't leave," he said quietly. "You're safe here. We'll just tell the bloody hacks to sod off if they try and get to you. Serena," he came back to sit next to her, "you're safer here with me, I mean working here," he corrected himself. "Than out there on your own. I can protect you."

She shook her head. A brief vision of Stephen rose before her, telling her how to do things, Alex trying to shield her from pain, and now Ed. Ed thinking she only had to hide behind him and she would be safe.

"Thank you. You're being kind beyond belief. But I have to do this on my own. No one owes me anything and this way I don't owe them anything either. I don't want that particular bag ever again. Believe me."

He swore loudly but she just smiled. "Hey, don't frighten me. A tacky letter and a visit from the fraud squad I can take. But not you cursing."

"You mean it, don't you?" He looked her over slowly as if seeing her for the first time.

"Uh huh," she nodded. "I'll fix when to leave with Mike. I'll just slip away so there'll be no big deal. I'll have to tell Tipper, he's a friend. He wouldn't believe any claptrap about being bored with the job. He knows how important it's been to me."

"Then for Christ's sake, woman, stay," Ed exploded.

"I'm out of here," she mimicked. "I'll say goodbye before I go."

He walked with her to the door. "Thanks, Ed." She turned and smiled at him as the lift appeared. "It's been great."

"Bloody women," he growled, as the lift doors closed.

*

Mike watched Ed emerge from the lift at nearly three in the morning. The club was emptying out, with just a few strays left in the bar. Serena had departed ten minutes before, having had a prolonged talk with Mike who, like Ed, had tried to persuade her to stay on.

"Tough about Serena," he said as Ed reached him. "She'll be hard to replace. There's quite a few faces who have ambitions in her direction."

Ed just grunted and lit a cigar. Mike looked slyly at him out of the corner of his eye. "And of course," he went on, taking a sudden close interest in the toe of his shoe, "I'll put money on it that now she's free from club rules, quite a few of them will be after her. Now," he repeated, just in case the point had not reached its target, "now she doesn't work for you any more, I mean."

"That's right," Ed blew a cloud of smoke. "Funny how things work out. I was just thinking that myself. Now that I'm not her boss, anything could happen."

Mike looked perplexed. It was not the reaction he'd been expecting and he should have known better than to listen to club gossip.

"What's that mean?"

"Oh bugger it, Ed. You know exactly what I mean."

Ed paused at the top of the stairs and studied the business end of his cigar.

"Do I?" he finally asked. "Now there's an odd thing, my old sunshine, because for once in my life, I'm not sure that I do."

Chapter Twenty-Eight

Alex looked pleased. "I hated you being there," he confessed. "But you needed to prove something and you have."

"Like I could earn a living?" Serena began to gather up the plates from dinner. "Not sure I had the luxury of proving anything. Still haven't."

Almost a month later she still found it odd to be at home in the evening. Each morning she fought down the panic whilst confronting another day searching for a job, and each night she went to bed comforting herself that this couldn't go on forever. It became a ritual, after Harry and Louise were safely in school, for her to sit down and check her finances. Secretly she hoped she would have miscalculated in her favour the day before, while knowing full well, long before she shoved the bills out of sight into the kitchen drawer, that she was fooling herself.

The money Frobisher's put into her bank account each month had stopped, and the security of knowing she could pay the rent and the bills that were eating into her carefully managed savings along with it. She had started to regret buying the car. At the end of the week she knew she should go and sign on. The thought depressed her. All those questions, justifying her life. But what else was there?

All of that she expected, but it was missing the bustle of the club and the camaraderie that was leaving an unexpected hollow. Shortly after she left she had called Don Trewless to tell him she was no longer at Frobisher's. But he knew.

"Serena, I think it might be worth firing a shot across the bows at chippy Cheryl," he suggested. "I'll get one of the lads to say they're checking any-one who's ever worked for you about the letter. Just routine. It might stop her trying the papers if she thinks she's under suspicion."

Serena was touched by the offer but knew its root was in preventing any undue publicity to scare off Stephen should he be thinking of making a secret visit to his deserted family. Or even more unlikely, to turn himself in. "Thanks, Don," she said. "That would help."

To be fair to Alex, she had kept all of this from him. Some of Ed's advice seemed to make more sense. Raking over old wounds was not always the best way to go forward. She looked over to where he was sipping his wine, elbows on the table, watching her lovingly over his glass.

"Well, another job of course," he agreed as she rose to start the washing up. "But I think you needed the chance to regain a sense of self worth. And," he raised his glass, "you've done that magnificently."

The dishes slid into the sink. Slowly she turned her head to look at him. "Is that what you think?" She wiped her hands on a cloth. "That I did all this," she paused, emphasizing the words, "for me?"

A flash of uncertainty crossed his face. "No, of course not." He got hastily to his feet and hugged her. "I don't think you ever think of yourself. Honestly, darling, it was a compliment."

She turned away from him and began soaking dishes. "Of course. Ignore me. I'm having an identity crisis in a big way." She forced a smile and threw a tea towel at him. "You can earn your supper. Start with the saucepans."

It was a rule Serena had established that Alex would not stay over with her. She had insisted it was because of the effect on the children but she knew it was as much to do with her own need for independence from him. It was also because she didn't know how to extricate herself from a relationship that had been born out of loneliness and need. In her own way she had come to love Alex. How could she not? He had been there for her, listened. There was of late, however, a feeling that was refusing to go away, a growing belief, now that she was his lover, that she had helped him just as much. Sometimes when he spoke of his relationship with Alice and, before her, Lorrayne, she suspected she had in fact helped him more than he realized.

"See you tomorrow." He gazed meaningfully at her as he left close to midnight, just as Serena was leaving to collect Louise from the friend's house where she had spent the evening.

Her hand flew to her mouth. "Alex, I'm sorry. I forgot. I've promised to take Bella and the children out to dinner. It's Bella's last night with us. I know, come with us. Oh do. It'll be fun."

He put his hands in the air to deflect her. "Whoa. Not for me. This is a special one for you and the children. Wish her luck from me, won't you?"

He strode off, throwing her a kiss. He was gone so quickly she didn't have time to say that Tipper and Stacey were coming too. Louise would be relieved if he wasn't there because she knew, absolutely *knew*, she told Serena, that he didn't like Damon, who was also going to be with them.

Stacey called at seven to say she wouldn't be able to join them after all. When she saw Bella's stormy face as she replaced the phone, Serena guessed.

"Not coming? Barry?"

"Jackpot. He's such a sod. He just didn't want her to be out of his reach," Bella fumed. "You know he doesn't love her, Serena. He's just a control freak, and she earns good money, so she's useful."

Serena slipped an arm round her shoulders. They were close, Bella and Stacey, and Serena knew from Bella that Stacey's parents were frantic with worry about their daughter even though they had disowned her while she was living with Barry.

"She's like an addict around him," Bella fretted. "Like a drunk. She won't listen. Would you stay with anyone that cuffs you for nothing? Oh God, what's the point, we've been over this a hundred times."

"Never mind," Serena consoled her. "There's nothing you or I can do until she wakes up. Now come on, it's your last night."

The phone rang as they were leaving the house. Louise ran back and answered it, fearful it might be Daphy hearing she was out with Damon without her and putting a stop to it.

"It's for you, Mum," she shrieked from the door, as Serena was piling everyone into her car. "It's Ed."

"Ed? Ed Stein?"

"And how many Eds do you know?" Tipper teased. "Course it's him. He got back last night."

"I'm told you're all going on the razzle," Ed said when she came on the line. "Don't let me hold you up. The shrink treating you all?"

Glad though she was to hear from him, surprised too — well, perhaps not totally surprised, she admitted to herself — she did not want Alex disparaged.

"Don't call him the shrink. And no. Family outing."

"Sounds healthy. I'll call you tomorrow to see what time you want me to pick you up."

"Pick me up?"

"Sure. Wednesday. Dinner and the dogs."

She tried not to laugh or to feel quite so pleased. "Ed. I think you know my feelings about —"

"Yeah, yeah, yeah," he interrupted. "But that was last month's excuse. You don't work for me now." There was a brief pause. "Do you? Look, Mrs Carmichael, you wouldn't want me to be totally humiliated in front of all my friends, now would you? Naturally I can see perhaps I should have cleared it with you first, but I thought, now who's the person I would like to see most go to the dogs ..."

She tried not to laugh. And she couldn't refuse. "You mentioned dinner as well. Is that part of the deal?"

"You drive a hard bargain. I'll collect you myself and annoy that old bat who lives across the road."

When she reached the car, Louise was squabbling with Tipper about Damon's haircut.

"If you mention it, he'll never speak to me again," she pleaded.

"Stop it, you two." She climbed behind the wheel.

"And?" Tipper prompted, trying to see her face.

"And what?" She pulled the car away from the kerb and headed for the main road.

"What did he say?"

"He says I'm finally going to the dogs."

*

Several hours later, the whole house was roused by the sound of someone leaning frantically on the doorbell. Dazed with sleep, Serena stumbled from her bed to collide with Bella on the landing. Louise emerged from her room rubbing her eyes.

"What is it, Mum?"

"Soon find out," Serena muttered, the noise from the door reaching a crescendo. "Harry, stay where you are," she called, running down the stairs, shouting above the din and pulling her robe around her.

Before she reached it she could hear Stacey. "Open it, Serena," she was sobbing. "Please help me."

"Dear God," she stifled an oath, pulling back the bolts. Leaning weakly against the doorframe, blood trickling down her face, Stacey stumbled into the hall.

Behind her Serena heard Bella scream as Stacey fainted at her feet.

After the doctor had left and the children had been persuaded to go back to sleep, Serena and Bella sat either side of Stacey, who was now tucked up in Serena's bed. A livid bruise was showing on her temple, one eye was closed, her mouth swollen. The doctor, because of her condition and only because Serena guaranteed she would make sure she got her to the hospital next day, had agreed to put a stitch above her eye himself. Stacey insisted she had fallen and became almost hysterical when Serena wanted to call the police. It was all Bella could do to stop crying at the sight of Stacey's beaten face. On the other side of the bed Serena considered the shocked girl and was rapidly trying to decide the next course of action.

Stacey was, by her own calculation, three months pregnant — the reason Barry had so savagely beaten her. Going home to her parents in Birmingham was not an option, in fact Bella had sounded as horrified at the very idea as Stacey when Serena suggested it. Their God-fearing family would be traumatized at having an unmarried mother in their midst. The irony of the un-Christian attitude of those who professed to love God but would turn their own daughter from the door was, Serena noticed, lost on the two young women sitting next to her.

"Can't do it to them," Stacey whispered. "Can I, Bel?"

The younger girl shook her head. "You won't go back to him, will you,

Stace?" she asked fearfully.

Stacey shook her head on the pillow, large tears rolling down her battered face. "Never. Never."

All three jumped as the phone next to the bed jangled. Mesmerized, they gazed at it insistently ringing. "It's him," Stacey panicked, starting to jump from the bed.

"Don't let him come here." She gripped Serena's arm.

"Of course not." Serena said reaching for the phone herself. "Wish he would though."

A stream of abuse identified the enraged Barry demanding Stacey's return. Serena listened, one hand over her free ear.

"Oh stop it," she yawned down the phone. "You're frightening me to death. Come round by all means but it won't change a thing. Beating Stacey — do be quiet, I'm not impressed with threats — was the last time you'll ever touch her. But you should know, Barry, that every call to my house is checked by the police and they're listening to you right now. By the morning they'll have your address, from me. But meanwhile they'll already know your number. Sometimes it helps to have a husband on the run. Don't call again unless it's to apologise. And don't be tiresome and start coming here. It won't take Einstein to figure out who's responsible if anything happens to anyone living here."

She replaced the phone.

"Is that true?" Stacey asked, awed by what she'd just heard. Serena shrugged. "'Fraid so. He won't call again. He's such a scumbag."

Stacey looked crushed. "You've always thought that, haven't you?"

The other two glanced at each other. "Yes," Serena answered bluntly. "But then we don't choose who to love, do we?"

"What'll I do?" Stacey asked. "I can't go to work like this. My stuff's at Barry's."

"You stay here, of course," Serena broke in briskly. "Until you want to go somewhere else. I'll ask Tip if he knows a heavy who can go round and get your stuff. But the main concern is the baby. Who's your doctor?"

Stacey stared numbly back at her. "Haven't got one. I didn't know who to go to. I was so scared."

In the course of the next ten minutes Serena discovered that getting pregnant had not been planned by either Stacey or her lover and nor had contraception figured very urgently in their relationship. Nor had Stacey any idea if she wanted the child. Until last week, when she gave up hope that her symptoms might be due to stress, she had never thought of having a baby. Now she didn't know where to start if she didn't want to keep it, and if she did, she didn't know how she could.

"What'll she do?" Bella asked nervously. They both turned to look at Serena, who saw in their faces their complete faith in her ability to sort this out.

She swallowed hard and tried to sound as though she knew what she was doing. In truth she was at just as great a loss as they were. "OK." She kept her voice brisk. "Bella, hop in with Stacey. I'll sleep in your bed for the rest of the night. Don't worry," she patted Stacey's hand. "First thing Monday morning we'll get the whole thing sorted out. Honestly. Trust me."

*

It was evident after an exhausting three days that Stacey's pregnancy was not going to be straightforward. For a start, pronounced the doctor, whom Serena had taken her to see, Stacey was nearer five months than three, which ruled out one decision, and a scan at the maternity unit at St Wilhemina's showed the baby was not as developed as they would have liked.

Too absorbed in what was being explained, neither the doctor imparting the news or Stacey herself, noticed Serena stiffen. While they talked, she planned. It was a long shot, but he owed her a favour. Many favours.

George Kincaid came hurriedly to the phone. She guessed from the affable way he greeted her that someone was listening. She waited while he got rid of them.

"What do you want?" he hissed down the phone.

"Not a lot, George. Stop panicking. I just want a favour from you."

*

At seven on Wednesday Ed collected her. Stacey was babysitting, her battered face still showing the legacy of her run-in with Barry. Harry was introduced, shyly nodding at him, but remained resolutely out of reach in case Ed should attempt to shake his hand. Serena was relieved to see Ed didn't try and the moment passed in the noise of Louise greeting him carelessly like an old friend.

"Nice kids," he observed, as Bob, his driver, pulled away.

"I think so." You couldn't help warming to someone who liked your children, she decided.

"Nice mother too," he added. "Great legs."

She stopped herself from tugging at her skirt. "Thank you," she replied politely, smoothing her hair instead. Alex, she reflected, would have said the colour suited her or that he loved women in black silk. He would have made her feel feminine and flirtatious. With Stephen she would have felt elegant, knowing the skirt worked with sheer black tights and heels. Ed, she decided irritably, made her feel wanton and in need of protection. At the first opportunity she surreptitiously wriggled her skirt down as far as it would go.

They had dinner high above the race track with a group of Ed's clearly regular cronies who included his tailor Lenny Horniman. She recognized the name of the man who headed a major film production company and another who had recently been in the news, having sold the world-wide television rights to the next heavyweight boxing championships for a multi-million dollar figure. They seemed to know she would be coming and only the wife of the film man, after a few drinks, drunkenly asked Serena why someone hadn't made a film about her husband. Her husband whispered sharply to her to leave films to him, throwing an apologetic look at Ed. Serena flushed but Ed chose that moment to take her hand and march her off for a tour of the ground.

It was, she knew, the kind of evening designed to make her forget the bills, the neighbours and Foster Street. Ed showed her how to place bets, laughing at her when she shrieked as her choice shot past the post and even harder at her dismay when she lost.

Halfway through the evening, she was vaguely aware that her hair had tumbled out of its moorings and she was suffused in a forgotten feeling of well-being. Ed had switched seats so that he was no longer sitting safely opposite her, but beside her, his arm resting lightly along the back of her chair. The expanse of leg she was revealing was a matter of indifference to her. Every now and then they were interrupted by people who knew him and occasionally he turned away from her to talk quietly to one or two of them. On these occasions she did not want to have to acknowledge that Ed Stein was extraordinary company in spite of the diamond and ruby tie pin the size of a bottletop that flashed when the light caught it.

He told her about his childhood in the East End and the shock of what had awaited his family in Australia — not the promised land at all, just a tin hut where they'd lived for two years. How he hated holidays lying on beaches unless it was somewhere on his own with just a book and, he held her gaze for a second longer than she thought was decent, a beautiful woman for company. Inexplicably she blushed and only just managed to concentrate on hearing about his preference for wandering around Prague or St Petersburg instead of Paris. She finally got to hear about Willow and the fact that Eve was a problem he was trying to solve.

She told him about her father and made him roar with laughter at her grandmother's insistence that they kept up standards when they were drained of money by insisting on consulting the cook even when they were just having a ham salad. Then she described the brutal Barry and the advantages of having the fraud squad linked to every facet of her life. Encouraged by his genuine interest she told him about Harry's difficulty with school, still not entirely solved, and of suspecting Louise of having marijuana in her room.

"What did you do?" He signalled to the waiter to refill their glasses. Everyone else had disappeared to the bar and they were alone at their table.

"Nothing. Alex told me what clues to look for, you know, secretive behaviour, no appetite, but I couldn't do it. It was like snooping and a tacit admission that I didn't trust her. So I just left it. Why? What would you have done?"

"That and bunged her a bit more pocket money for staying off the stuff."

"But that's assuming you knew she wasn't on it in the first place."

354

"This Alex of yours should be able to tell just by looking at her she's not into that. She's into annoying you. Loudly and usually at meal times when you told me she eats you out of house and home in spite of the diets she's always on. Doesn't sound — and nor does she look — like she's into dope."

Since this was what she herself believed, she felt relieved that her judgement was not as flawed as she thought, but defensive about Alex, who had been troubling her conscience for most of the evening.

"He's been so good with Harry," she pointed out.

"Harry's eleven," he replied bluntly. "He shouldn't be baring his soul to anyone. Can of worms and all that psycho stuff."

She bristled. "He's improved enormously. Alex says —"

"Mrs Carmichael." He threw down his napkin and leaned towards her, his face only an inch from hers. She noticed tiny lines at the corners of his eyes, he smelt faintly of cigars and an aftershave that she could not quite place. "The unsexiest phrase in the world is," he looked directly into her eyes. "Trust me on this, *'Alex says'*. Which is a shame because when I look at you," he spoke lazily, pushing a tendril of hair away from her face, "I want to do things to you that can't be done in a place as public as this, like ..."

He murmured into her ear.

A year ago she would have stalked out enraged. Instead she pushed him back, her face registering bewilderment.

"I do beg your pardon," she looked blank. "You want to do what?"

At first she thought he was going to repeat it, but he just shook his head.

"Only," she said confidingly, "I have no idea whether that's a suggestion or a specific activity and I wouldn't want to mislead you by pretending I know."

He looked both ways and then his shoulders began to shake. Finally he leaned forward and kissed her lightly on the cheek. "Mrs Carmichael, you've led a very sheltered life."

"Well, I wouldn't have put it quite like that," she dissented, but mildly. "But then I haven't had your wide circle of," she paused with deliberation, "*friends* ... to instruct me in more sophisticated practices such as ..." she frowned. "I'm sorry. What did you call it again?"

He threw her a suspicious look and then patted her cheek. "When I know you better I'll tell you."

"Good idea," she approved. "I can't think of anything less erotic than having to break off what you're doing to issue instructions."

He began to laugh. Loudly. Other diners glanced curiously in their direction. While he dispensed with the attack of mirth, she simply smiled calmly, glancing with interest at her surroundings, occasionally sipping her wine.

Finally he rose and held out his hand to her. "I have the strongest suspicion you're playing a game. But now I'll never know, will I? Home?"

"I think so." She gave him a beaming smile, placing her hand in his as he pulled her to her feet. She saw no reason to let him know, as she thanked him for a marvellous evening, that after almost a year at Frobisher's it would have been nothing short of a miracle if she hadn't understood precisely what he had had in mind, but thought her safest option lay in feigning innocence.

*

The lift doors opened on to the familiar corridor. The lilac carpet stretched one way towards the discreetly furnished private rooms, the other towards George Kincaid's suite of consulting rooms.

"Mrs Carmichael," the sister greeted her, astonishment in her face. "It's been a long time."

Serena returned the greeting and asked her to let George know that she and Miss Barclay were waiting. At the end of the corridor the door opened and George's secretary, new since Serena's time, came towards them. Together they trooped after her, past the room where Louise and Harry had been born and where Serena had been consoled the night Anna had died. This time she looked straight ahead. Coming back at all had taken a supreme effort since she was not at all sure she could find the courage, nor did she want to inflict pain on herself. There was no need for even the swiftest calculation. Serena knew her baby girl, had she lived, would have been sixteen.

George rose to his feet as they came in, buttoning his jacket as he did so. With more heartiness than he clearly felt he greeted Serena with a handshake. It was not lost on her that in the past a double kiss had been George's preferred mode of greeting. He knew why they were there and, after the introductions, Serena withdrew to the waiting room, giving Stacey's shoulder a reassuring pat on the way out.

To his credit George was giving Stacey as much time as he would any of his more well-heeled patients. Idly she flicked through some recent glossy magazines until, eventually, bored with gazing at fashions she could not afford and holidays she would never take, she picked up one that specialized in more domestic matters. There was not much to interest her among the ads for agencies supplying trained nannies and maternity nurses or the nursery schools for those older siblings in need of a good start in life.

And then she saw it. A small news item about the Stella Bonner Centre which actively campaigned for improving the life of single working mothers. It said they were now in a position to employ a fundraising manager responsible for raising their profile. Serena read it through twice and then looked thoughtfully into the middle distance. Finally, she tucked the magazine into her handbag and waited for George to finish with Stacey. As she had fully expected, George agreed to take Stacey without a fee and to deliver the baby himself in the Wendover Wing.

"Thank you, George." She was genuinely grateful. "I wanted her to have the best and to be somewhere safe if the baby is premature."

He looked at her over his glasses. "We both know why I'm doing this, Serena."

"Because I was instrumental in getting the prem unit in place," she replied evenly. "That's all, George. Of that you can be quite sure. There is, however, one other thing you can do for me, and then I'll disappear out of your life."

She saw him stiffen. "Here," she quickly handed him the magazine. "I need a job and this is one I could do."

"Well, of course," he handed it back to her. "But how does that concern me?"

"I need a reference, George. Not just any old reference but one from someone who counts."

"Anything else?" he asked drily. "As I seem to be the source of all bounty today?"

She smiled. "No. Not unless you want to come over to my place to do a little light hoovering."

Chapter Twenty-Nine

The new fundraising manager of the Stella Bonner Centre sat in a black leather chair behind a teak desk and surveyed her office with pleasure. Her name was on the door. The walls were lined with shelves stacked high with reports on the progress and potential funding for a company committed to improving support systems for single working mothers. A couple of pale grey armchairs were arranged in front of the desk. A wilting green plant leaned drunkenly towards the sunlight pouring through the window. Serena walked to the water cooler outside her door and filled a plastic carton which she poured on to the plant.

Sitting beside the computer terminal, two phones and a serious looking leather diary, there was also a basket of flowers from Ed, sent from New York with a message that had clearly been read by the secretary she had inherited and whom she would share with the accounts executive and the head of counselling. Serena hastily shoved the card into her bag for fear that the wrong impression might be given so early in her career there. Heaven knows what they would make of his message: "If you come across any words you don't know, call me."

With Ed, anything was possible. When he heard about her new job, he had promptly suggested Paris for the weekend and jeered lightly at her, the word coward being introduced, when she refused. He asked her if Alex had anything to say and she ignored that too. Alex had taken her to their restaurant to celebrate, genuinely thrilled for her. And proud. Serena could see he was also relieved that for once he didn't have to skirt around describing what she did to any of his friends.

The phone buzzed on her desk. "Mrs Carmichael? Miss Martindale says would you lunch with her today? You don't appear to have anything in your diary."

Serena grinned to herself. Windows every day, she acknowledged, but not for long. This was only her first day.

"Tell her that would be most kind," she told the secretary. "And Trish? I think 'Serena' will be fine."

Gilly Martindale had hired Serena. She wore tailored suits, crisp white shirts and had her russet curly hair cut into a square bob. She lived alone since her divorce seven years before, in a town house in Notting Hill. Hers had been the inspiration behind the centre, the campaigning zeal to change laws, fund creches and pester local councils until they caved in and agreed that they might find the money or a house to fund after-school and holiday care for the children of single working mothers. The Trustees to whom she was responsible were in awe of her. Serena was not surprised.

"Just get me the money." She pointed her fork at Serena. "There's plenty of it around. Just not going in our direction. I'm sick of this piecemeal stuff. I want security for us, as a team, not just for the work. What are your plans?"

Before they left the restaurant Serena raised the small matter of the diary item in that morning's paper that had brought her new job to the attention of their readers. It had a picture of Serena taken at the time of Stephen's disappearance looking gaunt and unsmiling. The one this morning was taken with her consent as she arrived for her first day at the entrance to her new office in Victoria Street. A small story accompanied it, sketchy in detail and short on facts. It ended by pointing out that almost three years on Serena remained tight-lipped about her missing husband. Friends were quoted as saying she had remained throughout a dignified and contained figure. Her children, now at local state schools, had been her priority. Her new job with a charity organization would now occupy her life. Not one word of censure had ever left her lips on the subject of her disgraced husband.

It was kind enough, but Serena was wary. Such mild descriptions usually signalled the softening up process so that she'd agree to a fuller interview later on.

"I spotted him first," Serena explained to Gilly about the photograph. "I didn't want a furtively snatched picture so I told him if he wanted a picture he only had to ask. Was that OK?"

Gilly dismissed it with another wave of her fork. "George Kincaid is an old schmoozer, but he said you were ace at raising money. That's all I care about."

"He probably didn't mention I'm also an expert now in sifting the genuine from the curious. So I'll know those who agree to see me who just want to gawp at me. I've had plenty of practice."

Gilly grinned. "I bet you have. Anyway, I've made sure everyone at the office understands no one talks to the press. And Serena? I can't say I know what you've been through, but as far as I'm concerned it's history. Who do you suppose the 'friends' are?"

Serena shook her head. "No one I can think of. Invented, I expect."

Two requests for interviews came within days. Both were politely deflected and the ensuing persistent calls were finally directed to Andrew Beresford's office. He thanked them for their continuing concern but even the handsome donation to the Stella Bonner Centre on offer in return for an interview was not going to alter Serena's decision.

Within weeks the initial flurry of interest in her had faded and Serena had become an expert on figures. Each night after supper while Harry watched television and Louise sat with her headphones or the telephone clamped to her ear, she mugged up statistics and facts. By day she relentlessly, telephoned, faxed or wrote to the marketing arms of corporate giants, drawing their attention to such an important social development and pricking their conscience so that some of their charity budget would come Stella Bonner's way. Some of it didn't. But a great deal more did. Alex joked about his rival, and he wasn't referring to another man, when evening after evening he was turned down in favour of preparation for a meeting or a presentation the following morning.

"I get thirty minutes, that's all, to get the message home. I can't risk getting a fact wrong. All that work down the tube, Gilly says."

She heard a slight groan. "Really, my precious, you've taken to saying 'Gilly says' such a lot."

Serena smiled. "You sound like someone else I know," the phone tucked under her chin, forking up the omelette that Stacey had whisked up for supper. "Anyway, you'll like Gilly. I'll get her round to supper. I think she's great. The weekend, I promise. See you then."

Her weekends were filled with the children's needs but in order to stop Alex fretting she invited Gilly, along with Charles and Melanie, to have supper. And she began cautiously looking for another house. A mortgage was no longer out of the question. A small one of course. But a move in the right direction in every sense.

Jasmine phoned to say she was proud of Serena. "Well done, my dear," she said. "You've been amazing. The children are a credit to you. I'm sorry not to have seen you with them, but I agree it was more important for you to get this job underway. Anyway," she dropped her voice to a conspiratorial whisper, "LouLou is so different when she's here. I'm sure Margot finds it so. I get a few days of city slicker mode and then she's too impatient to keep it up. Really, Serena, she's going to be a stunning girl."

Serena felt quite moved at such a display of solidarity from a woman who had once found it hard to disguise her impatience with her. But mostly it was relief that there was hope for Louise.

"I couldn't have managed without your support," she returned. "And next time, I'll be over. Better still, it would be great if you came here."

They parted, each more pleased with the other than they would have thought possible only a few years before, both privately aware that Stephen's name had not been mentioned.

Stacey's baby was due in two months, just before Christmas, and they all agreed they couldn't remember what it was like not having her live with them. Slowly, through Bella, Serena was encouraging Stacey to build bridges with her estranged family. This in itself was becoming easier, since the peace and security that Serena offered Stacey had calmed her into a greater optimism about her future. Tipper had collected her belongings from Barry, of whom she now heard nothing except that he had moved someone else in.

"Odd, isn't it? I do mind that he's done it. It's not a nice feeling knowing," she fought to control her voice, "that I was just a commodity." Stacey leaned back on the sofa. Harry curled up resting against her legs.

"Don't worry," she assured Serena. "I wouldn't go back now. Not now. This," she patted her swollen stomach. "Is far too important. I want him to have a peaceful family to grow up in."

"It's definitely a 'him' then?" Serena handed her a cup of tea. Stacey had refused the offer to know the sex of her child in advance.

Stacey smiled knowingly. "Absolutely. My grandma always said if you carry to the front it's a boy. So you see if it was a girl I'd be all bottom."

"Fancy that." Serena picked up the report she'd been studying and settled down to what the children called her homework.

After a moment she glanced across at Stacey. "Stacey? Anything from your mother?"

Stacey half smiled. "Not yet. Bel's done a great job on Grandma. She says they'll come round. Eventually."

Serena threw her a sympathetic look. "They will. If not you, they won't be able to resist — him."

"I'm banking on it," Stacey replied. "Hey, you should be working. Big day tomorrow. Get a move on. Harry? Bed."

*

Twice she had had dinner with Ed and on both occasions had calmly rejected his suggestions for the more exotic end to the evening he had in mind. When he then disappeared for weeks on end and didn't contact her at all she felt uneasy and couldn't think why she felt better knowing he was around, even if he disturbed her peace of mind. Eventually he would just turn up on the doorstep and she would find herself greeting him as though she was unaware he had been out of her life for up to a month. He flattered Louise and was capable of spending two hours playing Fantasy Football with Harry, who could be heard instructing him on why the highest paid player in the Championship would be too expensive when he needed two strikers to win the league.

"Ah, but you've forgotten the BS factor," he pointed out to Harry alongside him, both engrossed in the screen.

"What's that?"

A warning cough from Serena, sitting at the other end of the room surrounded by a pile of reports, stopped him.

"The er … Big Star factor," he amended. Serena smothered a laugh. "Overwhelms the opposition," Ed soldiered on, ignoring her. "Who are so busy proving he isn't worth the transfer fee they forget there are ten other blokes to deal with."

Harry looked impressed. "OK," he ordered. "Let's get him."

"I'll thank you to mind your language in front of such an impressionable child," Serena rebuked Ed, as he joined her, at the other end of the room.

"Baloney," Ed cheerfully retorted, picking up Louise's copy of a magazine Serena loathed, but knew would be read covertly if she banned it. "You think Harry hasn't heard worse than 'bullshit' in that playground?"

"Possibly," she replied calmly. "But he doesn't hear it in this house."

"He'll hear worse when he comes to the Arsenal–Spurs match next Saturday. Bloody hell, look at this," he lowered the magazine. "Is this what fifteen-year-olds read? Listen, it says —"

Serena's eyes flew open. "Saturday?" she cut across him, hardly listening. "Oh heavens, he must think I'm taking him. I'll never get tickets. I'd better ask Tip."

Ed dropped the magazine on to the table and leaned back, his hands linked behind his head, a smug grin on his face. "You're not going anywhere. He's coming with me, bringing three of his friends from school, and they're going to sit in the director's box and give Harry a bit of kudos on Monday morning."

She stiffened. "Ed. It's kind of you. But I don't think it's wise to let Harry think he can buy people off …"

"He's not. He's a great kid and he's beginning to make friends at that school of his. Besides, he needs a bit of fun instead of exploring his feelings through whatever it is he does on Saturday mornings."

"Alex says —" she began.

"Fuck Alex," Ed interrupted, with an irritated snap. "Oh, I forgot. You do."

"Please go," she rose to her feet. "You're intolerable."

"Possibly. But he's worse. He's a bloody bore. OK, I'm out of here."

If it hadn't been for the fact that Harry would have been devastated, Serena would have refused to let him go on Saturday. There was another reason she felt annoyed. It was the first time she had heard that Harry was making any friends at his new school. At weekends he relied on his art class on Saturday morning and Alana, but even she was less in evidence as the attractions of boys and dressing up had diluted her interest in watching computer games with Harry. It would, she thought furiously, have to be Ed who discovered the fact.

"They're all right," Harry mumbled when she enquired who they were. "I didn't think they'd let me play football with them, but Ed said they would, but not unless I asked and if they wouldn't let me, to say he was bigger than their dads and I'd send him round to sort them out."

Serena was horrified. "He said that? For heaven's sake ..."

"Oh, it's all right, Mum. I didn't have to mention Ed at all, I just said can I play and it was OK. Only you always said you should wait to be asked but Ed said that only applied to meal times and being invited to parties but not when you're getting nowhere with something you really want to do."

"He said that, did he?" she replied acidly. "I bet he did."

She slumped back on the bed. It was true she never invited him round. He just turned up. Alex wouldn't dream of doing that. But then invitations were issued to him so there was no need. He respected her need to work. Ed claimed he did too, but never quite convinced her he understood her need for independence. It was, she decided, irritating that she felt a compelling need to stay in his orbit, but not within his grasp. She preferred to play his game from a distance. She did, however, feel mortified that she had appeared so unwelcoming.

Tipper thought she was mad to feel worried about Ed's invitation to Harry, especially as he'd been included in the Saturday outing.

"Says he needs a bit of help with the lads. Doesn't want any women along. You know you should throw your lot in with him," he advised, and not for the first time. "Just think what you'd have. Money, security, never having to work again? Surely now, it's what every woman wants?"

"Not this one." She tucked her legs under her. "I've had that. It doesn't follow that you're secure or," she paused, "or loved. I'm not going to be anyone's mistress. And you all seem to forget, apart from the fact that I'm married, there's no sign of Eve dropping out of his life. No, I think I'm safer looking after myself. Besides I'm getting good at it."

And she was. Gone was the charming flirtatious woman knowing what to say to massage the egos of vain bankers and MPs. In her place was a woman who had emerged wiser, sharper, less trusting, but much smarter than the one who had been plunged into poverty.

It was part of her nature to be charming on public occasions — now it was allied to a genuine commitment to the cause she was pleading and a professionalism that, one captain of industry murmured to his deputy, was the sexiest combination he'd ever seen. Gilly rubbed her hands with pleasure when she could see the effect Serena was having on her audience.

"And that, gentlemen, is why your name behind this project will move your profile from the City pages to the women's pages which is where your customers are drawn from." Serena, bringing her presentation to a close, stepped down from the small dais and sat on the edge of the small stage.

"You don't need me to tell you the percentage of those who, for whatever reason, have been left with the full weight of a child or children to raise as good, decent citizens. Just think when that centre is open you will be able to say you helped — no, not helped, ensured — that they were kept off the streets and out of trouble."

As she spoke she crossed her legs and rested her hands either side of her on the stage. "Now I'm sure you have a question or two?"

"Yes." The head of marketing rose to his feet. "When can you start working for us?" A sally of laughter greeted his remark.

"We won't get it," Gilly said once, as they left after one such encounter. "They're really committed to women's health this year. But I bet we're on the list next time. Well done, star."

Her days were filled with meetings, lunches and presentations to drug companies, supermarket chains and high street stores which had money to bestow. It was all a million light years away from the way in which she used to prise money from her rich friends — a lady who lunched in a designer suit applauding the illustrious name recruited by a phone call from Stephen to the PM's private office or the private secretary of a spare royal.

Melanie met her for lunch in a small trattoria just off Victoria Street and told her she looked stunning. "I'm so proud of you," she told her fiercely. "Everyone says what an amazing person you are. Never complained, just got on with it."

"The picture in the newspaper, you mean?" Serena asked, noting there was no mention of Stephen.

"Well, yes, but George is taking the credit. Sorry, my ducks, but he is. Oh c'mon — what can you expect? Hard to tell whether he wants a knighthood or to be canonized. Pivotal role in your success, waiving his fee for a deserving cause," Melanie reeled off George's claims to saintliness. "How could he resist?"

"How indeed?"

Melanie signalled to the waiter for the bill, "I know you're in a rush to get back to work," she glanced at Serena, "and I envy you. It must be wonderful having something so fulfilling to do. Everyone says they'll buy tickets for this fundraiser you're doing."

Serena looked thoughtfully at her friend. "I'll let you know. Now tell me. How are the children?"

Each night she mugged up facts and figures and laid the foundations for the first big fundraising event she was trying to stage. Metro Radio had agreed to a tie-in with the Stella Bonner Centre for a fundraising concert and Gilly was ecstatic. Serena was terrified. Busking her way through a meeting she had engineered with the station's board of directors was a doddle compared with what now lay in front of her. Before, she could have relied on her social standing to call in any number of household names to lend their support, but now she was starting from scratch. She looked at her notes. It was all very well having a hard-hitting young radio station encouraging their listeners to buy tickets, but she had to find something for them to see.

It was Louise who nagged her to have a rock concert, but Serena who saw how it could be done with a difference. It had not escaped Serena's notice that a lot of Harry's heroes, when interviewed, said they would love to be a rock star. Louise tried to appear cool when Serena said Metro would back her, but in the end she squealed frantically, called Serena a star and raced to phone Daphy with the amazing news. With the station's help Serena rounded up five young footballers who she had seen happily modelling clothes in Louise's magazines and who were game to appear as rock singers. An ad in the music press brought her the offer of a couple of backing groups who said they would play in return for tickets to the next Cup Final.

The hard part was getting a big star name to pull the whole thing together, and at least three walk-on surprise guests. Glumly she leafed through her address book, feeling the gap between a smart address in Kensington and a rich husband and the less exalted environs of the Stella Bonner Centre and no husband at all. Well, not one in evidence.

*

Harry raced through the door. "Mum!" he yelled. "Mum, it was brill! We won. You should have been there."

Serena whooped with delight and hugged him. Tipper, coming in behind, was almost as ecstatic. "Right little buggers they were," he beamed. "But once the match started it was ace. And what's more," he stepped aside as Harry tore past to find Louise to tell her about his afternoon, "himself says if I want to work in Paris or New York he'll fix it."

She gave him a look of dismay. "Oh Tip. I couldn't bear it. How would I manage without you?"

"Ah now, you're worse than the Big Man himself. Full of blarney. You'd all manage a treat. The thing is I'm not really seeing anyone and I'm not over Jake — not quite yet. You've been good for me, Serena," he added. "I don't know what I'd have done without you and the kids. I feel you're my own, you know that?"

She gave him a quick hug. "Now who's full of blarney? By the way, big news. Breakthrough at last. Stacey's mother phoned. Good old Bella."

Tipper marched off to find Stacey to share her good news. Serena guessed they'd gossip for the next half-hour. Harry was in his room poring over the programme. Louise was holed up in the bathroom where she'd been for the past hour. Serena picked up the phone in the kitchen and dialled Ed's number.

"Just wanted to thank you," she said when Wally switched her through to him. "I've never, ever seen Harry so ecstatic."

"Nice kid," he replied briefly. There was a long pause.

"Well, that was it really," she broke the silence. "Just a grateful mother."

"How grateful?"

In front of her the notice board had a note from Alex saying he would call later about dinner.

"If you think," she said carefully, "that I would agree to dinner just because you entertained my son —"

"I haven't invited you," he pointed out.

"I know that," she snapped back.

"So?"

"*I'm* inviting *you*. But if you're going to be all heavy about it, conditions and that stuff, you can forget it."

"OK."

Serena waited. "What is that? OK you will or OK forget it?"

"OK where. You are tedious at times."

She gritted her teeth, regretting her resolution to be nicer to him. And even more the impulse to invite him over.

"Here. I can't afford your kind of restaurant and I haven't got anyone to sit with Harry. Stacey's going to see a friend and Tip's had enough for the day."

"In which case I'll be there at eight. Black tie?"

She banged the phone down. The note from Alex was staring at her.

"Alex? Can I take a rain check on tonight? Ed's coming to supper. Yes, I invited him. Harry had such a brilliant time, it was so kind of him and it's the least I can do."

"You know, Serena, I understand, I'm just a bit concerned that this rather superficial level of securing Harry's place in his peer group is fraught with dangers. It looks so privileged."

"Alex," she cut across him. "Harry is not privileged; he may have been once, but he's suffered. You know that better than anyone. I don't think a boost to his morale will damage him for life. After all, it's a one-off. Ed isn't a fixture in his life."

There was a small pause. She thought she detected a steelier note in Alex's voice. "I hope not," he said frostily.

Gilly called almost immediately to say would Serena and Alex like her two tickets to the National to see the Brecht, as the guest she was taking had cried off and she knew Alex adored Brecht.

Serena paused. "Gilly," she said, "I can't, but why don't you ask Alex?"

Chapter Thirty

Harry joined them for dinner. It was not what she had intended. After all, Ed had entertained him all afternoon and so generously. Alex's parting shot had, however, made her jittery enough to exercise more caution. After she phoned him and encouraged him to accept Gilly's invitation, she hastily relaid the table for three, snapped on lamps and removed candles. By the time she stood back and anxiously surveyed the setting for anything that could even mildly be construed as seductive, her resentment towards Alex had turned to mild gratitude. Supposing he was right and it had looked as though she was encouraging Ed to regard himself as a contender for something more permanent? Just in case, she replaced the French linen napkins with more serviceable cotton.

To her surprise, Ed appeared to expect nothing else. Louise, who was off to a party in a pair of skin-tight black trousers and a cropped T-shirt, greeted him with a high five and a giggle when he said she made him feel old.

"No you're not," she rushed to assure him. "You're cool."

"Tell your mother," he urged. "She says I can't go to her concert. I'm not," he leaned forward, looking mournful as Serena poured him a drink, and mouthed the rest of the sentence, "trendy enough."

Louise gaped. "Mum said that? And this from the woman who thinks *Arctic Monkeys* is a wildlife programme?"

Ed shook his head in disbelief. "You're kidding? Pathetic, isn't it?"

"Go on then," Serena handed him a drink. "Explain *Arctic Monkeys* to me. Pay attention, Lou. This'll be fascinating."

"Sorry," he shook his head sadly. "I wouldn't dream of humiliating the chef. I am a guest after all."

"Precisely. He hasn't a clue. And I've only told him he can't come unless he gives Tip the night off. Off you go, Lou. I'll send a cab at midnight."

*

As usual Ed confused her. Against her better judgement she allowed herself to be charmed by his wit and beguiled by his stories. He could make her laugh with the same ease with which he could mobilize fury, and it wasn't until he had despatched his driver to fetch Louise that Serena realized that not once had he treated her as anything more than an interesting companion.

In turn she told him about the house she had seen that week in Fulham which she could rent with the possibility of buying.

"I've got to let them know on Monday morning." She feigned panic.

"Good idea," he said, rather surprisingly. "Make sure it's what you want before you saddle yourself with buying it."

"Golly," she laughed. "I couldn't afford to buy for years. At least not before I get this concert out of the way."

She made him chuckle with a wicked impersonation of the agents vying with each other to get their footballers top of her bill and found herself confiding in him more than she had intended.

"Thing is, I can't make one any starrier than the others or the others will drop out. And, I've got this producer who phones eighty times a day saying I've got to find him a proper star."

"And have you?"

"I wish. I've got to have someone by the middle of next week, otherwise we've got to keep the ticket price down. A major name and we could double it. I've learned just how tough fundraising really is," she grimaced. "I didn't know the half of it before."

He looked at her with a careful expression. "Big miss, eh?"

"Miss?" She looked up, surprised. "Oddly enough, no. I wouldn't want to go back to that kind of fundraising. I did it —" She stopped. "I did it," she took a deep breath, "because I lost a child and she might not have died if there had been a prem baby unit there waiting. I don't think I thought beyond assuaging my own grief. It had to mean something. This is different. I'm at the cutting edge of fund raising, if you like. When I lost my daughter I didn't meet anyone who could say, "Yes, I know what you're going through"; I just contained it. Oh I cried and suffered and Stephen did too but I didn't meet other women like me."

Ed was sitting very still; his eyes never left her face.

"And now?"

"Now?" Serena tried to smile and failed. "I meet single mothers all the time."

"I meant about your child."

Ed did this to her. She told him things she never meant to tell anyone. Already she was regretting it. "I'm not a basket-case anymore. It's my problem. I deal with it. Let me get you some coffee."

"No." He reached over and took her hand. "No. Tell me about her. What was her name?"

For a long, long moment she held his gaze. "Anna," she said finally. "Just Anna. I had her for two days and she's buried with my father. No, a part of me has never recovered. When I dream, she's often there. I dream about her as well as think about her. Which is why I truly believe Stephen is alive. If he wasn't he would be in my dreams too. And he never is. Except once but now I think it was Anna I was dreaming about because she was with him."

She realized he was still holding her hand.

"Sorry," she gave him a bleak smile, gently sliding her hand away. "You don't want to hear this."

"I wouldn't have asked if I didn't. Tell me about Stephen. Where does he fit in now?"

"Stephen? Fit in?"

"I mean would you have him back?"

"Back?" She swallowed hard. "Of course. Why not? I mean where else would he go? He would need me."

"So we'll take that as not sure?"

"We'll take it that I am sure," she contradicted him. "He's my husband."

"That's not a reason. Still in love with him? That's got to be the only reason. Are you?"

Silence lay between them. From next door the sounds of Betty and Les laying into each other could be heard as they returned from their separate pubs. Upstairs Harry was probably asleep and Stacey had gone straight to bed after she had returned an hour before. Serena wished the car bringing Louise home would hurry.

"You've got to confront it sometime." Ed finally broke the silence. "How would he feel about, say, the shrink?"

"I'll deal with that." Her defiance clearly didn't impress him.

"Thought as much." He leaned back and crossed his legs.

"Meaning?"

"What Lou's comic would call Mr OK for Now."

She shook her head impatiently. "Ed, if you're going to mock Alex, please stop."

"I'm not interested in him. Not anymore. If he was important you wouldn't be sitting here entertaining me. He'd be here too."

"As a matter of fact he would have been, but Gilly Martindale had a spare ticket for the National tonight and she knows Alex adores Brecht so he's gone with her and it was my suggestion. Satisfied?"

"Don't avoid the issue. Would Stephen, trolling home after his jaunt to wherever it is, be happy for you to entertain another bloke while he was sidelined for the night?"

"Stop it, Ed," she warned, "I would never be disloyal to Stephen, to you or anyone else."

"He doesn't deserve even your loyalty let alone anything else."

"Don't say that," she rounded on him. "How do you know what he deserves? You never knew him. Until all this, he was the most marvellous man." She stumbled to a halt, horrified that she could feel tears pricking her eyes.

"I would never abandon him," she went on. "Whatever he's done, for whatever reason he's remained in hiding, he knows, even at this minute, wherever he is, he knows I will never turn away from him."

He listened dispassionately. "And trust? Could you ever trust him again?"

She nodded, not sure she could sound convincing.

He drained his glass and reached for the bottle. Mutely she watched him.

"A wiser man than me not a million miles from Descartes said, 'It is prudent never to trust wholly those who have deceived us even once.'"

Serena stared down at her clasped hands.

"Don't you ever want a life of your own?" He was angry with her now. A familiar surge of panic started to eat away in her chest. She wanted him to stop, but she could see that he couldn't. The energy she needed to stop him eluded her. She wouldn't look at him.

"You live for a day you have no idea will ever come," he persisted. "If it does, you're expecting the same man to come back. If I cared less about you I would say less. But I do care what happens to you. Oh for Christ's sake," he cut across her as she looked up startled, "it's obvious I do. So what are you going to do? Three years, Serena, that's what it's been, and you're still planning your future with him in it. And you know why? Because you can't face the truth."

"I don't want to hear." She pushed her chair back and walked away from him. He followed her and swung her round.

"Of course not. The truth is often not very wonderful is it? The truth is —"

She covered her ears with her hands. "Stop it. You don't know the truth."

"Tell me." He gave her a slight shake. "Go on, tell me what the truth is? I'm interested."

She could hear the car bringing Louise home drawing up. They both looked towards the window. She turned back to face him.

"The truth," she said dully, "is that until I've seen him, spoken to him, there is no future for me."

Louise could be heard in the hall. "Wonderful," Ed muttered, dropping his hands from her shoulders. "Bloody fucking wonderful. Hi, beautiful, how did it go?"

*

Halfway through the following Wednesday morning, just as she arrived back from agreeing to take the house in Parson's Green, a man announcing himself as the agent for the American movie star Brett Bruce asked to be put through to her. Twenty minutes later Serena raced along the corridor and burst in on Gilly whooping. "I've got a star. You won't believe it. Brett Bruce."

"Get her a chair," Gilly murmured aside to her secretary. "She's hallucinating. You've got Brett Bruce?" she asked in the manner of one humouring a lunatic. "In what way, exactly?"

"The concert. He's agreed to be host. We've cracked it. Harry will have a fit."

Gilly's secretary had sat heavily down on the chair she was about to offer Serena.

"Bugger Harry," she breathed. "What about me? I have to be there. Oh my God. Brett Bruce. Who can I tell first?"

"No one." Serena grabbed her arm as it went for the phone. "I have to call Metro first and then that poor producer. I can't believe it. We can charge double. He's here for the première of his next film, *Lethal Dogs* or something like that, and Ed — that's Ed Stein, a friend of mine — asked him if he would stay on for a couple of days and do it and he's said he would. I didn't even know he knew him. He never said. And I'm going to faint with happiness."

"Are you a fan?" Gilly asked nervously, watching Serena stride around her office. She had never heard her gabbling before.

"A fan? Not until this moment. Do you know what this means? It means treble the price of the ticket."

"Good grief," Gilly was as excited as Serena, "I'll join too."

"Join? Join what?"

"The Brett Bruce Appreciation Society or whatever it is."

Serena blinked. "What? Oh God no. Sorry, I was talking about Ed."

The only difficulty she faced was to call Ed to thank him. Mercifully he was in Paris so she wrote him a note instead.

*

It was hard to hear from Melanie that Paula and Miranda had asked for tickets for the concert. George Kincaid had taken a box. Shrewder than they were, he had recognised Serena's emerging status as a fundraiser and had begun to entertain unspoken thoughts that she might return to perk up the flagging coffers of *Babyways* and take back the reins from the appalling Brisley woman. Paula and Miranda's slow realisation that she was emerging from the dark days and might just, inconveniently and embarrassingly, reveal their less than supportive role in her life, had left them both racing to cover their social tracks in George's wake.

The wrestle Serena had had with her need to tell them to shove their tickets in the most inaccessible place of their anatomy was finally overcome by knowing that they would also pile on top of the ticket price a sizeable donation to Stella Bonner.

"They really do admire the way you've handled this whole thing," Charles told her over dinner. "Everyone does."

Serena raised an eyebrow at him. "You will understand if that doesn't overwhelm me."

Charles exchanged an apprehensive look with his wife. "I know. I don't blame you. On the other hand ..."

"Sorry, Charles, that wasn't fair." In spite of the disruptions to his own life, and she was in no doubt that he had suffered as a result of Melanie's devotion to her, he had never turned his back on her. "Of course I don't mind. Anyway it's the centre that will benefit."

"And you don't have to do anything other than say hello," Melanie broke in eagerly. "Not even that if I see them first."

The radio station team screamed with relief and braced themselves to deal with enquiries for tickets. Ed's secretary called Serena and said Ed had bought up two boxes and needed tickets for such an array of dazzling names Serena felt weak. Rock stars, boxers, a string of models who graced the pages of the glossies, and soap stars whose names Louise gazed at in awe. Ed's secretary said that Ed hoped that Louise and Harry would sit with his noisier guests in one of the two rows they had bought up because it might be more fun for them than with the wrinklies he was bringing. However, he hoped Serena would join him because he might need help entertaining Brett's companion.

"Of course," she agreed instantly. "Tell him I'd love to. Only I might have to duck in and out if there are any problems."

It was, Gilly breathed, their finest hour. Long before the show started, the road was packed with fans waiting for a glimpse of Brett Bruce, and the tickets could have been sold twice over. A parade of exotically dressed stars who would never have been considered for a *Babyways* evening drew cheers and screams from the crowd as they alighted from overstretched limos, surrounded by burly minders in the flashiest and most vulgar display of celebrity Serena had ever witnessed. Two models, both currently the subject of a tabloid claim that they rarely slept less than three in a bed, sashayed up the steps and disappeared inside the theatre.

Not a tiara was in sight and Serena loved every last, glittering, spellbinding moment of it. Louise and Harry arrived with their friends half an hour before the curtain went up, with a heavily pregnant Stacey in tow and all the hostesses from Frobisher's. Serena nearly died laughing as she greeted them. They were all to sit together and they had done her proud. If cleavage hadn't been invented, it would have been that night. Two of them were arm in arm with Harry and his friend while Daphy and Louise forgot they were cool dudes as their eyes flew from one famous name to another. She wanted to take them to their seats but Harry wouldn't permit it.

"I know where to go," he insisted. "They're all going to follow me."

She thought she would cry. "Good for you, my angel," she whispered. "See you afterwards."

The tricky question of Alex and Ed being present together had been solved by her suggesting he escorted Gilly, with whom he was now on good terms. They both hugged her and said they would see her after the show.

"I'm so proud of you," Alex whispered. "You must be feeling like hell having to deal with all these people and you're hiding it beautifully."

She hoped she might have a chance to see Ed before the show. A brief note and a couple of phone calls via his secretary had been her only contact with him.

There was, however, no escaping Paula and Miranda, even though Melanie and Charles had tried to prevent it. Serena kissed Charles warmly and hugged Melanie. To the others she merely nodded and said she hoped they enjoyed the show. Paula hastily covered the step forward she had taken to greet Serena with a kiss by kissing Charles instead. Since she had done this only a couple of minutes before, everyone assumed Paula must be very tired to have overlooked this fact.

"All support for the centre is appreciated," Serena added. "Excuse me. I have all these people to welcome." She turned away to introduce herself to the manager of a Premier League football team and his companion, trying not to laugh at the horror on Paula's face when she saw with whom she would be spending the evening.

George Kincaid greeted Serena as though they had never had an estrangement. And she didn't mind. He was being wonderful with Stacey and his knighthood was virtually assured now that he had swung his weight behind penniless mothers and the Stella Bonner Centre.

Brett Bruce arrived with Mike Griffith and a contingent of bodyguards who were as numerous as they were physically huge. All carried mobile phones and talked incessantly into them, updating each other on Brett's whereabouts. Brett was an absolute sweetheart. His companion, a real babe whose fame almost matched his, moulded her perfectly honed body to his side, clutched his hand and replied coyly to shouted enquiries that they hadn't discussed marriage. Yet.

The press, out in force, gleefully upped this next day to rumours that they were already married. Tipper, who had volunteered to help backstage, stared in unashamed lust at the blond handsome star whose face was currently gazing down from hoardings across London.

When they were introduced, Brett pulled Serena to him, kissed her full on the mouth and told her he'd heard about her from Ceri and Bernice and they were spot on. Ed really was a shit keeping her in London.

"Really?" she gasped, staggering back. "How kind."

And then Brett spotted Tipper and, as Serena told Melanie later, while it might not have been love at first sight, it was certainly lust.

"Don't give it a thought, honey," the babe breathed, slicking another layer of lipgloss over her surgically enhanced lips, the dress she was almost wearing hitching up to reveal smooth brown thighs. "He does the same for me."

"You?" Serena repeated blankly.

"Sure," winked the superbabe. "Who's the little number he's about to introduce to his tonsils?"

"A friend, Tipper." Serena glanced anxiously to where Brett was murmuring into Tipper's ear.

"Well, I'm off to get lucky," she drawled. "Matter of fact," she punched Serena playfully in the arm, "any time you want to swing, honey, just call me."

"Heavens," Serena murmured, peering into the gloom of Brett's dressing room where he was now pinning a very willing Tipper into the corner. "You'll be the first to know," she assured her.

And then they were on. From the wings she watched, nervously, praying she would remember her short speech when she was summoned on stage. Brett strolled out, unshaven, jeans and a Versace jacket swinging open to reveal a tight black T-shirt, the audience erupting as he stood, arms outstretched, revelling in the attention. For a few minutes he warmed them up, cracking jokes and proving why he was a star.

And then over the speakers she heard him saying he wanted them all to meet someone with the energy and love that only comes from a big heart. Her name came from somewhere. A blur of lights, the stage manager pushed her in the small of the back and she walked forward, no longer worried that she might trip over in her heels, that the dark blue satin trousers might split, or that it was too late to worry about the amount of cleavage her jacket revealed.

With a cheery wave to the audience who were clapping her arrival, she was kissed by Brett who stood with his arm draped around her while she spoke.

A white blur of light obliterated the audience. She couldn't see a thing but somehow she got through her five minutes about the charity and how grateful they all were for everybody's support. She paid a fulsome tribute to Gilly, whose vision and commitment had been the inspiration for the centre, along with a special thank you to Metro Radio, the football clubs who had so generously released their stars and most of all she wanted to say an extra special thank you to Ed Stein for his help. She finished with the fervent wish that the night would be a success and that she would wake up on Christmas morning and find Brett Bruce in her stocking.

To an appreciative gale of laughter, she walked off and found she was trembling from head to foot. She was immediately wrapped in a bear hug by Ed who was waiting for her in the wings.

"C'mon star," he teased, kissing her gently on the mouth. "There's a box full of people waiting to meet you. You were stunning."

*

Next morning the papers carried pictures of Brett and his babe and one or two of the few who bothered to mention the centre, even got the name right. Serena's name was mentioned by several of the diaries. The amount of money raised looked staggering.

The after-effects, the details that were of no interest to anyone except those concerned, were the more seismic. Tipper eventually emerged from the star's hotel room at midday and left a message for Serena saying he had to talk urgently. Louise and Harry, who had been allowed to attend the aftershow party for an hour and been driven home by Bob, Ed's driver, were still in their rooms. Stacey, who had gone straight home after the show, left a note for Serena saying if that didn't induce the baby nothing would; she had gone to spend the day with a friend and would be back by supper. Her answer machine, when Serena finally felt equal to handling the messages, had run out of space. Nothing from Alex or Gilly but a stream of calls from those who wanted to congratulate her. Serena sat in the kitchen and gingerly felt her head.

Black coffee, she decided. It was no use pretending any more. Nor could she, since she had fallen asleep with no other thought and woken shortly after nine knowing one thing. Ed was important. How important was something else. She wanted the dazzle to wear off, normality to resume, to make sure the euphoria of the occasion had not swept her along in the same dizzying wake of Tipper and his star or Gilly's clear besottedness with Alex. They had left long before the aftershow party had subsided, Alex looking grave and Gilly hugging her a bit too fiercely. It was not as though Ed had hovered over her all night, or suggested, as he was prone to do, that she threw her scruples to the wind and spent what remained of the night with him.

This is ridiculous, she scolded herself. You're behaving like a teenager, poring over moments, remarks, looks, loading them with a significance they don't merit. Now just forget it. Wait 'til he calls, then see. After which she promptly subsided into a reverie of the night's events.

All she knew was that she would find herself searching the room with her eyes till she found him and when she did he would smile, maybe raise his glass, and go on talking to whoever was claiming his attention. She watched him work the room, lowering his head to catch what someone was saying, throwing a joking remark over his shoulder to someone passing behind him. After a while she stopped trying to convince herself that the presence of a man as imposing as Ed was bound to be hard to avoid.

When she was finally persuaded to sit down by Melanie and Charles to eat she agreed, but could touch nothing until Ed slipped into the chair next to her and handed her a plate piled with chicken and salad, telling her simply to eat it. Which she obediently did whilst he entertained Charles and Ryland Holt to what Brett's shopping list had included in the deal.

"All pointless," he finished, as they howled with laughter. "If I'd known all it took was my own barman I wouldn't need to feed that gang over there." He pointed to a group of muscular male models denied the pleasure of Brett's company consoling themselves with enough champagne to ensure a hangover for days.

At this point Ed's arm was resting lightly around Serena's shoulders. She was so conscious of it she just wanted to lean back and never get up again. Instead, he gave her shoulders a squeeze, whispered into her hair that he'd be back and strolled off to talk to a captain of industry.

"Anything you'd like to tell me?" Melanie murmured, slipping into the seat vacated by Ed.

"Only that I think I need a shrink," she replied drily.

"Thought you had one of those," Melanie reminded her.

Serena gazed thoughtfully across the room to where Alex and Gilly were sitting with a group of people, all unknown to her. "No," she said firmly. "I haven't."

When the room started to empty out around three in the morning, Charles found Ed to say they were leaving, taking Serena with them if that was OK. He excused himself to the group he was talking to and came over to where Serena was leaning, exhausted, against the doorway.

"Poor baby." He smiled down at her, stroking her cheek. "Of course you must go. Charles, I can always get Bob to drop Serena."

"No trouble," Charles shook his head. "Wonderful night. We must see more of you. Melanie," he turned to his wife, not understanding for a second the pointed look she gave him, "arrange for Ed and Serena to come over. Can't think why you haven't."

Serena wanted the ground to open. "Neither can I," Ed grinned, giving Melanie a hug. "I've heard a lot about you. I'd like to hear more from the original. And as for you," he turned to Serena, still standing leaning weakly against the wall, and laughed down at her, "oh God, just look at her, nearly asleep. Charles, take the star home. Call you tomorrow," he said, pulling her to him and kissing the side of her hair. She then found herself being taken away by her oldest and best friends and in the whole of her life she had never wanted anything less.

Hopeless. She groaned, pushing the balls of her hands against her eyes. What was she thinking of? She was still sitting there when the doorbell rang. Probably someone for the kids. She yawned, pushing her hair away from her unmade-up face, and opened it.

For a moment she couldn't make sense of her visitor.

"Why, Don," she managed at last. "Come in."

She was vaguely aware of a police car outside and that another man was with him.

A cold stab of fear went through her. Her eyes flew to his. She could feel her heart beating painfully against her chest. He took the door from her hand and gently closed it.

"Don?" Small bursts of fear were exploding in her chest.

He just nodded. "I'm sorry, Serena," he placed a hand on her shoulder, "it's over."

Chapter Thirty-One

Not in Ireland but in France. He had chosen Marseilles because it was big enough to hide in and not, he had decided, an obvious place to search for a runaway banker. The logic of that escaped her, but then logic had not played a big part in Stephen's flight to freedom. Detection had not seemed to trouble him either. How could it, when his disguise was so efficient? Hair dyed grey, his nose reshaped on one of the frequent visits she heard he had been making to Bucharest. It was all that had been needed to make instant recognition almost impossible. That and his new occupation as a writer. He must have been planning it for months. Maybe even years. Serena buried her face in her hands.

A bank account established several years before under the name he had assumed, John Mallory, had been pumped up periodically with cash injections from a bank in Bucharest. His papers were impeccable, his work, allegedly as a specialist in East European history, the only cover he needed to cross borders undetected, replenish his needs and regain entry to France.

Don told her not to expect much from him. "He'll be brought back tonight. Held on remand in custody at the nick and then on Monday morning he'll appear before magistrates at Bow Street and be sent on remand to perhaps Wandsworth, until a trial can be fixed."

"What?" She looked up, dimly aware that he had spoken to her twice. "I'm sorry. What did you say?"

Poor cow, Don thought. More slowly and quite gently he repeated what was happening. "He's OK. He just thought he was safe."

"How?" Her eyes strayed to the photograph of Stephen in a small silver frame tucked between others on a side table. Prison. Stephen, so meticulous, so energetic, so flawed, in prison. She pressed her hand against her mouth to stop the scream rising up from the pit of her stomach.

"Speeding."

Of course, she thought dully. Always in a hurry. Impatient.

"Along the road out of Marseilles to Toulon. Just before Bandol," Don was saying. "When they checked his licence, the name John Mallory didn't match with anyone granted residential status. It's an odd thing, it's always something so simple, and on another day, crowded with tourists, when the traffic department were busy, they might not have noticed. They called us about a month ago —"

"A month ago?" A month? Her mind raced, what had she been doing? And last night when he was arrested she was ... she stopped. It didn't bear thinking about. Instead she repeated incredulously: "You've known? For a month?"

He nodded. She looked away. There was no need to ask why she hadn't been told.

"It didn't fall into place straight away. Someone over there became suspicious about his source of income. Ran a check on the books he said he was writing. None existed. After that it was easy. He was living alone. Nice house, pleasant road on the outskirts. A housekeeper who lived in a small annexe next door. Apart from that, a bit of a loner. Classic stuff."

A loner. Yes, that was Stephen. "They'll let you see him tomorrow," he went on. "No. Don't." He stopped her as she began to insist to be taken to him without delay.

"Has he," she stopped and took a deep breath. "Has he asked for me?"

"Yes. He said for you to get Andrew Beresford to act for him."

Her face wore a dazed look. "Is that all?"

Don's face remained impassive. "All that I've been told. I expect he has said more," he comforted, "but they just haven't passed it on. And of course getting him a lawyer is important."

"Yes of course. What shall I do? I'm sorry, I can't seem to think."

Don glanced out of the window. No one had yet twigged. In this street the sight of a police car was unlikely to arouse much interest other than to avoid it. A posse of photographers would cause a riot.

"Call the lawyer and get the children out of here," he advised, turning back to her. "The press will know in an hour or so. No way we can stop them."

A bewildered Harry and Louise were roused from their beds, the excitement of the night before forgotten in the haste to get them away. Margot was phoned and calmly agreed to be there in the early evening. Melanie, on the point of leaving for the country, responded by screeching to a halt outside Foster Street less than an hour later. Stacey was urgently contacted by phone at her friend's and ordered to stay there.

"The baby," Melanie told her firmly, as Charles threw hastily packed overnight cases into the boot of his car. "Think of the baby," she ordered when Stacey had at first refused, wanting to be with Serena.

By four, when the house was besieged, Harry and Louise were already at Melanie's weekend cottage in the Cotswolds and a policeman had been posted outside the door to deal with the clamour. Andrew Beresford was due back from New York on Sunday night. He would call her then. Alex and Gilly had arrived together and pleaded to be allowed to stay, but Serena refused. It was only later it occurred to her that no one had phoned them. They must have been coming to see her anyway.

"This is disgraceful." Alex was tight-lipped, angered that his entry had been made so difficult, forced to identify himself as a friend and counsellor to the children. "You must be given space to think about what you want to do."

They found Serena in her kitchen, as far away from the prying eyes of the press waiting outside as she could get. Afterwards Gilly said it was like seeing a victim of a road accident; a terrible haunted look clung to her. Shock was etched on her face. Gilly touched Alex's arm. "I don't think they agree." She nodded behind her to where Don was on the phone. A policewoman stood in the hallway, her mobile strapped to her shoulder crackling incomprehensibly. Occasionally she talked back to it.

"My mother's coming." Serena tried to concentrate, just wishing they would go. "She's the best person. All these people are known to her. And besides, I don't want you involved in this. You have your own lives. Think of what Lorrayne would say," Serena urged him wearily.

Inside her head, a small hammer was pounding relentlessly; the roof of her mouth was dry. Lack of sleep was now kicking in, her bones ached. Alex hesitated, consternation written all over his face. As much, Serena suspected, because of the situation she was in, as the realization that Lorrayne would have every reason to cut up rough about his time with the children if his name was connected with her so publicly.

"I'm sure Lorrayne would not expect me to abandon you," he began, but she could see the unease in his eyes. At this point Don Trewless stepped in. "It might be better, sir, if you go. Serena and I know each other well. Believe me, we'll take care of her."

A further interruption was caused by Betty and Les pitching up in the kitchen. This led to a mini security alert when they were briefly mistaken for the press. Seeing the front was impenetrable, they had simply scaled the back wall and offered the services of a couple of Les's friends to get her to a safe house. Serena told them it would be unnecessary.

"Chin up, love," Betty whispered, casting a scathing look at the assembled police officers. "You know where we are," she added, giving her a significant look. "Just yell."

And then, in a moment of uncustomary solidarity, they both hugged her and told the policewoman they would go as they had arrived, thank you very much, and provided a rare comic moment in a house where the tension was crackling like tissue paper. Les flirting with a stroke bent double while Betty used his back as a lever to scale the fence, paisley leggings straining at the seams over her ample bottom. Alana and Ellis screamed encouragement from the other side, which frightened Sovereign into a frenzy of howling.

Mr and Mrs Mojani stood outside, their eyes closed, and prayed for her. Bradley and his friends fired water-filled condoms at the press from the upstairs bedroom window.

Serena drew the blinds. The big picture. They were going to get it at last.

*

The nightmare had resumed. Flashbulbs exploded as anyone left her house, and what seemed like the whole road turned out to watch the amazing sight of the quiet and generally liked Mrs Carmichael being interviewed by the police.

"Arrested, is she?" asked the woman who lived on the other side of Betty Plaxton.

"Gawd almighty, you kidding?" retorted Betty, who had found it impossible to remain indoors. "Hadn't a due, poor cow. Always a bit," she waggled her hands, indicating a certain fragility, "you know, bit innocent about the world. I've been in of course. Collapsed," she confided quite untruthfully, since Serena was shocked but still functioning, but there were not many moments in Betty's life when she could experience the power that came with possessing exclusive information. It was Betty's finest hour and when a journalist twigged she was the next door neighbour and the pack closed in, she thought she would expire with happiness. As it happened Betty's view of newspapers had been largely derived from television soaps and films in which their presence was to be scorned and derided. She filled her role with such gusto that even the man from the biggest selling Sunday tabloid with money to burn retreated, telling anyone who cared to listen that the dog was a more reasonable bet.

"Innocent?" screamed Cheryl from the back of the crowd, hungrily devouring the scene in front of her. Not in her wildest dreams could she have envisaged such a gloriously humiliating scene.

"I told you," Cheryl's piercing voice penetrated the crowd of newsmen. "I said she was a tart. None of you would listen. 'Ere," she protested, as Don Trewless's assistant pushed his way through the newsmen and the crowd and took her arm, drawing her clear of the mob. Whatever he said made her flush and look defiant. He waited while she returned to her own home without saying another public word about her neighbour.

"Stupid bitch," he murmured, rejoining Don Trewless standing in the hallway. Don nodded. He'd grown fond of Serena, admired her courage even if he felt exasperated by her unswerving loyalty to a man who was being escorted back to England after three years on the run.

"What do you reckon?" his assistant murmured. "Did she know?"

Don shook his head. "She never did. Trouble is, I could never trust what she would do in the unlikely event he managed to contact her. He's just got such a hold over her. And now I'll never know."

His assistant jerked his head towards the closed door, impatient to be out of the fray. "Who's the big feller, just gone in?"

Don looked straight ahead, squinting at the darkening December sky. "Ed Stein. She used to work for him."

"Boyfriend?"

Don shook his head. "Don't think so. Chalk from cheese. I think the one who left just after he arrived is the main man. Anyway, she asked if she could have a couple of minutes alone with him."

Inside the house, away from the curious eyes of the policewoman, Serena faced Ed.

"You shouldn't have come." Her voice was as stiff as her body. It was what shock did to you. Her hair was pulled back from her face. At some point she must have got dressed but her efforts had stopped when it came to applying make-up. She forced herself to think. Her face was pale, her lips colourless. Nervously she pulled at the neck of her black roll-top sweater.

"And done what instead?" Ed demanded. He leaned against the sink, his hands dug deep into his pockets. "Read about it in the papers? Why didn't you call me? Or do you still think the shrink is better for you? I had to hear it from Mike. Thanks a bunch."

"Please," she whispered, "not now. Alex just came. I didn't call anyone. I wouldn't. Why would I involve you … I mean, anyone … in this mess?"

"Off the top of my head," he replied furiously. "Because maybe your independence is a pain in the arse and this might just be the moment when you let someone else into your life to help."

"I can't." She sagged down into a chair. "And I have to do this on my own. This …" A lead weight was resting on her eyes. What she wanted to do, what every inclination propelled her to do, was impossible. "This," she repeated, her hands clenched between her knees to stop herself from going near him, "is between me and Stephen. It always was, you see. He needs me."

There was a silence, broken only by the sound of Sovereign still howling in the back yard. Painfully she lifted her eyes to his face.

"Is that what you think, what you really want?" he asked. His face was drawn and he looked defeated.

"Yes," she whispered. "Oh yes. I've always known it would come to this." After a long silence in which she sat facing away from him she heard him say, "I see. Well, you know where to find me. Take care." And he was gone.

*

The shock was Stephen's hair. Almost grey. And his nose. It was straighter, weakening his face, robbing it of the strength she was so used to seeing there. He was deeply tanned, he looked fit, he looked well. Maybe she would have had to look closely to make sure it was him, but she would have known the eyes, the mouth, the curve of his neck, the way he frowned and the way he ran his hand impatiently through his hair. All of it would have betrayed him. But only to her.

Two prison officers stood at the back of the surprisingly light and simply furnished interview room. A plain square table with four chairs around it occupied the centre of the room. A narrow waist high shelf ran its length on which were two phones and a lamp. The window had bars and the door was guarded.

Stephen was sitting at the table. He rose unsteadily to his feet when she was ushered in; he was wearing jeans and a leather jacket. Serena had never known him to wear such clothes. Privacy was not an option. Don Trewless, who had accompanied her, walked to the window and turned his back. She went forward, the tears already flowing down her cheeks.

"Stephen." Her voice was hoarse. Her arms reached out for him. "Oh my God, Stephen. Are you all right?"

They clung together, Serena weeping uncontrollably, incoherent half-questions tumbling from her, until Stephen untangled her arms from his neck and urged her to sit down.

"Don't," he said urgently. "Don't cry. It won't do any good and it won't help me."

She blew her nose and began to apologize. "No, of course not, but oh, Stephen, why? Tell me, oh God help me, I can't think straight. Say something, tell me."

"I will, I will," he promised, taking her hands and pushing her into the seat opposite. The sound of his voice was strange, the smell of him, the faint aroma of a cologne she didn't recognise.

"Listen," he threw a watchful glance at Don and lowered his voice. "Andrew? Where is he? Is he coming?"

"Andrew?" she repeated blankly. "Yes. He's back tonight. He'll be in court in the morning."

"Serena. Darling." He gripped her hands. "We'll talk and you can tell me everything, but first I have to have Andrew on my case. I must see him the minute he gets back. You'll arrange that, won't you?"

She blinked. "I already have." She struggled to focus on what he was saying. It was a litany of bitterness, instruction on what she should do. Exhausted and drained by lack of sleep, she could not stop the tears flowing.

"Please," he urged her. "Please try to be calm. I've been through hell. Always keeping an eye on newspapers and the news. Watching every stranger in case it was one of them." He jerked his head towards Don. "Have you any idea what it's been like for me?"

"No. I mean yes. We were the same, the children. Oh God, Stephen, the children —"

"But you were here," he broke in. "With them. Not like me. Living in a different country. You didn't have to hide, change your identity."

"Why didn't you get in touch?"

"In touch?" He glanced behind him. He looked uneasily at her. "How? Without revealing where I was? While you didn't know where I was I was safe. And you were too, of course. Of course I tried to work out how I could get in touch, but it was just not possible."

The tissue she was holding was damp and shredded.

"Why?" She tried to control her voice. "Why did you do it? We were happy, weren't we? I've been nearly demented trying to think why."

"Why?" He let go of her hands and threw his head back in such a gesture of despair, her heart was wrung for him. While he talked she fumbled for another tissue in her bag. "I was sick of working," he told her bitterly. "Sick of being denied what should have been mine. Everything was within my grasp. My education, my skills should have opened doors. But no one ever thought I was quite good enough on my own. My father saw to that. Gambling everything away, not making a future for me — and he could have done. God, how he could have done."

Serena glanced nervously over at Don Trewless.

"Stephen," she interrupted, trying to warn him, "I'll hear this another time."

"Another time." He gave a derisive laugh. "That's all Malcolm ever said when I tried to talk to him. 'Another time, Stephen,' 'Later, old boy.' Me? The star negotiator, the trouble-shooter. Anything I took they owed me. Compensation if you like. Yes, that's all it was. And I deserved every penny. And then I discovered that Rupert was lined up for New York, not me. Rupert, with his dreary ancestry and his brain the size of a grape, was going to get my reward."

It was the first she'd heard about New York.

"I was going to surprise you," he muttered. "When I'd got it."

"Just drop everything and go?" Her voice was almost inaudible. He wasn't listening.

"And it would have been OK if Rupert hadn't fucked up one of the accounts and let them check it without asking me."

Serena knew all this. That simple error had led to the first question being asked. A butterfly flaps its wings in Peru, she thought, and there's an earthquake in China. Who had said that? And then she recalled who had quoted it to her and had to shake herself to concentrate.

"I knew then it was time to go."

"And you never told me?" The sobs rose to her throat.

He looked at her with impatience. "I've told you, we were all safer if you didn't know."

"Do you think I would have betrayed you? Not helped you, advised you?"

"What? To give myself up to this?" he returned with such savagery she physically recoiled. Immediately he was contrite.

"Not involve me?" she whispered, unable to keep the incredulity from her voice. "Didn't you think, just once, about my terror?" She pressed her fist into her chest. "My shock? Not knowing whether you were alive or dead. Not even a note left for me. Did I mean so little to you that you could not have given me just a moment's peace of mind, a little hope that I had not been such a failure as a wife?"

"Involve you?" He replied with such vehemence that Don Trewless looked round. Hurriedly he lowered his voice.

"Try and understand," he urged her in an undertone. "There wasn't time. I had at most three days to clear out before they closed in. I just thought once I was safe I might find a way."

Serena listened in shocked silence. Three days.

"I thought you were in Ireland," she said at last.

"Ireland?" It was his turn to look bewildered. "Why on earth Ireland?"

"Because you talked about it so much. You know, Yeats and your roots ..." Her voice tailed off. She did't mention the Irish newspapers she had bought, the maps she had pored over, wondering, searching, planning to go and find him. The posters she had gazed on with such longing she could hardly breathe.

"Did I?" he replied with a shrug. "Can't think why."

The door behind him opened. Don indicated it was time for her to go.

"Shall I bring the children?" she asked, not certain if her legs would support her.

"Of course." He appeared shocked she should even have to ask him. Her spirits rose just a little. "They'll want to see me as well, won't they?"

Shock, she told herself firmly. Just shock. Stephen was never a selfish man, but he clearly had to think of himself first to keep his freedom. That was it, and hadn't she, in the end, done the same?

She reached over and held him. As she did so he tipped her face up to his.

"There's my girl. As beautiful as ever. I knew you'd be all right. I knew you'd be there for me."

She said nothing, just nodded. "I won't be in court tomorrow," she said.

"But that doesn't mean I don't want to be. It's just that we, that is, Don, has said it will simply turn into a bunfight."

A look of alarm leapt to his face. "Don't listen to him," he bent his head to whisper. "Andrew will want you there. Publicly supporting me."

She released him and walked to the door.

"Andrew," he reminded her eagerly. "He'll get me out of here. Don't worry about money. Call Richard — or better still Giles Hooper. They'll stand bail. They owe me."

It was unbearable. They wouldn't touch him and they wouldn't touch her either.

"Why? Why won't they? After all I did for them?"

She turned and silently searched his face. Don was holding the door. She signalled to him to give her just a few moments and went back to where Stephen was standing, his expression one of bewildered indignation.

"You left me penniless and virtually friendless." She spoke as calmly as she could. "No one would touch me. I have lived in virtual poverty for three years. I can't believe you didn't know if you were reading English newspapers."

The colour in his face whitened under the tan. "Penniless? I thought that was all bluff to make me turn myself in. No one? Surely Richard —"

"After I refused to go to bed with him I never saw Richard again." Her voice was blunt. "I'm surprised you couldn't hear the doors slamming shut, there were so many of them. You may have led a lonely but comfortable existence, Stephen, but I led one in near destitution and terror. You haven't even asked where I'm living —"

"Richard did what?" His voice was incredulous. "But not now? You're OK now." It was a statement. "What about Charles? He must have helped. There you are," he went on eagerly as she nodded, "Charles will help."

It was hopeless. He was not even on nodding terms with reality. Shock, of course. From somewhere she mustered a smile. "I'll do my best."

Don stood aside as she left.

*

For the fourth time in an hour Margot boiled the kettle.

"They have to." She was blunt. "He's their father. They'll have to go."

Serena nodded, watching Margot pour scalding water into the teapot. "I know. But they don't know what's hit them." Her mother gave her a side-long look. No sleep again last night, she guessed, taking in the dark circles under her eyes. "Neither do you," she pointed out.

"I'll survive." Serena brushed aside the sympathy.

All she wanted was for no one to broach the subject of her feelings. Few things were private for her any more, but no one could get inside her head. No one.

*

The line of women and children ahead of her was no comfort to Serena as she waited with Harry and Louise for admittance to the visiting room. A dank, sickly smell assailed them as they finally entered the heavily secured door into the prison remand wing where Stephen had been sent to await his trial. Harry looked sick, Louise defiant.

No one was spared, no feelings counted, no privileges extended. All three shuffled along the depressing little queue of humanity waiting to see men who had let them down and reduced their relationships to an hour a month.

Serena had tried to prepare them both for how Stephen had changed. On Alex's advice she had sat them down and described the rituals of prison life, the searches, the meticulous regard for rules, the noise and above all the fact that after three long years they would be greeting their once so loved and idolised father wearing prison-issue clothes in a room full of strangers. Before she finished she knew that nothing could prepare them for what lay ahead.

"Let them do the talking," Alex urged. "They need answers to questions, they need to know he still loves them."

Before they reached the door leading into the inner courtyard of the prison she could see Harry was struggling not to cry. Louise was more stoic. Catching Serena's anxious eye, she grinned bravely.

"Daphy and Damon will think this is really cool. Won't they, Harry?"

For once Serena made no attempt to stop her. Whatever was going to get Louise through the next half-hour was to be welcomed. Harry's face was ashen as Louise leaned across to whisper in his ear. It brought a watery smile to his face. Louise slipped around to his other side and held his hand.

"OK, bruv," she affected a cockney accent, "let's do it." In that moment Serena had never loved her more.

The crowd surged forward across a black asphalt yard to a small door set in the wall on the far side. Then along a wide corridor to double doors at the end, guarded on both sides by prison officers, their arms folded across navy blue jerseys. It opened out on to a vast room dotted with tables and chairs. At the far end a small kiosk dispensed soft drinks and bars of chocolate. Small children cried or whined. Couples argued and some were pushing the restricted physical contact they were allowed to its limit. Her horror was hard to disguise. Not for herself, but for her children, who had already been through so much. She could not bring herself to imagine what it was like for Stephen.

And then she saw him at the back of the room. "There." She touched Louise's shoulder, guiding her to look in the right direction. "Harry?"

She led the way holding Harry's hand. She greeted Stephen with a kiss and then stood aside.

"Hey," Stephen's voice cracked. "Look who's here."

Awkwardly they allowed themselves to be hugged, but it was, she could see, one-way. To his credit, Stephen did his best, but his questions were contrived and they didn't know what to say to him. The smell and the noise overpowered them both. The company they found themselves in visibly distressed them. Anxiously they glanced from one parent to another for guidance, and in the end Serena, against all Alex's advice, stepped in and filled what was the longest half-hour she had ever spent in talking and sometimes answering for them to take the weight from her poor children. Stephen's embarrassment was obvious. Serena wondered if she would last long enough before she screamed.

And then it was over. Once again they were hugged. Serena told them to wait for her by the door, which they did, trying not to show their relief. When they were out of earshot, she turned to Stephen.

"I can't do that to them again. They've got used to life without you, they must have time to get used to having you back. You do understand?"

"Are you going to stop them coming here?" he asked. His hands were on his hips. He was making no attempt to hold her.

"No, of course not. I will just let them come when they want. Is that OK with you?"

Without speaking he nodded. "It's been tough on you," he said. "Tough on them. Harry's grown, hasn't he? I'm not sure I would have recognized Louise, she looks so grown up."

"No," she said quietly. "Three years is a long time in their lives, Stephen. Andrew said he's doing what you asked. Ring if you need to talk. Here," she shovelled a handful of phone cards into his hands. "He said you wanted these."

He looked down at them and slowly raised his eyes to hers.

"You're not going to abandon me?" he asked. "You wouldn't do that, would you?"

"No," she answered. "I won't abandon you. You looked after me for so long. Now it's my turn to care for you."

Relief flooded his face. They kissed. It was not passionate, nor was it the kiss of a man who had been celibate for three years. But then, she acknowledged as she gave him a last hug, neither had she.

Chapter Thirty-Two

Stephen admitted his adultery first. "It was nothing," he insisted. "Just sheer human comfort. Nothing special. Anyway," he gazed earnestly into her eyes. "No one could take your place."

It was like hearing a small gun go off in the back of her head. She couldn't look at him. Until that moment she had refused to confront it. It was her own fault she had made him tell her. And now she'd heard what she wanted to hear and solved nothing.

"I understand." She reached across the table and covered his hand with her own. He looked up and smiled eagerly at her, returning her warmth.

"You do, don't you? I knew once the shock had worn off you would be more understanding. You always were. And you," he levelled his gaze at her. "Have you met anyone?"

"If you mean," she had rehearsed what she would say. "Have I slept with anyone, yes. One person. Only in this last year. A dear man, he was good to me and Harry. Harry needed a lot of help."

She waited, expecting pain to show in his eyes. In the brief moment before he dropped his head it was hard to tell.

"Stephen?" she whispered urgently. "Please, look at me. I don't want to hurt you. Never did. I was just lonely."

He lifted his head and looked at her. His elbows on the table, the back of his fists pressed into his mouth. Finally, he reached over and took her hand. "I don't want to imagine you with anyone else. Is it still going on?" He was watching her carefully.

It was unbearable. In spite of everything Alex had drummed into her about honesty, the reality was that she could not hurt him any further. "No. Oh no," she eagerly assured him. "Not now. Not for ages."

It was almost true. Alex had told her about Gilly and his feelings for her;

it had seemed so rational and sensible to be totally honest. No dark corners, no uncertainty.

"It's what is left to the imagination that causes the real damage," Alex explained. "I didn't want you to think my feelings for Gilly had been going on for longer than you imagined because that would have meant my time with you was a lie. I wanted you to know quickly. That's why I think a fair and honest description of our relationship would be better for Stephen. You're hopeless at lying, Serena. You're so transparent."

Sitting now with Stephen, she knew this not to be true. If lying were required, she could have done it to spare him. But it wasn't necessary. Everything she'd said was true.

"So, no one else? Just the one. And now it's over?"

She nodded. "Don't let's talk about this anymore," she begged. "No one in either of our lives. Let's start again. It would never have happened," she talked rapidly. "If you hadn't done all this. I never looked at anyone else in the whole of our marriage and then not for two years. Please? Stephen? Please. I was so lonely. That's all."

"I can't pretend it doesn't hurt," he said, passing a hand across his eyes. "But I do understand. Or at least," he gave her a half-smile. "I'll try."

In so short a time she had to make sure he was not left with the kind of uncertain pain she had lived with for so long. It was like talking to someone she'd just met. Unreal because it was Stephen, who knew her so intimately, who knew that she had to have two cups of tea before she could start the day, would only read the paper as far as the sports pages, slept on her stomach, cried at sad movies and had never once gone to bed without checking the children were still breathing. And here they were confessing adultery to each other when they had scorned such behaviour in other couples.

"I understand so easily how it happens," she insisted. "So please try and do the same for me. I'm only human after all." The clock showed she had ten minutes left. "Stephen. Listen. This is so much more important. I want to talk to you about the trial."

Briefly she outlined how she could afford to pay for his defence, describing the strategy she had agreed with Andrew and the expert witnesses she had mustered to testify that he had suffered a nervous breakdown.

"I think that's it." She frowned over the file she was reading from. "Now is there anything you want? Anything I can do?"

He looked at her with narrowed eyes. "You've changed," he finally said.

"Of course I have." She returned the papers to her bag. She would not add to his misery with recriminations. Or add to hers with more guilt. He looked exhausted. Sleep, he had told her at the outset, was impossible, the noise and the threat of violence constant companions.

"Just as well I have changed," she added in a softer, more rallying voice. "Someone's got to get you out of here."

⁂

Stacey's baby daughter — to be called Clementine after her grandmother — was delivered safely and on time in the Wendover Wing one week before Christmas. On the same day, Serena heard that Edith had died. She was to be buried, at her own wish, alongside her husband who had died in the war.

The funeral was attended by eight people. Serena sat with Matron and the care worker, Carol, who had befriended Edith. While they waited in the hushed and cold chapel at the cemetery, Carol took a card from her bag and handed it to Serena.

"Christmas card," she whispered, "from Edith. We did them last week. I thought you'd still like to have it. She only wrote six."

The service was short but moving. Edith's coffin was covered in simple bouquets from those assembled. A spray of white roses lay on the steps to the chancel. An elderly couple, who lived next door to Edith and had taken in her cat when she was in the Maud Frierley ward, sang *The Lord Is My Shepherd* in wobbly voices along with the tiny congregation. Of the dreaded relative there was no sign but Edith's solicitor, Bernard Atkins, a round-faced, jolly young man in his thirties, had made the journey from Hove and was to give Mrs Harding and Carol a lift back.

The service over, they sang *Jerusalem* as the coffin was hoisted on to the shoulders of the pallbearers to be carried outside and laid in the grave. They waited while the elderly couple ahead of them left the pew and walked, heads bowed, after the coffin.

At the back of the chapel she saw Ed. Wally was with him. They came forward almost instantly and greeted the old couple, who appeared to know them both well, and talked quietly together as they walked out into the cold winter sunshine. The rest of them followed and stood at a little distance while the priest shook hands with Ed and Wally. At last aware that he was being watched with curiosity by three of the onlookers and consternation by the fourth, Ed walked to the rest of the group.

He was bareheaded and without a coat. His only concession to the biting wind was a cashmere scarf wound round his neck. Tipper said he had been in Barbados with the temperamental Eve, which must account for the tan. On the path behind him, the maroon Bentley was waiting with Bob standing respectfully a little distance away from the mourners.

"Hi," he nodded to her. "Bill and Poppy," he indicated the elderly couple. "Knew Lil as well. Wally grew up with their son."

"Of course." Serena nodded to Wally, who had raised his hand in a half-wave. She found it difficult to speak and hastily took refuge in introductions. "Mrs Harding," she managed at last, "have you met Ed Stein? And this is Carol who has been so kind to Edith. And Bernard Atkins I think you know."

At that moment the priest asked them to follow him for the burial so she was spared the necessity for further talk.

It was a bright but sharply cold day, a wintry sun succeeding now and then to cast shafts of dazzling light into their eyes before plunging them back under a heavy overcast sky. Serena pulled the narrow collar of her coat as close as she could around her neck. A bitterly cold wind wrapped itself around the straggling line of mourners as they followed the pallbearers across the soft damp grass, past graves entwined with festive red berries, glossy green leaves of holly wreaths tied in fluttering bright tartan ribbons fluttered in the wind, cutting swathes of colour against the grey silent headstones.

Serena shivered as Edith's coffin was lowered into the ground. She felt a slight movement beside her and then a warm scarf was wrapped around her neck. A fleeting look passed between them and then she followed Ed's lead and joined in the Lord's Prayer.

When it was over, Bill and Poppy, anxious to do the decent thing for their old friend, insisted they all come back to their terraced house nearby for a drink — to keep out the cold and cheer Edith on her way. It was the last thing Serena wanted, but she went as a mark of respect to Edith, driving her car behind Ed's, who had ushered the couple into the back with him and Wally. Stephen would have loathed the reception they had laid on. A lace cloth carefully covered a dining room table that must have been with them since their marriage fifty years before. A sofa that had seen better days, a two-bar electric fire in the fireplace over which was hung a copy of the famous Landseer painting, *Stag at Bay*. It overpowered a room filled with fussy little tables and school photographs of un-named grandchildren.

There was barely space for them all. Poppy handed around plates of sausage rolls and anxiously looked after her guests, four of whom were strangers to her, the Serena person that Edith had been so fond of looking quite pale and out of place. On the other hand, Ed looked perfectly at home, laughing and reminiscing with Bill and Wally, pouring beer from a can into a tall glass. Poppy gazed fondly at him.

"He's always been a one," she confided to Serena, who without knowing it was dazzling Bernard Atkins with her interest in the problems of convey-ancing in Hove. "If he hadn't been carted off to Australia, Gawd knows where he'd have ended up. Mind you," she dropped her voice, "Lil was a right tartar. The number of times I saw her cuff him all the way down the street when he'd nicked stuff from the sweet shop. He has done well though, hasn't he?

"Having said that," she leaned forward, holding the plates piled with fat sausage rolls, shielding her voice from the men grouped behind her. "She'd have been pleased to see him with someone like you, dear. Now don't you think for a moment you being here with him will get out. I'm not one to gossip. Lil was. Not the kind of thing you want to get back to the old man in chokey, is it? Oh dear. Something gone down the wrong way, has it?"

After the second drink, and feeling her stomach beginning to revolt against a lack of food, she took her leave and the small party from Hove took their cue from her.

Bernard, who had enjoyed himself hugely, kissed Serena like an old friend and said he would be in touch.

"She was fond of you," he said as Ed joined them. "She said you were a true friend. I didn't know you were from round here, though?"

"I'm not," she explained. "Edith occasionally confused me with someone else. She thought my mother worked for a bookie."

"No, it wasn't that." He scratched his head. "You were all bound up in her head with Ed here."

"No," Serena hastily said. "She was mistaken."

"OK to drive?" Ed asked when they were standing outside on the pavement.

"I'm going to walk," she explained. "I think the sherry's having an effect. It's not far. But thank you. How ... how are you?" She had studiously avoided him in Poppy's tiny sitting room, but with the benefit of time to recover her wits and a couple of drinks, she was feeling braver.

"I've known better times," he replied, squinting up at the sky. "You?"

"Oh, you know. Surviving."

For a moment he looked along the narrow road with its flat-fronted houses and small gardens and then abruptly turned away and called to his driver.

"Bob? Take Serena's keys. Drive her car to Foster Street. Wally, go with him and get a cab back. I'll drive myself."

They drove in near silence to Hans Crescent. In all honesty Serena was relieved; she was not at all certain she had even wanted to walk, let alone drive a car. Once there, he rang through to his housekeeper and told her he had a guest for lunch, ignoring Serena's insistence that she wasn't hungry. A drink would be fine. He looked a bit doubtful and then shrugged when she insisted.

"When's the trial?" he asked, handing her a vodka with a generous measure of tonic and splashing whiskey into a tumbler for himself.

"Beginning of March." She sat down, still with her coat on. "He's got no option but to plead guilty. The documents are in place, and Andrew says they've got space for it on the schedule. I just pray it will go in his favour. He didn't want to admit anything."

"What does Beresford say?"

"Not optimistic. Temporary mental instability is his best chance."

"And then what?" He stood leaning against the fireplace.

"Then? Oh God, I don't know," she said wearily. "I can't bear to think of him in that place. He hasn't killed anyone and he's going to be locked up with murderers and child molesters and ..." she cast wildly round for other examples of social deviancy. "Crooks."

Ed remained unmoved. "I was talking about you."

"Me? It depends on where Stephen is sent. I don't see how I can continue with Gilly if he's stuck miles away from London. Andrew said because he fled he's regarded as a bolter so he'll get a category B and that could be anywhere in the country. I thought he might get an open prison, but Andrew ruled that out for at least two years. When I know, I'll work out how to move nearer to him and get a job somehow."

"What about the house? The new one."

She hung her head. "It can't be done. I'll tell them after Christmas."

"And the children?"

"Yes. That's a problem. But they'll have to come with me. And I've been thinking, it may not be a bad thing. Away from all the fuss. As long as they're with me, they'll be OK. We'll all survive."

"Perhaps my memory is playing up, but wasn't there something you told me the night of the concert, that Gilly had recommended to the Trustees that you go on the board? It seemed to grab you at the time."

She nodded sadly, holding out her glass for him to refill. Her head was feeling a bit muzzy through lack of food. It was warm in this room and sleep suddenly seemed an attractive idea. "Yes," she gave herself a shake and sat more upright. "But I don't see that being possible. I'm just grateful Gilly didn't tell me to sling my hook when all this erupted."

"Not when she's nabbed the boyfriend?"

"That's unfair," she flashed back. The effort made her wince. "These things happen. Besides, Alex and I always knew we had no future together."

"Or with anyone until that crook tells you that you can."

Ed tried again, not puzzled by her loyalty to Stephen, but angry. "And once again, you're all going to dance to the tune of Stephen, bloody bent Stephen. Give me strength."

It occurred to her that she should just walk out, but the effects of the drink prevented her. She was frustrated and angry. No one understood. It was suddenly vital that she made him.

Serena never got drunk, but now she decided it to be imperative. Without asking, she pushed herself out of her chair and poured another shot of vodka into her glass.

"I don't think that's a good idea," Ed warned, indicating the bottle she was holding.

"Well, I think it's a brilliant one," she snapped back, tossing half the drink down her throat and leaning on the back of the chair. "Listen to me. No," she waved the hand still clutching her glass to stop him interrupting, "I want you to get something clear."

Getting no answer, she continued. "What none of you understand is that," she groped for the right words, determined not to sit in spite of that slight buckle she felt which had forced her to lean her arms across the back of the chair, "is that Stephen looked after me for fifteen years. He gave me everything." She took another gulp of her drink. "I wanted for nothing and I gave nothing in return. Didn't," she waved him aside, thinking he was disagreeing, "took everything and now," she took a deep breath, wondering why the curtains were weaving around like that. "And now I'm going to look after him."

While she was talking he had quietly pressed a bell behind him. As Wally entered Serena was explaining the difference between takers in the world and those who gave, and in case she had not made it perfectly clear she asked Ed if he quite understood that she included herself in the latter category. Each point was emphasized by tapping him on the chest with her finger. Ed appeared to be supporting her by her elbows.

"Black coffee," he mouthed, as Wally took in the scene. "In the guest room."

"Got you." Wally tapped the side of his nose.

*

Serena woke lying in the centre of a bed as big as a football pitch, in a room that was unfamiliar if extremely comfortable. Above her she could see a small gold corona from which a cascade of cream silk was framing the bed. The roof of her mouth appeared to be filled with sawdust, small red-hot daggers pricked at the back of her eyes and she had a raging thirst.

At first she couldn't move her legs until she realized there was a light rug over them. Cautiously she felt her feet. Her shoes were gone and a careful investigation showed that so too was her jacket. For a moment she tried to make sense of the soft glow of a lamp on the other side of the room and the heavily swathed cream curtains that swept in deep curves across two sets of windows, light from the street adding to the protective warmth surrounding her.

Carefully she eased herself on to her side, giving a slight groan as the movement sent shock waves through her head. A fire was burning cheerfully in the grate, either side of which were two armchairs. In front of the windows she could see the outline of a figure, feet up on a chaise-longue and reading a newspaper.

The movement attracted Ed's attention. He swung his legs to the floor and strolled over to the bed. "I hope you've got a hangover," he said, to the welcome sound of iced water being poured into a glass. "You deserve it. You must be mad doing what you did."

She waved a feeble hand in his direction, taking the glass he was holding out. "Don't," she said, pausing to sip the water. "I feel like death. What's the time?"

"Nearly five."

"I've got to get home." She inched her way to the side of the bed and swung her legs over the side. "Stacey's coming home with the baby. My mother will be frantic."

"No she won't. I told her you were with me."

"Sorry, Ed," she croaked. "What a mess I am. Honestly, I've never done that before. Jesus, my head. I don't think I can drive. Could you possibly get a car?"

He sat down beside her, supporting her with his arm. "All arranged. Can you concentrate just for a minute?"

She nodded. "No longer," she warned, "I think someone's wrapped my brain in wet cotton wool."

"You got drunk because you're unhappy."

"Excuse me," she contradicted, making an attempt to open one eye, "I got drunk because I had too much to drink."

"And what about the night of the concert? You drank then. Quite a lot of champagne, as I recall. You didn't get drunk then. And you know why? Because you were happy."

"How do you know? You hardly came near me. You treated me like … anyone else," she accused him.

He looked thoughtfully at her. "And you don't know why?"

"How should I know?" she said crossly, longing to drench her whole head under a cold shower.

"I'll tell you why." He pulled her round to face him. "I could have had you that night."

"How delicately you put it," she gritted.

"Oh knock it off. You'd have been up for it. What I didn't want was you to do it out of gratitude. The same as you are now with him. You're grateful to him. That's not the same as love. Know what you said to me before you, er … fell asleep?"

Dear God. What next? "Go on," she groaned, "surprise me. What did I say?"

"You said, 'You don't understand. I don't know what it's like not being in love with Stephen.'"

"I said that?"

"Amongst other things. All I want you to do — for your own sake — is to give it a whirl. Try finding out. What kind of man wants you there for him because you're grateful? Help him, but get on with your life. He hadn't planned to include you in his."

Slowly she stood up, holding on to his shoulder to steady herself. "This," she tried to recover some dignity, "is not a matter of gratitude. This is a debt."

He reached out and picked up the phone. "OK. When you've paid it, let me know. Until then you're on your own. Wally? Tell Bob to bring the car round. Serena's leaving, even though she hasn't quite woken up."

*

Clementine's presence in the house was felt by everyone, but more so by Margot, who departed the day after Boxing Day, taking Serena and the children with her until the New Year. Stacey's grandmother had finally persuaded her parents to visit. Serena insisted that they stay with them in Foster Street and convinced Stacey that, without strangers hanging around them, they had a better chance of healing the wounds that had separated them for so long. She stayed just long enough to greet them, trying not to laugh at the expressions on their faces that could have quailed even the Mojanis before following Margot down the motorway to the tranquillity of her cottage in the country.

Serena tried not to be relieved that there was no visiting allowed for Stephen on Christmas Day. The weekend before she had taken the children but the visit went slowly but not painfully. Halfway through, as she encouraged them to tell him about their lives, it came to her that it wasn't shyness but boredom that was preventing an easy flow of exchange between the children and their father. He knew nothing of their friends: Tipper and Stacey had to be explained. Alex was glided over and Ed spoken of with enthusiasm. Looking back, she wondered why it had never occurred to her why they were so uneasy in each other's company. Snatches of life at the cottage or Belvoir Square came to her. They had talked, as most children do, in bursts, not at length. This was so artificial. Louise had already told her she found it hard to think of him as her father.

"He doesn't look like him," she explained. "I mean, I do want to help. But I don't know what to say."

It was a few days before Harry felt able to confess that he felt the same.

As they were leaving, Stephen pulled Serena back. "I didn't realise," he said in a low voice. "You knew Ed Stein so well."

She stiffened. "I worked for him. I told you. He became a good friend."

"Keen on you, is he?"

"Not that I know of," she perjured herself. "Why?"

"He's got the right contacts. Money. He could help me. Oh look, I know it goes against the grain with you to consort with someone like him, but give it a go, eh? There's my girl."

*

Stephen went down for five years. It would have been longer except the psychologist's report was able to quite truthfully reveal that his separation from reality had been instrumental in his behaviour, caused by stress and unreasonably long hours at the bank. The fact that he had lived so well in his exile was not in his favour. There was little evidence of financial or physical suffering or indeed any record of a doctor being consulted to deal with stress.

It was dreadful to see him being led away. She couldn't cry. The time for tears had long gone. The tan had faded, the dye no longer necessary for a disguise made a sharp contrast between his dark, almost black hair and the skin now tinged with the prison pallor she had come to recognise.

Andrew, who knew the Lowry painting Serena had given him three years before well outstripped his fee, represented him. It was impossible to get anyone to speak up for Stephen except for his former secretary Barbara. No one even knew what had happened to her — the bank had dismissed her shortly afterwards — but she had come forward quite voluntarily and asked Serena if she might visit him from time to time. Stephen refused. What use was she to him now?

Jasmine made a flying visit from Lucca and only Serena, who had come to know and understand her, knew the toll it took to remain impassive when the verdict was announced. Both women were allowed to see him briefly in the cells before he was taken away to start his sentence.

It was clear he was shocked. What he had expected, although he had been well warned by Andrew, was at the very most an open prison for a couple of years. To his mother he was almost a stranger. To Serena he spoke urgently and almost frantically.

"I'll make everything up to you. You must start an appeal. You, Serena, you must fight for me."

"You know I will." She could hardly speak. "Take care. Oh God, take care."

*

The sentence, due to the expensive but persuasive power of his lawyer, was reduced to three years. With good behaviour, Andrew had said, and the time he'd spent on remand added in, it might easily be reduced to two. Serena clung to that.

Stephen had been in jail for a month when Serena was finally allowed to see him. He had asked that she didn't come until he felt like seeing her. Of Ed there was no news. Tipper said after the trial he had disappeared and told Mike he was not to be disturbed.

"I've got some news," Tipper told her, sitting in the kitchen. "I'm going to take up Ed's offer of New York."

Serena put the dishes away carefully. "Brett?" she asked, not looking at him, hoping he was not placing all his future in the hands of such a capricious man.

"Ah, Brett." He shook his head. "Now that is something else. I could go and live with him in LA and find myself in the same mess I was in with Jake. He says it won't be like that. But look at us, Serena. I'm an Irish barman and he's a big star. How long do you think that would last?"

She dried her hands on a cloth and sat opposite him. "I could say, if you love each other, forever. But life isn't like that. Risk is for the very young or the very rich. The rest of us like a little more going for us than a promise to be together forever. Go to New York. Have fun. Take it easy, but don't take it or Brett seriously. I'm going to miss you, Tip." She looked at him affectionately. "You've been so good to me."

"Ah, get away with you," he protested. But she could see he was pleased. "And you?" he asked gently. "What about you?"

She sighed and pushed the table away with her hands. "I'll move to Manchester when the kids break up from school in the summer. I can't ask Gilly to let me have two days off each month like this, just to go and see him. If

411

I'm nearer it won't be so difficult. Harry isn't so settled at that new school that a change will affect him and Louise — well, she'll get used to it."

Tip scanned her face. "Are you sure that's what you want? Is the house in Fulham absolutely gone? You did like it."

"Probably, and no, it's not what I want. It's what I have to do. Stephen needs me. Who else will visit or write to him? Look at him? He does deals on phone cards like there's no tomorrow. That's all he ever seems to care about."

"Who does he phone?"

"Me, Andrew, maybe Jasmine — although I doubt that — he just needs to keep in touch. And," she went on, enumerating the reasons that she counted like a mantra each night, "Stacey says she doesn't mind coming with me, which would be nice and no further away from her family than she is now. Gilly and Alex are practically living together and my mother is free to see us any time. And besides," she said, stacking a pile of envelopes and throwing them into the basket. "Apart from my job there's nothing to keep me here anymore, not now that you're going. Is there?"

"No one?" he asked, bending his head to see into her face.

"No," she said firmly. "No one, Tip. Believe me. Absolutely no. I've been through that pain barrier."

"The thing is," Tip confided to Mike an hour or so later, "has *he*?"

Chapter Thirty-Three

Alex pointed out, rather unnecessarily in her view, that three years on her own was a long time. After all, she had lived it. No one could know better what changes and what sacrifices such a time span entailed.

"You've all developed in such different directions," he explained. "You've swapped roles. Stephen is now dependent on you."

"The trouble is," she frowned. "He still seems so distant. Almost as though he's frightened to let me get near him. Maybe he feels so hurt because I was unfaithful."

"So was he," Alex pointed out.

"I know, but not, not in the same way. Drunken moments, that kind of thing. No real relationship. Not like me."

They were still not such good or indifferent friends that such a comparison didn't bring a moment's awkwardness.

"Maybe he couldn't risk it," Alex went on. "I mean, not get close to anyone in case they told the police."

Recalling his hurt when she had told him about Alex, she shook her head. "No. Stephen was never a womanizer. I can't be sure of many things but he was never emotionally unfaithful to me."

Alex summoned the waiter for the bill. "You look exhausted," he said. "I'm going to take you home. Gilly says you need a holiday. And she's right."

"Well," she drew a pattern on the cloth with her spoon, "I could go to Lucca with the children, but I also need to get Manchester sorted out. The visits are so short, Alex, there's hardly time to say hello before I've got to leave."

"Write to him about how you feel," he advised. "Sometimes it's so much easier. Encourage the children to write and to go with you."

Serena looked doubtful. "Parental ties are so important," he said as he signed the bill. "Get them to make scrapbooks of what they've done, include pictures of their friends. Photographs of their schools. Let him absorb them in his own time. He must find it all very bewildering."

She blinked. And they didn't? A vision of Louise solemnly pasting pictures of the new boyfriend into a scrapbook was hard to summon. These days she tended to find Alex's textbook advice a bit wearing. Perfectly sound, but wearing. Their relationship had endured the shift from lovers to friends and she was relieved. Lorrayne was, if anything, more hostile to Gilly, proving that her resistance to Serena had been rooted in her over-powering need to keep control of her former husband so that her own new life was accommodated before anyone else's. Until that moment, Serena had believed Alex was a willing colluder in this plan for their new lives. Even now it was hard to believe he could not see the manipulation of his own life by a determined woman. Occasionally he still saw Alice for lunch and more frequently he saw Serena for dinner. Serena joked with Melanie that if he fell out with Gilly there was only breakfast left. But for all that she had grown used to listening to his advice, even if these days she adhered to it less and less. But her fondness for him remained.

"How does Stephen feel about you moving to Manchester?" asked Alex, as they walked towards his car.

"Haven't told him. He still thinks I'm moving to Fulham."

Alex raised his brows in surprise. "How's Mr Stein these days?"

"Ed?" she asked carelessly. "No idea. Don't see him. Heavens, Alex, isn't that your friend Paul over there? No? Looked awfully like him. By the way, tell me about the children. Did they have a good time in Florida?"

Stephen was right. She had changed. No bad thing, she told herself as she climbed into bed. The anguish of living with not knowing how Stephen was managing without her, lonely and maybe frightened, had pared her feelings to the bone. Now, no one could do that to her. She snapped off the lamp and lay in the darkness gazing up at the ceiling. Life had touched her too much to believe in such fantasies. Clearly he had managed without her. Now he was back and the search for a way of being a couple again was on.

Nevertheless, as sleep claimed her, she was still wondering what might have been if Stephen had not returned so abruptly to her life.

*

Stephen's reaction was not what she expected.

"*Move?*" he shouted. Other visitors paused in their own conversations to look their way.

"I mean," he lowered his voice, "I don't want you living up here. Fulham's not brilliant but God, it's better than — what's it called? Foster Street. And what happens if I get moved?"

"That won't happen for at least two years," she reminded him, stung by his lack of enthusiasm. She was feeling tired and depressed after a long journey and a dreary trudge out to the prison by bus and did not, she told herself angrily, need to be greeted by such opposition.

In her sitting room there was a pile of work she would have to tackle when she got home, not to mention the presentation she had to prepare for a big fundraising push in the autumn that would be dealt with on the train back. She wanted to leave everything in place for her successor. All this way for an hour with him in a room full of half-functioning people and misery at every table.

The press had stopped asking her if she was going to stand by him. She clearly was. But they were not always kind. "Kept Woman Now Keeps Him" screamed one columnist:

"*We have grown used to the sight of betrayed wives being marshalled in front of the cameras to save a feckless husband's career. Serena Carmichael, abandoned for three years — and it would have been longer if he hadn't been caught — has given the ultimate green light to any errant husband who behaves badly. Of course he's locked up for his crimes, but when he emerges, she'll be waiting to include him in a life that he selfishly shattered and she has painfully rebuilt. Haven't four decades of feminism taught such women anything?*"

Standing in the sweltering heat of an August afternoon being shuffled in line to await Stephen's arrival, her despair at what such a once golden couple had become suffocated her thinking. Not even tearing the newspaper up before she threw it away had salvaged her feelings.

"And besides," she went on, dragging her dwindling reserves of energy to the surface. "It means the children will be able to see you more often. I can easily get a job. Remember, we're in this together." She tried to sound robust, instead she sounded resentful. "Besides, the house I wanted has gone back on the market."

Stephen glanced around and then leaned forward. "Look, darling. I live for your visits, you know that. But it isn't necessary for you to move. I don't know why you don't do as I suggest and apply for a longer visit once a month?"

"Not see you for a month?"

"Sweetheart, it's not forever. I'm doing this for you. You look shattered. And besides, when I get out what on earth would I do in Manchester?"

That evening, Stacey asked if Stephen was perhaps finally beginning to see what he had put her through. Serena frowned and hoisted Clemmie on to her shoulder, who gave a satisfying burp as she did so.

"Yes," she said absently, patting Clemmie's back, holding out her hand for her bottle. "I do believe he is. I suppose he has more time to think now that all the fuss has died down and he knows that's it for the foreseeable future. There's my good girl," she crooned to the small warm bundle lying in the crook of her arm. "Don't marry a banker," she advised the feeding child. "Not the best idea in the world."

*

She broke the news to Jasmine over the phone that she was moving to Manchester to be nearer Stephen.

"And this is his idea or yours?" his mother asked.

"Mine. He was really very noble about it," she told her. "He was even prepared to sacrifice a visit so that I didn't have to travel up and down so much. But honestly, I couldn't do that to him. There isn't anyone else. It's so awful for him."

"It isn't exactly paradise for you, my dear, either."

A week after her conversation with Jasmine she was sitting in her bath-robe, her hair washed and wrapped in a towel, when she heard an excited squeal from downstairs.

"Mum," shrieked Louise. "Come quickly. Look who's here."

In the living room, she blinked. Jasmine stood hugging her grandchildren, a rather ancient suitcase lying behind her.

"Minnie," Serena exclaimed, joining in the embraces. "What on earth brings you here? You never said."

"Tea. Good strong English tea, and then I'll tell you all about it."

"Why didn't you say? I could have met you at the airport or at least sent a cab."

Minnie folded her long skirt neatly over her knees and sank gratefully into an armchair, Harry straddling one arm, Louise the other. They were truly now very fond of her.

"Because," Minnie said, looking up at her daughter-in-law, "I flew in early this morning. I've been to Manchester. To see Stephen."

Long after the children had gone to bed and after Minnie had showered and hoped that Louise didn't mind giving up her bed for her, she and Serena were still talking. As she watched her, Serena was struck by her likeness to Stephen.

It was a physical resemblance. Both were lean with strong bones and well defined jaws. The same blue eyes. Once Jasmine's iron-grey hair, coiled loosely on top of her head, had been the same dark colour as Stephen's. Her eyebrows were still black. After that all similarities between them ended. Particularly as her face had retained the strength that cosmetic surgery had weakened in Stephen.

Jasmine was an extraordinary woman; she wondered why she had taken so long to notice it. She had always seen her through Stephen's eyes and as a result had missed the value of her advice and the strength of her support. Now she was utterly confused.

"Don't go to Manchester," Minnie told her. "Get on with your life here. There was a time when Stephen would have taken precedence over you and the children, but not now. I've always cared about them, but I've now grown to love them. Do what he says. I love him, but he's just like his father. Many times I wanted to say to you; love him less, help him more. Now, for your own sake, do it. He's his father all over again with more brains."

That day at her wedding all those years before, she had not seen what Minnie was trying to alert her to. Wilfred Carmichael had been a vain man and Minnie the victim of his vanity. Just like his father, she had said. And she was wrong in only one respect. Stephen had taken his father's greed for the good life just one stage further. At least Wilfred had only squandered his own money, even if he left his family penniless.

"This is so hard for me." Jasmine pressed her fingers against the bridge of her nose. "And I'm tired so perhaps I'm not making any great sense. I do love him. How could I not? But I'm not blind to what's happening here. Even at this stage I wonder if you love him enough to help him."

Serena gazed mutely at her. Of course she loved Stephen. It was still there, it was just taking time to surface in another way.

"He doesn't see that you owe him very little. When he gets out, in three — alright maybe two year's time — do you really believe you can live together and be happy?"

"Well, it will take some adjusting," Serena began, feeling flustered, "but if we both work at it …"

Minnie studied the contents of her cup, swirling it around in an absent little gesture.

"If you were still the same person I might agree with you. But you're not. What he saw in you was perfect breeding, and he failed to see your strength. It was there all the time. Look around you. Look at the children. Who else but a woman with strength could have found the resources to have survived so well with everything against you? Could you really love him enough to let him take over once again?"

In the kitchen Serena could hear Stacey moving around preparing Clementine's late-night bottle. Harry's games were splayed out across the floor and her own workspace, stacked on two shelves. The idea of Stephen living in such a place, coping with a teenage son and a daughter who had learned to live without his approval, had indeed learned to live without him at all, was difficult to imagine. When, as Minnie said, he got out, it would be seven years since they had all lived together. It didn't bear thinking about.

"Love isn't the answer. Not after a while," Minnie said. "Once, a long time ago, I loved too much as well. It wore me out. That's why when Wilfred was buried I went to Lucca and found myself."

She looked at Serena's surprised face and gave a small laugh. "You look surprised. Even sixty-year-olds can start again. So can you. Do it, my dearest girl. Do it."

"I can't," Serena whispered miserably. "It would be the final betrayal. How could I do that to any human being, let alone Stephen? How?"

*

Jasmine left three days later, not entirely optimistic that her visit had achieved much in the way of boosting a calmer future for them all.

Ed's phone call came as Serena arrived home the next evening, the thought of the long haul to Manchester the next day an unwelcome weight. Between them she and Stephen had agreed that the children's schools were not to be disrupted, confining visits to half term and holidays. In truth Serena had made that decision long before she consulted Stephen.

After months of silence Ed simply said, "I'm coming over."

She glanced frantically around. Clemmie was sleeping peacefully in her carry cot in the corner, Stacey helping Harry with his homework, Louise lounging in front of *Eastenders*.

"No. Wait. Why? I mean, what can you possibly have to say?"

"Charming. I've missed you, Mrs Carmichael. I'm bored with missing you."

"Ed, please. It won't do any good. I'm moving."

"I know."

"You don't. I'm going to Manchester. To be near Stephen."

"All the more reason to see you. Before you go." There was a long pause. "And you might have said you missed me. Course you have. I can tell."

"I miss anyone who has been kind and good to me," she replied stiffly. "And you have."

"I must have been away longer than I thought." He sounded thoughtful. "I can't recall you were ever boring before. Serena, I've got to talk to you. Just once and then I'll stay out of your life. You owe me nothing. This is a request."

It was not true. The debt she owed him was huge. For once she didn't want her common sense to triumph. "Ed," she said hurriedly. "If you wouldn't mind, could you come now?"

It was done. Barely an hour later, she saw his car pull up. A near riot greeted him from Harry and Louise who berated him for his absence.

"Hi," he greeted her over their heads. "Listen, you guys, I've got some serious stuff to discuss with your mother. Let me just take a look at Clementine. Stacey? What are you feeding this child on? She's a cracker."

Stacey beamed with pleasure. Ed tried not to wince when he was invited to hold the little treasure, saying he'd like to see Stacey in action first so that he'd know what to do.

"Coward," Stacey told him cheerfully. She cast a quick glance to where Serena was standing by the door, remaining mostly silent, and then back at Ed. "I'm sure you want a drink, and you two," she turned to the children, "supper. Kitchen. Now."

"But I want to talk to Ed," Louise protested. "Oh, OK," she caved in, meeting a very pointed stare from Stacey. "Yeah, sure. Harry? You heard what Stacey said. Go on, I'll bring Clem."

Alone they just nodded at each other.

"We could sit," he suggested after a moment.

So they did. She poured him a drink and very carefully, and in full view, a soft drink for herself. He smiled. "You're a charming drunk. We must do it together sometime."

"I can't wait," she replied. "What is it, Ed? I know that look. What was it you wanted to ask me?"

"You can't imagine the pleasure of knowing you've studied me so closely. Sorry. This is serious. I want you to tell me straight. No messing. No honourable stuff. Are you seriously planning to stick by this bloke?"

She nodded.

"What would it take to stop you?" He swirled the drink around in his glass.

For one awful moment she thought he was going to suggest money and then felt ashamed, knowing it would never occur to him.

"More than anyone can suggest," she replied quietly. "Oh, I don't know," she shrugged when he persisted. "That he no longer loved me in any way or asked me not to come near him. Ed, this is a pointless conversation. Because he does."

He shook his head. "Maybe. What if he had been unfaithful, that there was someone else?"

She rose quickly to her feet. "For heaven's sake, Ed. He has been. He told me. But then I was too. Now there isn't …" she couldn't look at him, "anyone in either of our lives. So that's that."

She was staring out of the window. Behind her she heard the snap as his glass was put down. He came over to her and turned her round. Foster Street was bathed in an odd kind of light, the heavy sultriness that comes just before a storm.

"I don't play games," he reminded her. "And I'm not playing one now. Look at me, Serena. Tell me what you really feel. Tell me that you feel nothing for me and I'll go away. Tell me."

"Don't, Ed," she pleaded. "Please don't." She looked at him and there was something in his face that made her halt. Afterwards she could not explain why she had chosen that moment. But her strength left her, the need to unburden herself was too strong.

"All right, all right, all right," she cried. "I'm not in love with him anymore. I haven't been for a long time. There," she looked up defiantly. "And it changes nothing. I could no more abandon him now than Harry or Louise. Call it what you like, duty, honour, affection — yes, now I come to think of it, affection for what we had. So," she finished brightly, "where has that got us? Nothing's changed."

It was easier to study the top button of his shirt. When he reached out and tipped her face towards him, she averted her gaze.

"Thank you," he said softly. He leaned forward and very gently kissed her. An odd thing happened to her legs and she had to clutch his lapels. Her eyes were still closed when he pushed her carefully away from him.

"That was much harder to do than what I have to tell you," he said, moving her hair away from her face. The base of his thumb was by the corner of her mouth. She felt absurdly weak.

"Tell me?" Her voice sounded like a croak. "Of course," she tried to recall why he was here. "You wanted to tell me something."

And he did. Gently and without preamble and without taking his eyes from her face he told her about Chantal and Stephen's two-year-old son, living in Marseilles. He told her how he'd never believed a man like Stephen would have been living for so long without someone in his life. Through Wally he had heard that in prison Stephen was phoning France on as regular a basis as his phone cards would allow. When the trial was over and Serena so determined to stand by him he thought he might as well take some time and find out about the man standing between him and, he smiled, a good time.

A son. Aged two. Ed watched her face, knowing what she was working out. "It doesn't take a rocket scientist, my petal," he interrupted. Her face was a mask.

"Three months after he left," she faltered. "He must have met her and … did he know her," she asked, the pain not quite kicking in. She knew it would. Later. The sequence of shock was no longer new to her. "I mean, know her before?"

"Seems not. I found her with the help of a couple of guys who do the odd private job for me. Most people, including the police, bought the story that she was a widow caring for her son by working for him. They didn't socialise much, her family are from Grasse, she'd come down to the coast to work as a waitress and met Stephen. When he was arrested, she knew, I gather, that was the moment to pack up and go until he could send for her."

Serena only half listened to the rest. Her mind had gone back to the day she had pleaded with Stephen to forgive her for her brief affair with Alex and the guilt that had assailed her all the way home. No one, he'd said, no one but her.

"To be honest, for the first few months after he was arrested the girl did as she was told. Kept up the pretence to the police that she was his house-keeper and now that Stephen had been arrested she was going back to her parents. Only she didn't. She went into hiding."

"But why?" Serena took the brandy he gave her. "Why?"

"Because she loves him and did what he told her to do. Oh yes, she knew exactly who he was. Apparently once she was pregnant he told her. Potty about him, she is. Matter of fact," Ed scratched his head. "I wish I could meet him to see what it is that makes women so blind to him."

"Please, Ed," she stopped him. "Not now. Why did he tell her to lie, what was the point?"

Ed gave a dry laugh. "My flower. He knew if he was arrested, his best chance of being treated lightly was to present a tragic figure, separated from his wife and children. Amazing guy. Even when he was screwing her he was planning ahead. Oh I know, he assumed his friends would stick by him if he was still linked with you. They didn't, but you did. That was the shock. Hardly the moment to confess a second family was waiting for the word to join him. Would Andrew have acted for him without you? Of course not. What could a poor penniless French girl, no more than about twenty-five, I'd say, do to help him? You held his future. And there's no doubt that with Andrew's resources behind him he got off bloody lightly."

Her eyes were filled with horror. Nausea rose to the back of her throat. Hastily she gulped the brandy.

"His son? What will happen?"

"God knows. Chantal now wants to come to England but she says Stephen keeps saying not yet. She wants to be near him. Serena," he leaned forward. "She loves him. Not like you, out of duty, or honour, or because of Lou and Harry. God knows why, but she thinks she can sit it out till he's freed. Actually," he paused and looked down at his glass, "she wants to come to England. He said in time he would divorce you and marry her. Frankly she thinks that time has come."

"Ed," she touched his arm. "Would you mind leaving me now? I need to think."

"Sure?"

"Sure. Ed? Did you see the child?"

He nodded. "Briefly. Why?"

She swallowed hard. "Does he ... does he look like Stephen?"

"You mean there might be a mistake? Passing the kid off as his?"

"Well ..." She flushed. "It happens."

"I've no idea," he rose to his feet. The softened expression vanished. "I've never seen Stephen except in photographs and on television news reports and Chantal didn't look like a trollop on the make to me. So I can't be certain. Personally I thought I was looking at Louise. No mistake there."

"Ed ..." she called as he went through the door. "I'll call you."

He hadn't heard. He was already out of the door.

Chapter Thirty-Four

He waited until she finished, his face expressionless, occasionally examining intently the signet ring on his left hand or looking off over her shoulder. Only fleetingly did he meet her eye.

"It was the only disguise I could think of," he said when she finally came to a halt making no attempt to deny any of it. "They were looking for a single man, living alone. A man with a partner and a child was not so obvious."

Disbelief gripped her. "You planned this? Planned a family?"

"No. No. Not until I was on the boat going to France."

Serena stifled a gasp.

"Chantal knew almost from the first something was wrong. And then when — well, when we knew she was pregnant with Jean Patric, I told her."

"Told her what?"

"You, the children. Why I had to hide. She was frightened for me. But I trusted her because I knew she was in love with me. As long as she stayed that way I was secure."

If he noticed her wincing, he made no sign of it. Since he appeared to think his actions were those of a rational man and since she could not bring herself to ask, "And was that how you saw me? Was that all I was?" she let him talk. Most of it was meaningless. All she saw in front of her was a man who needed help. But not — anymore — hers.

"Could you — eventually — be happy with her?" She was more curious now than caring. "Live that kind of life. Stephen?"

When had he planned to tell her? How did he think he would get away with it? She closed her eyes. Because he always did get away with it. Or nearly did. "Stephen," she leaned forward, making him look at her. "Think. Do you love her?"

"In a way," he conceded without hesitation or apparent surprise at the question. "I don't see why I have to make that decision. I can make money — eventually," he mimicked her. "It's one thing I do know about. Chantal will be OK. She has always understood."

Serena looked at her hands, twisting her wedding ring. "Understands what exactly?" she asked, steadily meeting his eyes.

He shrugged. "That I'll see Jean Patric as much as I can, but I'm married to you."

If she looked hard enough maybe the strangeness would disappear, the familiar face of Stephen would re-emerge. The dark eyes, so intense, so passionate, must still be lurking behind the blank, watchful gaze now meeting hers across the table.

Speaking slowly, carefully considering each word, she said, "Stephen? What did you do with the Yeats book?"

"The Yeats book? Not sure. In France somewhere I expect. Why? Is it important?"

"No." She gave a small smile. "Not important at all. But this is."

She took a deep breath and began. "I will always love you for the happy years — and I was happy, believe me I was. And loved you. So much. For such a long time. But I can't anymore. I want to. My head says you can't stop loving someone you care about. But I have. I do care. I can't stop that. But we're not the same people we were. I'm not the girl you married — and," she paused, knowing tears were not far away, "you're not," she finished brokenly, "my Stephen anymore."

He didn't move. She thought he would reach out and touch her. But he didn't. It had been too long. Instead she leaned across the gap between them and closed her fingers over his. For a moment they just stared down at their hands gripped tightly together.

In the end she made the first move. She leaned over, half rising out of her chair, and kissed him lightly on the cheek, gently releasing her hand from his. Her chair scraped noisily as she pushed it back and then she turned and walked to the door. As she was ushered through by the warden, she composed her face into a smile, fighting back tears, and turned to look back. But Stephen's seat was already empty.

*

"It's like this, you see." She was standing in Ed's library in Hans Crescent. "I'm free now. But I need time to get used to that freedom. I need to move, get Lou and Harry back on course, and — of course — make sure they see Stephen whenever they want."

"And how often will that be?" Ed asked. At almost nine in the evening he had been unprepared for Serena's visit. In the dining room, several guests were assembled, about to start dinner. He loosened his tie as she spoke.

She knew she was looking dishevelled, but if she hadn't come straight from the train she would never have come at all. "I don't know," she confessed. "I suspect not a lot."

"Why are you telling me all this?"

"Because ..." It was the first time she had ever seen insecurity in his eyes. "Because you're important to me. And I need time to find out just how important. Ed," she asked nervously as his tie dropped to the floor, "what are you doing? You've got guests. Ed, please," she protested weakly as he pulled her on to the sofa next to him. "I'll wait," she offered.

"But I can't," was the last sensible thing either of them said for some time.

Half an hour after Wally had shown Serena into the library and summoned Ed from his guests murmuring urgent business, he was despatched to discover what was keeping their host. A light tap on the door elicited no reply. Wally bent his ear to the door and strained to hear signs of life. He even tried the handle but the door was locked. With a broad grin, he straightened his shoulders and returned to the dining room, where several faces turned expectantly to his.

"Very serious," he nodded solemnly. "Matter of fact it wouldn't surprise me if it didn't take all night."

Chapter Thirty-Five

The removal van was blocking Foster Street. Since early morning Cheryl's curtains had been twitching convulsively. Now enraged at not having heard until the removal van turned up that the family she hated most were moving out, she abandoned all attempts at concealment and stood in her living room speed-dialling the police to complain about the van. Mrs Mojani left a Bible on the doorstep and scurried away while Betty broke off from screaming at Bradley to bring round a mug of tea.

"Thought you might need this," she called, sweeping in unannounced. Serena brushed sawdust from the knees of her jeans and, tucking a lock of hair behind her ear, took the cup.

"Movin's 'ell," Betty continued cheerfully. "I'm always saying to Les, you can get through anything on a nice cuppa. Keep the mug. Going away present. Oh my gawd," she broke off, taking in the half-empty packing cases and piles of books waiting to be loaded on to the van and to be taken to Valery Road. "What a mess."

Their new home was not the one they had wanted, but one just as nice around the corner. Well, it would be once she'd finished with it. The rush to close the deal had suited Serena. Three weeks from the day she had heard about Chantal and Jean Patric she was ready to move on.

"Take my advice," Betty was saying. "Keep the lead to the kettle where you can find it. Nice cuppa at the other end should set you to rights. Ta ta, love. Can't say I'll miss the noise your two make, but it's been nice knowin' you."

"*Noise?* My two?" Serena's jaw dropped as Betty waved over her head as she sailed back down the path and disappeared into her own chaotic world.

Harry was already at the new house with Stacey, Clemmie and Tipper, waiting to see in the first of their belongings.

She smiled. In fact, she smiled a lot these days. Alex said it was delayed reaction and suggested that Serena found time to attend a course taking place at a country retreat where she could work through all her anguish and uncertainty. It was called *Repositioning Your Life and Ditching the Past*. Serena gazed blankly at him. What *was* he talking about? She loved Alex, always would, but recently she had begun to think he was not always rooted in the real world.

Once, over dinner, he had told her gently that Louise and Harry's different and exhausting reactions to moving to Foster Street were bound up with not being in on the decision making.

"Send Harry on ahead," he advised. "Give him a sense of belonging in his next home. Let him be there to welcome you."

"All right," she agreed, making a mental note to stop Harry letting it slip that the decision had already been made on more practical grounds that his room was to be the first to be emptied here and the first to be reassembled at Valery Street.

The anguish was over. The past dealt with. There was only the future to tackle. No more decisions to make about Stephen. Chantal had written to Serena to say she wanted to marry Stephen and begging her to divorce him. Her child needed a father. And mine don't, she thought sourly, staring at the looped writing, the precise English.

Her letter to Stephen enclosing Chantal's was brief. She would leave it to him to say when he next wanted to see her but to assure Chantal that she was not the obstacle to a divorce. There was no reply. A truly lucky man, she reflected, to have found such devotion twice in a lifetime. Her instinct was to warn Chantal to stay put, but it was no longer her affair. She'd done enough.

Her mother had said it was a chance to start again. "It's not," Serena told her. She gave her a hug. "I did that a long time ago. It's more getting there."

The phone rang and she glanced round for a space to put the scalding mug emblazoned with the smiling faces of a couple of royals, longed divorced, picked out in swirling gold letters. Louise, who had been closeted in her room since breakfast with Daphy and Damon, clumped down the stairs.

Serena braced herself. "Hold on," she said into the receiver. Every now and then Louise, her face streaked with tears, would stand in the kitchen doorway, ignoring the packing boxes and her mother pointedly ticking off lists, and inform her that she had ruined her life and why couldn't she move in with Damon's family?

"Because you are fifteen. Because Fulham isn't on another planet and Damon is very welcome to visit you any time he wants. And I've just found your history prep which you told me had been stolen."

Louise turned and stomped back upstairs, her boots sounding like a demolition team moving in for the final fell as she pounded the bare boards. Serena winced as the door slamming echoed through the empty house, followed by an even louder clatter as all three marched out into the street.

"I should go after her," Serena sighed into the phone, walking to the window to look out.

"I shouldn't," Ed replied.

"Why? In case it confirms her position as negotiable instead of absurd?"

"No," he said laughing. "Because she'll need someone to blame when she can't be bothered to see him once she's installed in her new home. Much easier for her to say you've forbidden them to meet rather than saying she's gone off him."

"And which," she asked pulling the only chair left near with her foot and sitting down, "of the one hundred and twenty-seven schools of thought on behaviour taught you that?"

"None of them," he laughed. "It was on some television show. Pretty girl Daft as a brush. How's it going?"

"Going." She surveyed the kitchen and cringed at the mess. "I wouldn't put it any higher. See you later?"

"Absolutely," he said. "I need some advice."

"You?"

"Mm. I'm not sure what to do next. I just thought that with your decision-making skills so finely honed you might be just the person to consult."

She put her hand over the receiver as the removal men came back in and pointed to the last of the boxes to go out. Louise and her friends had taken up a new position on the outside wall, taking it in turns to share a cigarette. Serena leaned forward, peering at them through the curtainless window. It was a cigarette, she thought doubtfully. The stage. That was it. Louise would be brilliant. All that drama and theatrical overreaction.

"Sorry, Ed. Consult me about what?"

"I've sold out of Frobisher's."

Serena gasped. "When? When did this happen? Why didn't you tell me?"

Ed gave a small cough. "Well, you've been a bit preoccupied and I've never really wanted it. Actually I was on the point of pulling out when you turned up and I had to have an excuse to go on meeting you, so it's no big deal. I mean I don't need a whole club now just to see you, do I?"

He was impossible. "But Ed. What now?"

"I thought I might find out your plans first."

"Well," she began, slowly tracing a pattern on the floor with the toe of her canvas sneakers, "I'm going to move house, work hard to pay the mortgage. Bring my kids up, hope they'll be decent about their father, want to see him from time to time. I hope they'll want to see me and won't blame me too much. And in between, find time to be happy with this man I've met. Only he's not good at telling me important things like giving up a major part of his business life."

"I would, if you ever stopped still long enough," he retorted. "I come quite low down on that list," he pointed out. She thought he sounded hurt but she knew him well enough to know he would never admit it.

"No you don't," she contradicted him. "You come very high on a quite separate one. You know you do. I just need time to merge them. The kids need time. And Ed? You need time. I don't exactly come uncluttered. Love isn't enough, I learned that the hard way."

He sighed. "Doesn't sound like a bad start to me. Oh bugger. I have to go. I'm late. I'll call later."

She hung up and balanced the phone on the window sill.

*

When she left she didn't look back. The door of forty-two clicked after her. Out of habit she gave it a second tug and heard the lock shut firmly and familiarly into place. The removal van was already at the bottom of the street, turning left into the main road. Parked further down the road, her car was crammed to the roof. Just enough room left for her and Louise.

As Louise caught sight of her mother she began to sob afresh. Oh God, thought Serena, slipping a comforting arm around her daughter and leading her to the car. Not this all the way to Parson's Green? She slid behind the wheel, reaching over to hand her swollen-eyed daughter a box of tissues, and her heart melted. "Don't cry, my petal," she said, stroking her hair, hugging her. "Daphy will take care of him."

"Daphy?" shrieked Louise in disgust, tearing a handful of tissues out of the box. "That cow's been trying to snog him for weeks. And I bet he'll let her. Oh God, I hate them all. Where's my iPod?"

Serena reached over, recognizing with relief the imminent signs of recovery and handed Louise her most treasured possession. She smiled, giving a swift sideways look at her daughter whose eyes were closed as she automatically began to mouth the words. Serena glanced in the rear mirror as she pulled away. Bradley Plaxton was running down the centre of the road. She felt a thud as he hurled a stone after them. Cheryl, arms folded, stood at her gate furiously berating the man next door, all tattoos and tight muscle, dismantling the engine of his car. An interested knot of people had gathered, attracted by the possibility of something physical developing, melting back to their homes as a stray police car pulled over.

At the end of the road Serena waited for a gap in the traffic and turned towards the city centre. No one noticed she'd gone. Foster Street receded into the distance, shrinking, freezing into an image already shaping into a memory, then it vanished behind a stream of traffic as she rounded a bend in the road. Serena suddenly found herself straining to keep familiar landmarks in sight, not wanting to let go, knowing she must. Ahead was a different view. Panic flickered. There was a knot in her stomach. She drove on, blindly following the stream of traffic taking her to the empty house. They drove in silence. Louise, forgetting she was heartbroken, rummaged in the glove compartment for a toffee.

Decision time, Serena told herself. Her decision, like all the others these

432

last three years. Twice she went to pull the car over and twice she changed her mind. She could hear her own voice justifying her place in Stephen's life echoing through her head. "Not unimportant, just on a different list." Oh God. Had she really said that? There was a knot in her stomach.

"Mum," Louise said impatiently. "What are you looking for? What do you want?"

Up ahead on the other side of the road, Serena saw a gap in the traffic. She pulled in and got out. "I'll tell you later. Hang on," she called through the window, "I'll only be a minute."

She dived between the traffic to reach the centre of the road, then raced through a gap between a bus lumbering heavily along near the kerb and a delivery van whose driver swore robustly after her as she reached the safety of the pavement. Inside the small florist, she ordered a bunch of the biggest, most overblown red roses, she could find, arranged to send them to Hans place. Out on the street, she tapped out a number and waited. Wally's familiar voice intoned the fact that she had reached Mr Stein's residence.

"'Allo, S'reena," he greeted her like an old friend. "Sorry he's not here," he apologized. Won't be back until much later. What shall I say?"

She bit her lip. "OK," she decided. "Tell him, I've made a new list. Tell him he's right up there with Fantasy Football and *Arctic Monkeys*. Tell him —" she stopped. She was going to say she'd changed her mind, that love *was* enough. Instead she said: "That's it, Wally, I'll tell him the rest myself."

Then she hung up and leaned her head against the door, briefly closing her eyes, a small smile on her face, blotting out the snarling tide thundering past outside and shaking the glass pane of the little shop. It was enough. More than enough. Across the street she could see Louise craning her head out of the car looking for her. She took a deep breath and ran back through the traffic.

If you enjoyed *A Kept Woman*, you may enjoy *A Better Life*, also by Frankie McGowan and published by Endeavour Press.

Extract from *A Better Life* by Frankie McGowan

Chapter One

The studio lights went down. Ben Goodwright raised his arms above his head and began to vigorously applaud, which he had told the audience was their cue to yell, whistle and stamp their feet.

'So obedient,' he muttered, as the noise erupted around him. At least, he thought to himself, as floor manager he was paid to endorse an hour of unadulterated crap. Those of the studio audience who had dodged past him — and there were always a determined handful who did — surrounded Max for autographs. The rest began to shuffle out, blinking in the sudden sunlight of the studios' foyer.

The six-strong line of human frailty who had ensured that Max Warner's acquisition of a second home in Manhattan and that his penchant for fine wines was secure, remained seated on the podium looking around uncertainly. Three of them had just entertained several million viewers with brutally painful revelations of the infidelity perpetrated on them by the other three, but with no lights, or the heady adrenalin rush of a cheering audience to validate their presence, they were now uncertain of their role.

'Ben?' Anna Minstrel came through his earpiece. 'Make sure those people are looked after. No booze. Don't want a repetition of yesterday.'

'*Sun* been on?' Ben chuckled.

'Tell me about it,' she murmured. 'And get them out before Max erupts. He can't sign autographs for ever.'

'Will do. Stupid berk,' Ben muttered without looking above to where Anna was sitting out of sight behind a stretch of black glass high above the studio floor. 'Just ignores me. I might as well be signalling to the *QE2*. Oh, God, here he goes again. Vesuvius is erupting.'

Much better, he decided, as the first explosion from the silver-haired Max reached him, to leave the fall out to Anna. She never let him get to her.

*

From where she sat in the control room, Anna could see Max Warner slamming his unread script against the floor manager's chest. If that was as bad as it got, Ben could handle it. After all, it was she and not Ben who would take the brunt of Max's fury. His was the name that lured the audience to switch on, but it was Anna who made sure that his performance was worth the effort. Max hated any suggestion that his thoughtful or provocative questions, his witty asides, the homily he delivered at the end of the show owed anything to anyone but himself. When an interview with him appeared in the papers analysing his knack of pushing his subject to even greater heights of intimacy, he would be quoted as saying it was down to a natural and instinctive feel for the hearts and minds of his guests. On such days he convinced himself that Anna would have read the article and was privately laughing at him. His resentment of her doubled. Since his second wife had left him, he had to hate someone.

Now Anna watched as Max stormed off the set on his way to confront her.

'Just look,' Anna leaned with a mock shiver, towards the man next to her, who was nursing his head in his hands. 'Frightening me to death, he is.' Slowly she removed her headphones and stretched her arms above her head, wondering why she didn't search out, as Oliver constantly urged, something else to do. Something more upmarket, something political that went out in the evening, instead of all this trailer-park trash in the morning. Maybe she would. But then again, maybe she'd think about it another time. Not thinking about it at all, of course, was easiest.

She smiled wryly at the dejected-looking Henry Spedding and linked her hands behind her head as the control room began to empty. Aggie Finch, Henry's deputy, wedged her chair against the door to let in some air. Stuart, the director, had already vanished on a fruitless errand to head off Max.

Tessa, the show's PA, was collecting up styrofoam cups and discarded running orders. 'More coffee, Anna? Henry? Or something stronger?' She giggled, knowing what was coming and not wanting to miss it. She could see herself now sitting in the wine bar that evening regaling her friends, who in Tessa's view had dull jobs not worth hearing about, with descriptions of these thrilling clashes between Max Warner and his producer.

'Not for me, Tess,' Anna yawned, knowing it would take Max less than two minutes to reach her. 'So what's it to be, Henry? My resignation or his reputation? Don't look at me like that. You hired him.'

'I think,' Henry said, dragging his hands down his face. 'I think I've lost the will to live.'

Anna grimaced. 'And they'll renew his contract,' she said.

'He's loved,' Henry moaned. 'Millions of viewers say so.'

'Shame millions of viewers can't see there's only a pulse where there should be a brain,' she retorted.

'They don't see it because you don't let them,' Henry objected. 'Why do you do it? Why don't you just let him fall flat on his smirking face and then we could be rid of him?'

'Because I'm paid not to,' she sighed, hearing raised voices through the open door. 'And the strange thing is, Henry, if he would just stop being afraid of accepting help, he'd probably be quite good. Henry? Do me a favour. He'll be up here in a minute and I've got eight zillion phone calls to make before the meeting. I haven't got time for all this. Tell him you bawled me out and I'm sobbing in the loo. Tell him anything. Just give me ten minutes to get life restarted.'

Henry, balding, thin, and with the prospect of school fees to find for three children out of his very average salary, shot out a hand and grabbed her arm.

He had planned to slip out to Boots for some aftershave before his lunchtime assignation with Melissa Arkwright, the PA on *Chic Chefs* with whom he was having the most unsatisfactory affair or non-affair, really, since furtive gropings in discreet restaurants had been his lot so far. An hour spent soothing Max's monstrous ego — and it would certainly be an hour — would sabotage his hopes of anything more satisfying, something that would still the terrible sense of time rushing past in a chaotic tide of children, school runs and his own horizons, which seemed rapidly to be closing in on him.

He thought of the small hotel to which he had taken Charlotte, last year's 'final' fling, who now worked for CBS and who, in Henry's bitter view, had sunk her six-inch Prada heels into his back for the advancement of her career and little else. He thought of the concierge, who had asked no questions, and the room with its crisp cotton sheets and double bed, the heavy brocade curtains that blotted out daylight and reality. The vision of Melissa's legs gripping his frame as she gasped for more had sustained him throughout the torment of *Max Meets*. He couldn't bear to let it go. He gave a stifled moan.

'No. Oh, God, no,' he implored Anna. 'You? Sobbing in the loo? He'll never believe it. No one would. Anna, please, don't leave me alone with him. I'll hit him. And I can't afford to hit him. And I don't want your resignation. And you know you don't mean it. I'd have to go as well if you did. It's only knowing he hates you more than he despises me that keeps me here.'

Anna patted his shoulder as she got to her feet. 'And the only thing keeping me here is —' She broke off and frowned comically. 'Good heavens. Remind me what it is. I've forgotten. Listen, if Oliver rings tell him I'll call him later.' She gathered up sheaves of papers and hooked her bag over her shoulder. 'Uh-oh.' She groaned. 'Here he is. I'm out of here.'

She stopped at the door of the control room which led on to a corridor along which hung portraits of the station's most famous faces just as Max Warner reached it, blocking her exit. The benevolence of the on-screen host of *Max Meets*, who encouraged the stream of dysfunctional people he encountered each day to confide in him before viciously confronting each other, stretched only as far as the edge of the studio floor. Anna marvelled that a man with such a limited vocabulary had ever found fame on such a scale.

As he caught sight of her, a tirade, liberally laced with expletives was unleashed. Henry leapt to his feet in protest.

'Now, just a minute, Max,' he raised his voice to get the enraged man's attention. 'That's not on. Absolutely out of order.'

Max ignored him. 'Stay out of this,' he screamed, jabbing a finger at Henry. 'Are you listening to me?' He turned on Anna again, but she had wriggled past him and was already heading for the stairs.

'Show's over, Max. Look,' she clapped her bag to one ear and a folder to the other as she walked backwards down the corridor. 'Can't hear you anymore.'

'Let me remind you,' Max yelled, at her retreating back. 'That without me this show would die on its feet and you'd be out on the fucking street. Let me further remind you,' he bawled, following her to the head of the stairs and leaning perilously into the stairwell, 'That I could fucking well have you sacked.'

Anna turned her face up at him and blew him a kiss. 'You know you'd miss me, Max. You know you love me whispering in your ear.'

'Whispering?' He went an odd shade of purple. 'You call ordering me around like the fucking SAS *whispering?*'

Anna halted. Everyone waited for her to retaliate. Briefly she considered where it would lead and then, since none of the options open to her appealed, she shrugged and strode on to her office.

Later, she knew, there would be a bottle of champagne on her desk. After lunch Max would search her out and justify his behaviour by drawing her attention to his professionalism which, he would claim, demanded so much more of him than of anyone else. He would bend his head just a little to one side and say, 'Forgive?' with that hesitant, boyish smile and in the tone that made millions of women adore him and left Anna feeling queasy.

For Max, the show was not about the emotional messes who paraded their untidy lives in front of the viewers each morning, it was about him. Especially him perched casually on a high stool at the end of the programme, delivering, straight to camera, his lines about the quality of relationships, the importance of integrity and trust. Every word written for him by Anna. Today when Anna had murmured into his earpiece that his line of questioning with a self-confessed wife-abuser sounded sympathetic and to stick to the script, he had ignored her. Now he was convinced she had taken her revenge by running the credits over his closing address.

All of this Anna knew. She didn't care much about it. She wasn't sure she ever had. It was a job. That was all.

There wasn't, in fact, very much these days, that she did care about, except her father and Oliver. Everything else rolled around her and slid away.

Which was odd because, when she thought about it, it was the future, once filled with plans and hope, that she had stopped contemplating and the past that preoccupied her.

Anna arrived at her office door and went in with Aggie following her muttering under her breath all the things she wanted to say to Max but had never summoned the courage to voice.

'I don't know why you don't just tell the stupid sod where to go,' she grumbled. 'He just doesn't read the brief. It's like watching a ventriloquist. Out of here,' she pointed to her mouth, 'and into here,' she tapped her ears.

'Or not,' Anna reminded her. 'Like today.'

'Honest to God, Anna,' Aggie shook her head disbelievingly. 'Doesn't he get it? There are millions of women watching him, and they don't want to hear a wife-beater getting a soft ride.'

'Tell Max, not me.' Anna glanced down a list of messages already planning the next day's show. 'Ag? Be an angel and check with Charlie we've got hotels for all these people tonight. And if we haven't, check Henry hasn't nabbed one with you-know-who and get it back.'

Aggie rolled her eyes. 'The idea of bumping into him and bloody Melissa. Spare me. Don't worry. Tess says his poor wife rang and left a message that he wasn't to forget parents' evening, so he's using up his lunch break. He's booked in at one.'

'In which case,' Anna kept a straight face, 'he'll be out by five past.'

Aggie giggled.

'What's that piece of paper you're waving at me?'

'Oh, sorry.' Aggie unfolded the sheet in her hand. 'About tomorrow. Good news. At least, I think it is. Tess says Freda — the one who was adopted at five and has now found her sister? — will come on and say … Let me see …' She consulted her notes. 'Ah, here it is. "I wasn't adopted. I was discarded. I was an inconvenience who got thrown out with all the other rubbish in their life."'

Anna looked up. 'Good Lord. What else?'

'Can't get Brenda Forsyth. Says her credibility as a leading psychologist is being damaged with all this soundbite therapy. Forgetting, of course, that we made her "leading" in the first place. And we've got a yes from Gordon, who's going to say he's never given up hope of finding his mother, that he's spent nearly ten grand trying and has just remortgaged his house so he can go to Australia and pick up a lead he's got there.'

Aggie put down the piece of paper. 'Why,' she demanded. 'Why go all that way when he could just phone or pay a detective? So much cheaper. Know what? I think it's the search he's hung up on. Probably be a disaster when he finally gets to meet her. That's it,' she finished handing Anna the sheet. 'Except we need to get Max to really wind up the rejected bit.'

Anna glanced down the list. 'I suppose.' She agreed. 'On the other hand, not everyone feels rejected.'

'No, but they're not so interesting, are they?' Aggie objected.

Anna smiled. 'No, I'm not,' she teased.

'Oh, Lord. Sorry Anna.' Aggie's hand flew to her mouth. 'Forgot. You know what I mean, though. You should be on this programme.'

'I'd need a brain transplant first. Tempting, though. Imagine what it would do to Max. He'd end up screaming, "And can you blame them for giving her away?" And anyway, I've had a great life. I just feel sorry for whoever was my real mother because she just couldn't keep me. So, as you said, boring. And now you'd better buck up, Ag.' Anna grabbed the nearest phone as she saw Max bearing down on her, and thrust a list into the other woman's hand. 'Give this to Henry,' she said, ignoring Max, who was now giving an elaborate performance of snubbing her. 'I've just got to call my father. He rang while we were in the studio.'

Aggie noticed the look on her face. 'Nothing wrong, is there?'

'Hope not.' Anna slid into a chair. 'But it's unusual for him to ring so early.'

'How is he?' Aggie asked.

'Okay-ish.' Anna frowned. 'He's been visiting an old friend in Scotland who lives near where he grew up. I expect it's helping. But it takes time — you don't get over someone like my mother in just a couple of years, believe me.'

'No, of course not,' Aggie said sympathetically. 'Poor man. Thank God he's got you.'

'Thank God, I've got him.'

Anna meant it. Without her father her life might have been so differ-ent. She pressed some rewind buttons on the screen in front of her then pressed her father's telephone number on the speed dial of her phone. While she waited for him to answer, she began to look more closely at the footage from Friday's programme, which the legal department said had libelled a cabinet minister and which she was convinced had not. She heard her father's familiar voice. 'Hi, Pa,' she greeted him. 'Hold on, just got to get rid of this. Okay, I'm with you. Aggie,' she mouthed. 'Urgento. Tell Henry no way libel. Sorry, Dad,' she turned away as Aggie went off to find Henry. 'Frantic? No, just the usual. Missed you. You're not to go off for that long again. Unless you take me too.'

Colin Minstrel had decided to break the news of his impending marriage to Anna over dinner at their usual meeting-place. The small Italian restau-rant, just along the road from Anna's office, was several blocks from where Colin got off the bus that had brought him from his home in Clapham to Waterloo. He made the same journey once a week and he liked to walk the last half-mile. If Anna had to go back to work afterwards he sometimes went on to a concert. Until about six months ago he hadn't been to one in years when Meryl had suggested it on a weekend she had spent in London. While Colin hadn't particularly cared for the performance, he had liked all the business of buying tickets, choosing where to sit, studying the pro-gramme. Meryl, he recalled, had dismissed the pianist as mediocre, which pleased him because he had thought so too.

On the way home he would, if the weather held, walk along the Embank-ment, perhaps as far as Battersea Bridge, where he would wait for a bus to take him to Clapham. He had plenty of time: retirement had followed rapidly on the heels of widowhood and had left two chasms in his life that needed to be filled, which neither friends nor Anna could do for him.

Anna had become his companion, protector, housekeeper, but it wasn't what Colin wanted of her or of anyone. Sometimes when she had turned up three times in the same week, after only days in a new job, he could see the exhaustion on her face and wanted to say: 'I'm okay. Come again next week, not tomorrow. You have your life. You must live it. It's what your mother would have wanted,' But he had known she would take no notice. She was so kind, just like her mother, doing everything for everyone. Now, of course, there was Oliver to be considered.

Colin quite liked Oliver. He had warmed to him on two counts: first, he was encouraging Anna to move on from that ghastly programme, and second, he had encouraged Colin to retire, which had horrified Anna.

'Not now,' she had argued. 'Now, more than ever, you don't need another change. In a year or two when the pain's more bearable. Oliver doesn't understand. I do. I'm there too, in the same place as you. Remember?'

He could have continued to teach for a while longer but he didn't want to. Colin had had enough of the boys who faced him each day in his maths classes. 'When I retire,' he had vowed, before Barbara's death. 'I shall never impart so much as the date to any child ever again. I shall take myself off around every historic castle in England then write a book. I shall be happy and become a total bore on the subject.'

'I'll come with you,' Anna had teased. 'I'll turn it into a series. You'll be famous.'

'No, thank you,' he replied promptly. 'You've only just started a job. And besides you'd have that wretched mobile phone with you and cameramen telling me what to do and a soundman ordering me to speak properly. I shall make your mother come with me and she can take notes,' he had ended grandly.

Instead, Barbara had set off one morning to the parade of shops around the corner from their home when a motorbike overtaking a bus that had slowed to let her cross at the pedestrian crossing opposite, had put paid to thirty-five years of marriage.

Colin could see that staying on at school would have filled his days. But no one seemed to understand how much pain it would have caused him. He and Barbara had met at that school. She'd been running the headmaster's office when Colin had arrived from Scotland to take up his first teaching job. It hadn't been long before she had been looking after him too: finding him a bedsitter, showing him where to shop, inviting him home to her own small flat for supper. Of course, he had fallen in love with her, and they had married a year after they'd met.

When they were told they could have Anna, Barbara had given up work until Anna was at school and then only part time so she could collect her each day to walk home.

They first saw their daughter when she was just a few days old, lying in a crib, and Barbara had cried and said she could not believe that anyone, no matter what, could have given up such a beautiful child. And then she promptly thanked God for the Italian au pair who had been forced to part with her baby.

Small gusts of rain whipped at Colin's coat as, head down, he plunged towards the restaurant through the office workers surging either side of him. Punctually at seven he pushed open the outer door of Mancetti's. A low babble of voices met him, the scent of ciabatta wafted from the kitchen. Usually, at this point, Colin was assailed by a wave of comfort at its homeliness but tonight he felt mildly apprehensive. He smiled a greeting to the owner, who came towards him, hand extended, beaming with pleasure.

'Mr Minstrel,' Bernardo exclaimed, wiping his hands on the black apron wrapped around his ample waist. 'We missed you last week. How was your holiday? Come in, come in. Here, let me take your coat. As you can see we're busy tonight, but business is bad. I said to my wife just this morning that at this rate we'll have to sell up. But who would buy?'

As Colin removed his coat and settled into a chair Bernardo grumbled about the state of the catering industry, which was not, he lowered his voice, what it once was. Colin enjoyed these exchanges, knowing that he was not expected to argue in favour of change — and change was what Bernardo would have to face up to if he was to survive — but to be a comrade in arms. They were both members of a generation who mourned falling standards. He ordered a beer, unfolded his paper and waited for Anna to join him.

'She's late,' Bernardo remarked setting down Colin's glass. 'Nothing changes, eh?'

Colin gave him a thoughtful look. 'Sometimes it does,' he said.

'You mean you live in hope?' Bernardo laughed heartily at his own joke.

'Something like that,'Colin said. 'Anyway, she says it's not that she's late, just that I'm always early.'

'Since when has punctual been early?' Bernardo threw up his hands. 'Take my business. They make reservations for eight o'clock and think that means nine and then wonder why I have to give the table away. I have to live.'

Of course she was late, Colin reflected, but she had warned him she might be. Each time the door opened he glanced up. Twenty minutes later, after he had completed the sports section and read the concert reviews, which always demolished even the bravest performance, Anna arrived, full of smiles and hugs and apologies. He watched as she settled herself into the seat opposite, ordered mineral water and whipped her hair out of the band looped at the nape of her neck.

'That's better.' She grinned, massaging her shoulders.

'Tired?' he asked, as Bernardo brought her drink.

She shook her head. 'Just Max. As ever.'

'What was it today?' Colin asked sympathetically.

'Same as ever. Won't read the brief I give him, and when he gets it wrong he blames everyone else. I can only do so much from the gallery. Once he's on the studio floor he should know what he's meant to do — which he would if he read his notes. He shouldn't need me whispering into his earpiece. Which he ignores anyway. Ends up looking the prat he is. Ugh.'

'Oh dear.' Colin pulled the corners of his mouth down. 'I didn't watch this morning. Was it dreadful?'

'You missed nothing,' she assured him. 'Now, what was it that was so urgent? How was Scotland? It's lovely to see you, Dad.' She reached across the table and squeezed his hand. 'So what's new?'

Chapter Two

Anna paused. 'I'm sorry, Dad? You're doing *what?* 'Married?' She was unable to take her eyes off his face, searching it for a sign that this was just a joke. But even as she scanned the thick grey hair, the laughter lines fanning out from the blue eyes, she knew it wasn't. 'You're going to marry Meryl? But why? Why Meryl?'

'Oh, Anna.' He gave a deep sigh and laid the menu across the heavily patterned plate in front of him. He clasped his hands on top of it. 'I can see I'm doing this very badly.' He removed his glasses and rubbed the bridge of his nose. 'You must have guessed,' he said replacing them. 'No?' He looked faintly disbelieving as she shook her head.

'No, I didn't,' she replied, in a voice unlike her own. 'I didn't guess at all.' Her mind roved rapidly over the last few months, the two occasions when she had briefly met Meryl, the widow of Colin's best friend Giles Carlton. Small, neat, bustling Meryl Carlton lived in Scotland. She had grey hair cut into short wisps around her face, doll-like eyes and a dislike of inactivity, a trait that Colin personified. If there had been clues Anna had not seen them. 'When … when was all this — I mean, is it decided? Definitely?'

'Ah.' Bernardo swept up to the table. Anna stared at her father. 'You are here.' Bernardo beamed. 'Now you make up for keeping your father waiting by eating well, yes?'

'What?' Anna looked blankly at her menu. 'Oh, yes. Sorry. Just a salad. Dad?'

Colin folded the menu and handed it to Bernardo. 'The, er … the chicken. That's all. I'm sorry? Oh, yes. Vegetables, too.'

When Bernardo had bustled off Colin glanced at Anna and cleared his throat. 'Well, we were just standing there at the check-in yesterday afternoon and I said, 'This is silly. You're in Scotland and I'm in London and apart from being round the corner from Anna, what possible reason is there for me to stay in that empty house?'

Anna winced. He had changed, she could see that. He didn't look younger or happier, but, now that she looked closely at him, he had an air of well-being. As though he had just returned from a bracing holiday. He was clear-eyed, more purposeful. Clearly the change had come from inside. But it was too soon for marriage. Surely?

On the far side of the restaurant Anna could see Aggie engrossed in a conversation with her friend who worked in personnel and from whom no secret was safe. Henry was there too, staring morosely into a wine glass at a table by the door clearly praying that a bulging coat stand would camouflage Melissa's presence. If Anna could have guessed at what was coming she would not have chosen to meet her father in what amounted to the office canteen. She turned back to him. He tried to take her hand, but she lifted her glass and took a sip of water.

Colin's shoulders dropped. 'It's not the way it was with your mother. But it's every bit as good in a totally different way. I didn't think it would happen to me again. But,' he lifted his hands in a small, helpless gesture. 'There you are. Smitten. We have no way of knowing when it's going to happen. I feel very blessed to have known it twice in my life.'

On a sensible, practical level Anna knew love could strike at any time, but now she felt neither sensible nor practical, only that her father was sixty-two and she did not want what was left of her peace of mind invaded by images of him with Meryl. She did not want to imagine her father involved in such intimacy with a virtual stranger. She could not have been more shocked if he had told her he had been unfaithful to her mother.

Suddenly she understood why all those people who pleaded to come on the show to unburden themselves to the dreadful Max Warner wanted to do it — why they wanted to scream abuse at the Other Woman, to unload the guilt of affairs, to rail at the injustices of fate. At that moment she felt like shouting herself, trying to talk him out of it. But as she studied her father's face, she knew she could not. His cautious statements were not negotiable. She gave it one last try anyway.

'Dad, please, it's none of my business — I mean, good God, how could it be at my age? And of course I'm pleased for you. But — after, you know,' she mumbled. 'Mum.'

He reached across the table and placed his hand over hers. This time she let him. 'I will never forget your mother,' he said. 'I don't want to. How could I? You must never, ever think that. And it *is* your business,' he said. 'You know it is. I wouldn't do anything that you didn't like, but you've never said you disliked Meryl —'

'I don't,' Anna broke in. 'Meryl's fine. I just don't know her.'

'No,' he conceded. 'You're right.' He sighed, squeezed her hand and let it go. 'I suppose it's because you've been busy — what with your job and poor Oliver wedged in between me and Max Warner. What odd men there are in your life.'

She smiled reluctantly. 'And,' he went on, 'I'm rather surprised myself. It just seemed sensible, the right thing to do. I've known Meryl since Giles and I were in our first year at Aberdeen.' He looked away. 'I was always fond of her. She's a good woman, Anna.'

Anna did not want to hear of Meryl's goodness. 'Dad, I'm sure she is,' she said abruptly. 'And you must do whatever you think is right. I just wasn't expecting this, that's all. Just let it sink in for a day or two, eh? Wow. Married. When? And where?'

'Six weeks' time.' Relief flooded Colin's voice. 'A small church service. Just the family. Athol and Sheridan and their families. We thought it would be nice if you came up to Carrigh for a weekend first, to meet everyone before the day.'

Anna nodded mechanically. After Barbara had died, she remembered now, Meryl had sent flowers and an invitation for Colin to spend a week or two with her. And he had. They had gone walking in the hills around Carrigh, north of Perth, where Meryl had lived all her married life and only twenty miles from where Colin had been born. They had renewed friendships, revisited old haunts. They had talked about times they both remembered, happier times when Meryl had married Giles and Colin had come south to his first teaching job.

Of course Anna had been interested in his visits to his old home, but her own grief and shock at her mother's death had kept her from the realization that while she was still desperately missing Barbara, her father was moving on. While Anna had thought that this old friend and her family were helping distract him from the emptiness of his life without Barbara, the widowed Mrs Carlton had been intent on filling it.

They left soon after, neither having done justice to Bernardo's food. He had been especially reproachful of Anna who had eaten hardly anything.

'Meryl said you could fly up on, the last shuttle from Heathrow on Friday,' her father told her, as they walked along the wet pavements towards the studios. Anna said she would get the midday flight on Saturday.

*

Sitting at the front of the bus taking him back over the bridge to the south side of the river, Colin stared fixedly ahead. The roads were too familiar to be of interest and he had a lot to consider. Later he would call Meryl and tell her that he would be there on Thursday as planned and that work prevented Anna from joining them until after lunch on Saturday.

Anna was all the family Colin cared about, his and Barbara's only child. After they had been told that Barbara could not have children, it had taken them a year to decide on adoption. By the time she was seven, Anna also shared what little they knew of her birth-mother and, so that she grew up with no sense of having been rejected or any fanciful ideas about her parentage, they told her endlessly of how they had chosen her from all the other babies they could have had.

Anna, therefore, had always known that she had not been abandoned by the star of a travelling circus or a careless royal, but that she was the result of an ill-judged love affair between a teenage Italian au pair and an unknown man. One of her natural parents, Barbara and Colin told each other, had given Anna that restless energy, the self-deprecating sense of humour and that nose. In childhood, it had been too large for such a small face. The skinny little girl with the dark, serious eyes could never have been their natural child, but she was Barbara in every other way, resilient, strong and funny. And indeed Colin had loved them both. Anna had grown into an unusually striking young woman. Not beautiful, never that. But arresting, was how most people described her. By the time she was sixteen she towered over Barbara and could look Colin in the eye. Her nose now looked strong rather than out of place, and when she smiled, heads turned.

Colin alighted from the bus at the end of his road. It had stopped raining, the air was damp and cold and for once, in a very long time, he was anxious to be home. He began to walk quickly, turning away from the busy main road into the more dimly lit Granton Street, into which he and Barbara had moved when they brought Anna home at just a few weeks' old. At the time the house had seemed perfect if rather alarming when they looked at the monthly mortgage repayments. Now it had hardly changed, and the area was much the same, except for the butcher's, which was now a betting shop, and where there had once been a greengrocer there was now a minimart that also sold, alongside the daily needs of milk and bread — stamps and lottery tickets. It was owned by a pleasant man called Mr Viraswami, who liked to think that in the street among those he regarded as riff-raff there was a professional man like Mr Minstrel.

He was just starting to close up when Colin looked round the door. 'Ah, sorry to disturb,' Colin began. 'But is there time for me to ...?'

'Of course, Mr Minstrel.' Mr Viraswami ushered him in. 'Of course. Please. Take your time. I'll be a few minutes more. You're late tonight?'

'A little,' Colin agreed. 'Dinner in town with my daughter.'

'Ah.' Mr Viraswami nodded. He did not approve of *Max Meets* and was constantly rushing into the back room to remonstrate with his wife and daughters when he found them gathered round the set instead of sorting deliveries. Since they had also ignored his stricture that they should not wear jeans, he had little faith in his words being heeded. In Mr Minstrel he felt he had a kindred spirit. It was never quite clear to him why this was so, because Colin always met his references to the waywardness of young people with the response that they could be puzzling but that they had their own ways.

Out of respect for Colin's feelings Mr Viraswami never referred to Barbara's death but it was obvious to him that Colin was poorly served in the family department. He had just the one daughter, unmarried although she was at least thirty, and living alone — if just ten minutes away. What support was she to him? Should the same fate befall Mr Viraswami, he had numerous sons and daughters-in-law to fall back on to tend his every need.

'Just some milk and a small loaf,' Colin said, placing them on the counter. 'And to say I'll be moving at the end of the month so I won't be needing my newspaper after that.'

Mr Viraswami looked dismayed. 'That is a shame,' he said, handing Colin his change. 'We'll miss you. Where are you going? To your daughter?'

Colin laughed and shook his head. 'No. I'm to be married and I'm going to live in Scotland. The house will be on the market tomorrow.'

'Married?' Mr Viraswami exclaimed, making a mental note to contact the estate agent first thing. His son could do with living nearer the shop. 'That is very good news. Very good. Your daughter will be pleased. You've been a very good father to her. She's done so well. Goodnight. Be sure to come and say goodbye.'

Mr Viraswami had taken over the shop when Anna was in her final term at university so he had no way of knowing that Colin felt he had played little part in his daughter's upbringing. Except to give her a good, loving home, the one he was walking to now. And while Colin knew he loved Anna, he didn't really understand her. He had truly believed she would be pleased that he was to remarry. But clearly she was not. He paused, key in hand. No that wasn't right. She had been shocked not angry. But he had to move on. Only a few days before, he had made a solitary pilgrimage to the spot where Barbara's ashes were to be found and in a private exchange he had sought her blessing. All he needed now was Anna's.

Oliver had been right. Anna needed a change, particularly from that job. Delving into the lives of people who were dysfunctional and exhibitionist was not Colin's idea of entertainment any more than it was Oliver Manners'. In Anna's present mood, he thought it wiser not to mention that Meryl had said the same thing.

Chapter Three

Later that night, in a crowded tube train Anna decided to be positive about her father and Meryl. She still thought he was making a huge mistake, but Oliver had said — and he was probably right, she sighed — that only her father could know that. The darkened windows reflected a jarring reflection of her face as the train rattled through the tunnel. Anna knew that her mother would have wanted him to be happy, but now she suddenly felt displaced in his affections. They roared into the station, and Anna hoisted her bag on to her shoulder, rummaging in it for her travel card.

When she walked in Oliver was opening a bottle of wine he had retrieved from the fridge. He was still in his suit, his tie loosened. Most people described him as glamorous, and he was, with his untidy blond hair and that Englishness about him that his background had ensured he would never lose. The moment she met him Anna had decided that she had rarely encountered anyone as handsome and could understand why a procession of left-wing political groups employed him to put the right spin on their public utterances. She had grown to love his private utterances too. And to depend on him. She had phoned him the minute she had left Colin after dinner.

'If he's wrong,' he said now, nuzzling her neck as she leaned against the kitchen table, 'he'll soon find out. And, besides, at their age it's much more likely to be companionship, nothing more passionate, so where's the disloyalty to your mother — which is what all this is about, isn't it?'

'No. Yes. I mean possibly,' she cried. 'How do I know? And he said smitten,' she reminded him. 'Smitten isn't a word normally associated with comfort, is it? And, Oliver, he *looked* smitten. There was a glow about him. That's it,' she said earnestly. 'He looked *pleased* with himself.'

'Well, I expect he was pleased.' Oliver sounded exasperated. 'Marriage isn't generally associated with misery. Well, not at first,' he added, with a grin. She didn't smile back. 'And anyway after all he's been through, and Meryl has been on her own for — how many years?'

'Ten,' Anna said. 'Two grown-up sons. Married. With kids,' she added, trying to remember all she could of the family that was now her father's.

'Well, there you are. I think it sounds perfectly okay. Anna, don't look like that. You said to me once that you hoped he'd marry again one day, so now he's going to. Look, you're right. I do think he could have found a better way of telling you. But men of his generation are like that — a bit brisk where emotional stuff's concerned. My father's just the same.'

'But why's he got to do it so quickly?'

'Anna, you're being stupid.'

'I know, I know.' She groaned. 'It's just that he's lonely for my mother. I just know he is. And that's not fair on Meryl,' she added unconvincingly.

'That's Meryl's problem,' Oliver insisted, taking her wineglass from her and placing it with his on the draining-board. 'And it's not fair on me that you haven't made me feel at home and I've been here a good thirty minutes.'

'You *are* at home,' she objected, leaning against him. 'My home. And I *am* welcoming. Look,' she indicated the wine. 'And I've got the pizza-delivery number at my fingertips.' She flexed her fingers. 'See?'

She was tired and the thought of a hot bath had sustained her all the way from the studio to Braverton Street. Even so, she felt a pang of guilt. Her father had said that poor Oliver was wedged in between him and Max. 'Sorry, sorry.' She rubbed her nose against his chin. 'What a misery I am. I just haven't got over Mum. Sometimes I feel she's somewhere near by, and I can't handle it when I look round and of course she isn't there. Why doesn't he feel it?'

'Anna.' He gave her a gentle shake. 'Darling. Please just let it go. The wedding's in a few weeks. I understand how you feel, you loved your mother, so did your dad, but he's got to move on. If you try to stop him, he might resent you for it. You might even resent yourself. Then you'd be impossible to live with. You're impossible now. I haven't seen you for three days ... and you are doing unspeakably wonderful things to me in that shirt which

I think would look better off.' He bent his head and kissed her tentatively, then more forcefully all the while manouevering her on to the nearest horizontal surface which happened to be the table.

'You're right,' she agreed, helpfully pulling off his jacket. She just wished it were that simple. Instead she said, as solemnly as the moment would allow: 'I warn you, I've been in these clothes all day and I'm feeling very grubby.'

'What a coincidence,' he muttered thickly into her neck. 'So am I.'

*

On a good day, Anna usually reached her house in Braverton Street around eight, after a ten-minute walk from the tube. She had lived alone for the past eight years, the last three in this terraced house, in a road that contained a mix of aspiring young executives and ethnic minorities. The area was an eclectic jumble of affluent squares, worn-out streets and high-rise flats, not far from where she had grown up, and was what Oliver called real. Everything about Anna struck Oliver as real and everything about him had saved her. It was his stability, his decisiveness, that had given a shape to her life in the first awful months after her mother's death.

Having been brought up along with his younger brother, in a splended centuries old house in Somerset by a wealthy landowner father and his genteely raised mother who had never been obliged to work, Oliver had never experienced at close quarters, a life like Anna's. Now with a decent degree from Cambridge behind him he lived in a smart block in St John's Wood, but he preferred Anna's terraced house in Clapham to his own conventional surroundings. What often puzzled him, was Anna's lack of ambition to live in such a house as his father's. He found that puzzled he might well be since Rachel adored it, he still loved her for it.

The terraced house that Oliver so loved, was a constant drain on Anna's slim budget but as he never thought of it as the permanent home they would one day share, he thought she worried too much. It was bought after years of paying an exorbitant rent for a flat she had shared with Carrie Hunt until Carrie had gone to live with the father of her baby, Euan. Anna's mother had encouraged her to buy it, largely because it was less than twenty minutes away from her, and had hired a neighbour's son, who was looking for work, to paint the dingy grey outside white and the inside walls lemon. There were only two rooms downstairs and a tiny kitchen, so Anna had asked him to find someone to knock through the small dark room at the back to make a kitchen she could live in.

Books, paintings and cushions crowded every corner in a riot of colour but plans for anything more substantial had crumbled under the size of the mortgage repayments. But Barbara had been in her element, ferreting out bargains to furnish the house. Once it had been eight — almost matching — chairs for the kitchen, then a chance meeting in a local furniture shop had led to an odd-coloured second-hand blue carpet being laid for nothing. Now a deep blue sofa filled the window recess, flanked on either side by two round tables crammed with pictures of Anna's friends clustered round a central photograph of her mother. Anna loved that picture: Barbara had been engrossed in a book until Anna had called her then clicked the camera as she looked up. Behind the sofa, a large sash window was framed with green and blue curtains pulled back on cords to reveal window-boxes dripping with red geraniums. It looked, her mother had said, marvelling at Anna's fearlessness with colour, like a house that should be sitting in the sun, not wasted on a road like Braverton Street.

While her mother made curtains and filled the freezer, Anna embarked on restoring the little roof garden, cleaved out of the space left when an attic room had been added at the top of the house. It overlooked what only the very generous called an interesting view. A high-rise block of flats could be seen to the immediate east, and to the west an uneven skyline of factory roofs, garages and a derelict park identified by a valiant but uninspiring cluster of trees. Anna didn't care: its pink-washed walls, the deep Mediterranean blue of the iron railings that surrounded it, the terracotta pots of all sizes crammed with hardy plants were the result of two weekends of her own hard work. It was where she did her best thinking. It also represented the only — minor — source of contention between her and Oliver. He felt it needed toning down with cream walls, black railings and a couple of director's chairs, rather than the rickety pair Anna had put there.

'But I've got Italian blood in my veins.' She laughed at him.

'Of course.' He looked carefully at her. 'I keep forgetting because you don't have a — a — I mean you don't have anything like a fiery temperament at all, do you?'

'Yes, I do,' she said indignantly. 'And I'll demonstrate it if you mention tasteful white walls and black railings again.'

But otherwise Oliver loved everything about her, apart from her neighbour, Eamonn Bingham, who lived next door and worked tirelessly for the homeless. In Oliver's view Eamonn had an overpowering and quite irrational sense of social injustice. In his turn Eamonn felt Oliver's socialist leanings were more fashionable than fundamental. And then there was Dottie. Dorothy Fellowes lived next door on the other side and alarmed Oliver with her reliance on Anna. At eighty-odd she still defiantly proclaimed her independence to a series of exasperated social workers who retreated down her path composing paeans to their own forbearance in the face of her stubbornness in the reports they were obliged to write. Oliver thought Dottie should be in a home. Only Carrie, was regarded by Oliver as a delight. Carrie who had long since ejected Euan's father from her life when she realised one particularly fraught day in the hundreds that, since Euan's arrival, had challenged her each day with increasing mercilessness, that while she was running ragged taking Euan each morning to the child minder and rushing home to get him by six, Euan's father — a writer who had failed spectacularly to show her anything he had written in the long days he spent at home — had become so averse to work on any level and in any form, he was often still in bed when they staggered through the doorway.

Oliver was sympathetic. In fact if it hadn't been for Carrie, he might never have met Anna. One of Oliver's clients, an MP with much to say about single working mothers, had — to Oliver's horror — accepted Anna's invitation to appear on *Max Meets* to confront a warring band of women who had publicly announced they wanted to put an end to his career since he had recently revealed that he thought these outraged women the authors of their own misfortune. Responsible for the breakdown of family life and the rise in juvenile crime, had been the thrust of the article that had brought him to Carrie's attention and thus to Anna's.

On that occasion Oliver had stuck valiantly by his client's side, ready to reverse any of his more insensitive comments, but found as the morning progressed that his eye strayed almost hypnotically to the programme's producer, white shirt tucked loosely into khaki combat trousers, loafers and her astonishing mane of hair pulled into the nape of her neck into which he had an overpowering urge to sink his teeth. He could not recall that she had once raised her voice more than was necessary. He thought the control she exerted over the whole production was the sexiest thing he had ever witnessed. He thought he might be in love.

The next day he had phoned her and asked if he could take her to lunch. A month later he had parted from his long-term girlfriend, Rachel, and launched himself into making sure that Anna could not do without him. And she couldn't. His purposeful approach to life, the way he organized his clients and understood just how hard her job was, drew her to him at a time when any decision beyond what to wear each day seemed overwhelming.

Oliver liked her friends and his friends liked her, except perhaps Rachel, who had every reason not to. Oliver still had lunch with Rachel, and Anna wasn't sure she liked it, but of course they worked together. Even so.

More of a problem, but one she felt was Oliver's to resolve, were his parents. Or, at least, his mother, Christina. She had welcomed Anna warmly but was clearly nervous about her. *Max Meets* was bad enough but Oliver had swapped Rachel, whose pedigree embraced a diplomat for a father and a mother who was the younger daughter of an earl, for Anna, the adopted child of a schoolmaster from South London and parentage from God alone knew where.

When Anna turned into Braverton Street, twenty-four hours after she had known that the landscape of her life was about to change, she was thinking about Oliver possibly having lunch with Rachel while she was in Carrigh over the weekend. If she had said don't, which Anna sometimes suspected he wanted her to do, she knew he would not. But she didn't ask because it was not in her nature to ask for anything. Pride, she knew. But there it was.

Today had run relatively smoothly. Max had been in high spirits about getting away to New York, and the chief guest on the programme, Freda, who had been adopted at birth, had, as promised, complained loudly that she had not been given away. Chucked away, she had cried, like an old shoe. With no evidence that anyone could establish that the nice couple who brought her up had mistreated her, she stuck rigidly to her view that, as a result of being adopted, she had had a rotten life. '*Emo-shunally*,' she thumped her chest with a clenched fist. 'I've been damaged, know what I mean?'

Having met Freda's kindly but worried adoptive parents, Anna thought that Freda had been more fortunate than damaged. She much preferred Gordon.

'I want to know where I come from,' he had said simply. 'It's got nothing to do with my mum and dad — the ones who adopted me — it's to do with wanting to look at a family album and see my nose, my eyes. Now, take my dad. My adoptive Dad, I mean. He loves sailing and I can't stand it. You could say that might happen in any family, and you're right, but my mum says to him, 'Oh, you're so like your father. There'd have to be a hurricane to get him off the river. See? Whatever I do, no one can tell me where I get anything from, except my real mother. Is that so hard to understand?'

Up in the control room Anna's eyes were fixed on him. 'No,' she said to herself. 'Not hard at all.'

Now she was glad to be almost home. Tomorrow she would fly up to Carrigh. As her house came into view, the sight of the elderly woman, standing outside leaning heavily on a frame with one hand, made her quicken her step. Under Dottie's other arm was her skinny cat, Mister, legs dangling untidily as he mewed for contact with the floor. He was almost blind but this did nothing to deter him from making a bid for freedom if Dottie left the door open too long.

Anna groaned. If Mister got away, it behoved her or Eamonn to spend the next hour trying to retrieve him. And it was much too cold for Dottie to be standing outside but she always did if Anna was bringing her shopping for her. Eamonn had offered to help, but Dottie had spurned him.

Eamonn got all the wrong things, she complained to Anna. Butter when she'd said marge, sardines instead of pilchards. Hopeless, he was. How he ever found homes for the homeless when he couldn't find his way round her shopping list was beyond her. Dottie knew that Anna would simply bring her shopping and listen while she roundly abused the manager of the supermarket that she refused to set foot in. Afterwards she would go to her own home next door and not bother her, until Dottie summoned her with an imperious thud on the adjoining wall.

'Can't find a damn thing in there,' Dottie had grumbled, when Anna had first offered to collect her shopping. 'And when I do I can't reach it. No, you do it, dear. Taller than me, you are. Give me the wrong change, he did. Waved a five-pound note at me saying that's what I'd given that cheeky little minx at the checkout. I might be slow but I'm not stupid. Course it was a tenner. She pocketed it. No, you go, dear. Much better.'

Dottie had been widowed after the war and had never remarried. Years of independence had given her a fighting spirit that accounted for her survival and insistence on living alone. At first when Anna had moved next door she had been alarmed at Dottie's fragile strength but even more wary of her temper. Once upon a time Dottie's hair had been a fiery red, which had suited her in every possible way, and there were still traces of it in her strange, shaggy eyebrows. 'Fierce, I was,' she cackled delightedly. 'Still can be. You just watch.'

'When one of us notices she's started to sleep downstairs,' Anna suggested to Eamonn, when they had become friendly enough to discuss their joint neighbour's welfare, 'or that she hasn't washed up her cup, we'll do something about it.'

Dottie's only and now very middle-aged son, who lived on the other side of London, showed up perhaps twice in a good year and each time he left in a hurry. Once he had distressed Dottie so much by urging her to go into a home that when he'd gone Anna and Eamonn, on the way back from Carrie's, had found her standing in great agitation in the street. They had made her tea, found Mister, who had made his escape, and assured her that there was no way her son would be allowed to move her while they were around. The only person who felt her son might have a point, even if it was self-interest, was Oliver.

'Is everything all right, dear?' Dottie asked, as Anna reached her. 'You look tired. That job getting you down? Freaks, aren't they?' She adored *Max Meets*.

'None bigger than Max,' Anna muttered. 'Now, I've got you two small sliced white, Dottie,' she explained, putting the fresh bread into the tiny bread-bin beside the sink. 'They didn't have any large. I didn't think you'd want ciabatta. Is that okay?'

'Honest, I don't know,' Dottie grumbled, leaning heavily on her frame as she followed Anna around, watching her deftly putting things in the right cupboards. 'Bloody foreign bread. No large indeed. Chibbawhat? Well, really,' she mumbled on, enjoying the mild annoyance which, in the end, was largely what kept her going.

*

It had been Meryl who had suggested a wedding before Christmas, Meryl who had opted for a family-only weekend a fortnight before the wedding so they could all get to know each other. It had been Meryl too who had quietly told Anna, when her father had driven to the village to collect some last-minute shopping, that he would not be retiring, after all.

'But he has.' Anna smiled, puzzled. 'He wants to do what he's always said he would do once he left teaching. Roam around historic castles, picnic lunches, long walks. He's had enough of grubby schoolboys.'

'Well, of course he can still find time for that.' Meryl's colour was just fractionally heightened. 'He'll only be working part-time, coaching for exams, that kind of thing. It's not good for a man like Colin to give up too soon.'

'He hasn't given up,' Anna protested. 'You don't know Dad. He truly loathed those last few years before Mum died. All those ambitious parents with unambitious little boys blaming him when they didn't get into Westminster or Harrow. Heavens,' she rolled her eyes in mock horror, 'Don't suggest teaching to him.'

'Well, we'll see,' Meryl replied briskly. 'Now, I'm sure you want a rest before you change for dinner. Rose and Gordon are meeting us at the restaurant.'

'Rose and Gordon?' Anna asked politely, as Meryl led the way upstairs.

'Gordon Picard,' Meryl explained. 'He was in your father's year at Aberdeen. Now married to Rose, of course, not Janet. I must remind Colin in case he forgets. Here we are. Now, have I remembered everything?' Meryl cast a quick glance around the low-ceilinged room with its brown carpet and virtuous single bed covered with a pale yellow counterpane that matched the curtains.

'This is lovely,' Anna said. 'I'm sure you haven't forgotten a thing.'

'Then I'll leave you. Don't rush. It doesn't matter if we're a few minutes late. Gordon and Rose know we have a guest for the weekend.'

Anna blinked. 'Of course,' she said.